"AT THE RENDEZVOUS OF VICTORY"
by Nadine Gordimer

Pulitzer-prize winner Nadine Gordimer explores the dark side of national unity in a powerful and poignant tale of a former South African freedom fighter's troubling struggle to preserve his dignity . . . and that of his native land.

"THE DEATH OF HIS EXCELLENCY
THE EX-MINISTER"
by Nawal el-Saadawi

An Egyptian feminist uses a stream-of-consciousness monologue to develop this dramatic episode about a deposed official who finds his nemesis in an assertive woman employee.

"THE STRENGTH OF THE STRONG"
by Jack London

In the hands of Jack London, a simple tale of early tribal life becomes a deeply allegorical exploration of man's first attempts at political organization.

"THE BUST OF THE EMPEROR"
by Joseph Roth

This great writer of the decline of the Austro-Hungarian Empire pens a haunting tale set in what was once Eastern Galicia about the life of an aging Polish aristocrat and the dangers of nationalism.

PLUS MORE GREAT STORIES FROM AROUND THE
WORLD

Other Laurel Editions of Interest

REBELS AND
REACTIONARIES

·

An Anthology of
Great Political Stories

Edited with an Introduction
by Mitchell Cohen

A LAUREL BOOK
Published by
Dell Publishing
a division of
Bantam Doubleday Dell Publishing Group, Inc.
666 Fifth Avenue
New York, New York 10103

The trademark Laurel® is registered in
the U.S. Patent and Trademark Office.

The trademark Dell® is registered in
the U.S. Patent and Trademark Office.
ISBN: 0-440-20816-5

Printed in the United States of America

Published simultaneously in Canada

August 1992

10 9 8 7 6 5 4 3 2 1
RAD

CONTENTS

For my friends at *Dissent*

Stories of Politics
by Mitchell Cohen

Here's a book of stories about politics and political life. Mostly short, some are a little longer; mostly fiction, but not all; generally serious, though satire and humor are to be found too (and humor and satire can, of course, be quite serious). Some are realistic, others fablelike. The selection is diverse and far reaching, although not comprehensive. "It is hard to put together any representative selection of stories," Randall Jarrell once wrote. "It is like starting a zoo in a closet: the giraffe alone takes more space than one had for the collection . . ."

In the "political short story," two realms, politics and literature, come together in a small space. The two realms are often uneasy with each other. True, modern history has seen literary figures assume prominent political roles, from Benjamin Disraeli, a novelist-politician who became British prime minister in the nineteenth century, to Vaclav Havel, a playwright-dissident who became Czechoslovakia's president in the late twentieth. They tend, however, to be exceptions, and some critics would argue that their political accomplishments surpass their literary achievements.

Usually it is through their craft—as voices of conscience, of warning, or as troubling scrutinizers—that great writers engage political questions. Political fiction can elucidate; it can intervene. It can cry out: "Look here, something is wrong." It can capture a historical moment. In some cases it can even shape the terms of political debate. Think of how the vocabulary of George Orwell's classic antitotalitarian novel *1984*—phrases like "Big Brother is watching" and "doublethink"—became part of our common usage.

Each selection in this anthology explicitly or implicitly reveals something about the political world. Most are political short stories per se, that is, self-contained works of short prose fiction. There are exceptions: "The Legend of the Grand Inquisitor," though it stands on its own as a meditation in fable form about human nature, politics, and many other things, is also a chapter from Dostoyevsky's novel *The Brothers Karamazov*. "Shooting an Elephant" is George Orwell's remarkable memoir of dilemmas he faced while a member of the British imperial police in Burma. Both are classics, and like the short stories in this volume, say something important about the world of power—about its nature, its impact, its institutions.

Short stories generally fasten to a moment or an incident—or a few moments and a few incidents. Thus political stories cannot—and don't aim to—give us the fictional version of a political treatise, let alone a country's political history. Their subject matter, politics, distinguishes them, but their literary attributes tend to be similar to those of all short stories. The most important is the most obvious one—brevity. The short story, remarks Nadine Gordimer, "suits modern consciousness." It is a "fragmentary and restless form . . ." Though short tales and storytelling have a genealogy dating back to biblical parables and ancient oral traditions, the short story is a distinctly modern literary form, which flowered first in the nineteenth century, making it more recent than the novel.

Edgar Allan Poe, writing about Nathaniel Hawthorne's *Twice Told Tales* (in a review generally considered to be the first attempt at a "theory" of the short story), insisted that "the brief tale" had to be "perusable" in one sitting. He calculated this as no more than two hours' reading. An author is thereby allowed to "carry out the fullness of his intention, be it what it may," achieving the "deepest effects" on the reader. This impact, said Poe, can come only from "unity of impression" and an experience of "totality" in reading. In other words, brevity allows an intense experience of wholeness. By definition the short story captures only a fragment of life, yet ironically we experience the fragment as a "totality." It gives us not length but keen focus and intensity; and a political short story does this with political subjects.

Novelists have spatial luxuries denied to the short story writer. Political short stories and political novels share the same subject matter, but not the same medium. Still, a common subject matter imposes common problems and questions. A work of political fiction, Irving Howe writes in his classic study *Politics and the Novel*, must transform ideas into "something other than the ideas of a political program." One does not approach a novel or short story with the motivations or expectations that might be brought to a political pamphlet or essay. Political fiction is, after all, fiction; it endeavors through imagination to discern some truth(s) about political reality and the human condition. A novel, Howe writes, "tries to confront experience in its immediacy and closeness, while ideology is by its nature general and inclusive." Politics is of course entwined with our experience, but the human condition is not only political. Remembering this is surely one rule for good political fiction.

It is a prescription for balance and tension, as we can see by briefly examining several of the stories in this anthology. A good political story never soothes, even if written by a conservative. Take, for example, Joseph Conrad, who thrashes radicals (especially anarchists) in several of his novels and stories. Although—perhaps because—he was the son of a Polish nationalist rebel, Conrad was profoundly conservative in both his instincts and world-view. Resignation, he asserted in his memoir, *A Personal Record*, "is the only one of our feelings for which it is impossible to become a sham." The "revolutionary spirit," he insisted, "frees one from all scruples as regards ideas." Yet for all his contempt for revolutionaries—there is a pathology for every anarchist he invents —he never presents to his readers an innocent picture of the forces of order. He writes not as a persuader, not to convince us of a political idea; he writes as a troubling scrutinizer of politics and the human condition in general.

Conrad's "An Anarchist" gives us Paul, a good-hearted but gullible French worker. He is seduced by the slogans of some seedy anarchists and lands with them in a penal colony. He escapes during a prison break, killing two erstwhile "comrades" en route, but is then trapped into working for B.O.S. Ltd., an exploitative cattle estate.

Conrad's portrait of anarchists, much like that in his renowned novel *The Secret Agent*, is unremittingly hostile—virtually a caricature. They are presented as venal and violent enunciators of alluring but invidious bromides. Here Conrad is less than fair (as numerous critics have noted). An innocent reader would never know that anarchism was not a monolithic doctrine, that among its adherents were not only nihilistic bomb-throwers, but pacifists and utopian idealists who dreamed of the world reborn as a federation of workers' cooperatives. (The latter type of anarchist is the target of John Sayles's affectionate satire in "At the Anarchists' Convention.")

Yet Conrad almost argues against himself. Having thrust his pen like a rapier at the anarchists in his story, the author has his narrator, in an aside, declare: "Comrade! Monsieur! Ah, what a good word! And they, men such as these two, had made it accursed!" The brief against revolutionaries does not become a mere paean for the status quo. Indeed, its sores are so exposed that someone less resigned than Conrad might find a good case for radicalism in his story. At its end, the protagonist is in the avaricious clutches of B.O.S. Ltd. Was it not against such exploitation that anarchists first raised their fists—against authority, against bosses? Indeed, Conrad opens the story with a wry commentary on B.O.S. Ltd.'s advertising. It is no less fraudulent, in the author's eyes, than the anarchists' slogans. In the small space of a short story Conrad is politically multifarious and shows us the negatives of both parties—that of order and that of disorder. While he is resigned, surely he comforts no reader, of whatever political persuasion.

In Conrad, the discomfort comes from a simple tale of a simple man enveloped. Compare "An Anarchist" to "Theme of the Traitor and the Hero." The portrait of revolutionaries and the human condition in this extraordinary piece by Jorge Luis Borges is infinitely more complex and enigmatic, yet in an even smaller space. A single word or page, Borges once commented, is never simple, because "each thing implies the universe whose obvious trait is complexity." The theme of Borges's story, which reads almost as if it were a report, is the multiplicity of human reality. The author gives us Ryan writing a biography of his great grandfather, the revolutionary martyr Kilpatrick. The latter—it turns out—was not what legend made of him. His dramatic death, it seems, was scripted by yet another, Nolan, partly with future historians like Ryan in mind. And Borges, author of the story of Ryan writing about Kilpatrick according to Nolan's script, proposes that the story is unfinished. In any event, it has "zones" that have "not yet been revealed to me."

Where does it occur? In Dublin in the early nineteenth century, but Borges tells us that it is set there "for convenience"—it might be in any oppressed land, from Ireland to Poland to South America. The story, the circumstances of Kilpatrick's death, are as universal and allusive as the human condition is for the author. Borges prefaces his account with a quote from a Yeats poem written during the 1919 Irish upheavals. In it men are dancers on the whirling treads of right and wrong. Eventually we will discern that questions of right and wrong, like those of politics and history, are answered, even posed, only with ambiguity.

On the eve of revolutionary upheaval Kilpatrick, "captain of conspirators" and national hero, is murdered in a theater. The gunman was never found and the police are suspected. Such is popular memory. However, Ryan discovers the "truth." Shortly before his death, Kilpatrick warned his plotting colleagues that a traitor was in their midst. He charged his old comrade, Nolan, with revealing him. Nolan, the translator into Gaelic of Shakespeare's *Julius Caesar* and a student of the *Festspiele* (a form of Swiss public theater in which historical episodes are reenacted with a town's participation) discovers that the traitor is no other than the revolutionary leader himself.

Kilpatrick, having led his comrades to himself, signs his

own death warrant. But he wishes his death to serve, not harm, the cause. Word of his treason would be a catastrophe for the revolution; better for his execution to be "an instrument for the country's emancipation." So Nolan proposes a scenario. Kilpatrick will be felled dramatically while attending—where else for such an historical spectacle?—the theater. He will appear to be a hero assassinated rather than a traitor executed. Thereby the national upheaval will be hurried and Kilpatrick redeemed. He goes bravely to his stage-managed death in a theater box. For Ryan, as for Borges and his twentieth-century readers, this seems reminiscent of Lincoln's murder—although it is actually presagement, since the assassination in Dublin occurs three decades before that of the American president. And on Kilpatrick's person, like that of the slain Julius Caesar, is discovered an unopened letter warning of impending doom (penned, one presumes, by Nolan).

Political history is enacted, reenacted, and foreshadowed on the whirling treads of right and wrong. As Kilpatrick dies, he mumbles some words that a later player in the intrigue—Ryan—suspects were to direct future historians to "the truth." Yet, having discovered "the truth," Ryan resolves to keep the secret and write solely of valiant Kilpatrick. "He understands that he too forms part of Nolan's plot." As the hero is the traitor, the historian-biographer-sleuth becomes a falsifier-concealer. But only of the treason, for Kilpatrick is truly a hero too. Like his great-grandfather, Ryan embraces his part; perhaps it was all foretold, though it is told to us afterward. It is as if Ryan is following the scenarios of both Noland and Borges.

Still, the script is not yet fully written. . . . Here then, a crucial difference between Conrad's resigned tale and Borges's metaphysical report; Conrad's world in "An Anarchist" is politically equivocal but the characters themselves are not. His anarchists are one dimensional, Paul's personality is plain. Borges, by contrast, doesn't seek to fathom his own characters and doesn't portray their political world or ideologies. We are left, instead, with the metaphysical uncertainty of the human condition, yielding only one possible conclusion (if one can call it a conclusion): politics and history are ambiguous. After all, who, or what, is Kilpatrick? Despicable traitor? Heroic rebel? Both?

In writing these stories, neither Borges nor Conrad summons the reader to political action. Though they write of political themes, Borges's metaphysical ambiguities and Conrad's resignation are ultimately private stances. George Orwell's political commitment was a public one. He sought to persuade; no political writer contrasts to Conrad's resignation or Borges's ambiguities more sharply than he. If resignation begot Conrad's insights into politics and ambiguities begot Borges's, Orwell's were born of engagement. This is what gave them such force. Reflecting on his life's work in 1946 he declared, "I see that it is invariably where I lacked *political* purpose that I wrote lifeless books, and was betrayed into purple passages, sentences without meaning, decorative adjectives and humbug generally." His experiences as an imperial cop in Burma, then as a pauper in London and Paris, then as a participant in the Spanish Civil War, and finally as witness to Stalin and Hitler—all these imposed his subject matter on him, and didn't permit ambiguity. He took it all quite personally, and the result was politically engaged writing. Consider the opening sentence of his dissection of imperialism, "Shooting an Elephant": "In Moulmein, in Lower Burma, I was hated by large numbers of people . . ."

And yet while Orwell is perhaps most celebrated for his political novels, *Animal Farm* and *1984*, he tells us in his celebrated essay "Why I Write" that he would have preferred not to write about politics. Indeed, in the mid-1930s he penned a short poem ending with this verse:

> I dreamed I dwelt in marble halls,
> And woke to find it true;
> I wasn't born for an age like this;
> Was Smith, was Jones, were you?

Here was his problem: given "an age like this" how could he not write about politics? And without committed urgency? "Every line of serious work that I've written since 1936," he insisted a decade later, "has been written directly or indirectly, *against* totalitarianism and *for* democratic Socialism, as I understand it . . . And the more conscious of one's political bias, the more chance one has of acting politically without sacrificing one's aesthetic and intellectual integrity." What did this mean for him as a writer? "The job," he asserted, "is to reconcile my ingrained likes and dislikes with the essentially public, nonindividual activities that this age forces on all of us."

The problem is, again, balance, tension, synthesis: aesthetic vision is easily dissolved in the imperatives of political purpose; political acuity can by lyrically lost in aesthetic pursuit. Romantics are often guilty of the latter sin. Orwell's political novels are often charged with the former. It is the danger of becoming "a sort of pamphleteer," as he once referred to himself. Indeed, *1984* becomes, at points, a pamphlet-as-novel, with an inevitable loss of literary texture, of balance. But its power, its political pungency are the direct consequences of his sense of political urgency.

Similar urgency animates Luisa Valenzuela's "The Censors," although her story never becomes pamphletlike. Her theme, censorship as a vital feature of political repression, is central too in *1984*. In Orwell's mind were Stalin and Hitler; in that of Valenzuela, an Argentinean, are the brutal right-wing dictatorships that have so often marred contemporary Latin American history. Her protagonist, Juan, is sucked into the regime's logic when, after sending a letter to a girlfriend living in Parisian safety, he fears that the government, now possessing her address, may stretch its claws across the ocean. The censors, as a matter of course, will examine his letter, "sniff, feel and read" between its lines, scrutinizing commas and the "most accidental stain" for subversive suggestions.

So Juan seeks employment in the government censor's office to intercept his own letter, "to beat them to the punch . . ." In Orwell's novel the protagonists, Winston and Julia, work in the regime's middle echelon—he is a functionary in the Ministry of Truth, the locus of censorship—and they seek freedom by creating a space for themselves outside the state's control. This is inadmissible in a totalitarian society, for it would allow them to step out of its seamless dominion. Captured, their souls are broken and put back together so that they are at one with the state's machinery. In Valenzuela's story, the private realm is also threatened. The censor's searing eye can make what it wants of Juan's personal correspondence with Mariana, and condemn them both for it; the logic of dominance spews illogic when it comes to guilt and innocence. Juan leaves his private life and enters that of the state when he goes to work in the censor's office. It is a building festive on the outside and staid inside. Power must always mask itself. In the end, Juan is not only enveloped by the regime, he internalizes it. He becomes increasingly habituated to its rhythms through his tasks, and his faithful service brings promotion upon promotion.

Eventually his mind becomes that of a censor, at one with the regime and its mania. He now fulfills his role as obsessively as the regime pursues its foes—"any distraction could make him lose his edge . . . He had a truly patriotic task, both self-denying and uplifting." The final self-denial: his own letter comes to him, he censors it "naturally . . . without regret"—and is executed. The fate of this individual, of human experience, is fused first in soul, and then in body, with dominance. Valenzuela's impact is achieved by an intensity that comes of the story's brevity and the author's compelling drive. And the reader recognizes immediately that this short fiction is not only an exercise in troubling scrutiny but a political *cri de coeur*: "Look here, something is terribly, terribly wrong."

Such cries also can be terribly risky. The Juans are usually anonymous sufferers of censorious tyrannies, but those who write about them often become celebrated victims. Conscience, scrutiny, warning—such interventions are often unappreciated by those in power. Asking questions that Power prefers to avoid is perhaps one of the essential political functions that political literature can play, blatantly or subversively. Several authors in this anthology paid for their writings with censorship, exile, imprisonment, or worse. Something to think about while reading these stories . . .

Nathaniel Hawthorne

Nathaniel Hawthorne *(1804–1864) was born in Salem, Massachusetts. He is one of the most celebrated of American novelists and short-story writers. Among his works are* The Scarlet Letter, The House of Seven Gables, *and* Twice-Told Tales.

MY KINSMAN,
MAJOR MOLINEUX

After the kings of Great Britain had assumed the right of appointing the colonial Governors, the measures of the latter seldom met with the ready and general approbation which had been paid to those of their predecessors, under the original charters. The people looked with most jealous scrutiny to the exercise of power which did not emanate from themselves, and they usually rewarded their rulers with slender gratitude for the compliances by which, in softening their instructions from beyond the sea, they had incurred the reprehension of those who gave them. The annals of Massachusetts Bay will inform us that of six Governors in the space of about forty years from the surrender of the old charter, under James II, two were imprisoned by a popular insurrection; a third, as Hutchinson inclines to believe, was driven from the province by the whizzing of a musket ball; a fourth, in the opinion of the same historian, was hastened to his grave by continual bickerings with the House of Representatives; and the remaining two, as well as their successors, till the Revolution, were favored with few and brief intervals of peaceful sway. The inferior members of the court party, in times of high political excitement, led scarcely a more desirable life. These remarks may serve as a preface to the following adventures, which chanced upon a summer night, not far from a hundred years ago. The reader, in order to avoid a long and dry detail of colonial affairs, is requested to dispense with an account of the train of circumstances that had caused much temporary inflammation of the popular mind.

It was near nine o'clock of a moonlight evening, when a boat crossed the ferry with a single passenger, who had obtained his conveyance at that unusual hour by the promise of an extra fare. While he stood on the landing place, searching in either pocket for the means of fulfilling his agreement, the ferryman lifted a lantern, by the aid of which, and the newly risen moon, he took a very accurate survey of the stranger's figure. He was a youth of barely eighteen years, evidently country bred, and now, as it should seem, upon his first visit to town. He was clad in a coarse gray coat, well worn, but in excellent repair; his undergarments were durably constructed of leather, and fitted tight to a pair of serviceable and well-shaped limbs; his stockings of blue yarn were the incontrovertible work of a mother or a sister; and on his head was a three-cornered hat, which in its better days had perhaps sheltered the graver brow of the lad's father. Under his left arm was a heavy cudgel formed of an oak sapling, and retaining a part of the hardened root; and his equipment was completed by a wallet, not so abundantly stocked as to incommode the vigorous shoulders on which it hung. Brown, curly hair, well-shaped features, and bright, cheerful eyes were nature's gifts, and worth all that art could have done for his adornment.

The youth, one of whose names was Robin, finally drew from his pocket the half of a little province bill of five shillings, which, in the depreciation in that sort of currency, did but satisfy the ferryman's demand, with the surplus of a sexangular piece of parchment, valued at threepence. He then

walked forward into the town, with as light a step as if his
day's journey had not already exceeded thirty miles, and with
as eager an eye as if he were entering London city, instead of
the little metropolis of a New England colony. Before Robin
had proceeded far, however, it occurred to him that he knew
not whither to direct his steps; so he paused, and looked up
and down the narrow street, scrutinizing the small and mean
wooden buildings that were scattered on either side.

"This low hovel cannot be my kinsman's dwelling," thought
he, "nor yonder old house, where the moonlight enters at the
broken casement; and truly I see none hereabouts that might
be worthy of him. It would have been wise to inquire my way
of the ferryman, and doubtless he would have gone with me,
and earned a shilling from the Major for his pains. But the
next man I meet will do as well."

He resumed his walk, and was glad to perceive that the
street now became wider, and the houses more respectable in
their appearance. He soon discerned a figure moving on
moderately in advance, and hastened his steps to overtake it.
As Robin drew nigh, he saw that the passenger was a man in
years, with a full periwig of gray hair, a wide-skirted coat of
dark cloth, and silk stockings rolled above his knees. He carried a long and polished cane, which he struck down perpen-
dicularly before him at every step; and at regular intervals he
uttered two successive hems, of a peculiarly solemn and sepulchral intonation. Having made these observations, Robin
laid hold of the skirt of the old man's coat, just when the light
from the open door and windows of a barber's shop fell upon
both their figures.

"Good evening to you, honored sir," said he, making a low
bow, and still retaining his hold of the skirt. "I pray you tell
me whereabouts is the dwelling of my kinsman, Major Molineux."

The youth's question was uttered very loudly; and one of
the barbers, whose razor was descending on a well-soaped
chin, and another who was dressing a Ramillies wig, left their
occupations, and came to the door. The citizen, in the mean-

time, turned a long-favored countenance upon Robin, and answered him in a tone of excessive anger and annoyance. His two sepulchral hems, however, broke into the very center of his rebuke, with most singular effect, like a thought of the cold grave obtruding among wrathful passions.

"Let go my garment, fellow! I tell you, I know not the man you speak of. What! I have authority, I have—hem, hem—authority; and if this be the respect you show for your betters, your feet shall be brought acquainted with the stocks by daylight tomorrow morning!"

Robin released the old man's skirt, and hastened away, pursued by an ill-mannered roar of laughter from the barber's shop. He was at first considerably surprised by the result of his question, but, being a shrewd youth, soon thought himself able to account for the mystery.

"This is some country representative," was his conclusion, "who has never seen the inside of my kinsman's door, and lacks the breeding to answer a stranger civilly. The man is old, or verily, I might be tempted to turn back and smite him on the nose. Ah, Robin, Robin! even the barber's boys laugh at you for choosing such a guide! You will be wiser in time, friend Robin."

He now became entangled in a succession of crooked and narrow streets, which crossed each other, and meandered at no great distance from the waterside. The smell of tar was obvious to his nostrils, the masts of vessels pierced the moonlight above the tops of the buildings, and the numerous signs, which Robin paused to read, informed him that he was near the center of business. But the streets were empty, the shops were closed, and lights were visible only in the second stories of a few dwelling houses. At length, on the corner of a narrow lane through which he was passing, he beheld the broad countenance of a British hero swinging before the door of an inn, whence proceeded the voices of many guests. The casement of one of the lower windows was thrown back, and a very thin curtain permitted Robin to distinguish a party at supper, round a well-furnished table. The fragrance of the good cheer steamed forth into the outer air, and the youth could not fail to recollect that the last remnant of his traveling stock of provisions had yielded to his morning appetite, and that noon had found and left him dinnerless.

"Oh, that a parchment threepenny might give me a right to sit down at yonder table!" said Robin, with a sigh. "But the Major will make me welcome to the best of his victuals; so I will even step boldly in, and inquire my way to his dwelling."

He entered the tavern, and was guided by the murmur of voices and the fumes of tobacco to the public room. It was a long and low apartment, with oaken walls, grown dark in the continual smoke, and a floor which was thickly sanded, but of no immaculate purity. A number of persons—the larger part of whom appeared to be mariners, or in some way connected with the sea—occupied the wooden benches, or leather-bottomed chairs, conversing on various matters, and occasionally lending their attention to some topic of general interest. Three or four little groups were draining as many bowls of punch, which the West India trade had long since made a familiar drink in the colony. Others, who had the appearance of men who lived by regular and laborious handicraft, preferred the insulated bliss of an unshared potation, and became more taciturn under its influence. Nearly all, in short, evinced a predilection for the Good Creature in some of its various shapes, for this is a vice to which, as Fast Day sermons of a hundred years ago will testify, we have a long hereditary claim. The only guests to whom Robin's sympathies inclined him were two or three sheepish countrymen, who were using the inn somewhat after the fashion of a Turkish caravansary; they had gotten themselves into the darkest corner of the room, and heedless of the nicotian atmosphere, were supping on the bread of their own ovens, and the bacon cured in their own chimney smoke. But though Robin felt a sort of brotherhood with these strangers, his eyes were attracted from them to a person who stood near the door, holding whispered conversation with a group of ill-dressed associates. His features were separately striking almost to grotesqueness, and the whole face left a deep impression on the memory. The forehead bulged out into a double prominence, with a vale between; the nose came boldly forth in an irregular curve, and its bridge was of more than a finger's breadth; the eyebrows were deep and shaggy, and the eyes glowed beneath them like fire in a cave.

While Robin deliberated of whom to inquire respecting his kinsman's dwelling, he was accosted by the innkeeper, a little man in a stained white apron, who had come to pay his professional welcome to the stranger. Being in the second generation from a French Protestant, he seemed to have inherited the courtesy of his parent nation; but no variety of circumstances was ever known to change his voice from the one shrill note in which he now addressed Robin.

"From the country, I presume, sir?" said he, with a profound bow. "Beg leave to congratulate you on your arrival, and trust you intend a long stay with us. Fine town here, sir, beautiful buildings, and much that may interest a stranger. May I hope for the honor of your commands in respect to supper?"

"The man sees a family likeness! The rogue has guessed that I am related to the Major!" thought Robin, who had hitherto experienced little superfluous civility.

All eyes were now turned on the country lad, standing at the door, in his worn three-cornered hat, gray coat, leather breeches, and blue yarn stockings, leaning on an oaken cudgel, and bearing a wallet on his back.

Robin replied to the courteous innkeeper, with such an assumption of confidence as befitted the Major's relative. "My honest friend," he said, "I shall make it a point to patronize your house on some occasion, when"—here he could not help lowering his voice—"when I may have more than a parchment threepence in my pocket. My present business," continued he, speaking with lofty confidence, "is merely to inquire my way to the dwelling of my kinsman, Major Molineux."

There was a sudden and general movement in the room,

which Robin interpreted as expressing the eagerness of each individual to become his guide. But the innkeeper turned his eyes to a written paper on the wall, which he read, or seemed to read, with occasional recurrences to the young man's figure.

"What have we here?" said he, breaking his speech into little dry fragments. " 'Left the house of the subscriber, bounden servant, Hezekiah Mudge—had on, when he went away, gray coat, leather breeches, master's third-best hat. One pound currency reward to whosoever shall lodge him in any jail of the province.' Better trudge, boy; better trudge!"

Robin had begun to draw his hand towards the lighter end of the oak cudgel, but a strange hostility in every countenance induced him to relinquish his purpose of breaking the courteous innkeeper's head. As he turned to leave the room, he encountered a sneering glance from the bold-featured personage whom he had before noticed; and no sooner was he beyond the door, than he heard a general laugh, in which the innkeeper's voice might be distinguished, like the dropping of small stones into a kettle.

"Now, is it not strange," thought Robin, with his usual shrewdness, "is it not strange that the confession of an empty pocket should outweigh the name of my kinsman, Major Molineux? Oh, if I had one of those grinning rascals in the woods, where I and my oak sapling grew up together, I would teach him that my arm is heavy though my purse be light!"

On turning the corner of the narrow lane, Robin found himself in a spacious street, with an unbroken line of lofty houses on each side, and a steepled building at the upper end, whence the ringing of a bell announced the hour of nine. The light of the moon, and the lamps from the numerous shop windows, discovered people promenading on the pavement, and amongst them Robin hoped to recognize his hitherto inscrutable relative. The result of his former inquiries made him unwilling to hazard another, in a scene of such publicity, and he determined to walk slowly and silently up the street, thrusting his face close to that of every elderly gentleman, in search of the Major's lineaments. In his progress, Robin encountered many gay and gallant figures. Embroidered garments of showy colors, enormous periwigs, gold-laced hats, and silver-hilted swords glided past him and dazzled his optics. Traveled youths, imitators of the European fine gentlemen of the period, trod jauntily along, half dancing to the fashionable tunes which they hummed, and making poor Robin ashamed of his quiet and natural gait. At length, after many pauses to examine the gorgeous display of goods in the shop windows, and after suffering some rebukes for the impertinence of his scrutiny into people's faces, the Major's kinsman found himself near the steepled building, still unsuccessful in his search. As yet, however, he had seen only one side of the thronged street; so Robin crossed, and continued the same sort of inquisition down the opposite pavement, with stronger hopes than the philosopher seeking an honest man, but with no better fortune. He had arrived about midway towards the lower end, from which his course began, when he overheard the approach of someone who struck down a cane on the flagstones at every step, uttering, at regular intervals, two sepulchral hems.

"Mercy on us!" quoth Robin, recognizing the sound.

Turning a corner, which chanced to be close at his right hand, he hastened to pursue his researches in some other part of the town. His patience now was wearing low, and he seemed to feel more fatigue from his rambles since he crossed the ferry than from his journey of several days on the other side. Hunger also pleaded loudly within him, and Robin began to balance the propriety of demanding, violently, and with lifted cudgel, the necessary guidance from the first solitary passenger whom he should meet. While a resolution to this effect was gaining strength, he entered a street of mean appearance, on either side of which a row of ill-built houses was straggling towards the harbor. The moonlight fell upon no passenger along the whole extent, but in the third domicile which Robin passed there was a half-opened door, and his keen glance detected a woman's garment within.

"My luck may be better here," said he to himself.

Accordingly, he approached the door, and beheld it shut closer as he did so; yet an open space remained, sufficing for the fair occupant to observe the stranger, without a corresponding display on her part. All that Robin could discern was a strip of scarlet petticoat, and the occasional sparkle of an eye, as if the moonbeams were trembling on some bright thing.

"Pretty mistress"—for I may call her so with a good conscience, thought the shrewd youth, since I know nothing to the contrary—"my sweet pretty mistress, will you be kind enough to tell me whereabouts I must seek the dwelling of my kinsman, Major Molineux?"

Robin's voice was plaintive and winning, and the female, seeing nothing to be shunned in the handsome country youth, thrust open the door, and came forth into the moonlight. She was a dainty little figure, with a white neck, round arms, and a slender waist, at the extremity of which her scarlet petticoat jutted out over a hoop, as if she were standing in a balloon. Moreover, her face was oval and pretty, her hair dark beneath the little cap, and her bright eyes possessed a sly freedom, which triumphed over those of Robin.

"Major Molineux dwells here," said this fair woman.

Now, her voice was the sweetest Robin had heard that night, the airy counterpart of a stream of melted silver; yet he could not help doubting whether that sweet voice spoke Gospel truth. He looked up and down the mean street, and then surveyed the house before which they stood. It was a small, dark edifice of two stories, the second of which projected over the lower floor, and the front apartment had the aspect of a shop for petty commodities.

"Now, truly, I am in luck," replied Robin, cunningly, "and so indeed is my kinsman, the Major, in having so pretty a housekeeper. But I prithee trouble him to step to the door; I will deliver him a message from his friends in the country, and then go back to my lodgings at the inn."

"Nay, the Major has been abed this hour or more," said the

lady of the scarlet petticoat, "and it would be to little purpose to disturb him tonight, seeing his evening draught was of the strongest. But he is a kindhearted man, and it would be as much as my life's worth to let a kinsman of his turn away from the door. You are the good old gentleman's very picture, and I could swear that was his rainy-weather hat. Also, he has garments very much resembling those leather small-clothes. But come in, I pray, for I bid you hearty welcome in his name."

So saying, the fair and hospitable dame took our hero by the hand; and the touch was light, and the force was gentleness, and though Robin read in her eyes what he did not hear in her words, yet the slender-waisted woman in the scarlet petticoat proved stronger than the athletic country youth. She had drawn his half-willing footsteps nearly to the threshold, when the opening of a door in the neighborhood startled the Major's housekeeper, and, leaving the Major's kinsman, she vanished speedily into her own domicile. A heavy yawn preceded the appearance of a man who, like the Moonshine of Pyramus and Thisbe, carried a lantern, needlessly aiding his sister luminary in the heavens. As he walked sleepily up the street, he turned his broad, dull face on Robin, and displayed a long staff, spiked at the end.

"Home, vagabond, home!" said the watchman, in accents that seemed to fall asleep as soon as they were uttered. "Home, or we'll set you in the stocks by peep of day!"

"This is the second hint of the kind," thought Robin. "I wish they would end my difficulties, by setting me there tonight."

Nevertheless, the youth felt an instinctive antipathy towards the guardian of midnight order, which at first prevented him from asking his usual question. But just when the man was about to vanish behind the corner, Robin resolved not to lose the opportunity, and shouted lustily after him:

"I say, friend! will you guide me to the house of my kinsman, Major Molineux?"

The watchman made no reply, but turned the corner and

was gone; yet Robin seemed to hear the sound of drowsy laughter stealing along the solitary street. At that moment, also, a pleasant titter saluted him from the open window above his head; he looked up, and caught the sparkle of a saucy eye; a round arm beckoned to him, and next he heard light footsteps descending the staircase within. But Robin, being of the household of a New England clergyman, was a good youth, as well as a shrewd one; so he resisted temptation, and fled away.

He now roamed desperately, and at random, through the town, almost ready to believe that a spell was on him, like that by which a wizard of his country had once kept three pursuers wandering, a whole winter night, within twenty paces of the cottage which they sought. The streets lay before him, strange and desolate, and the lights were extinguished in almost every house. Twice, however, little parties of men, among whom Robin distinguished individuals in outlandish attire, came hurrying along; but, though on both occasions they paused to address him, such intercourse did not at all enlighten his perplexity. They did but utter a few words in some language of which Robin knew nothing, and perceiving his inability to answer, bestowed a curse upon him in plain English and hastened away. Finally, the lad determined to knock at the door of every mansion that might appear worthy to be occupied by his kinsman, trusting that perseverance would overcome the fatality that had hitherto thwarted him. Firm in this resolve, he was passing beneath the walls of a church, which formed the corner of two streets, when, as he turned into the shade of its steeple, he encountered a bulky stranger, muffled in a cloak. The man was proceeding with the speed of earnest business, but Robin planted himself full before him, holding the oak cudgel with both hands across his body as a bar to further passage.

"Halt, honest man, and answer me a question," said he, very resolutely. "Tell me, this instant, whereabouts is the dwelling of my kinsman, Major Molineux!"

"Keep your tongue between your teeth, fool, and let me

pass!" said a deep, gruff voice, which Robin partly remembered. "Let me pass, I say, or I'll strike you to the earth!"

"No, no, neighbor!" cried Robin, flourishing his cudgel, and then thrusting its larger end close to the man's muffled face. "No, no, I'm not the fool you take me for, nor do you pass till I have an answer to my question. Whereabouts is the dwelling of my kinsman, Major Molineux?"

The stranger, instead of attempting to force his passage, stepped back into the moonlight, unmuffled his face, and stared full into that of Robin.

"Watch here an hour, and Major Molineux will pass by," said he.

Robin gazed with dismay and astonishment on the unprecedented physiognomy of the speaker. The forehead with its double prominence, the broad hooked nose, the shaggy eyebrows, and fiery eyes were those which he had noticed at the inn, but the man's complexion had undergone a singular, or, more properly, a twofold change. One side of the face blazed an intense red, while the other was black as midnight, the division line being in the broad bridge of the nose; and a mouth which seemed to extend from ear to ear was black or red, in contrast to the color of the cheek. The effect was as if two individual devils, a fiend of fire and a fiend of darkness, had united themselves to form this infernal visage. The stranger grinned in Robin's face, muffled his parti-colored features, and was out of sight in a moment.

"Strange things we travelers see!" ejaculated Robin.

He seated himself, however, upon the steps of the church door, resolving to wait the appointed time for his kinsman. A few moments were consumed in philosophical speculations upon the species of man who had just left him; but having settled this point shrewdly, rationally, and satisfactorily, he was compelled to look elsewhere for his amusement. And first he threw his eyes along the street. It was of more respectable appearance than most of those into which he had wandered; and the moon, creating, like the imaginative power, a beautiful strangeness in familiar objects, gave something of romance to a scene that might not have possessed it in the light of day. The irregular and often quaint architecture of the houses, some of whose roofs were broken into numerous little peaks, while others ascended, steep and narrow, into a single point, and others again were square; the pure snow white of some of their complexions, the aged darkness of others, and the thousand sparklings, reflected from bright substances in the walls of many; these matters engaged Robin's attention for a while, and then began to grow wearisome. Next he endeavored to define the forms of distant objects, starting away, with almost ghostly indistinctness, just as his eye appeared to grasp them; and finally he took a minute survey of an edifice which stood on the opposite side of the street, directly in front of the church door, where he was stationed. It was a large, square mansion, distinguished from its neighbors by a balcony, which rested on tall pillars, and by an elaborate Gothic window, communicating therewith.

"Perhaps this is the very house I have been seeking," thought Robin.

Then he strove to speed away the time, by listening to a murmur which swept continually along the street, yet was scarcely audible, except to an unaccustomed ear like his; it was a low, dull, dreamy sound, compounded of many noises, each of which was at too great a distance to be separately heard. Robin marveled at this snore of a sleeping town, and marveled more whenever its continuity was broken by now and then a distant shout, apparently loud where it originated. But altogether it was a sleep-inspiring sound, and, to shake off its drowsy influence, Robin arose, and climbed a window frame, that he might view the interior of the church. There the moonbeams came trembling in, and fell down upon the deserted pews, and extended along the quiet aisles. A fainter yet more awful radiance was hovering around the pulpit, and one solitary ray had dared to rest upon the open page of the great Bible. Had Nature, in that deep hour, become a worshiper in the house which man had builded? Or was that heavenly light the visible sanctity of the place—visible because no earthly and impure feet were within the walls? The scene made Robin's heart shiver with a sensation of loneliness stronger than he had ever felt in the remotest depths of his native woods; so he turned away and sat down again before the door. There were graves around the church, and now an uneasy thought obtruded into Robin's breast. What if the object of his search, which had been so often and so strangely thwarted, were all the time moldering in his shroud? What if his kinsman should glide through yonder gate, and nod and smile to him in dimly passing by?

"Oh, that any breathing thing were here with me!" said Robin.

Recalling his thoughts from this uncomfortable track, he sent them over forest, hill, and stream, and attempted to imagine how that evening of ambiguity and weariness had been spent by his father's household. He pictured them assembled at the door, beneath the tree, the great old tree, which had been spared for its huge twisted trunk and venerable shade, when a thousand leafy brethren fell. There, at the going down of the summer sun, it was his father's custom to perform domestic worship, that the neighbors might come and join with him like brothers of the family, and that the wayfaring man might pause to drink at that fountain, and keep his heart pure by freshening the memory of home. Robin distinguished the seat of every individual of the little audience; he saw the good man in the midst, holding the Scriptures in the golden light that fell from the western clouds; he beheld him close the book and all rise up to pray. He heard the old thanksgivings for daily mercies, the old supplications for their continuance, to which he had so often listened in weariness, but which were now among his dear remembrances. He perceived the slight inequality of his father's voice when he came to speak of the absent one; he noted how his mother turned her face to the broad and knotted trunk; how his elder brother scorned, because the beard was rough upon his upper lip, to permit his features to be moved; how the younger sister drew down a low-hanging branch before her eyes; and how the little one of all, whose sports had hitherto broken the decorum of the scene, understood the prayer for her playmate, and burst into clamorous grief. Then he saw them go in at the door; and when Robin would have entered also, the latch tinkled into its place, and he was excluded from his home.

"Am I here, or there?" cried Robin, starting; for all at once, when his thoughts had become visible and audible in a dream, the long, wide, solitary street shone out before him.

He aroused himself, and endeavored to fix his attention steadily upon the large edifice which he had surveyed before. But still his mind kept vibrating between fancy and reality; by turns, the pillars of the balcony lengthened into the tall, bare stems of pines, dwindled down to human figures, settled again into their true shape and size, and then commenced a new succession of changes. For a single moment, when he deemed himself awake, he could have sworn that a visage—one which he seemed to remember, yet could not absolutely name as his kinsman's—was looking towards him from the Gothic window. A deeper sleep wrestled with and nearly overcame him, but fled at the sound of footsteps along the opposite pavement. Robin rubbed his eyes, discerned a man passing at the foot of the balcony, and addressed him in a loud, peevish, and lamentable cry.

"Hallo, friend! must I wait here all night for my kinsman, Major Molineux?"

The sleeping echoes awoke, and answered the voice; and the passenger, barely able to discern a figure sitting in the oblique shade of the steeple, traversed the street to obtain a nearer view. He was himself a gentleman in his prime, of open, intelligent, cheerful, and altogether prepossessing countenance. Perceiving a country youth, apparently homeless and without friends, he accosted him in a tone of real kindness, which had become strange to Robin's ears.

"Well, my good lad, who are you sitting here?" inquired he. "Can I be of service to you in any way?"

"I am afraid not, sir," replied Robin, despondingly, "yet I

shall take it kindly if you'll answer me a single question. I've been searching, half the night, for one Major Molineux; now, sir, is there really such a person in these parts, or am I dreaming?"

"Major Molineux! The name is not altogether strange to me," said the gentleman, smiling. "Have you any objection to telling me the nature of your business with him?"

Then Robin briefly related that his father was a clergyman, settled on a small salary, at a long distance back in the country, and that he and Major Molineux were brothers' children. The Major, having inherited riches, and acquired civil and military rank, had visited his cousin, in great pomp, a year or two before; had manifested much interest in Robin and an elder brother, and, being childless himself, had thrown out hints respecting the future establishment of one of them in life. The elder brother was destined to succeed to the farm which his father cultivated in the interval of sacred duties; it was therefore determined that Robin should profit by his kinsman's generous intentions, especially as he seemed to be rather the favorite, and was thought to possess other necessary endowments.

"For I have the name of being a shrewd youth," observed Robin, in this part of his story.

"I doubt not you deserve it," replied his new friend, good-naturedly, "but pray proceed."

"Well, sir, being nearly eighteen years old, and well grown, as you see," continued Robin, drawing himself up to his full height, "I thought it high time to begin the world. So my mother and sister put me in handsome trim, and my father gave me half the remnant of his last year's salary, and five days ago I started for this place, to pay the Major a visit. But, would you believe it, sir! I crossed the ferry a little after dark, and have yet found nobody that would show me the way to his dwelling; only, an hour or two since, I was told to wait here, and Major Molineux would pass by."

"Can you describe the man who told you this?" inquired the gentleman.

"Oh, he was a very ill-favored fellow, sir," replied Robin, "with two great bumps on his forehead, a hook nose, fiery eyes; and, what struck me as the strangest, his face was of two different colors. Do you happen to know such a man, sir?"

"Not intimately," answered the stranger, "but I chanced to meet him a little time previous to your stopping me. I believe you may trust his word, and that the Major will very shortly pass through this street. In the meantime, as I have a singular curiosity to witness your meeting, I will sit down here upon the steps and bear you company."

He seated himself accordingly, and soon engaged his companion in animated discourse. It was but of brief continuance, however, for a noise of shouting, which had long been remotely audible, drew so much nearer that Robin inquired its cause.

"What may be the meaning of this uproar?" asked he. "Truly, if your town be always as noisy, I shall find little sleep while I am an inhabitant."

"Why, indeed, friend Robin, there do appear to be three or four riotous fellows abroad tonight," replied the gentleman. "You must not expect all the stillness of your native woods here in our streets. But the watch will shortly be at the heels of these lads and—"

"Ay, and set them in the stocks by peep of day," interrupted Robin, recollecting his own encounter with the drowsy lantern-bearer. "But, dear sir, if I may trust my ears, an army of watchmen would never make head against such a multitude of rioters. There were at least a thousand voices went up to make that one shout."

"May not a man have several voices, Robin, as well as two complexions?" said his friend.

"Perhaps a man may; but Heaven forbid that a woman should!" responded the shrewd youth, thinking of the seductive tones of the Major's housekeeper.

The sounds of a trumpet in some neighboring street now became so evident and continual that Robin's curiosity was strongly excited. In addition to the shouts, he heard frequent bursts from many instruments of discord, and a wild and confused laughter filled up the intervals. Robin rose from the steps, and looked wistfully towards a point whither people seemed to be hastening.

"Surely some prodigious merrymaking is going on," exclaimed he. "I have laughed very little since I left home, sir, and should be sorry to lose an opportunity. Shall we step round the corner by that darkish house, and take our share of the fun?"

"Sit down again, sit down, good Robin," replied the gentleman, laying his hand on the skirt of the gray coat. "You forget that we must wait here for your kinsman; and there is reason to believe that he will pass by, in the course of a very few moments."

The near approach of the uproar had now disturbed the neighborhood; windows flew open on all sides; and many heads, in the attire of the pillow, and confused by sleep suddenly broken, were protruded to the gaze of whoever had leisure to observe them. Eager voices hailed each other from house to house, all demanding the explanation, which not a soul could give. Half-dressed men hurried towards the unknown commotion, stumbling as they went over the stone steps that thrust themselves into the narrow footwalk. The shouts, the laughter, and the tuneless bray, the antipodes of music, came onwards with increasing din, till scattered individuals, and then denser bodies, began to appear round a corner at the distance of a hundred yards.

"Will you recognize your kinsman, if he passes in this crowd?" inquired the gentleman.

"Indeed, I can't warrant it, sir; but I'll take my stand here, and keep a bright lookout," answered Robin, descending to the outer edge of the pavement.

A mighty stream of people now emptied into the street, and came rolling slowly towards the church. A single horseman wheeled the corner in the midst of them, and close behind him came a band of fearful wind instruments, sending forth a fresher discord now that no intervening buildings kept it from the ear. Then a redder light disturbed the moon-beams, and a dense multitude of torches shone along the street, concealing, by their glare, whatever object they illuminated. The single horseman, clad in a military dress, and bearing a drawn sword, rode onward as the leader, and, by his fierce and variegated countenance, appeared like war personified; the red of one cheek was an emblem of fire and sword; the blackness of the other betokened the mourning that attends them. In his train were wild figures in the Indian dress, and many fantastic shapes without a model, giving the whole march a visionary air, as if a dream had broken forth from some feverish brain, and were sweeping visibly through the midnight streets. A mass of people, inactive, except as applauding spectators, hemmed the procession in; and several women ran along the sidewalk, piercing the confusion of heavier sounds with their shrill voices of mirth or terror.

"The double-faced fellow has his eye upon me," muttered Robin, with an indefinite but an uncomfortable idea that he was himself to bear a part in the pageantry.

The leader turned himself in the saddle, and fixed his glance full upon the country youth, as the steed went slowly by. When Robin had freed his eyes from those fiery ones, the musicians were passing before him, and the torches were close at hand; but the unsteady brightness of the latter formed a veil which he could not penetrate. The rattling of wheels over the stones sometimes found its way to his ear, and confused traces of a human form appeared at intervals, and then melted into the vivid light. A moment more, and the leader thundered a command to halt; the trumpets vomited a horrid breath, and then held their peace; the shouts and laughter of the people died away, and there remained only a universal hum, allied to silence. Right before Robin's eyes was an uncovered cart. There the torches blazed the brightest, there the moon shone out like day, and there, in tar-and-feathery dignity, sat his kinsman, Major Molineux!

He was an elderly man, of large and majestic person, and strong, square features, betokening a steady soul; but steady as it was, his enemies had found means to shake it. His face was pale as death, and far more ghastly; the broad forehead was contracted in his agony, so that his eyebrows formed one grizzled line; his eyes were red and wild, and the foam hung white upon his quivering lip. His whole frame was agitated by a quick and continual tremor, which his pride strove to quell, even in those circumstances of overwhelming humiliation. But perhaps the bitterest pang of all was when his eyes met those of Robin; for he evidently knew him on the instant, as the youth stood witnessing the foul disgrace of a head grown gray in honor. They stared at each other in silence, and Robin's knees shook, and his hair bristled, with a mixture of pity and terror. Soon, however, a bewildering excitement began to seize upon his mind; the preceding adventures of the night, the unexpected appearance of the crowd, the torches, the confused din and the hush that followed, the specter of his kinsman reviled by that great multitude—all this, and, more than all, a perception of tremendous ridicule in the whole scene, affected him with a sort of mental inebriety. At that moment, a voice of sluggish merriment saluted Robin's ears; he turned instinctively, and just behind the corner of the church stood the lantern-bearer, rubbing his eyes, and drowsily enjoying the lad's amazement. Then he heard a peal of laughter like the ringing of silvery bells; a woman twitched his arm, a saucy eye met his, and he saw the lady of the scarlet petticoat. A sharp, dry cachinnation appealed to his memory, and, standing on tiptoe in the crowd, with his white apron over his head, he beheld the courteous little innkeeper. And lastly, there sailed over the heads of the multitude a great, broad laugh, broken in the midst by two sepulchral hems, thus: "Haw, haw, haw—hem, hem—haw, haw, haw, haw!"

The sound proceeded from the balcony of the opposite edifice, and thither Robin turned his eyes. In front of the Gothic window stood the old citizen, wrapped in a wide gown, his gray periwig exchanged for a nightcap, which was thrust back from his forehead, and his silk stockings hanging about his legs. He supported himself on his polished cane in a fit of convulsive merriment, which manifested itself on his solemn old features like a funny inscription on a tombstone. Then Robin seemed to hear the voices of the barbers, of the guests of the inn, and of all who had made sport of him that night. The contagion was spreading among the multitude, when all at once it seized upon Robin, and he sent forth a shout of laughter that echoed through the street—every man shook his sides, every man emptied his lungs, but Robin's shout was the loudest there. The cloud spirits peeped from their silvery islands, as the congregated mirth went roaring up the sky! The Man in the Moon heard the far bellow. "Oho," quoth he, "the old earth is frolicsome tonight!"

When there was a momentary calm in that tempestuous sea of sound, the leader gave the sign, the procession resumed its march. On they went, like fiends that throng in mockery around some dead potentate, mighty no more, but majestic still in his agony. On they went, in counterfeited pomp, in senseless uproar, in frenzied merriment, trampling all on an old man's heart. On swept the tumult, and left a silent street behind.

"Well, Robin, are you dreaming?" inquired the gentleman, laying his hand on the youth's shoulder.

Robin started, and withdrew his arm from the stone post to which he had instinctively clung, as the living stream rolled by him. His cheek was somewhat pale, and his eye not quite as lively as in the earlier part of the evening.

"Will you be kind enough to show me the way to the ferry?" said he, after a moment's pause.

"You have, then, adopted a new subject of inquiry?" observed his companion, with a smile.

"Why, yes, sir," replied Robin, rather dryly. "Thanks to you, and to my other friends, I have at last met my kinsman, and he will scarce desire to see my face again. I begin to grow weary of a town life, sir. Will you show me the way to the ferry?"

"No, my good friend Robin—not tonight, at least," said the

gentleman. "Some few days hence, if you wish it, I will speed you on your journey. Or, if you prefer to remain with us, perhaps, as you are a shrewd youth, you may rise in the world without the help of your kinsman, Major Molineux."

Guy de Maupassant

Guy de Maupassant (1850–1893) was born near Dieppe, France, and is one of the nineteenth-century masters of the short story. This story takes place in the aftermath of the French defeat at Sedan in the Franco-Prussian war (1870), which led to the collapse of the French Empire and the birth of the French Third Republic.

A COUP D'ÉTAT

Paris had just learned of the disaster at Sedan. The Republic had been proclaimed. The whole of France huffed and puffed at the onset of the madness which lasted until after the Commune. Throughout the length and breadth of the land, grown men played at being soldiers.

Haberdashers had the rank of colonels and the functions of generals; revolvers and daggers were flaunted on large peace-loving paunches wreathed in red sashes; ordinary towns-people-turned-warriors for the duration commanded battalions of loud-mouthed volunteers and swore like troopers to give themselves a suitably martial air.

The simple fact that they were armed and handling service rifles went to the heads of men who otherwise had never previously handled anything more lethal than a pair of weighing-scales, and made them, for no reason at all, terrifying to anyone they encountered. They executed innocent people just to show that they could kill. As they roamed through fields as yet innocent of Prussians, they shot stray dogs, cows gently masticating, and sick horses grazing in meadows. Each man believed that he had been called upon to play a great military role. Cafés in the most out-of-the-way villages, bursting with shopkeepers in uniform, looked like barracks or field-stations.

The town of Canneville had still as yet to receive the appalling news about the army and the capital. But for a month now it had been in a state of extreme turmoil and the opposing parties stood eyeball to eyeball.

The Mayor, the Vicomte de Varnetot, who was small and thin and prematurely aged, a Bourbon legitimist who had lately transferred his loyalties to the Empire, of which he had hopes of preferment, had been confronted by a sudden burst of determined opposition in the person of Doctor Massarel, a large man with a brick-red face, leader of the local Republican Party, worshipful master of the region's masonic lodge, president of the Farmers' Club and the Firemen's Circle, and the man responsible for organizing the rural militia which was to be the salvation of the province.

Within a fortnight he had managed to rally to the defence of their territory no fewer than sixty-three volunteers, all married men with children—canny farmers from the country and shopkeepers from the town—and each morning he drilled them on the square in front of the Town Hall.

Whenever the Mayor happened to turn up at the civic offices, Commandant Massarel, bristling with pistols, sabre in hand, and strutting proudly in front of his squad, ordered them to shout: "Long live the Nation!" This cry, people noticed, upset the Vicomte who probably interpreted it as a threat, a challenge, and, to boot, an odious reminder no doubt of the Revolution of 1789.

On the morning of 5 September, the doctor, wearing full uniform and with his revolver lying on the table in front of him, was seeing two of his patients, an elderly country couple —the husband had been suffering with varicose veins for seven years but had waited until his wife was in the same state before coming to consult the doctor—when the postman delivered the newspaper.

Monsieur Massarel opened it, turned pale, stood up abruptly, and, raising his arms in a gesture of exultation, began shouting at the top of his voice while the bewildered yeoman and his wife looked on: "Long live the Republic! Long live the Republic! Long live the Republic!" Then he sat down again just as suddenly, quite faint with emotion.

When the farmer went on: "It all started when I got like pins and needles all up and down me legs," Doctor Massarel screamed: "Not another word! I haven't got time to bother with your stupid legs. The Republic has been declared, the Emperor has been taken prisoner, and France is saved. Long live the Republic!" And, making a dash for the door, he bellowed: "Céleste! Quickly! Céleste!"

The maid came running, frightened out of her wits. He spoke so fast that he tripped over his words: "My boots, my sabre, my cartridge belt, and the Spanish dagger you'll find on the table by my bed: hurry!"

The old farmer, making the most of a moment of silence, carried on stubbornly: "Then I got these sort of lumps on me veins wot gave me gip when I walked."

Beyond patience, the doctor yelled: "Don't bother me now, man, for God's sake. If you'd washed your feet a bit more often, you'd never have got yourself into this state." Grasping him by the collar, he barked at him: "Don't you realize that we now live in a Republic, you stupid oaf?"

But almost at once his sense of professional propriety brought him back to earth and he shooed out the bewildered couple, repeating: "Come back tomorrow, come back tomorrow, there's good people. I just don't have time today."

While he kitted himself out from head to foot, he gave a new series of urgent orders to his maid: "Run around to Lieutenant Picart's and Sub-Lieutenant Pommel's, and say I want them here immediately. And get Torcheboeuf to come too: tell him to bring his drum. Look lively! Sharp about it!"

When Céleste had gone he collected his thoughts, steadying himself to face the difficult situation ahead.

The three men arrived together, in their working clothes. The Commandant, who had been expecting to see them in uniform, was appalled:

"My God! Haven't you heard what's happened? The Emperor has been captured. The Republic has been proclaimed. We must take action. My position is delicate. I'd even go so far as to say dangerous!"

He paused briefly for thought while his subordinates looked on highly alarmed, then went on:

"We must take action. We must not dither. Minutes are as precious as hours at times like this. The key is the speed with which we take decisive action. You, Picart, go and find the padre and order him to ring the church bell to rally the people so that I can let them know what's going on. You, Torcheboeuf, take your drum all round the commune as far as the hamlets of La Gerisaie and Salmare and call out the militia: they're to assemble, armed, in the square. You, Pommel, get into uniform at the double, cap and tunic will do. The two of us are going to occupy the Town Hall and order Monsieur de Varnetot to hand over his powers to me. Understood?"

"Yes."

"Get on with it, then, and quick about it. Pommel, I'll come round to your house with you since we shall be operating together."

Five minutes later, the Commandant and his subaltern, both armed to the teeth, reached the square just as the diminutive figure of the Vicomte de Varnetot, walking briskly, wearing gaiters as though he were setting out on a hunting expedition, and with his Lefaucheux rifle over his shoulder, emerged from the other street, flanked by his three gamekeepers dressed in green tunics, with knives strapped to their thighs and guns slung across their backs.

While the doctor halted in astonishment, the four men went into the town hall. The door closed behind them.

"Beaten us to it," muttered the doctor. "We'll have to wait for reinforcements. Nothing to be done for the moment."

Lieutenant Picart turned up: "The curé said he wouldn't," he reported. "He's even gone and shut himself up in the church with the beadle and the churchwarden." And on the other side of the square, opposite the white, impassive civic hall, the silent black church flaunted its great iron-studded oak door.

Then, as the intrigued townspeople were beginning to poke their heads out of their windows and come out onto their doorsteps, there was a sudden roll on a drum and Torcheboeuf came into view, beating out the rapid triple call to arms. He crossed the square at a brisk trot, then disappeared along the road that led away to the fields.

The Commandant drew his sabre and advanced alone until he was about halfway between the two buildings in which the Enemy had barricaded himself. Then, waving his weapon above his head, he shouted as loudly as he could:

"Long live the Republic! Death to traitors!"

Then he turned and walked back to his officers.

The butcher, the baker, and the chemist anxiously put up their shutters and shut their shops. Only the grocer remained open.

Meanwhile the men of the militia were arriving in ones and twos, all dressed differently but each wearing a black cap with red-braid round the peak, a cap being all the corps had by way of uniform. They were armed with their own rusty old guns which had been hanging above kitchen fireplaces for thirty years, and they looked for all the world like a detachment of foresters.

When he had collected thirty or so around him, the Commandant quickly briefed them on recent events. Then, turning to his staff-officers, he said: "And now we go into action."

The townspeople were gathering, watching, and chatting among themselves.

The doctor soon had his plan of campaign worked out: "Lieutenant Picart, you will advance until you are in full view from the windows of the Town Hall and you will order Monsieur de Varnetot, in the name of the Republic, to hand over all civic buildings to me."

But the Lieutenant, who was a master mason, refused: "You wasn't born yesterday, was you? Go and get meself shot? Not likely. Them blokes inside don't miss, you know. Do your own dirty work."

The Commandant turned red in the face. "I order you! This is insubordination!"

The Lieutenant said mutinously: "Think I want to go getting me head blown off without knowin' why?"

The town's clever set had gathered in a little knot nearby. They began to laugh. One of them called out: "Quite right, Picart. It's a bad time for it!"

The doctor muttered: "Cowards!" And handing his sabre and his revolver to one of his men, he advanced slowly, his eyes fixed on the windows, expecting to see the barrel of a rifle aimed at him at any moment.

When he was within a few paces of the building, the doors at both ends, which gave access to the town's schools, suddenly opened and a flood of small children streamed out, boys on one side and girls on the other, and started playing in the wide, empty square, shouting and shrieking like a flock of geese around the doctor who could not now make himself heard. When the last pupils were outside, both doors closed again.

Most of the children drifted away eventually and the Commandant called out loudly: "Monsieur de Varnetot!"

A first-floor window opened. Monsieur de Varnetot appeared.

The Commandant began: "Monsieur, you are aware of the momentous happenings which have lately changed the face of Government. The administration which you represent has ceased to exist. That which I represent has come to power. In this difficult but decisive situation, I am here to ask you, in the name of the new Republic, to place in my hands the authority vested in you by the outgoing power."

"My dear doctor," Monsieur de Varnetot replied; "*I am the Mayor of Canneville, appointed by duly constituted authority, and Mayor of Canneville I shall remain until I have been removed from office and replaced by order of my superiors. As Mayor, I have every right to be in the Town Hall and here I intend to stay. Anyway, just you try getting me out.*" And he shut the window.

The Commandant returned to his men. But before reporting to them, he looked Lieutenant Picart up and down: "Some brave soldier you are! Rabbits aren't as lily-livered as you. You're a disgrace to the army. I'm reducing you to the ranks!"

The Lieutenant answered: "Fat lot I care." And he strolled over to the knot of muttering townsfolk.

The doctor hesitated. What was he to do next? Launch an attack? But would his men obey the order? And in any case, did he have the authority to give it?

He had a bright idea.

He hurried over to the telegraph office which faced the Town Hall on the other side of the square. There he sent three telegrams:

To the members of the Republican Government in Paris;

To the new Republican Prefect for the Seine-Inférieure at Rouen;

To the new Republican Sub-Prefect of Dieppe.

He reported the situation fully, said what danger the commune was running by being left at the mercy of the former monarchist Mayor, offered his loyal services, requested orders, and signed his name, taking care to add all his letters and qualifications. Then he rejoined his company and, taking ten francs from his pocket, said: "Here you are, men, go and get yourselves something to eat and a drink. Just leave a detachment of ten men here to make sure no one leaves the Town Hall."

But ex-Lieutenant Picart, who was chatting with the watchmaker, overheard him. He began to snigger and shouted; "Hang on. If they come out, that would be your chance to get in. Otherwise, I don't ever see you ever managing to make it inside!"

The doctor did not reply and went off to have his lunch.

In the course of the afternoon he set up posts all round the commune as though there were a threat of a surprise attack. On several occasions he walked past the doors of the Town Hall and the church without seeing anything suspicious; both buildings might have been deserted.

The butcher, the baker, and the chemist re-opened their shops.

There was a lot of talk in people's houses. If the Emperor had been captured, there must have been some dirty work behind it. No one knew exactly which Republic had been restored.

Night fell.

At about nine o'clock, the doctor, alone and treading silently, advanced as far as the entrance to the Town Hall, convinced that his opponent had gone home to bed. Just as he was shaping up to break down the door with a pickaxe, a loud voice belonging to one of the gamekeepers suddenly barked: "Who goes there?"

Monsieur Massarel beat a hasty retreat.

Day broke with the situation unchanged.

The armed militia still occupied the square. The entire population had gathered round them, waiting for a solution to be found. People from the surrounding villages kept arriving, to see for themselves.

Then the doctor, realizing that his reputation was at stake, decided to get the whole business over and done with one way or another. He was on the point of deciding on a course of action—he did not know what but it would of course be decisive—when the door of the telegraph office opened and out came the little girl who worked for the woman who ran it, holding two pieces of paper in her hand.

First she made for the Commandant and gave him one of the telegrams. Then, crossing the deserted middle of the square, crushed by all the eyes that were fixed on her, head lowered and walking with small, quick steps, she proceeded to knock timidly at the barricaded building, as though quite unaware that a party of armed men was hidden inside.

The door opened halfway. A man's hand took the paper and the girl walked back again, blushing scarlet and close to tears, aware that the whole locality was staring at her.

The doctor called out in a ringing voice: "Can I have silence, please!" And when the hoi-polloi had fallen silent, he went on grandly: "Here is the message which I have this moment received from the Government." And holding up the telegram, he read it out:

> Former mayor removed from office. Please advise promptly. Further instructions follow.
>
> For the Sub-Prefect,
>
> SAPIN, Councillor."

He had won! His heart thumped with joy. His hands shook. But Picart, his ex-subaltern, shouted out from the group nearby: "That's all very well. But if the other gang won't come out, a fat lot of good your bit of paper'll do you!"

Monsieur Massarel turned pale. If in fact the others did not come out, then he would have to make a move. It was not only a question of rights now, but of duty.

He looked anxiously towards the Town Hall, hoping to see its doors open and his opponent withdraw. The doors remained closed. What was he to do? The crowd argued amongst themselves and pressed close round the militia. Some were laughing.

The doctor was especially tormented by one thought. If he ordered an attack, he would have to march at the head of his troops. And since confrontation would cease if he were killed, it was at him and him alone that Monsieur de Varnetot and his three gamekeepers would shoot. And they were good shots, very good, as Picart now reminded him once more. But he had in idea and, turning to Pommel, said: "Go and ask the chemist to lend me a towel and a pole. At the double!"

The Lieutenant hurried off.

He would make a flag of truce, a white one, the sight of

which might possibly rejoice the former Mayor's legitimist heart.

Pommel returned with the piece of cloth he had been asked to fetch plus a broomhandle. With some pieces of string they organized a standard which Monsieur Massarel seized with both hands. Then, brandishing it before him, he set out once more for the Town Hall. When he faced the door, he again called out: "Monsieur de Varnetot?" The door opened suddenly and Monsieur de Varnetot appeared on the threshold accompanied by his three gamekeepers.

Instinctively, the doctor took one step back. Then he saluted his adversary courteously and, choking with emotion, managed to say: "I am here to inform you of the instructions which I have received."

Without returning his salute, his high-born enemy replied: "Sir, I withdraw. But do not think that I do so out of fear or out of deference to the odious government which has usurped power." And stressing each word separately, he declared: "I have no wish to appear to serve the Republic, not even for a single day. That is all."

Quite at a loss for words, Massarel did not answer. Monsieur de Varnetot broke into a quick march and disappeared around one of the corners of the square, still flanked by his escort.

Then the doctor, drunk with pride, walked back to the waiting crowd. The moment he was near enough to be heard, he shouted: "Hooray! Hooray! The Republic is winning up and down the line!" This brought no reaction whatsoever.

The doctor continued: "The people are free. You are free and independent. You should be proud!" The inert villagers stared at him. No glory shone in their eyes.

Then he in turn stared at them, appalled by their indifference, and he cast round for something he could say or do which would produce a mighty effect, electrify this sleepy township, and fulfil his mission as champion of a new order.

He was visited by inspiration. Turning to Pommel, he said: "Lieutenant, go and see if you can find the bust of the former

Emperor which is in the Council debating chamber, then bring it here with a chair."

Pommel soon returned carrying on his right shoulder the plaster bust of Louis-Napoleon and holding in his left hand a chair with a straw seat.

Monsieur Massarel stepped forward to meet him, took the chair, set it on the ground, placed the white bust on it, and, stepping back a few paces, addressed it in a sonorous voice:

"Oh tyrant! How fallen are the mighty, fallen into mud and mire. The dying nation groaned beneath thy foot. Avenging fate has struck thee down. Defeat and shame have jumped onto thy back; thou hast fallen in defeat, a prisoner to the Prussian. But out of the ruins of thy crumbling empire, the Republic rises, young and radiant, picking up thy broken sword . . ."

He waited for the applause. There was no acclamation, no spontaneous burst of clapping. The startled yokels remained silent. Meanwhile the bust, with its waxed moustaches extending beyond the cheeks on both sides, and its head held quite still and combed as immaculately as a barber's model, seemed to be watching Monsieur Massarel with its indelible, mocking, plaster smile.

And so they faced each other, Napoleon on his chair and the doctor standing three paces away. The Commandant was suddenly filled with anger. But what was he to do? What could he do to rouse the people and carry off public opinion victoriously and definitively? By chance, his hand came to rest on his hip and, under his red sash, he felt the butt of his revolver.

At this moment no inspiration, no words came to him. Instead, he drew out his pistol, took two paces forward, and, at point blank range, blasted the fallen Emperor.

The bullet made a little black hole in the forehead. It might have been a spot and was nothing to speak of. The effect had been missed. Monsieur Massarel fired a second shot, which made another hole, then a third, and, without pausing, loosed off his last three bullets. Louis-Napoleon's forehead flew up in a cloud of white dust, but his eyes, his nose, and the fine points of his moustaches remained intact.

At the end of his patience, the doctor knocked the chair over with a flick of the wrist and, placing one foot in the pose of a conqueror on what remained of the bust, turned to the bewildered crowd bellowing: "And so perish all traitors!"

But since no display of enthusiasm was as yet forthcoming and the spectators seemed to have been struck dumb with astonishment, the Commandant called to the men of the militia: "You may return to your homes now, men!" And he himself walked off quickly towards his house, as though he were running away.

As soon as he appeared, his maid said he had patients who had been waiting in the surgery for more than three hours. He hurried along to see. It was the country people with the varicose veins. They had come back and had been stubbornly, patiently sitting there since early morning.

The old farmer immediately carried on with what he had been saying:

"It started when I got like pins and needles all up and down me legs . . ."

Joseph Conrad

Joseph Conrad (1857–1924) was Polish in origin but became a British subject in 1886. He was born Teodor Josef Konrad Korzeniowski in Russian controlled Ukraine, but wrote in English (which was his third language, after Polish and French). Among his works are The Secret Agent, The Heart of Darkness, Lord Jim *and* Nostromo.

AN ANARCHIST

That year I spent the best two months of the dry season on one of the estates—in fact, on the principal cattle estate—of a famous meat-extract manufacturing company.

B. O. S. Bos. You have seen the three magic letters on the advertisement pages of magazines and newspapers, in the windows of provision merchants, and on calendars for next year you receive by post in the month of November. They scatter pamphlets also, written in a sickly enthusiastic style and in several languages, giving statistics of slaughter and bloodshed enough to make a Turk turn faint. The "art" illustrating that "literature" represents in vivid and shining colours a large and enraged black bull stamping upon a yellow snake writhing in emerald-green grass, with a cobalt-blue sky for a background. It is atrocious and it is an allegory. The snake symbolizes disease, weakness—perhaps mere hunger, which last is the chronic disease of the majority of mankind. Of course everybody knows the B. O. S. Ltd., with its unrivalled products: Vinobos, Jellybos, and the latest unequalled perfection, Tribos, whose nourishment is offered to you not only highly concentrated, but already half digested. Such apparently is the love that Limited Company bears to its fellow-men—even as the love of the father and mother penguin for their hungry fledglings.

Of course the capital of a country must be productively employed. I have nothing to say against the company. But being myself animated by feelings of affection towards my fellow-men, I am saddened by the modern system of advertising. Whatever evidence it offers of enterprise, ingenuity, impudence, and resource in certain individuals, it proves to my mind the wide prevalence of that form of mental degradation which is called gullibility.

In various parts of the civilized and uncivilized world I have had to swallow B. O. S. with more or less benefit to myself, though without great pleasure. Prepared with hot water and abundantly peppered to bring out the taste, this extract is not really unpalatable. But I have never swallowed its advertisements. Perhaps they have not gone far enough. As far as I can remember they make no promise of everlasting youth to the users of B. O. S., nor yet have they claimed the power of raising the dead for their estimable products. Why this austere reserve, I wonder? But I don't think they would have had me even on these terms. Whatever form of mental degradation I may (being but human) be suffering from, it is not the popular form. I am not gullible.

I have been at some pains to bring out distinctly this statement about myself in view of the story which follows. I have checked the facts as far as possible. I have turned up the files of French newspapers, and I have also talked with the officer who commands the military guard on the *Ile Royale,* when in the course of my travels I reached Cayenne. I believe the story to be in the main true. It is the sort of story that no man, I think, would ever invent about himself, for it is neither grandiose nor flattering, nor yet funny enough to gratify a perverted vanity.

It concerns the engineer of the steam-launch belonging to

the Marañon cattle estate of the B. O. S. Co., Ltd. This estate is also an island—an island as big as a small province, lying in the estuary of a great South American river. It is wild and not beautiful, but the grass growing on its low plains seems to possess exceptionally nourishing and flavouring qualities. It resounds with the lowing of innumerable herds—a deep and distressing sound under the open sky, rising like a monstrous protest of prisoners condemned to death. On the mainland, across twenty miles of discoloured muddy water, there stands a city whose name, let us say, is Horta.

But the most interesting characteristic of this island (which seems like a sort of penal settlement for condemned cattle) consists in its being the only known habitat of an extremely rare and gorgeous butterfly. The species is even more rare than it is beautiful, which is not saying little. I have already alluded to my travels. I travelled at that time, but strictly for myself and with a moderation unknown in our days of round-the-world tickets. I even travelled with a purpose. As a matter of fact, I am—"Ha, ha, ha!—a desperate butterfly-slayer. Ha, ha, ha!"

This was the tone in which Mr. Harry Gee, the manager of the cattle station, alluded to my pursuits. He seemed to consider me the greatest absurdity in the world. On the other hand, the B. O. S. Co., Ltd., represented to him the acme of the nineteenth century's achievement. I believe that he slept in his leggings and spurs. His days he spent in the saddle flying over the plains, followed by a train of half-wild horsemen, who called him Don Enrique, and who had no definite idea of the B. O. S. Co., Ltd., which paid their wages. He was an excellent manager, but I don't see why, when we met at meals, he should have thumped me on the back, with loud, derisive inquiries: "How's the deadly sport to-day? Butterflies going strong? Ha, ha, ha!"—especially as he charged me two dollars per diem for the hospitality of the B. O. S. Co., Ltd., (capital £1,500,000, fully paid up), in whose balance-sheet for that year those monies are no doubt included. "I don't think I can make it anything less in justice to my company," he had remarked, with extreme gravity, when I was arranging with him the terms of my stay on the island.

His chaff would have been harmless enough if intimacy of intercourse in the absence of all friendly feeling were not a thing detestable in itself. Moreover, his facetiousness was not very amusing. It consisted in the wearisome repetition of descriptive phrases applied to people with a burst of laughter. "Desperate butterfly-slayer. Ha, ha, ha!" was one sample of his peculiar wit which he himself enjoyed so much. And in the same vein of exquisite humour he called my attention to the engineer of the steam-launch, one day, as we strolled on the path by the side of the creek.

The man's head and shoulders emerged above the deck, over which were scattered various tools of his trade and a few pieces of machinery. He was doing some repairs to the engines. At the sound of our footsteps he raised anxiously a grimy face with a pointed chin and a tiny fair moustache. What could be seen of his delicate features under the black smudges appeared to me wasted and livid in the greenish shade of the enormous tree spreading its foliage over the launch moored close to the bank.

To my great surprise, Harry Gee addressed him as "Crocodile," in that half-jeering, half-bullying tone which is characteristic of self-satisfaction in his delectable kind:

"How does the work get on, Crocodile?"

I should have said before that the amiable Harry had picked up French of a sort somewhere—in some colony or other—and that he pronounced it with a disagreeable forced precision as though he meant to guy the language. The man in the launch answered him quickly in a pleasant voice. His eyes had a liquid softness and his teeth flashed dazzlingly white between his thin, drooping lips. The manager turned to me, very cheerful and loud, explaining:

"I call him Crocodile because he lives half in, half out of the creek. Amphibious—see? There's nothing else amphibious living on the island except crocodiles; so he must belong to the species—eh? But in reality he's nothing less than *un citoyen anarchiste de Barcelone.*"

"A citizen anarchist from Barcelona?" I repeated, stupidly, looking down at the man. He had turned to his work in the engine-well of the launch and presented his bowed back to us. In that attitude I heard him protest, very audibly:

"I do not even know Spanish."

"Hey? What? You dare to deny you come from over there?" the accomplished manager was down on him truculently.

At this the man straightened himself up, dropping a spanner he had been using, and faced us; but he trembled in all his limbs.

"I deny nothing, nothing, nothing!" he said, excitedly.

He picked up the spanner and went to work again without paying any further attention to us. After looking at him for a minute or so, we went away.

"Is he really an anarchist?" I asked, when out of ear-shot.

"I don't care a hang what he is," answered the humorous official of the B. O. S. Co. "I gave him the name because it suited me to label him in that way. It's good for the company."

"For the company!" I exclaimed, stopping short.

"Aha!" he triumphed, tilting up his hairless pug face and straddling his thin, long legs. "That surprises you. I am bound to do my best for my company. They have enormous expenses. Why—our agent in Horta tells me they spend fifty thousand pounds every year in advertising all over the world! One can't be too economical in working the show. Well, just you listen. When I took charge here the estate had no steam-launch. I asked for one, and kept on asking by every mail till I got it; but the man they sent out with it chucked his job at the end of two months, leaving the launch moored at the pontoon in Horta. Got a better screw at a sawmill up the river—blast him! And ever since it has been the same thing. Any Scotch or Yankee vagabond that likes to call himself a mechanic out here gets eighteen pounds a month, and the next you know he's cleared out, after smashing something as likely as not. I give you my word that some of the objects I've had for engine-drivers couldn't tell the boiler from the funnel. But this fellow understands his trade, and I don't mean him to clear out. See?"

And he struck me lightly on the chest for emphasis. Disregarding his peculiarities of manner, I wanted to know what all this had to do with the man being an anarchist.

"Come!" jeered the manager. "If you saw suddenly a barefooted, unkempt chap slinking amongst the bushes on the sea face of the island, and at the same time observed less than a mile from the beach, a small schooner full of niggers hauling off in a hurry, you wouldn't think the man fell there from the sky, would you? And it could be nothing else but either that or Cayenne. I've got my wits about me. Directly I sighted this queer game I said to myself—'Escaped Convict.' I was as certain of it as I am of seeing you standing here this minute. So I spurred on straight at him. He stood his ground for a bit on a sand hillock crying out: *'Monsieur! Monsieur! Arrêtez!'* then at the last moment broke and ran for life. Says I to myself, 'I'll tame you before I'm done with you.' So without a single word I kept on, heading him off here and there. I rounded him up towards the shore, and at last I had him corralled on a spit, his heels in the water and nothing but sea and sky at his back, with my horse pawing the sand and shaking his head within a yard of him.

"He folded his arms on his breast then and stuck his chin up in a sort of desperate way; but I wasn't to be impressed by the beggar's posturing.

"Says I, 'You're a runaway convict.'

"When he heard French, his chin went down and his face changed.

" 'I deny nothing,' says he, panting yet, for I had kept him skipping about in front of my horse pretty smartly. I asked him what he was doing there. He had got his breath by then, and explained that he had meant to make his way to a farm which he understood (from the schooner's people, I suppose) was to be found in the neighbourhood. At that I laughed aloud and he got uneasy. Had he been deceived? Was there no farm within walking distance?

"I laughed more and more. He was on foot, and of course the first bunch of cattle he came across would have stamped him to rags under their hoofs. A dismounted man caught on the feeding-grounds hasn't got the ghost of a chance.

"'My coming upon you like this has certainly saved your life,' I said. He remarked that perhaps it was so; but that for his part he had imagined I had wanted to kill him under the hoofs of my horse. I assured him that nothing would have been easier had I meant it. And then we came to a sort of dead stop. For the life of me I didn't know what to do with this convict, unless I chucked him into the sea. It occurred to me to ask him what he had been transported for. He hung his head.

"'What is it?' says I. 'Theft, murder, rape, or what?' I wanted to hear what he would have to say for himself, though of course I expected it would be some sort of lie. But all he said was—

"'Make it what you like. I deny nothing. It is no good denying anything.'

"I looked him over carefully and a thought struck me.

"'They've got anarchists there, too,' I said. 'Perhaps you're one of them.'

"'I deny nothing whatever, monsieur,' he repeats.

"This answer made me think that perhaps he was not an anarchist. I believe those damned lunatics are rather proud of themselves. If he had been one, he would have probably confessed straight out.

"'What were you before you became a convict?'

"'Ouvrier,' he says. 'And a good workman, too.'

"At that I began to think he must be an anarchist, after all. That's the class they come mostly from, isn't it? I hate the cowardly bomb-throwing brutes. I almost made up my mind to turn my horse short round and leave him to starve or drown where he was, whichever he liked best. As to crossing the island to bother me again, the cattle would see to that. I don't know what induced me to ask—

" 'What sort of workman?'

"I didn't care a hang whether he answered me or not. But when he said at once, *'Mécanicien, monsieur,'* I nearly jumped out of the saddle with excitement. The launch had been lying disabled and idle in the creek for three weeks. My duty to the company was clear. He noticed my start, too, and there we were for a minute or so staring at each other as if bewitched.

" 'Get up on my horse behind me,' I told him. 'You shall put my steam-launch to rights.' "

These are the words in which the worthy manager of the Marañon estate related to me the coming of the supposed anarchist. He meant to keep him—out of a sense of duty to the company—and the name he had given him would prevent the fellow from obtaining employment anywhere in Horta. The vaqueros of the estate, when they went on leave, spread it all over the town. They did not know what an anarchist was, nor yet what Barcelona meant. They called him Anarchisto de Barcelona, as if it were his Christian name and surname. But the people in town had been reading in their papers about the anarchists in Europe and were very much impressed. Over the jocular addition of "de Barcelona" Mr. Harry Gee chuckled with immense satisfaction. "That breed is particularly murderous, isn't it? It makes the sawmills crowd still more afraid of having anything to do with him— see?" he exulted, candidly. "I hold him by that name better than if I had him chained up by the leg to the deck of the steam-launch.

"And mark," he added, after a pause, "he does not deny it. I am not wronging him in any way. He is a convict of some sort, anyhow."

"But I suppose you pay him some wages, don't you?" I asked.

"Wages! What does he want with money here? He gets his food from my kitchen and his clothing from the store. Of course I'll give him something at the end of the year, but you don't think I'd employ a convict and give him the same money I would give an honest man? I am looking after the interests of my company first and last."

I admitted that, for a company spending fifty thousand pounds every year in advertising, the strictest economy was obviously necessary. The manager of the Marañon Estancia grunted approvingly.

"And I'll tell you what," he continued: "if I were certain he's an anarchist and he had the cheek to ask me for money, I would give him the toe of my boot. However, let him have the benefit of the doubt. I am perfectly willing to take it that he has done nothing worse than to stick a knife into somebody—with extenuating circumstances—French fashion, don't you know. But that subversive sanguinary rot of doing away with all law and order in the world makes my blood boil. It's simply cutting the ground from under the feet of every decent, respectable, hard-working person. I tell you that the consciences of people who have them, like you or I, must be protected in some way; or else the first low scoundrel that came along would in every respect be just as good as myself. Wouldn't he, now? And that's absurd!"

He glared at me. I nodded slightly and murmured that doubtless there was much subtle truth in his view.

The principal truth discoverable in the views of Paul the engineer was that a little thing may bring about the undoing of a man.

"Il ne faut pas beaucoup pour perdre un homme," he said to me, thoughtfully, one evening.

I report this reflection in French, since the man was of Paris, not of Barcelona at all. At the Marañon he lived apart from the station, in a small shed with a metal roof and straw walls, which he called *mon atelier*. He had a work-bench there. They had given him several horse-blankets and a saddle—not that he ever had occasion to ride, but because no other bedding was used by the working-hands, who were all vaqueros—cattlemen. And on this horseman's gear, like a son of the plains, he used to sleep amongst the tools of his trade, in a litter of rusty scrap-iron, with a portable forge at his head, under the work-bench sustaining his grimy mosquito-net.

Now and then I would bring him a few candle ends saved from the scant supply of the manager's house. He was very thankful for these. He did not like to lie awake in the dark, he confessed. He complained that sleep fled from him. *"Le sommeil me fuit,"* he declared, with his habitual air of subdued stoicism, which made him sympathetic and touching. I made it clear to him that I did not attach undue importance to the fact of his having been a convict.

Thus it came about that one evening he was led to talk about himself. As one of the bits of candle on the edge of the bench burned down to the end, he hastened to light another.

He had done his military service in a provincial garrison and returned to Paris to follow his trade. It was a well-paid one. He told me with some pride that in a short time he was earning no less than ten francs a day. He was thinking of setting up for himself by and by and of getting married.

Here he sighed deeply and paused. Then with a return to his stoical note:

"It seems I did not know enough about myself."

On his twenty-fifth birthday two of his friends in the repairing shop where he worked proposed to stand him a dinner. He was immensely touched by this attention.

"I was a steady man," he remarked, "but I am not less sociable than any other body."

The entertainment came off in a little café on the Boulevard de la Chapelle. At dinner they drank some special wine. It was excellent. Everything was excellent; and the world—in his own words—seemed a very good place to live in. He had good prospects, some little money laid by, and the affection of two excellent friends. He offered to pay for all the drinks after dinner, which was only proper on his part.

They drank more wine; they drank liqueurs, cognac, beer,

then more liqueurs and more cognac. Two strangers sitting at the next table looked at him, he said, with so much friendliness, that he invited them to join the party.

He had never drunk so much in his life. His elation was extreme, and so pleasurable that whenever it flagged he hastened to order more drinks.

"It seemed to me," he said, in his quiet tone and looking on the ground in the gloomy shed full of shadows, "that I was on the point of just attaining a great and wonderful felicity. Another drink, I felt, would do it. The others were holding out well with me, glass for glass."

But an extraordinary thing happened. At something the strangers said his elation fell. Gloomy ideas—*des idées noires*—rushed into his head. All the world outside the café appeared to him as a dismal evil place where a multitude of poor wretches had to work and slave to the sole end that a few individuals should ride in carriages and live riotously in palaces. He became ashamed of his happiness. The pity of mankind's cruel lot wrung his heart. In a voice choked with sorrow he tried to express these sentiments. He thinks he wept and swore in turns.

The two new acquaintances hastened to applaud his humane indignation. Yes. The amount of injustice in the world was indeed scandalous. There was only one way of dealing with the rotten state of society. Demolish the whole *sacrée boutique*. Blow up the whole iniquitous show.

Their heads hovered over the table. They whispered to him eloquently; I don't think they quite expected the result. He was extremely drunk—mad drunk. With a howl of rage he leaped suddenly upon the table. Kicking over the bottles and glasses, he yelled: *"Vive l'anarchie!* Death to the capitalists!" He yelled this again and again. All round him broken glass was falling, chairs were being swung in the air, people were taking each other by the throat. The police dashed in. He hit, bit, scratched and struggled, till something crashed down upon his head. . . .

He came to himself in a police cell, locked up on a charge of assault, seditious cries, and anarchist propaganda.

He looked at me fixedly with his liquid, shining eyes, that seemed very big in the dim light.

"That was bad. But even then I might have got off somehow, perhaps," he said, slowly.

I doubt it. But whatever chance he had was done away with by a young socialist lawyer who volunteered to undertake his defence. In vain he assured him that he was no anarchist; that he was a quiet, respectable mechanic, only too anxious to work ten hours per day at his trade. He was represented at the trial as the victim of society and his drunken shoutings as the expression of infinite suffering. The young lawyer had his way to make, and this case was just what he wanted for a start. The speech for the defence was pronounced magnificent.

The poor fellow paused, swallowed, and brought out the statement:

"I got the maximum penalty applicable to a first offence."

I made an appropriate murmur. He hung his head and folded his arms.

"When they let me out of prison," he began, gently, "I made tracks, of course, for my old workshop. My *patron* had a particular liking for me before; but when he saw me he turned green with fright and showed me the door with a shaking hand."

While he stood in the street, uneasy and disconcerted, he was accosted by a middle-aged man who introduced himself as an engineer's fitter, too. "I know who you are," he said. "I have attended your trial. You are a good comrade and your ideas are sound. But the devil of it is that you won't be able to get work anywhere now. These bourgeois'll conspire to starve you. That's their way. Expect no mercy from the rich."

To be spoken to so kindly in the street had comforted him very much. His seemed to be the sort of nature needing support and sympathy. The idea of not being able to find work had knocked him over completely. If his *patron*, who knew

him so well for a quiet, orderly, competent workman, would
have nothing to do with him now—then surely nobody else
would. That was clear. The police, keeping their eye on him,
would hasten to warn every employer inclined to give him a
chance. He felt suddenly very helpless, alarmed and idle; and
he followed the middle-aged man to the *estaminet* round the
corner where he met some other good companions. They assured him that he would not be allowed to starve, work or no
work. They had drinks all round to the discomfiture of all
employers of labour and to the destruction of society.

He sat biting his lower lip.

"That is, monsieur, how I became a *compagnon,*" he said.
The hand he passed over his forehead was trembling. "All the
same, there's something wrong in a world where a man can
get lost for a glass more or less."

He never looked up, though I could see he was getting
excited under his dejection. He slapped the bench with his
open palm.

"No!" he cried. "It was an impossible existence! Watched
by the police, watched by the comrades, I did not belong to
myself any more! Why, I could not even go to draw a few
francs from my savings-bank without a comrade hanging
about the door to see that I didn't bolt! And most of them
were neither more nor less than housebreakers. The intelligent, I mean. They robbed the rich; they were only getting
back their own, they said. When I had had some drink I believed them. There were also the fools and the mad. *Des
exaltés—quoi!* When I was drunk I loved them. When I got
more drink I was angry with the world. That was the best
time. I found refuge from misery in rage. But one can't be
always drunk—*n'est-ce pas, monsieur?* And when I was sober
I was afraid to break away. They would have stuck me like a
pig."

He folded his arms again and raised his sharp chin with a
bitter smile.

"By and by they told me it was time to go to work. The
work was to rob a bank. Afterwards a bomb would be thrown

47

to wreck the place. My beginner's part would be to keep watch in a street at the back and to take care of a black bag with the bomb inside till it was wanted. After the meeting at which the affair was arranged a trusty comrade did not leave me an inch. I had not dared to protest; I was afraid of being done away with quietly in that room; only, as we were walking together I wondered whether it would not be better for me to throw myself suddenly into the Seine. But while I was turning it over in my mind we had crossed the bridge, and afterwards I had not the opportunity."

In the light of the candle end, with his sharp features, fluffy little moustache, and oval face, he looked at times delicately and gaily young, and then appeared quite old, decrepit, full of sorrow, pressing his folded arms to his breast.

As he remained silent I felt bound to ask:

"Well! And how did it end?"

"Deportation to Cayenne," he answered.

He seemed to think that somebody had given the plot away. As he was keeping watch in the back street, bag in hand, he was set upon by the police. "These imbeciles" had knocked him down without noticing what he had in his hand. He wondered how the bomb failed to explode as he fell. But it didn't explode.

"I tried to tell my story in court," he continued. "The president was amused. There were in the audience some idiots who laughed."

I expressed the hope that some of his companions had been caught, too. He shuddered slightly before he told me that there were two—Simon, called also Biscuit, the middle-aged fitter who spoke to him in the street, and a fellow of the name of Mafile, one of the sympathetic strangers who had applauded his sentiments and consoled his humanitarian sorrows when he got drunk in the café.

"Yes," he went on, with an effort, "I had the advantage of their company over there on St. Joseph's Island, amongst some eighty or ninety other convicts. We were all classed as dangerous."

St. Joseph's Island is the prettiest of the *Iles de Salut.* It is rocky and green, with shallow ravines, bushes, thickets, groves of mango-trees, and many feathery palms. Six warders armed with revolvers and carbines are in charge of the convicts kept there.

An eight-oared galley keeps up the communication in the daytime, across a channel a quarter of a mile wide, with the *Ile Royale,* where there is a military post. She makes the first trip at six in the morning. At four in the afternoon her service is over, and she is then hauled up into a little dock on the *Ile Royale* and a sentry put over her and a few smaller boats. From that time till next morning the island of St. Joseph remains cut off from the rest of the world, with the warders patrolling in turn the path from the warders' house to the convict huts, and a multitude of sharks patrolling the waters all round.

Under these circumstances the convicts planned a mutiny. Such a thing had never been known in the penitentiary's history before. But their plan was not without some possibility of success. The warders were to be taken by surprise and murdered during the night. Their arms would enable the convicts to shoot down the people in the galley as she came alongside in the morning. The galley once in their possession, other boats were to be captured, and the whole company was to row away up the coast.

At dusk the two warders on duty mustered the convicts as usual. Then they proceeded to inspect the huts to ascertain that everything was in order. In the second they entered they were set upon and absolutely smothered under the numbers of their assailants. The twilight faded rapidly. It was a new moon; and a heavy black squall gathering over the coast increased the profound darkness of the night. The convicts assembled in the open space, deliberating upon the next step to be taken, argued amongst themselves in low voices.

"You took part in all this?" I asked.

"No. I knew what was going to be done, of course. But why should I kill these warders? I had nothing against them. But I was afraid of the others. Whatever happened, I could not escape from them. I sat alone on the stump of a tree with my head in my hands, sick at heart at the thought of a freedom that could be nothing but a mockery to me. Suddenly I was startled to perceive the shape of a man on the path near by. He stood perfectly still, then his form became effaced in the night. It must have been the chief warder coming to see what had become of his two men. No one noticed him. The convicts kept on quarrelling over their plans. The leaders could not get themselves obeyed. The fierce whispering of that dark mass of men was very horrible.

"At last they divided into two parties and moved off. When they had passed me I rose, weary and hopeless. The path to the warders' house was dark and silent, but on each side the bushes rustled slightly. Presently I saw a faint thread of light before me. The chief warder, followed by his three men, was approaching cautiously. But he had failed to close his dark lantern properly. The convicts had seen that faint gleam, too. There was an awful savage yell, a turmoil on the dark path, shots fired, blows, groans: and with the sound of smashed bushes, the shouts of the pursuers and the screams of the pursued, the man-hunt, the warder-hunt, passed by me into the interior of the island. I was alone. And I assure you, monsieur, I was indifferent to everything. After standing still for a while, I walked on along the path till I kicked something hard. I stooped and picked up a warder's revolver. I felt with my fingers that it was loaded in five chambers. In the gusts of wind I heard the convicts calling to each other far away, and then a roll of thunder would cover the soughing and rustling of the trees. Suddenly, a big light ran across my path very low along the ground. And it showed a woman's skirt with the edge of an apron.

"I knew that the person who carried it must be the wife of the head warder. They had forgotten all about her, it seems. A shot rang out in the interior of the island, and she cried out to herself as she ran. She passed on. I followed, and presently I saw her again. She was pulling at the cord of the big bell which hangs at the end of the landing-pier, with one hand, and with the other she was swinging the heavy lantern to and fro. This is the agreed signal for the *Ile Royale* should assistance be required at night. The wind carried the sound away from our island and the light she swung was hidden on the shore side by the few trees that grow near the warders' house.

"I came up quite close to her from behind. She went on without stopping, without looking aside, as though she had been all alone on the island. A brave woman, monsieur. I put the revolver inside the breast of my blue blouse and waited. A flash of lightning and a clap of thunder destroyed both the sound and the light of the signal for an instant, but she never faltered, pulling at the cord and swinging the lantern as regularly as a machine. She was a comely woman of thirty—no more. I thought to myself, 'All that's no good on a night like this.' And I made up my mind that if a body of my fellow-convicts came down to the pier—which was sure to happen soon—I would shoot her through the head before I shot myself. I knew the 'comrades' well. This idea of mine gave me quite an interest in life, monsieur; and at once, instead of remaining stupidly exposed on the pier, I retreated a little way and crouched behind a bush. I did not intend to let myself be pounced upon unawares and be prevented perhaps from rendering a supreme service to at least one human creature before I died myself.

"But we must believe the signal was seen, for the galley from *Ile Royale* came over in an astonishingly short time. The woman kept right on till the light of her lantern flashed upon the officer in command and the bayonets of the soldiers in the boat. Then she sat down and began to cry.

"She didn't need me any more. I did not budge. Some soldiers were only in their shirt-sleeves, others without boots, just as the call to arms had found them. They passed by my bush at the double. The galley had been sent away for more; and the woman sat all alone crying at the end of the pier, with the lantern standing on the ground near her.

"Then suddenly I saw in the light at the end of the pier the red pantaloons of two more men. I was overcome with astonishment. They, too, started off at a run. Their tunics flapped unbuttoned and they were bare-headed. One of them panted out to the other, 'Straight on, straight on!'

"Where on earth did they spring from, I wondered. Slowly I walked down the short pier. I saw the woman's form shaken by sobs and heard her moaning more and more distinctly, 'Oh, my man! my poor man! my poor man!' I stole on quietly. She could neither hear nor see anything. She had thrown her apron over her head and was rocking herself to and fro in her grief. But I remarked a small boat fastened to the end of the pier.

"Those two men—they looked like *sous-officiers*—must have come in it, after being too late, I suppose, for the galley. It is incredible that they should have thus broken the regulations from a sense of duty. And it was a stupid thing to do. I could not believe my eyes in the very moment I was stepping into that boat.

"I pulled along the shore slowly. A black cloud hung over the *Iles de Salut*. I heard firing, shouts. Another hunt had begun—the convict-hunt. The oars were too long to pull comfortably. I managed them with difficulty, though the boat herself was light. But when I got round to the other side of the island the squall broke in rain and wind. I was unable to make head against it. I let the boat drift ashore and secured her.

"I knew the spot. There was a tumbledown old hovel standing near the water. Cowering in there I heard through the noises of the wind and the falling downpour some people tearing through the bushes. They came out on the strand. Soldiers perhaps. A flash of lightning threw everything near me into violent relief. Two convicts!

"And directly an amazed voice exclaimed, 'It's a miracle!' It was the voice of Simon, otherwise Biscuit.

"And another voice growled, 'What's a miracle?'

" 'Why, there's a boat lying here!'

" 'You must be mad, Simon! But there is, after all. . . . A boat.'

"They seemed awed into complete silence. The other man was Mafile. He spoke again, cautiously.

" 'It is fastened up. There must be somebody here.'

" 'I spoke to them from within the hovel: 'I am here.'

"They came in then, and soon gave me to understand that the boat was theirs, not mine. 'There are two of us,' said Mafile, 'against you alone.'

"I got out into the open to keep clear of them for fear of getting a treacherous blow on the head. I could have shot them both where they stood. But I said nothing. I kept down the laughter rising in my throat. I made myself very humble and begged to be allowed to go. They consulted in low tones about my fate, while with my hand on the revolver in the bosom of my blouse I had their lives in my power. I let them live. I meant them to pull that boat. I represented to them with abject humility that I understood the management of a boat, and that, being three to pull, we could get a rest in turns. That decided them at last. It was time. A little more and I would have gone into screaming fits at the drollness of it."

At this point his excitement broke out. He jumped off the bench and gesticulated. The great shadows of his arms darting over roof and walls made the shed appear too small to contain his agitation.

"I deny nothing," he burst out. "I was elated, monsieur. I tasted a sort of felicity. But I kept very quiet. I took my turns at pulling all through the night. We made for the open sea, putting our trust in a passing ship. It was a foolhardy action. I persuaded them to it. When the sun rose the immensity of water was calm, and the *Iles de Salut* appeared only like dark specks from the top of each swell. I was steering then. Mafile, who was pulling bow, let out an oath and said, 'We must rest.'

'The time to laugh had come at last. And I took my fill of it, I can tell you. I held my sides and rolled in my seat, they had such startled faces. 'What's got into him, the animal?' cries Mafile.

"And Simon, who was nearest to me, says over his shoulder to him, 'Devil take me if I don't think he's gone mad!'

"Then I produced the revolver. Aha! In a moment they both got the stoniest eyes you can imagine. Ha, ha! They were frightened. But they pulled. Oh, yes, they pulled all day, sometimes looking wild and sometimes looking faint. I lost nothing of it because I had to keep my eyes on them all the time, or else—crack!—they would have been on top of me in a second. I rested my revolver hand on my knee all ready and steered with the other. Their faces began to blister. Sky and sea seemed on fire round us and the sea steamed in the sun. The boat made a sizzling sound as she went through the water. Sometimes Mafile foamed at the mouth and sometimes he groaned. But he pulled. He dared not stop. His eyes became blood-shot all over, and he had bitten his lower lip to pieces. Simon was as hoarse as a crow.

" 'Comrade——' he begins.

" 'There are no comrades here. I am your *patron.'*

" *'Patron,* then,' he says, 'in the name of humanity let us rest.'

"I let them. There was a little rainwater washing about the bottom of the boat. I permitted them to snatch some of it in the hollow of their palms. But as I gave the command, *'En route!'* I caught them exchanging significant glances. They thought I would have to go to sleep sometime! Aha! But I did not want to go to sleep. I was more awake than ever. It is they who went to sleep as they pulled, tumbling off the thwarts head over heels suddenly, one after another. I let them lie. All the stars were out. It was a quiet world. The sun rose. Another day. *Allez! En route!*

"They pulled badly. Their eyes rolled about and their tongues hung out. In the middle of the forenoon Mafile croaks out: 'Let us make a rush at him, Simon. I would just as soon be shot at once as to die of thirst, hunger, and fatigue at the oar.'

"But while he spoke he pulled; and Simon kept on pulling too. It made me smile. Ah! They loved their life these two, in this evil world of theirs, just as I used to love my life, too, before they spoiled it for me with their phrases. I let them go on to the point of exhaustion, and only then I pointed at the sails of a ship on the horizon.

"Aha! You should have seen them revive and buckle to their work! For I kept them at it to pull right across that ship's path. They were changed. The sort of pity I had felt for them left me. They looked more like themselves every minute. They looked at me with the glances I remembered so well. They were happy. They smiled.

" 'Well,' says Simon, 'the energy of that youngster has saved our lives. If he hadn't made us, we could never have pulled so far out into the track of ships. Comrade, I forgive you. I admire you.'

"And Mafile growls from forward: 'We owe you a famous debt of gratitude, comrade. You are cut out for a chief.'

"Comrade! Monsieur! Ah, what a good word! And they, such men as these two, had made it accursed. I looked at them. I remembered their lies, their promises, their menaces, and all my days of misery. Why could they not have left me alone after I came out of prison? I looked at them and thought that while they lived I could never be free. Never. Neither I nor others like me with warm hearts and weak heads. For I know I have not a strong head, monsieur. A black rage came upon me—the rage of extreme intoxication —but not against the injustice of society. Oh, no!

" 'I must be free!' I cried, furiously.

" *'Vive la liberté!'* yells that ruffian Mafile. *'Mort aux bourgeois* who send us to Cayenne! They shall soon know that we are free.'

"The sky, the sea, the whole horizon, seemed to turn red, blood red all round the boat. My temples were beating so loud that I wondered they did not hear. How is it that they did not? How is it they did not understand?

"I heard Simon ask, 'Have we not pulled far enough out now?'

" 'Yes. Far enough,' I said. I was sorry for him; it was the other I hated. He hauled in his oar with a loud sigh, and as he was raising his hand to wipe his forehead with the air of a man who has done his work, I pulled the trigger of my revolver and shot him like this off the knee, right through the heart.

"He tumbled down, with his head hanging over the side of the boat. I did not give him a second glance. The other cried out piercingly. Only one shriek of horror. Then all was still.

"He slipped off the thwart on to his knees and raised his clasped hands before his face in an attitude of supplication. 'Mercy,' he whispered, faintly. 'Mercy for me!—comrade.'

" 'Ah, comrade,' I said, in a low tone. 'Yes, comrade, of course. Well, then, shout *Vive l'anarchie.'*

"He flung up his arms, his face up to the sky and his mouth wide open in a great yell of despair. *'Vive l'anarchie! Vive——'*

"He collapsed all in a heap, with a bullet through his head.

"I flung them both overboard. I threw away the revolver, too. Then I sat down quietly. I was free at last! At last. I did not even look towards the ship; I did not care; indeed, I think I must have gone to sleep, because all of a sudden there were shouts and I found the ship almost on top of me. They hauled me on board and secured the boat astern. They were all blacks, except the captain, who was a mulatto. He alone knew a few words of French. I could not find out where they were going nor who they were. They gave me something to eat every day; but I did not like the way they used to discuss me in their language. Perhaps they were deliberating about throwing me overboard in order to keep possession of the boat. How do I know? As we were passing this island I asked whether it was inhabited. I understood from the mulatto that there was a house on it. A farm, I fancied, they meant. So I asked them to put me ashore on the beach and keep the boat for their trouble. This, I imagine, was just what they wanted. The rest you know."

After pronouncing these words he lost suddenly all control over himself. He paced to and fro rapidly, till at last he broke into a run; his arms went like a windmill and his ejaculations became very much like raving. The burden of them was that he "denied nothing, nothing!" I could only let him go on, and sat out of his way, repeating, *"Calmez vous, calmez vous,"* at intervals, till his agitation exhausted itself.

I must confess, too, that I remained there long after he had crawled under his mosquito-net. He had entreated me not to leave him; so, as one sits up with a nervous child, I sat up with him—in the name of humanity—till he fell asleep.

On the whole, my idea is that he was much more of an anarchist than he confessed to me or to himself; and that, the special features of his case apart, he was very much like many other anarchists. Warm heart and weak head—that is the word of the riddle; and it is a fact that the bitterest contradictions and the deadliest conflicts of the world are carried on in every individual breast capable of feeling and passion.

From personal inquiry I can vouch that the story of the convict mutiny was in every particular as stated by him.

When I got back to Horta from Cayenne and saw the "Anarchist" again, he did not look well. He was more worn, still more frail, and very livid indeed under the grimy smudges of his calling. Evidently the meat of the company's main herd (in its unconcentrated form) did not agree with him at all.

It was on the pontoon in Horta that we met; and I tried to induce him to leave the launch moored where she was and follow me to Europe there and then. It would have been delightful to think of the excellent manager's surprise and disgust at the poor fellow's escape. But he refused with unconquerable obstinacy.

"Surely you don't mean to live always here!" I cried. He shook his head.

"I shall die here," he said. Then added moodily, "Away from *them.*"

Sometimes I think of him lying open-eyed on his horseman's gear in the low shed full of tools and scraps of iron—the anarchist slave of the Marañon estate, waiting with resignation for that sleep which "fled" from him, as he used to say, in such an unaccountable manner.

Fyodor Dostoyevsky

Fyodor Dostoyevsky (1821–1881) was born in Moscow. He is one of the greatest literary figures of the nineteenth century, author of Crime and Punishment, Notes from Underground, *and* The Possessed. *"The Grand Inquisitor" is a chapter in his classic novel* The Brothers Karamazov.

THE GRAND INQUISITOR

"But now that I think of it, I can't just start without some preliminary remarks. I mean it needs a sort of literary introduction . . . Ah, hell," Ivan laughed, "what kind of an author am I? Well, I want you to understand that the action takes place in the sixteenth century, and in those days, as you may remember from school, it was usual to bring heavenly powers down to earth—in poetical writing, that is. Not to even mention Dante, in France the clerks and the monks in monasteries staged plays in which the Virgin, angels, saints, Christ, and even God Himself were brought out onto the stage. It was done very naturally then. Victor Hugo's *Notre Dame de Paris* has a passage about such a play—*Le bon jugement de la très sainte et gracieuse Vierge Marie*—performed under Louis XI in the city hall of Paris on the Dauphin's birthday. It was considered an edifying play and admission was free. In the course of the performance, the Virgin comes out on stage and announces her *bon jugement* in person. We, too, occasionally had plays like that performed in Moscow in the old days, before the rule of Peter the Great, plays based mostly on Old Testament stories . . . But, besides plays, many stories and 'poems' circulated all over the world at that time, in which saints, angels, and even the supreme heavenly powers appeared whenever their presence was required. In our monasteries, too, monks copied, translated, and even composed such poems, back at the time of the Tartar invasion. One of these monastery-written poems, for instance, is called *The Virgin's Journey Through Hell,* and it contains some scenes and descriptions as bold as Dante's. In the play, which is obviously influenced by the Greeks, the Mother of God visits hell, where the Archangel Michael is her guide. She sees the sinners being tortured. Incidentally, there is one very interesting category of sinners there: they float on a lake of fire, trying to swim out, but in vain, because 'God has forgotten about them'—extremely powerful and meaningful words, I think. Shocked and weeping, the Holy Virgin kneels before the throne of God and beseeches Him to forgive all those she has seen in hell, every one of them, without exception. Her dialogue with God is absolutely fascinating. She pleads, she refuses to give up. God points to the wounds left by the nails on her son's hands and feet and asks, 'How can I forgive His tormentors?' She then summons all the saints, all the martyrs, and all the angels and archangels to kneel with her before Him and pray for the pardon of all the sinners without exception. In the end, she obtains from God a yearly suspension of all torture between Good Friday and Trinity Sunday, and the sinners in hell thank the Lord and cry out: 'You are just in Your judgment, O Lord!'

"Well, what I'm trying to tell you is that my own little piece is a bit along such lines, as if it had been written in those days. In my piece, He comes on the scene, although He doesn't say a word; He just appears and vanishes again.

"Fifteen centuries have passed since He promised to come in His glory, fifteen centuries since His prophet wrote, 'Behold, I come quickly.' 'Of that day and hour knoweth no man, neither the Son, but the Father,' as He Himself announced when He was still on earth. But men still wait for Him with the same faith, with the same love. Nay, with even greater faith, for fifteen centuries have passed without a sign from heaven to mankind.

> Trust to what your heart will tell you,
> For from heaven no sign comes.

"And there is nothing but the faith still alive in the heart! It is true, though, that many miracles happened in those days. There were saints who worked miraculous cures. To some holy men, according to the stories of their lives, the Mother of God came down in person. But the devil was not idle and, among men, some started questioning the truth of these miracles. Just then there appeared a deadly new heresy in the North, in Germany. 'A huge star bright as a luminary'—i.e., the Church—'fell upon the sources of the waters and they became bitter.' The heretics blasphemously dismissed miracles. But that only made the faith of those who still believed more ardent. And, as of old, human tears rose up to Him; people still awaited His coming and loved Him; and men still placed their hopes in Him and were prepared to suffer and die for Him. For centuries, men had beseeched Him with faith and fervor: 'O Lord, our God, hasten Your coming.' And He, in His infinite mercy, had come down to them. He had visited saints, martyrs, and holy hermits while they were still on earth, just as it says in their *Lives*. In Russia our poet Tyuchev, believing deeply in the truth of his words, wrote:

> Through our mother earth entire
> Wandering, His cross He bore,
> The Heavenly King in slave's attire,
> Blessing all He came before.

And that is just what happened, believe me. He decided to show Himself, if only for a moment, to His people, long-suffering, tormented, sinful people who loved Him with a child-like love. My story takes place in Spain, in Seville, during the grimmest days of the Inquisition, when throughout the country fires were burning endlessly to the greater glory of God and

> In autos-da-fé resplendent
> Wicked heretics were burned.

"Of course, this was not the coming in which He had promised to appear in all His heavenly glory at the end of time and which would be as sudden as a bolt of lightning cutting the sky from east to west. No, He wanted to come only for a moment to visit His children and He chose to appear where the fires were crackling under the heretics.

"In His infinite mercy He came among men in human form, just as He had walked among them fifteen centuries before. He came down to that sun-baked Southern city the day after nearly a hundred heretics had been burned all at once *ad majorem gloriam Dei,* in a resplendent auto-da-fé by the order of the Cardinal, the Grand Inquisitor, and in the presence of the King, the royal court, knights, beautiful ladies-in-waiting, and the entire population of Seville.

"He came unobserved and moved about silently but, strangely enough, those who saw Him recognized Him at once. This might, perhaps, be the best part of my poem—I mean if I could explain what made them recognize Him . . . People are drawn to Him by an irresistible force, they gather around Him, follow Him, and soon there is a crowd. He walks among them in silence, a gentle smile of infinite compassion on His lips. The sun of love burns in His heart; light, understanding, and spiritual power flow from His eyes and set people's hearts vibrating with love for Him. He holds His hands out to them, blesses them, and just from touching Him, or even His clothes, comes a healing power. An old man who has been blind from childhood suddenly cries out to Him: 'Cure me, O Lord, so that I may see You too!' And it is as if scales had fallen from his eyes, and the blind man sees Him.

People weep and kiss the ground on which He walks. Children scatter flowers in His path and cry out to Him, 'Hosannah!' 'It is He, He Himself!' people keep saying. 'Who else could it be!' He stops on the steps of the cathedral of Seville at a moment when a small white coffin is carried into the church by weeping bearers. In it lies a girl of seven, the only daughter of a prominent man. She lies there amidst flowers. 'He will raise your child from the dead!' people shout to the weeping mother. The priest, who has come out of the cathedral to meet the procession, looks perplexed and frowns. But now the mother of the dead child throws herself at His feet, wailing, 'If it is truly You, give me back my child!' and she stretches out her hands to Him. The procession stops. They put the coffin down at His feet. He looks down with compassion, His lips form the words *'Talitha cumi'*—arise, maiden— and the maiden arises. The little girl sits up in her coffin, opens her little eyes, looks around in surprise, and smiles. She holds the white roses that had been placed in her hand when they had laid her in the coffin. There is confusion among the people, shouting and weeping . . .

"Just at that moment, the Cardinal, the Grand Inquisitor himself, crosses the cathedral square. He is a man of almost ninety, tall and erect. His face is drawn, his eyes are sunken, but they still glow as though a spark smoldered in them. Oh, now he is not wearing his magnificent cardinal's robes in which he paraded before the crowds the day before, when they were burning the enemies of the Roman Church; no, today he is wearing just the coarse cassock of an ordinary monk. He is followed by his grisly assistants, his slaves, his 'holy guard.' He sees the crowd gathered, stops, and watches from a distance. He sees everything: the placing of the coffin at His feet and the girl rising from it. His face darkens. He knits his thick white brows; his eyes flash with an ominous fire. He points his finger and orders his guards to seize Him.

"The Grand Inquisitor's power is so great and the people are so submissive and tremblingly obedient to him that they immediately open up a passage for the guards. A death-like silence descends upon the square and in that silence the guards lay hands on Him and lead Him away.

"Then everyone in the crowd, to a man, prostrates himself before the Grand Inquisitor. The old man blesses them in silence and passes on.

"The guards take their prisoner to an old building of the Holy Inquisition and lock Him up there in a dark, narrow, vaulted prison cell. The day declines and is replaced by the stifling, black Southern night of Seville. The air is fragrant with laurel and lemon.

"Suddenly, in the complete darkness, the iron gate of the cell opens and there stands the Grand Inquisitor himself, holding a light in his hand. The old man enters the cell alone and, when he is inside, the door closes behind him. He stops and for a long time—one or even two minutes—he looks at Him. At last he sets the light down on the table and says: 'You? Is it really You?' Receiving no answer, he continues in great haste:

" 'You need not answer me. Say nothing. I know only too well what You could tell me now. Besides, You have no right to add anything to what You said before. Why did You come here, to interfere and make things difficult for us? For You came to interfere—You know it. But shall I tell You what will happen tomorrow? Well, I do not know who You really are, nor do I want to know whether You are really He or just a likeness of Him, but no later than tomorrow I shall pronounce You the wickedest of all heretics and sentence You to be burned at the stake, and the very people who today were kissing Your feet will tomorrow, at a sign of my hand, hasten to Your stake to rake the coals. Don't You know it? Oh yes, I suppose You do,' he added, deeply immersed in thought, his eyes fixed for a moment on his prisoner."

"I don't quite understand what you're trying to say, Ivan," Alyosha said with a smile. Until then he had listened in silence. "Is it just some wild fantasy or is there a mistake in identity, a *quid pro quo*, by your grand inquisitor?"

"Why, you may assume the latter if you wish," Ivan said

laughingly, "since, as I see, you have been so spoiled by our contemporary brand of realism that you cannot accept anything that is a bit fantastic. If you wish to call it an error of identity, all right, so be it! It is a fact though," he said, starting to laugh again, "that the Inquisitor is ninety years old, so he has had plenty of time to have been driven completely out of his mind by his *idée fixe*. As to his prisoner, he may have been struck by the man's looks. Or perhaps he was just having hallucinations, which can easily happen to a ninety-year-old man close to death, and what's more, excited by the previous day's burning at the stake of a hundred heretics. But, really, why should we care whether it is a wild fantasy or a *quid pro quo?* What matters is that the old man must speak his mind. At ninety this is the first time that he is saying aloud something about which he has kept silent all those ninety years."

"And the prisoner—He just looks at him and says nothing?"

"Why, yes," Ivan laughed once more, "and that's as it should be in any case. Besides, the old man himself reminds Him that He may not add a single word to what He has said before. I might add that this may be the most crucial feature of Roman Catholicism, at least the way I see it. It's as if the Grand Inquisitor said to Him: 'You have transmitted all Your authority to the Pope and now he wields it. As to You, You had better stay away or, at any rate, not interfere with us for the time being.' They don't just say that, they even have it in writing, at least the Jesuits have. I've read it myself in the works of their theologians.

" 'Do You think You have the right to reveal even a single mystery of the world from which You come?' the Grand Inquisitor asks Him and then answers himself: 'No, You do not, for You may not add anything to what has been said before and You may not deprive men of the freedom You defended so strongly when You were on earth. Anything new that You might reveal to them now would encroach upon the freedom of their faith, for it would come to them as a miracle, and fifteen centuries ago it was freely given faith that was most important to You. Didn't You often tell them then that You wanted to make them free. Well, then,' the old man adds with a grin, 'so now You have seen *free* men. Yes, that business cost us a great deal,' he continues, looking sternly at Him, 'but at last, in Your name, we saw it through. For fifteen hundred years we were pestered by that notion of freedom, but in the end we succeeded in getting rid of it, and now we are rid of it for good. You don't believe that we got rid of it, do You? You look at me so gently, and You do not even consider me worthy of Your anger? I want You to know, though, that on this very day men are convinced that they are freer than they have ever been, although they themselves brought us their freedom and put it meekly at our feet. This is what we have achieved, but was it really what You wanted, was this the freedom that You wanted to bring them?' "

"I'm afraid I'm lost again," Alyosha interrupted Ivan, "is he being sarcastic? Is he laughing at Him?"

"He certainly is not. Indeed, he is claiming for himself and his church the credit for having done away with freedom and having thus given happiness to mankind.

" 'It is only now,' he says, obviously thinking of the Inquisition, 'that it has become possible, for the first time, to think of men's happiness. Man is a rebel by nature and how can a rebel be happy? You were warned,' he says to Him. 'There was no lack of warnings and signs, but You chose to ignore them. You spurned the only way that could have brought happiness to men. Fortunately, though, You allowed us to take over from You when You left. You made commitments to us, You sealed them with Your word, You gave us the right to loosen and to bind their shackles, and, of course, You cannot think of depriving us of that right now. Why, then, have You come to interfere with us now?' "

"What does that mean—there was no lack of warnings and signs?" Alyosha said.

"Well, that's precisely the most important point the old man must make.

" 'The wise and dreaded spirit of self-destruction and non-existence,' the old man went on, 'spoke to You in the desert and we learn from the books that he tried to tempt You. Was he really trying to *tempt* You, though? Could anything be truer than what he revealed to You in his three questions that You rejected, questions that were called "temptations" in the books? And yet, if a truly blinding miracle has ever happened on this earth, it happened on that day in the form of those three temptations. And it was precisely in those three questions that the miracle lay. If, for instance, those three questions asked by the dread spirit had been lost and we had had to rediscover and reinvent them, we would have had to assemble for that purpose all the world's wise men—rulers, high priests, scholars, philosophers, and poets—and to ask them to formulate three questions that would not only fit the magnitude of the occasion but also express in a few words, in three brief human sentences, the whole future history of the world and of mankind. Do You really believe that the combined wisdom of the earth could produce anything comparable in strength and depth to those three questions that the wise and powerful spirit asked You that day in the desert? From those questions alone, from the miracle of their formulation, it must be clear that it is not a matter of a transient human mind, but of something absolute and outside time. For those three questions contain the entire future history of man and they offer three symbols that reconcile all the irreconcilable strivings on earth which derive from the contradictions of human nature. It was not as clear at that time, because the future was still unknown. But now, fifteen centuries later, we can see that in those questions everything was perfectly foreseen and predicted and has proved so true that there is nothing we can add or subtract anymore.

" 'Judge for Yourself, then: who was right, You or the one who questioned You? Do You remember the first question? It was worded differently, but this is its purport: "You wanted to come into the world and You came empty-handed, with nothing but some vague promise of freedom, which, in their simple-mindedness and innate irresponsibility, men cannot even conceive and which they fear and dread, for there has never been anything more difficult for man and for human society to bear than freedom! And now, do You see those stones in this parched and barren desert? Turn them into loaves of bread and men will follow You like cattle, grateful and docile, although constantly fearful lest You withdraw Your hand and they lose Your loaves." But You did not want to deprive man of freedom and You rejected this suggestion, for, You thought, what sort of freedom would they have if their obedience was bought with bread? You replied that man does not live by bread alone, but do You know that for the sake of that earthly bread, the spirit of the earth will rise up against You, will confront and conquer You, and they will all follow him, shouting, "Who is there to match the beast who has brought us fire from heaven?" Do You know that more centuries will pass and men of wisdom and learning will proclaim that there is no such thing as crime, that there is therefore no sin either, that there are only hungry people. "Feed us first, then ask for virtue"—that will be the motto on the banners of those who will oppose You, of those who will raze Your temple and build in its place a new, terrifying tower of Babel. And although they will never complete it, any more than they did the last one, nevertheless You could have prevented men from making this second attempt to build the tower and thus have shortened their sufferings by a thousand years, for in the end it is to us that they will come, after this unnecessary thousand years of torment! They will find us hiding somewhere underground, hiding again in the catacombs —for we shall again be persecuted and tortured—and they will beg us: "Give us food, for those who promised us fire from heaven have not given it to us!" And that will be the day when we shall finish building their tower for them, for the one who feeds them will be the one who finishes building it, and we will be the only ones capable of feeding them. And we shall give them bread in Your name and lie, telling them that it is in Your name. Oh, never, never would they be able to feed themselves without us! There is no knowledge that could supply them with bread as long as they remain free. So, in the end, they will lay their freedom at our feet and say to us: "Enslave us, but feed us!" And they will finally understand that freedom and the assurance of daily bread for everyone are two incompatible notions that could never coexist! They will also discover that men can never be free because they are weak, corrupt, worthless, and restless. You promised them heavenly bread but, I repeat, how can that bread compete against earthly bread in dealing with the weak, ungrateful, permanently corrupt human species? And even if hundreds or thousands of men follow You for the sake of heavenly bread, what will happen to the millions who are too weak to forego their earthly bread? Or is it only the thousands of the strong and mighty who are dear to Your heart, while the millions of others, the weak ones, who love You too, weak as they are, and who are as numerous as the grains of sand on the beach, are to serve as material for the strong and mighty? But we are concerned with the weak too! They are corrupt and undisciplined, but in the end they will be the obedient ones! They will marvel at us and worship us like gods, because, by becoming their masters, we have accepted the burden of freedom that they were too frightened to face, just because we have agreed to rule over them—that is how terrifying freedom will have become to them finally! We shall tell them, though, that we are loyal to You and that we rule over them in Your name. We shall be lying, because we do not intend to allow You to come back. And it is in this deception that our suffering will consist, because we will have to lie! So this is the meaning of the first question You were asked in the desert, and this is what You rejected in the name of the freedom that You put above all else. And yet that question contains one of the great mysteries on which our world is founded. Had You been willing to give them bread, You would have satisfied the eternal craving of both individual man and human society as a whole—to have someone to worship. There is nothing a free man is so anxious to do as to find something to worship. But it must be something unquestionable, that all men can agree to worship communally. For the great concern of these miserable creatures is not that every individual should find something to worship that he personally considers worthy of worship, but that they should find something in which they can *all* believe and which they can all worship *in common;* it is essential that it should be in common. And it is precisely that requirement of *shared* worship that has been the principal source of suffering for individual man and the human race since the beginning of history. In their efforts to impose universal worship, men have unsheathed their swords and killed one another. They have invented gods and challenged each other: "Discard your gods and worship mine or I will destroy both your gods and you!" And this is how it will be until the end of time, even after gods have vanished from the earth—for they are bound, in the end, to yield to idols. You knew, You couldn't help knowing, this fundamental mystery of human nature and, knowing it, You nevertheless spurned the only banner that was offered You, that would have made them follow You and worship You without a murmur—the banner of earthly bread. But You chose to reject it in the name of freedom, in the name of spiritual bread! And look what You did after that, again in the name of freedom. I tell You once more that man has no more pressing, agonizing need than the need to find someone to whom he can hand over as quickly as possible the gift of freedom with which the poor wretch comes into the world. But only one who can appease a man's conscience can take his freedom from him. In bread, You were offered something that could have brought You indisputable loyalty: You would give man bread and man would bow down to You, because there is nothing more indisputable than bread. But if, at the same time, someone else succeeded in capturing his conscience, then man might even spurn Your bread and follow the one who ensnared his conscience. This is something about which You were right. For the mystery of human existence lies not in just staying alive, but in finding something to live for. Without a concrete idea of what he is living for, man would refuse to live, would rather exterminate himself than remain on this earth, even if bread were scattered all around him.

" 'That is so, but what came of it? Instead of seizing men's freedom, You gave them even more of it! Have You forgotten that peace, and even death, is more attractive to man than the freedom of choice that derives from the knowledge of good and evil? There is nothing more alluring to man than freedom of conscience, but neither is there anything more agonizing. And yet, instead of giving them something tangible to calm their consciences forever, You came to them with words that were unfamiliar, vague, and indefinite; You offered them something that was quite beyond them; it even looked as if You didn't love them, You who came to give them Your life! Instead of ridding men of their freedom, You increased their freedom, and You imposed everlasting torment on man's soul. You wanted to gain man's love so that he would follow You of his own free will, fascinated and captivated by You. In place of the clear and rigid ancient law, You made man decide about good and evil for himself, with no other guidance than Your example. But did it never occur to You that man would disregard Your example, even question it, as well as Your truth, when he was subjected to so fearful a burden as freedom of choice? In the end they will shout that You did not bring them the truth, because it is impossible to have left them in greater confusion and misery than You did, leaving them with so many anxieties and unsolved problems. You see, then, You Yourself sowed the seeds of destruction for Your own kingdom, and no one else is to blame. And think now, was this the best that You could offer them?

" 'There are three forces, only three, on this earth that can overcome and capture once and for all the conscience of these feeble, undisciplined creatures, so as to give them happiness. These forces are miracle, mystery, and authority. But You rejected the first, the second, and the third of these forces and set up Your rejection as an example to men. When the wise and dreaded spirit placed You on the pinnacle of the temple and said, "If You would know whether You are the Son of God then cast Yourself down, for it is written: The angels shall hold Him up lest He fall and bruise Himself; and You shall know then whether You are the Son of God and shall prove how great is Your faith in Your Father," You heard him out, then rejected his advice, withstood the temptation, and did not plunge from the pinnacle. Oh, of course, You acted proudly and magnificently; indeed, You acted like God, but can You expect as much of men, of that weak, undisciplined, and wretched tribe, who are certainly no gods? Oh, You knew very well at that moment that if You had made the slightest move to jump, You would have tempted God, proving You had lost Your faith in Him, and You would have been smashed against the earth that You had come to save, and would thus have gladdened the wise spirit who was tempting You. But again, how many are there like You? Could You possibly imagine, even for one second, that men would be able to withstand such temptation? Is human nature such that it can reject a miracle when confronted with the most frightening choices, the most heartbreaking dilemmas, and remain facing them with nothing but freedom of choice? And You knew only too well that Your act would be recorded in books, that it would reach the remotest corners of the earth and be passed on down to the end of time. Did You really expect that man would follow Your example and remain with God without recourse to miracles? Didn't You know that whenever man rejects miracles he rejects God, because he seeks not so much God as miracles? And since man cannot live without miracles, he will provide himself with miracles of his own making. He will believe in witchcraft and sorcery, even though he may otherwise be a heretic, an atheist, and a rebel.

" 'You did not come down from the cross when they shouted, taunting and challenging You, "Come down from the cross and we will believe that You are He." You did not come down, again because You did not want to bring man to You by miracles, because You wanted their freely given love rather than the servile rapture of slaves subdued forever by a display of power. And, here again, You overestimated men, for they are certainly nothing but slaves, although they were created rebels by nature. Look around and judge for Yourself. Fifteen centuries have passed. Examine them. Whom have You raised up to Yourself? I swear that man is weaker and viler than You thought! How could he possibly do what You did? By paying him such respect, You acted as if You lacked compassion for him, because You demanded too much of him—and that from You, who love him more than Yourself! Had You respected him less, You would have demanded less of him and that would have been more like love, for the burden You placed on him would not have been so heavy. Man is weak and despicable. What if, today, he rebels everywhere against our authority and is proud of his rebellion? It is a childish pride, the pride of a schoolboy, of little children rioting in their classroom and driving out their teacher. But the end will come soon and they will have to pay dearly for their fun. They will raze churches and flood the earth with blood, but the stupid children will finally realize themselves that, although they are rebels, they are weak and are unable to bear their own rebellion. Shedding their silly tears, they will finally admit that He who created them rebels intended to mock them and no more. They will say it in despair and it will be blasphemy, and then they will be even more unhappy, because human nature cannot bear blasphemy and in the end always punishes itself for it. And so man's lot is nothing but unrest, confusion, and unhappiness—after all the suffering You bore for their freedom! Your great prophet had a vision and told us in an allegory that he had seen all those who were in the first resurrection and that there were twelve thousand of them from each tribe. But if there were so many, they must have been gods rather than men. They bore Your cross, they endured years and years of hunger in a barren wilderness, living on roots and locusts—and, of course, You can point proudly at these children of freedom, at their freely given love, and at their magnificent suffering for Your sake. Remember, though, there were only a few thousand of them and even these were gods rather than men. But what about the rest? Why should the rest of mankind, the weak ones, suffer because they are unable to stand what the strong ones can? Why is it the fault of a weak soul if he cannot live up to such terrifying gifts? Can it really be true that You came only for the chosen few? If that is so, it is a mystery that we cannot understand; and if it is a mystery, we have the right to preach to man that what matters is not freedom of choice or love, but a mystery that he must worship blindly, even at the expense of his conscience. And that is exactly what we have done. We have corrected Your work and have now founded it on *miracle, mystery,* and *authority.* And men rejoice at being led like cattle again, with the terrible gift of freedom that brought them so much suffering removed from them. Tell me, were we right in preaching and acting as we did? Was it not our love for men that made us resign ourselves to the idea of their impotence and lovingly try to lighten the burden of their responsibility, even allowing their weak nature to sin, but with our permission? Why have You come to interfere with our work? And why do You look at me silently with those gentle eyes of Yours? Be angry with me. I do not want Your love, because I do not love You myself. Why should I go on pretending that I do not know to whom I am speaking? Everything I have to say You already know—I can read it in Your eyes. How could I expect to hide our secret from You? But perhaps You want to hear it from my own lips. Listen then: we are not with You, we are with *him*—and that is our secret, our mystery! We have been with *him* and not with You for a long time, for eight centuries already. Exactly eight centuries ago we accepted from him what You had rejected with indignation, the last gift he offered You—all the kingdom of earth. We accepted Rome and Caesar's sword from *him,* and we proclaimed ourselves the sole rulers of the earth, although to this day we have not yet succeeded in bringing our work to final completion. But You know who is to blame for that. Our work is only beginning, but at least it has begun. And, although its completion is still a long way off and the earth will have to face much suffering until then, in the end we shall prevail, we will be Caesars, and then we shall devise a plan for universal happiness. But You, You could have taken Caesar's sword when You came the first time. Why did You reject that last gift? Had You accepted the third offering of the mighty spirit, You would have fulfilled man's greatest need on earth. That is, the need to find someone to worship, someone who can relieve him of the burden of his conscience, thus enabling him finally to unite into a harmonious ant-hill where there are no dissenting voices, for the unquenchable thirst for universal unity is the third and last ordeal of man. Men have always striven to be organized into a universal whole. There have been many great nations with a glorious past history, but the higher the stage of development they reached, the greater was their discontent, because they became more and more obsessed with the need for universal unification. The great conquerors, the Tamerlanes and the Genghis Khans, who swept like whirlwinds across the earth, striving to subdue the whole world, were also, even if they were unaware of it themselves, obeying that eternal human craving for universal union. Had You accepted Caesar's purple, You would have founded a universal empire and given men everlasting peace. For who can rule men if not one who holds both their consciences and their bread? So we took Caesar's sword and, by taking it, we rejected You and followed *him*. Oh, there will still be centuries of chaos, in which men will be guided by their own unbridled thinking, by their science, and by their cannibal instincts, for, since they started building their tower of Babel without us, they will end up devouring each other. But it will be just at that moment that the beast will crawl to us, lick our feet, and spatter them with tears of blood. And we shall saddle and mount the beast and raise the cup on which the word "mystery" is engraved. Then, and only then, will the reign of peace and happiness come to men. You pride Yourself on Your chosen ones, but You have only the chosen, while we will bring peace of mind to all men. And that is not all: how many of those strong enough to be among the chosen have already or will in the future take their mighty minds and ardent hearts away from You and give them to some other cause, in the end raising their *free* banner against You? Yet You were the one who gave them that banner.

" 'Under us it will be different. Under us they will all be happy and they will not rise in rebellion and kill one another all the world over, as they are doing now with the freedom You gave them. Oh, we will convince them that they will only be free when they have surrendered their freedom and submitted to us. And that will be the truth, will it not? Or do You think we will be deceiving them? They will find out for themselves that we are right, for they will remember the horrors of chaos and enslavement that Your freedom brought them. Freedom, free-thinking, and science will lead men into such confusion and confront them with such dilemmas and insoluble riddles that the fierce and rebellious will destroy one another; others who are rebellious but weaker will destroy themselves, while the weakest and most miserable will crawl to our feet and cry out to us: "Yes, you were right. You alone possessed His secret, and we have come back to you. Save us from ourselves!" And when they receive bread from us, they will be clearly aware that it is bread they have earned with their own hands, the same bread we took away from them, that we perform no miracles by turning stones into bread, and yet the fact that they receive it from our hands will make them happier than the bread itself! For they will remember only too well that, without us, this same bread that they earned turned to stones in their hands, whereas, after they came to us, the stones in their hands were turned back into bread. Ah, they will value all too highly the advantages to be derived from submitting to us once and for all. And as long as men do not understand this, they will be unhappy. Now tell me, who is most to blame for their failure to understand? Who was it who broke up the human herd and sent men along innumerable unexplored paths? The herd will be gathered together and tamed again, however, and this time for good. And then we shall give them tranquil, humble happiness, suitable for such weak creatures. Oh, we shall have to convince them, finally, that they must not be proud, for, by overestimating them, You instilled pride in them. We shall prove to them that they are nothing but weak, pathetic children, but that a child's happiness is the sweetest of all. They will grow timid and cling to us in fear, like chicks to a hen. They will admire us, be terrified of us, and be proud of the strength and wisdom that enabled us to subdue a turbulent herd of many millions. They will tremble abjectly before our wrath; they will become timorous; their eyes will fill with tears as readily as those of women and children; but at the slightest sign from us, they will just as readily change to mirth, laughter, and untarnished joy, and they will burst into a happy children's song. Yes, we shall force them to work but, in their leisure hours, we shall organize their lives into a children's game in which they will sing children's songs together and perform innocent dances. Oh, we shall allow them to sin too, for, weak and defenseless as they are, they will love us like children if we allow them to sin. We shall tell them that every sin they commit with our permission can be expiated, that we allow them to sin because we love them, and that we shall take upon ourselves the punishment for their acts. And we shall indeed take their sins upon ourselves, and they will adore us as their saviors, who will answer to God for the sins they, the weak, commit. And they will have no secrets from us. We shall allow them or forbid them to live with their wives or mistresses, to have or not have children—all according to the degree of their obedience to us—and they will submit to us with cheerfulness and joy. They will tell us the secrets that most torment their consciences, they will tell us everything, and we shall solve all their problems, and they will trust to our solutions completely, because they will be rid of the terrible worry and the frightening torment they know today when they have to decide for themselves how to act.

" 'And everyone will be happy, all the millions of beings, with the exception of the hundred thousand men who are called upon to rule over them. For only we, the keepers of the secret, will be unhappy. There will be millions upon millions of happy babes and one hundred thousand sufferers who have accepted the burden of the knowledge of good and evil. They will die peacefully with Your name on their lips, but beyond the grave they will find nothing but death. But we shall keep the secret and, for their own happiness, we shall dangle before them the reward of eternal, heavenly bliss. For we know that, even if there is something in the other world, it is certainly not for such as they. They say and prophesy that You will come again with Your proud, strong chosen ones and that You will be triumphant. But our answer will be that those around You have saved only themselves, whereas we have saved all mankind. It is said that the whore who rides the beast and holds the *mystery* in her hands will be put to shame, that the weak will rise and rend her royal robes and expose her vile naked body. But I will rise then and show You the millions upon millions of happy babes who have known no sin. And we, who have taken their sins upon us to give them happiness, will stand up and say to You: "Judge us if You can and if You dare!" Know that I am not afraid of You; know that I, too, lived in the wilderness, fed upon roots and locusts, that I, too, blessed the freedom which You bestowed upon men, and that I, too, was prepared to take my place among the strong chosen ones, aspiring to be counted among them. But I came to my senses and refused to serve a mad cause. I turned away and joined those who were endeavoring to *correct Your work.* I left the proud and turned to the meek, for the happiness of the meek. What I have told You will happen and our kingdom will come. I repeat, tomorrow You will see obedient herds, at the first sign from me, hurry to heap coals on the fire beneath the stake at which I shall have You burned, because, by coming here, You have made our task more difficult. For if anyone has ever deserved our fire, it is You, and I shall have You burned tomorrow. *Dixi!*' "

Ivan stopped. His emotion had gradually increased as he

spoke, reaching its highest point at the end. But when he stopped, he suddenly smiled.

Alyosha, who at first had listened in silence, had also become very agitated toward the end; he looked as if he wanted to interrupt his brother and was restraining himself with great difficulty. Now, when Ivan stopped, words gushed from him, as if he could no longer hold them back.

"But it makes no sense!" he cried, turning red. "Your poem is no disparagement of Jesus, as you intended—it is in praise of Him! And who will accept what you say of freedom in the way you want it to be understood? Is that the way the Russian Orthodox Church interprets it? That is the reasoning of a Roman Catholic, but it doesn't even give a fair picture of their views either. It represents only the worst there is in Catholicism—its inquisitors and Jesuits! Besides, your inquisitor is too fantastic; such a character is quite impossible. And what sort of sins of others do these people take upon themselves? And also, who are these keepers of the secret—of the *mystery*—who are willing to bear some peculiar curse for the sake of the happiness of mankind? Who has ever heard of them? We know there are Jesuits with a pretty bad reputation, but they are nothing like what you describe. They are nothing, nothing, like that; in fact, they're simply the Pope's army, preparing the way for the establishment of their future empire on earth, with the Roman pontiff at its head. That is their actual goal and there is no *mystery* or sad, noble resignation in it: theirs is a plain and simple lust for power, low, despicable material advantages, enslavement of the people— something like Russian serfdom used to be, with them as the landowners . . . That's all they are after. They may not even believe in God for all I know. No, your tormented inquisitor is nothing but a figment of your fantasy."

"Wait a minute, don't get so excited," Ivan laughed. "You say it is a fantasy. Very good, I concede, it most certainly is a fantasy. Tell me one thing, though: Do you really believe that, during these centuries, the Catholics have directed all their efforts merely at seizing power in order to gain what you call low, despicable material advantages? Did you get that, by any chance, from that Father Paisii of yours?"

"No, no, not at all . . . In fact, once Father Paissi said something that resembles a bit what you were saying . . . But, no, of course it wasn't the same thing at all!" Alyosha added hurriedly, as if as an afterthought.

"I'm delighted to hear it, although you say it wasn't the same thing at all. What I'm asking you is this: Do you really think that the Jesuits and inquisitors would plot like that for the sake of mere despicable material advantages? Why couldn't there be among them one martyr, a man filled with great sadness and love for his fellow men? Just assume that, among all those interested only in material gain, there is one, only one, man like my grand inquisitor, who has lived on roots by himself in the wilderness, who has writhed in agony to overcome the needs of the flesh, in his efforts to gain freedom and perfection. Then that man, who has always loved his fellow men, suddenly realizes how puny is the moral satisfaction of achieving a triumph of will when he is convinced that millions of other children of God have been created as a sort of mockery, that they will never be able to cope with the freedom that has been forced upon them, that these wretched rebels will never grow into giants who will complete the construction of the tower of Babel. It was not geese such as these that our great idealist visualized joining in the final harmony. And so, having understood that, he turns around and joins the . . . well, the intelligent people. Why can't you imagine that something like that could happen?"

"Whom did he join, did you say? Who are these intelligent people?" Alyosha cried, almost angrily. "There's nothing so very intelligent about them, nor do they have any secrets or mysteries . . . Their only secret is their godlessness, and your inquisitor's only secret is that he doesn't believe in God, that's all!"

"Fine! Let's assume you are right. You've guessed it at last! And it's true—that is the only secret he has. But wouldn't a man who had spent his whole life in the wilderness performing acts of self-sacrifice and devotion without curing himself of his love and concern for mankind, wouldn't such a man suffer? In the last years that are left to him, it becomes clear to him that only the guidance of the great, wise, and dreaded spirit would make it possible to organize feeble and undisciplined men in such a way as to make their lives bearable, for they are just unfinished, ridiculous attempts, created in mockery. He becomes convinced that his duty is to follow the instructions of the wise spirit of death and destruction. And so he is willing to use lies and deception to lead men consciously to their death and destruction, while at the same time deceiving them, so that they will not see where they are being led, so that, at least on the way, these wretched, blind creatures may think they are happy. And I want you to note that the old inquisitor will be deceiving them in the name of the one in whom he believed so ardently for most of his life! Isn't that suffering, tell me? And if even just one man like that finds himself at the head of the whole army of those who crave nothing but power and despicable material gains, even so, wouldn't one such man be enough to make it a tragedy? I'll go even further: I say that, with one such man at their head, they would be a true, guiding ideal for the whole Roman Church with its armies and its Jesuits. I am also absolutely convinced that there has never been any lack of such individuals among those who head their movement; possibly even some of the popes themselves were such exceptional individuals. And who knows, perhaps a tormented old man who loves mankind as stubbornly as my inquisitor exists today, perhaps there is even a whole army of such individuals, and perhaps they exist not by mere chance but as the result of combined efforts to form an alliance whose aim is to keep the secret from the weak and the wretched, in order to make them happy. This, I am sure, is true, because it is bound to be. I even have the impression that the Freemasons are founded on a mystery of that sort, which would explain why the Catholics hate them, seeing in them competitors threatening to split their unifying idea; for they believe that there must be only one shepherd and one herd . . . But, in defending my idea this way, I sound like an author who cannot bear criticism. So we might as well talk about something else."

"Perhaps you're a Mason yourself!" Alyosha blurted out angrily, but then added at once with great sadness: "You don't really believe in God." He had the impression that his brother was looking at him sarcastically; he lowered his eyes and asked: "Does it have an ending, your poem, or is that how it ends?"

"Here's how I propose to end it," Ivan said, continuing.

"The Grand Inquisitor falls silent and waits for some time for the prisoner to answer. The prisoner's silence has weighed on him. He has watched Him; He listened to him intently, looking gently into his eyes, and apparently unwilling to speak. The old man longs for Him to say something, however painful and terrifying. But instead, He suddenly goes over to the old man and kisses him gently on his old, bloodless lips. And that is His only answer. The old man is startled and shudders. The corners of his lips seem to quiver slightly. He walks to the door, opens it, and says to Him, 'Go now, and do not come back . . . ever. You must never, never come again!' And he lets the prisoner out into the dark streets of the city. The prisoner leaves."

"And what about the old man?"

"The kiss glows in his heart . . . But the old man sticks to his old idea."

"And you too, you stick to it?" Alyosha cried out bitterly. Ivan laughed.

"You know what," he said, "it's all nonsense really, a meaningless poem by a scatter-brained student who's never written two lines of poetry in his life. Why must you take it so seriously? Or do you expect me to rush off at once and join the crowd of Jesuits devising corrections of His work? Don't you understand that I really don't give a damn about anything, that, as I told you before, I'm only interested in lasting out until I'm thirty, because by then I'll be willing to throw down the cup of life."

"And what about your sticky little leaves and the graves that are so dear to you and the blue sky and the woman you love?" Alyosha said bitterly. "How will you be able to live until then and love all those things with the hell that is in your heart and in your head? No, you *are* going to join them now or else you will kill yourself, because you won't be able to stand it!"

"There is a drive in me that can withstand anything," Ivan said coldly, with a twisted grin.

"What drive?"

"The Karamazov drive—the vile, earthly drive."

"You mean you plan to drown yourself in debauchery, to disintegrate your soul by rotting it? Is that what you want?"

"Something like that . . . I guess, though, I'll avoid it until I'm thirty, but after that, well yes . . ."

"And how do you intend to avoid it until then? How will you manage it, with those ideas of yours?"

"There again, I'll act like a Karamazov."

"By that you mean you'll act as if 'everything is permitted'? For you feel that's true—whatever you do is all right?"

Ivan frowned and suddenly turned very pale.

"Now you've picked up the phrase that shocked Miusov so much yesterday and that Dmitry picked up and repeated rather naively," Ivan said, smiling crookedly. "Well, since you've brought it up—I suppose everything is permitted, just as I said; I don't take it back. And I don't dislike our dear Mitya's formulation either."

Alyosha stared at him in silence.

"Ah, my little Alyosha, I thought that when I left this town you would be the only friend I had in the world," Ivan said with sudden feeling, "but now I realize that there is no room for me even in your heart, my dear recluse. Well, I won't go back on my idea that everything is permitted, but then, will you, too, turn your back on me?"

Alyosha stood up, walked over to him, and, without a word, kissed him on the lips.

"That's plagiarism!" Ivan shouted, suddenly beaming with

delight. "You stole it from my poem! But it's time we were on our way, Alyosha. We've got things to do, both of us."

They went downstairs, but stopped outside the inn.

"Know what, Alyosha?" Ivan said with deliberation. "If I last long enough to get around to the sticky little leaves, I will love them only thinking of you. The thought that you are somewhere here will be enough for me not to lose all desire to live. Is that good enough for you? If you want, you may take this as a declaration of my affection for you. But for now, you're turning right and I'm turning left, and that's that, understand? I mean that if I'm still in town tomorrow (which is extremely unlikely, for I expect to leave today) and if we happen to meet, I don't want to even mention any of these topics, not a word. Please, remember that. And also I'd like you never to mention our brother Dmitry to me, never!" he added irritatedly. "So now we've exhausted all possible topics, discussed everything. But I promise you this: when I'm close to thirty and decide to throw down my cup of life, I'll come especially to have one more talk with you—wherever I may be, even if I'm in America, I'll come all the way back to see you. Besides, I'll be very curious to have a look at you and see what you're like then. This is a rather solemn promise, as you can see, but then, we may be parting now for as long as seven, perhaps even ten, years. Well, go and join your Pater Seraphicus then, since he's dying, and if he happens to have died without you, you may be angry with me for having held you up. Good-by then, kiss me once more. Good. Now be off."

Ivan turned away abruptly and walked off. He did not once look back. It was a bit the way Dmitry had left Alyosha the day before, but it was also somehow quite different. That impression flashed like a red streak among the painful, sorrowful thoughts that were churning in Alyosha's head. He stood for a while, following Ivan with his eyes. Suddenly it struck him that Ivan rolled slightly as he walked, listing to the right, so that from behind it seemed to Alyosha that his right shoulder was lower than his left. Alyosha had never noticed that Ivan walked like that before. Then, all of a sudden Alyosha turned in the opposite direction, hurrying off toward the monastery. The day was already fading and he suddenly felt a strange fear creeping over him. Some new, unknown shadow was rising before him and he could not find an answer to it. As on the previous evening, a strong wind was rising and the ageless pine trees rustled gloomily on either side of him as he crossed the little wood between the monastery and the hermitage. He was almost running. "Where did he get that Pater Seraphicus from?" flashed through his head. "Ah, poor, poor Ivan, when will I see you again? Here's the hermitage. Oh, God! Yes, yes, he *is* Pater Seraphicus, he'll save me . . . he'll save me from him, save me forever . . ."

Later in his life, Alyosha often wondered how he could have forgotten so completely about Dmitry after he left Ivan —Dmitry, whom that very morning he had been determined to find at all costs, even if it made it impossible for him to return to the monastery that night.

Saki

Saki (1870–1916) is the pen name of Hector Hugh
Munro, a British writer who was born in Burma and died
in World War I. He is best known for his short stories.

THE INFERNAL PARLIAMENT

In an age when it has become increasingly difficult to accomplish anything new or original, Bavton Bidderdale interested
his generation by dying of a new disease. "We always knew he
would do something remarkable one of these days," observed
his aunts; "he has justified our belief in him." But there is a
section of humanity ever ready to refuse recognition to meri-
torious achievement, and a large and influential school of
doctors asserted their belief that Bidderdale was not really
dead. The funeral arrangements had to be held over until the
matter was settled one way or the other, and the aunts went
provisionally into half-mourning.

Meanwhile, Bidderdale remained in Hell as a guest pend-
ing his reception on a more regular footing. "If you are not
really supposed to be dead," said the authorities of that region, "we don't want to seem in an indecent hurry to grab
you. The theory that Hell is in serious need of population is a
thing of the past. Why, to take your family alone, there are
any number of Bidderdales on our books, as you may discover later. It is part of our system that relations should be
encouraged to live together down here. From observations
made in another world we have abundant evidence that it

promotes the ends we have in view. However, while you are a guest we should like you to be treated with every consideration and be shown anything that specially interests you. Of course, you would like to see our Parliament?"

"Have you a Parliament in Hell?" asked Bidderdale in some surprise.

"Only quite recently. Of course we've always had chaos, but not under Parliamentary rules. Now, however, that Parliaments are becoming the fashion, in Turkey and Persia, and I suppose before long in Afghanistan and China, it seemed rather ostentatious to stand outside the movement. That young Fiend just going by is the Member for East Brimstone; he'll be delighted to show you over the institution."

"You will just be in time to hear the opening of a debate," said the Member, as he led Bidderdale through a spacious outer lobby, decorated with frescoes representing the fall of man, the discovery of gold, the invention of playing cards, and other traditionally appropriate subjects. "The Member for Nether Furnace is proposing a motion 'that this House do arrogantly protest to the legislatures of earthly countries against the wrongful and injurious misuses of the word "fiendish," in application to purely human misdemeanours, a misuse tending to create a false and detrimental impression concerning the Infernal Regions.'"

A feature of the Parliament Chamber itself was its enormous size. The space allotted to Members was small and very sparsely occupied, but the public galleries stretched away tier on tier as far as the eye could reach, and were packed to their utmost capacity.

"There seems to be a very great public interest in the debate," exclaimed Bidderdale.

"Members are excused from attending the debates if they so desire," the Fiend proceeded to explain; "it is one of their most highly valued privileges. On the other hand, constituents are compelled to listen throughout to all the speeches. After all, you must remember, we are in Hell."

Bidderdale repressed a shudder and turned his attention to the debate.

"Nothing," the Fiend-Orator was observing, "is more deplorable among the cultured races of the present day than the tendency to identify fiendhood, in the most sweeping fashion, with all manner of disreputable excesses, excesses which can only be alleged against us on the merest legendary evidence. Vices which are exclusively or predominatingly human are unblushingly described as inhuman, and, what is even more contemptible and ungenerous, as fiendish. If one investigates such statements as 'inhuman treatment of pit ponies' or 'fiendish cruelties in the Congo,' so frequently to be heard in our brother Parliaments on earth, one finds accumulative and indisputable evidence that it is the human treatment of pit ponies and Congo natives that is really in question, and that no authenticated case of fiendish agency in these atrocities can be substantiated. It is, perhaps, a minor matter for complaint," continued the orator, "that the human race frequently pays us the doubtful compliment of describing as 'devilish funny' jokes which are neither funny nor devilish."

The orator paused, and an oppressive silence reigned over the vast chamber.

"What is happening?" whispered Bidderdale.

"Five minutes Hush," explained his guide; "it is a sign that the speaker was listened to in silent approval, which is the highest mark of appreciation that can be bestowed in Pandemonium. Let's come into the smoking-room."

"Will the motion be carried?" asked Bidderdale, wondering inwardly how Sir Edward Grey would treat the protest if it reached the British Parliament; an *entente* with the Infernal Regions opened up a fascinating vista, in which the Foreign Secretary's imagination might hopelessly lose itself.

"Carried? Of course not," said the Fiend; "in the Infernal Parliament all motions are necessarily lost."

"In earthly Parliaments nowadays nearly everything is found," said Bidderdale, "including salaries and travelling expenses."

He felt that at any rate he was probably the first member of his family to make a joke in Hell.

"By the way," he added, "talking of earthly Parliaments, have you got the Party system down here?"

"In Hell? Impossible. You see we have no system of rewards. We have specialized so thoroughly on punishments that the other branch has been entirely neglected. And besides, Government by delusion, as you practise it in your Parliament, would be unworkable here. I should be the last person to say anything against temptation, naturally, but we have a proverb down here 'in baiting a mouse-trap with cheese, always leave room for the mouse.' Such a party-cry, for instance, as your 'ninepence for fourpence' would be absolutely inoperative; it not only leaves no room for the mouse, it leaves no room for the imagination. You have a saying in your country I believe, 'there's no fool like a damned fool'; all the fools down here are, necessarily, damned, but—you wouldn't get them to nibble at ninepence for fourpence."

"Couldn't they be scolded and lectured into believing it, as a sort of moral and intellectual duty?" asked Bidderdale.

"We haven't all your facilities," said the Fiend; "we've nothing down here that exactly corresponds to the Master of Elibank."

At this moment Bidderdale's attention was caught by an item on a loose sheet of agenda paper: "Vote on account of special Hells."

"Ah," he said, "I've often heard the expression 'there is a special Hell reserved for such-and-such a type of person.' Do tell me about them."

"I'll show you one in course of preparation," said the Fiend, leading him down the corridor. "This one is designed to accommodate one of the leading playwrights of your nation. You may observe scores of imps engaged in pasting notices of modern British plays into a huge press-cutting book, each under the name of the author, alphabetically arranged. The book will contain nearly half a million notices, I suppose, and it will form the sole literature supplied to this specially doomed individual."

Bidderdale was not altogether impressed.

"Some dramatic authors wouldn't so very much mind spending eternity poring over a book of contemporary press-cuttings," he observed.

The Fiend, laughing unpleasantly, lowered his voice.

"The letter 'S' is missing."

For the first time Bidderdale realized that he was in Hell.

Rudyard Kipling

Rudyard Kipling (1865–1936) was born in Bombay and was the first English author to be awarded the Nobel prize. Among his best known works are Kim *and* The Jungle Books, *from which the following story comes.*

HOW FEAR CAME

> The stream is shrunk—the pool is dry,
> And we be comrades, thou and I;
> With fevered jowl and dusty flank
> Each jostling each along the bank;
> And by one drouthy fear made still,
> Foregoing thought of quest or kill.
> Now 'neath his dam the fawn may see,
> The lean Pack-wolf as cowed as he,
> And the tall buck, unflinching, note
> The fangs that tore his father's throat.
> The pools are shrunk—the streams are dry,
> And we be playmates, thou and I,
> Till yonder cloud—Good Hunting!—loose
> The rain that breaks our Water Truce.

The law of the Jungle—which is by far the oldest law in the world—has arranged for almost every kind of accident that may befall the Jungle-People, till now its code is as perfect as time and custom can make it. You will remember that Mowgli spent a great part of his life in the Seeonee Wolf-Pack, learning the Law from Baloo, the Brown Bear; and it was Baloo who told him, when the boy grew impatient at the constant orders, that the Law was like the Giant Creeper, because it dropped across every one's back and no one could escape! "When thou hast lived as long as I have, Little Brother, thou wilt see how all the Jungle obeys at least one Law. And that will be no pleasant sight," said Baloo.

This talk went in at one ear and out at the other, for a boy who spends his life eating and sleeping does not worry about anything till it actually stares him in the face. But, one year, Baloo's words came true, and Mowgli saw all the Jungle working under the Law.

It began when the winter Rains failed almost entirely, and Ikki, the Porcupine, meeting Mowgli in a bamboo-thicket, told him that the wild yams were drying up. Now everybody knows that Ikki is ridiculously fastidious in his choice of food, and will eat nothing but the very best and ripest. So Mowgli laughed and said, "What is that to me?"

"No much *now,*" said Ikki, rattling his quills in a stiff, uncomfortable way, "but later we shall see. Is there any more diving into the deep rock-pool below the Bee-Rocks, Little Brother?"

"No. The foolish water is going all away, and I do not wish to break my head," said Mowgli, who, in those days, was quite sure that he knew as much as any five of the Jungle-People put together.

"That is thy loss. A small crack might let in some wisdom." Ikki ducked quickly to prevent Mowgli from pulling his nose-bristles, and Mowgli told Baloo what Ikki had said. Baloo looked very grave, and mumbled half to himself: "If I were alone I would change my hunting-grounds now, before the others began to think. And yet—hunting among strangers ends in fighting; and they might hurt the Man-cub. We must wait and see how the *mohwa* blooms."

That spring the *mohwa* tree, that Baloo was so fond of, never flowered. The greeny, cream-coloured, waxy blossoms were heat-killed before they were born, and only a few bad-smelling petals came down when he stood on his hind legs and shook the tree. Then, inch by inch, the untempered heat crept into the heart of the Jungle, turning it yellow, brown, and at last black. The green growths in the sides of the ravines burned up to broken wires and curled films of dead stuff; the hidden pools sank down and caked over, keeping the last least footmark on their edges as if it had been cast in iron; the juicy-stemmed creepers fell away from the trees they clung to and died at their feet; the bamboos withered, clanking when the hot winds blew, and the moss peeled off the rocks deep in the Jungle, till they were as bare and as hot as the quivering blue boulders in the bed of the stream.

The birds and the Monkey-People went north early in the year, for they knew what was coming; and the deer and the wild pig broke far away to the perished fields of the villages, dying sometimes before the eyes of men too weak to kill them. Chil, the Kite, stayed, and grew fat, for there was a great deal of carrion, and evening after evening, he brought the news to the beasts, too weak to force their way to fresh hunting-grounds, that the sun was killing the Jungle for three days' flight in every direction.

Mowgli, who had never known what real hunger meant, fell back on stale honey, three years old, scraped out of deserted rock-hives—honey black as a sloe, and dusty with dried sugar. He hunted, too, for deep-boring grubs under the bark of the trees, and robbed the wasps of their new broods. All the game in the Jungle was no more than skin and bone, and Bagheera could kill thrice in a night, and hardly get a full meal. But the want of water was the worst, for though the Jungle-People drink seldom they must drink deep.

And the heat went on and on, and sucked up all the moisture, till at last the main channel of the Waingunga was the only stream that carried a trickle of water between its dead banks; and when Hathi, the wild elephant, who lives for a hundred years and more, saw a long, lean blue ridge of rock show dry in the very centre of the stream, he knew that he was looking at the Peace Rock, and then and there he lifted up his trunk and proclaimed the Water Truce, as his father before him had proclaimed it fifty years ago. The deer, wild pig, and buffalo took up the cry hoarsely; and Chil, the Kite, flew in great circles far and wide, whistling and shrieking the warning.

By the Law of the Jungle it is death to kill at the drinking-places when once the Water Truce has been declared. The reason of this is that drinking comes before eating. Every one in the Jungle can scramble along somehow when only game is scarce; but water is water, and when there is but one source of supply, all hunting stops while the Jungle-People go there for their needs. In good seasons, when water was plentiful, those who came down to drink at the Waingunga—or any-where else, for that matter—did so at the risk of their lives, and that risk made no small part of the fascination of the night's doings. To move down so cunningly that never a leaf stirred; to wade knee-deep in the roaring shallows that drown all noise from behind; to drink, looking backward over one shoulder, every muscle ready for the first desperate bound of keen terror; to roll on the sandy margin, and return, wet-muzzled and well plumped out, to the admiring herd, was a thing that all tall-antlered young bucks took a delight in, pre-cisely because they knew that at any moment Bagheera or Shere Khan might leap upon them and bear them down. But now all that life-and-death fun was ended, and the Jungle-People came up, starved and weary, to the shrunken river,—tiger, bear, deer, buffalo, and pig, all together,—drank the fouled waters, and hung above them, too exhausted to move off.

The deer and the pig had tramped all day in search of something better than dried bark and withered leaves. The buffaloes had found no wallows to be cool in and no green crops to steal. The snakes had left the Jungle and come down to the river in the hope of finding a stray frog. They curled round wet stones, and never offered to strike when the nose of a rooting pig dislodged them. The river-turtles had long ago been killed by Bagheera, cleverest of hunters, and the fish had buried themselves deep in the dry mud. Only the Peace Rock lay across the shallows like a long snake, and the little tired ripples hissed as they dried on its hot side.

It was here that Mowgli came nightly for the cool and the companionship. The most hungry of his enemies would hardly have cared for the boy then. His naked hide made him seem more lean and wretched than any of his fellows. His hair was bleached to tow colour by the sun; his ribs stood out like the ribs of a basket, and the lumps on his knees and elbows, where he was used to track on all fours, gave his shrunken limbs the look of knotted grass-stems. But his eye, under his matted forelock, was cool and quiet, for Bagheera was his adviser in this time of trouble, and told him to go quietly, hunt slowly, and never, on any account, to lose his temper.

"It is an evil time," said the Black Panther, one furnace-hot evening, "but it will go if we can live till the end. Is thy stomach full, Man-cub?"

"There is stuff in my stomach, but I get no good of it. Think you, Bagheera, the Rains have forgotten us and will never come again?"

"Not I! We shall see the *mohwa* in blossom yet, and the little fawns all fat with new grass. Come down to the Peace Rock and hear the news. On my back, Little Brother."

"This is no time to carry weight. I can still stand alone, but —indeed we be no fatted bullocks, we two."

Bagheera looked along his ragged, dusty flank and whispered: "Last night I kill a bullock under the yoke. So low was I brought that I think I should not have dared to spring if he had been loose. *Wou!*"

Mowgli laughed. "Yes, we be great hunters now," said he. "I am very bold—to eat grubs," and the two came down together through the crackling undergrowth to the river-bank and the lace-work of shoals that ran out from it in every direction.

"The water cannot live long," said Baloo, joining them. "Look across. Yonder are trails like the roads of Man."

On the level plain of the farther bank the stiff jungle-grass had died standing, and, dying, had mummied. The beaten tracks of the deer and the pig, all heading toward the river, had striped that colourless plain with dusty gullies driven through the ten-foot grass, and, early as it was, each long avenue was full of first-comers hastening to the water. You could hear the does and fawns coughing in the snuff-like dust.

Up-stream, at the bend of the sluggish pool round the Peace Rock, and Warden of the Water Truce, stood Hathi, the wild elephant, with his sons, gaunt and gray in the moonlight, rocking to and fro—always rocking. Below him a little were the vanguard of the deer; below these, again, the pig and the wild buffalo; and on the opposite bank, where the tall trees came down to the water's edge, was the place set apart for the Eaters of Flesh—the tiger, the wolves, the panther, the bear, and the others.

"We are under one Law, indeed," said Bagheera, wading into the water and looking across at the lines of clicking horns and starting eyes where the deer and the pig pushed each other to and fro. "Good hunting, all you of my blood," he added, lying down at full length, one flank thrust out of the shallows; and then, between his teeth, "But for that which is the Law it would be *very* good hunting."

The quick-spread ears of the deer caught the last sentence, and a frightened whisper ran along the ranks. "The Truce! Remember the Truce!"

"Peace there, peace!" gurgled Hathi, the wild elephant. "The Truce holds, Bagheera. This is no time to talk of hunting."

"Who should know better than I?" Bagheera answered, rolling his yellow eyes up-stream. "I am an eater of turtles—a fisher of frogs. *Ngaayah!* Would I could get good from chewing branches!"

"We wish so, very greatly," bleated a young fawn, who had only been born that spring and did not at all like it. Wretched as the Jungle-People were, even Hathi could not help chuck-

ling; while Mowgli, lying on his elbows in the warm water, laughed aloud, and beat up the scum with his feet.

"Well spoken, little bud-horn," Bagheera purred. "When the Truce ends that shall be remembered in thy favour," and he looked keenly through the darkness to make sure of recognising the fawn again.

Gradually the talking spread up and down the drinking-places. One could hear the scuffling, snorting pig asking for more room; the buffaloes grunting among themselves as they lurched out across the sandbars, and the deer telling pitiful stories of their long foot-sore wanderings in quest of food. Now and again they asked some question of the Eaters of Flesh across the river, but all the news was bad, and the roaring hot wind of the Jungle came and went between the rocks and the rattling branches, and scattered twigs and dust on the water.

"The men-folk, too, they die beside their ploughs," said the young sambhur. "I passed three between sunset and night. They lay still, and their Bullocks with them. We also shall lie still in a little."

"The river has fallen since last night," said Baloo. "O Hathi, hast thou ever seen the like of this drought?"

"It will pass, it will pass," said Hathi, squirting water along his back and sides.

"We have one here that cannot endure long," said Baloo; and he looked toward the boy he loved.

"I?" said Mowgli indignantly, sitting up in the water. "I have no long fur to cover my bones, but—but if *thy* hide were taken off, Baloo——"

Hathi shook all over at the idea, and Baloo said severely:

"Man-cub, that is not seemly to tell a Teacher of the Law. *Never* have I been seen without my hide."

"Nay, I meant no harm, Baloo; but only that thou art, as it were, like the cocoanut in the husk, and I am the same cocoanut all naked. Now that brown husk of thine——" Mowgli was sitting cross-legged, and explaining things with his forefinger in his usual way, when Bagheera put out a paddy paw and pulled him over backward into the water.

"Worse and worse," said the Black Panther, as the boy rose spluttering. "First Baloo is to be skinned, and now he is a cocoanut. Be careful that he does not do what the ripe cocoanuts do."

"And what is that?" said Mowgli, off his guard for the minute, though that is one of the oldest catches in the Jungle.

"Break thy head," said Bagheera quietly, pulling him under again.

"It is not good to make a jest of thy teacher," said the bear, when Mowgli had been ducked for the third time.

"Not good! What would ye have? That naked thing running to and fro makes a monkey-jest of those who have once been good hunters, and pulls the best of us by the whiskers for sport." This was Shere Khan the Lame Tiger, limping down to the water. He waited a little to enjoy the sensation he made among the deer on the opposite bank; then he dropped his square, frilled head and began to lap, growling: "The Jungle has become a whelping-ground for naked cubs now. Look at me. Man-cub!"

Mowgli looked—stared, rather—as insolently as he knew how, and in a minute Shere Khan turned away uneasily. "Man-cub this, and Man-cub that," he rumbled, going on with his drink, "the cub is neither man nor cub, or he would have been afraid. Next season I shall have to beg his leave for a drink. *Augrh!*"

"That may come, too," said Bagheera, looking him steadily between the eyes. "That may come, too—Faugh, Shere Khan! —what new shame hast thou brought here?"

The Lame Tiger had dipped his chin and jowl in the water, and dark, oily streaks were floating from it down-stream.

"Man!" said Shere Khan cooly, "I killed an hour since." He went on purring and growling to himself.

The line of beasts shook and wavered to and fro, and a whisper went up that grew to a cry: "Man! Man! He has killed Man!" Then all looked towards Hathi, the wild elephant, but he seemed not to hear. Hathi never does anything till the time comes, and that is one of the reasons why he lives so long.

"At such a season as this to kill Man! Was no other game afoot?" said Bagheera scornfully, drawing himself out of the tainted water, and shaking each paw, cat-fashion, as he did so.

"I killed for choice—not for food." The horrified whisper began again, and Hathi's watchful little white eye cocked itself in Shere Khan's direction. "For choice," Shere Khan drawled. "Now come I to drink and make me clean again. Is there any to forbid?"

Bagheera's back began to curve like a bamboo in a high wind, but Hathi lifted up his trunk and spoke quietly.

"Thy kill was from choice?" he asked; and when Hathi asks a question it is best to answer.

"Even so. It was my right and my Night. Thou knowest, O Hathi." Shere Khan spoke almost courteously.

"Yes, I know," Hathi answered; and, after a little silence, "Hast thou drunk thy fill?"

"For to-night, yes."

"Go, then. The river is to drink, and not to defile. None but the Lame Tiger would so have boasted of his right at this season when—when we suffer together—Man and Jungle-People alike. Clean or unclean, get to thy lair, Shere Khan!"

The last words rang out like silver trumpets, and Hathi's three sons rolled forward half a pace, though there was no need. Shere Khan slunk away, not daring to growl, for he knew—what every one else knows—that when the last comes to the last, Hathi is the Master of the Jungle.

"What is this right Shere Khan speaks of?" Mowgli whispered in Bagheera's ear. "To kill man is *always* shameful. The Law says so. And yet Hathi says——"

"Ask him. I do not know, Little Brother. Right or no right, if Hathi had not spoken I would have taught that lame butcher his lesson. To come to the Peace Rock fresh from a kill of Man—and to boast of it—is a jackal's trick. Besides, he tainted the good water."

Mowgli waited for a minute to pick up his courage, because no one cared to address Hathi directly, and then he cried: "What is Shere Khan's right, O Hathi?" Both banks echoed his words, for all the People of the Jungle are intensely curious, and they had just seen something that none, except Baloo, who looked very thoughtful, seemed to understand.

"It is an old tale," said Hathi, "a tale older than the Jungle. Keep silence along the banks, and I will tell that tale."

There was a minute or two of pushing and shouldering among the pigs and the buffalo, and then the leaders of the herds grunted, one after another, "We wait," and Hathi strode forward till he was nearly knee-deep in the pool by the Peace Rock. Lean and wrinkled and yellow-tusked though he was, he looked what the Jungle knew him to be—their master.

"Ye know, children," he began, "that of all things ye most fear Man"; and there was a mutter of agreement.

"This tale touches thee, Little Brother," said Bagheera to Mowgli.

"I? I am of the Pack—a hunter of the Free People," Mowgli answered. "What have I to do with Man?"

"And ye do not know why ye fear Man?" Hathi went on. "This is the reason. In the beginning of the Jungle, and none know when that was, we of the Jungle walked together, having no fear of one another. In those days there was no drought, and leaves and flowers and fruit grew on the same tree, and we ate nothing at all except leaves and flowers and grass and fruit and bark."

"I am glad I was not born in those days," said Bagheera. "Bark is only good to sharpen claws."

"And the Lord of the Jungle was Tha, the First of the Elephants. He drew the Jungle out of deep waters with his trunk; and where he made furrows in the ground with his tusks, there the rivers ran; and where he struck with his foot, there rose ponds of good water; and when he blew through his trunk,—thus,—the trees fell. That was the manner in which the Jungle was made by Tha; and so the tale was told to me."

"It has not lost fat in the telling," Bagheera whispered, and Mowgli laughed behind his hand.

"In those days there was no corn or melons or pepper or sugar-cane, nor were there any little huts such as ye have all seen; and the Jungle-People knew nothing of Man, but lived in the Jungle together, making one people. But presently they began to dispute over their food, though there was grazing enough for all. They were lazy. Each wished to eat where he lay, as sometimes we can do now when the spring rains are good. Tha, the First of the Elephants, was busy making new jungles and leading the rivers in their beds. He could not walk in all places; therefore he made the First of the Tigers the master and the judge of the Jungle, to whom the Jungle-People should bring their disputes. In those days the First of the Tigers ate fruit and grass with the others. He was as large as I am, and he was very beautiful, in colour all over like the blossom of the yellow creeper. There was never stripe nor bar upon his hide in those good days when this the Jungle was new. All the Jungle-People came before him without fear, and his word was the Law of all the Jungle. We were then, remember ye, one people.

"Yet upon a night there was a dispute between two bucks— a grazing-quarrel such as ye now settle with the horns and the fore-feet—and it is said that as the two spoke together before the First of the Tigers lying among the flowers, a buck pushed him with his horns, and the First of the Tigers forgot that he was the master and judge of the Jungle, and, leaping upon that buck, broke his neck.

"Till that night never one of us had died, and the First of the Tigers, seeing what he had done, and being made foolish by the scent of the blood, ran away into the marshes of the North, and we of the Jungle, left without a judge, fell to fighting among ourselves; and Tha heard the noise of it and came back. Then some of us said this and some of us said that, but he saw the dead buck among the flowers, and asked who had killed, and we of the Jungle would not tell because the smell of the blood made us foolish. We ran to and fro in circles, capering and crying out and shaking our heads. Then Tha gave an order to the trees that hang low, and to the trailing creepers of the Jungle, that they should mark the killer of the buck so that he should know him again, and he said, 'Who will now be master of the Jungle-People?' Then up leaped the Gray Ape who lives in the branches, and said, 'I will now be master of the Jungle.' At this Tha laughed, and said, 'So be it,' and went away very angry.

"Children, ye know the Gray Ape. He was then as he is now. At the first he made a wise face for himself, but in a little while he began to scratch and to leap up and down, and when Tha came back he found the Gray Ape hanging, head down, from a bough, mocking those who stood below; and they mocked him again. And so there was no Law in the Jungle—only foolish talk and senseless words.

"Then Tha called us all together and said: 'The first of your masters has brought Death into the Jungle, and the second Shame. Now it is time there was a Law, and a Law that ye must not break. Now ye shall know Fear, and when ye have found him ye shall know that he is your master, and the rest shall follow.' Then we of the Jungle said, 'What is Fear?' And Tha said, 'Seek till ye find.' So we went up and down the Jungle seeking for Fear, and presently the buffaloes—"

"Ugh!" said Mysa, the leader of the buffaloes, from their sand-bank.

"Yes, Mysa, it was the buffaloes. They came back with the news that in a cave in the Jungle sat Fear, and that he had no hair, and went upon his hind legs. Then we of the Jungle followed the herd till we came to that cave, and Fear stood at the mouth of it, and he was, as the buffaloes had said, hairless, and he walked upon his hinder legs. When he saw us he cried out, and his voice filled us with the fear that we have now of that voice when we hear it, and we ran away, tramping upon and tearing each other because we were afraid. That night, so it was told to me, we of the Jungle did not lie down together as used to be our custom, but each tribe drew off by itself—the pig with the pig, the deer with the deer; horn to horn, hoof to hoof,—like keeping to like, and so lay shaking in the Jungle.

"Only the First of the Tigers was not with us, for he was still hidden in the marshes of the North, and when word was brought to him of the Thing we had seen in the cave, he said: 'I will go to this Thing and break his neck.' So he ran all the night till he came to the cave; but the trees and the creepers on his path, remembering the order that Tha had given, let down their branches and marked him as he ran, drawing their fingers across his back, his flank, his forehead, and his jowl. Wherever they touched him there was a mark and a stripe upon his yellow hide. *And those stripes do his children wear to this day!* When he came to the cave, Fear, the Hairless One, put out his hand and called him 'The Striped One that comes by night,' and the First of the Tigers was afraid of the Hairless One, and ran back to the swamps howling."

Mowgli chuckled quietly here, his chin in the water.

"So loud did he howl that Tha heard him and said, 'What is the sorrow?' And the First of the Tigers, lifting up his muzzle to the new-made sky, which is now so old, said: 'Give me back my power, O Tha. I am made ashamed before all the Jungle, and I have run away from a Hairless One, and he has called me a shameful name.' 'And why?' said Tha. 'Because I am smeared with the mud of the marshes,' said the First of the Tigers. 'Swim, then, and roll on the wet grass, and if it be mud it will wash away,' said Tha; and the First of the Tigers swam, and rolled and rolled upon the grass, till the Jungle ran round and round before his eyes, but not one little bar upon all his hide was changed, and Tha, watching him, laughed. Then the First of the Tigers said, 'What have I done that this comes to me?' Tha said, 'Thou hast killed the buck and thou hast let Death loose in the Jungle, and with Death has come Fear, so that the people of the Jungle are afraid one of the other, as thou art afraid of the Hairless One.' The First of the Tigers said, 'They will never fear me, for I knew them since the beginning.' Tha said, 'Go and see.' And the First of the Tigers ran to and fro, calling aloud to the deer and the pig and the sambhur and the porcupine and all the Jungle-Peoples, and they all ran away from him who had been their judge, because they were afraid.

"Then the First of the Tigers came back, and his pride was broken in him, and, beating his head upon the ground, he tore up the earth with all his feet and said: 'Remember that I was once the Master of the Jungle. Do not forget me, O Tha! Let my children remember that I was once without shame or fear!' And Tha said: 'This much I will do, because thou and I together saw the Jungle made. For one night in each year it shall be as it was before the buck was killed—for thee and for thy children. In that one night, if ye meet the Hairless One—and his name is Man—ye shall not be afraid of him, but he shall be afraid of you, as though ye were judges of the Jungle and masters of all things. Show him mercy in that night of his fear, for thou hast known what Fear is.'

"Then the First of the Tigers answered, 'I am content'; but when next he drank he saw the black stripes upon his flank and his side, and he remembered the name that the Hairless One had given him, and he was angry. For a year he lived in the marshes, waiting till Tha should keep his promise. And upon a night when the Jackal of the Moon (the Evening Star) stood clear of the Jungle, he felt that his Night was upon him, and he went to that cave to meet the Hairless One. Then it happened as Tha promised, for the Hairless One fell down before him and lay along the ground, and the First of the Tigers struck him and broke his back, for he thought that there was but one such Thing in the Jungle, and that he had killed Fear. Then, nosing above the kill, he heard Tha coming down from the woods of the North, and presently the voice of the First of the Elephants, which is the voice that we hear now—"

The thunder was rolling up and down the dry, scarred hills, but it brought no rain—only heat-lightning that flickered along the ridges—and Hathi went on. *"That* was the voice he heard, and it said: 'Is this thy mercy?' The First of the Tigers licked his lips and said: 'What matter? I have killed Fear.' And Tha said: 'O blind and foolish! Thou hast untied the feet of Death, and he will follow thy trail till thou diest. Thou hast taught Man to kill!'

"The First of the Tigers, standing stiffly to his kill, said: 'He is as the buck was. There is no Fear. Now I will judge the Jungle-Peoples once more.'

"And Tha said: 'Never again shall the Jungle-Peoples come to thee. They shall never cross thy trail, nor sleep near thee, nor follow after thee, nor browse by thy lair. Only Fear shall follow thee, and with a blow that thou canst not see he shall bid thee wait his pleasure. He shall make the ground to open under thy feet, and the creeper to twist about thy neck, and the tree-trunks to grow together about thee higher than thou canst leap, and at the last he shall take thy hide to wrap his cubs when they are cold. Thou hast shown him no mercy, and none will he show thee.'

"The First of the Tigers was very bold, for his Night was still on him, and he said: 'The Promise of Tha is the Promise of Tha. He will not take away my Night?' And Tha said: 'The one Night is thine, as I have said, but there is a price to pay. Thou hast taught Man to kill, and he is no slow learner.'

"The First of the Tigers said: 'He is here under my foot, and his back is broken. Let the Jungle know I have killed Fear.'

"Then Tha laughed, and said: 'Thou hast killed one of many, but thou thyself shalt tell the Jungle—for thy Night is ended.'

"So the day came; and from the mouth of the cave went out another Hairless One, and he saw the kill in the path, and the First of the Tigers above it, and he took a pointed stick—"

"They throw a thing that cuts now," said Ikki, rustling down the bank; for Ikki was considered uncommonly good eating by the Gonds—they called him Ho-Igoo—and he knew something of the wicked little Gondee axe that whirls across a clearing like a dragonfly.

"It was a pointed stick, such as they put in the foot of a pit-trap," said Hathi, "and throwing it, he struck the First of the Tigers deep in the flank. Thus it happened as Tha said, for the First of the Tigers ran howling up and down the Jungle till he tore out the stick, and all the Jungle knew that the Hairless One could strike from far off, and they feared more than before. So it came about that the First of the Tigers taught the Hairless One to kill—and ye know what harm that has since done to all our peoples—through the noose, and the pitfall, and the hidden trap, and the flying stick, and the stinging fly that comes out of white smoke (Hathi meant the rifle), and the Red Flower that drives us into the open. Yet for one night in the year the Hairless One fears the Tiger, as Tha promised, and never has the Tiger given him cause to be less afraid. Where he finds him, there he kills him, remembering how the First of the Tigers was made ashamed. For the rest, Fear walks up and down the Jungle by day and by night."

"Ahi! Aoo!" said the deer, thinking of what it all meant to them.

"And only when there is one great Fear over all, as there is now, can we of the Jungle lay aside our little fears, and meet together in one place as we do now."

"For one night only does Man fear the Tiger?" said Mowgli.

"For one night only," said Hathi.

"But I—but we—but all the Jungle knows that Shere Khan kills Man twice and thrice in a moon."

"Even so. *Then* he springs from behind and turns his head aside as he strikes, for he is full of fear. If Man looked at him he would run. But on his one Night he goes openly down to the village. He walks between the houses and thrusts his head into the doorway, and the men fall on their faces, and there he does his kill. One kill in that Night."

"Oh!" said Mowgli to himself, rolling over in the water. *"Now* I see why it was Shere Khan bade me look at him! He got no good of it, for he could not hold his eyes steady, and—and I certainly did not fall down at his feet. But then I am not a man, being of the Free People."

"Umm!" said Bagheera deep in his furry throat. "Does the Tiger know his Night?"

"Never till the Jackal of the Moon stands clear of the evening mist. Sometimes it falls in the dry summer and sometimes in the wet rains—this one Night of the Tiger. But for the First of the Tigers, this would never have been, nor would any of us have known fear."

The deer grunted sorrowfully, and Bagheera's lips curled in a wicked smile. "Do men know this—tale?" said he.

"None know it except the tigers, and we, the elephants—the children of Tha. Now ye by the pools have heard it, and I have spoken."

Hathi dipped his trunk into the water as a sign that he did not wish to talk.

"But—but—but," said Mowgli, turning to Baloo, "why did not the First of the Tigers continue to eat grass and leaves and trees? He did but break the buck's neck. He did not *eat*. What led him to the hot meat?"

"The trees and the creepers marked him, Little Brother, and made him the striped thing that we see. Never again would he eat their fruit; but from that day he revenged himself upon the deer, and the others, the Eaters of Grass," said Baloo.

"Then *thou* knowest the tale. Heh? Why have I never heard?"

"Because the Jungle is full of such tales. If I made a beginning there would never be an end to them. Let go my ear, Little Brother."

Jack London

Jack London (1876–1916) was born in San Francisco and is most famous for novels such as The Call of the Wild, The Sea Wolf, *and* Martin Eden. *He was an active socialist, and his story "The Strength of the Strong," published in 1910, expresses his politics.*

THE STRENGTH
OF THE STRONG

Parables don't lie, but liars will parable.

—LIP-KING

Old Long-Beard paused in his narrative, licked his greasy fingers and wiped them on his naked sides where his one piece of ragged bearskin failed to cover him. Crouched around him, on their hams, were three young men, his grandsons, Deer-Runner, Yellow-Head and Afraid-of-the-Dark. In appearance they were much the same. Skins of wild animals partially covered them. They were lean and meager of build, narrow-hipped and crooked-legged, and at the same time deep-chested with heavy arms and enormous hands. There was much hair on their chests and shoulders, and on the outsides of their arms and legs. Their heads were matted with uncut hair, long locks of which often strayed before their eyes, beady and black and glittering like the eyes of birds.

They were narrow between the eyes and broad between the cheeks, while their lower jaws were projecting and massive.

It was a night of clear starlight, and below them, stretching away remotely, lay range on range of forest-covered hills. In the distance the heavens were red from the glow of a volcano. At their backs yawned the black mouth of a cave, out of which, from time to time, blew draughty gusts of wind. Immediately in front of them blazed a fire. At one side, partly devoured, lay the carcass of a bear, with about it, at a respectable distance, several large dogs, shaggy and wolflike. Beside each man lay his bow and arrows and a huge club. In the cave-mouth a number of rude spears leaned against the rock.

"So that was how we moved from the cave to the tree," old Long-Beard spoke up.

They laughed boisterously, like big children, at recollection of a previous story his words called up. Long-Beard laughed, too, the five-inch bodkin of bone thrust midway through the cartilage of his nose leaping and dancing and adding to his ferocious appearance. He did not exactly say the words recorded, but he made animal-like sounds with his mouth that meant the same thing.

"And that is the first I remember of the Sea Valley," Long-Beard went on. "We were a very foolish crowd. We did not know the secret of strength. For behold, each family lived by itself and took care of itself. There were thirty families, but we got no strength from one another. We were in fear of each other all the time. No one ever paid visits. In the top of our tree we built a grass house, and on the platform outside was a pile of rocks which were for the heads of any that might chance to try to visit us. Also, we had our spears and arrows. We never walked under the trees of the other families, either. My brother did, once, under old Boo-oogh's tree, and he got his head broken and that was the end of him.

"Old Boo-oogh was very strong. It was said he could pull a grown man's head right off. I never heard of him doing it, because no man would give him a chance. Father wouldn't. One day when father was down on the beach, Boo-oogh took after mother. She couldn't run fast, for the day before she had got her leg clawed by a bear when she was up on the mountain gathering berries. So Boo-oogh caught her and carried her up into his tree. Father never got her back. He was afraid. Old Boo-oogh made faces at him.

"But father did not mind. Strong-Arm was another strong man. He was one of the best fishermen. But one day, climbing after sea-gull eggs, he had a fall from the cliff. He was never strong after that. He coughed a great deal, and his shoulders drew near to each other. So father took Strong-Arm's wife. When he came around and coughed under our tree, father laughed at him and threw rocks at him. It was our way in those days. We did not know how to add strength together and become strong."

"Would a brother take a brother's wife?" Deer-Runner demanded.

"Yes, if he had gone to live in another tree by himself."

"But we do not do such things now," Afraid-of-the-Dark objected.

"It is because I have taught your fathers better." Long-Beard thrust his hairy paw into the bear meat and drew out a handful of suet, which he sucked with a meditative air. Again he wiped his hands on his naked sides and went on. "What I am telling you happened in the long ago, before we knew any better."

"You must have been fools not to know better," was Deer-Runner's comment, Yellow-Head grunting approval.

"So we were, but we became bigger fools, as you shall see. Still, we did learn better, and this was the way of it. We Fish-Eaters had not learned to add our strength until our strength was the strength of all of us. But the Meat-Eaters, who lived across the divide in the Big Valley, stood together, hunted together, fished together, and fought together. One day they came into our valley. Each family of us got into its own cave and tree. There were only ten Meat-Eaters, but they fought together, and we fought each family by itself."

Long-Beard counted long and perplexedly on his fingers.

"There were sixty men of us," was what he managed to say with fingers and lips combined. "And we were very strong, only we did not know it. So we watched the ten men attack Boo-oogh's tree. He made a good fight, but he had no chance. We looked on. When some of the Meat-Eaters tried to climb the tree, Boo-oogh had to show himself in order to drop stones on their heads, whereupon the other Meat-Eaters, who were waiting for that very thing, shot him full of arrows. And that was the end of Boo-oogh.

"Next, the Meat-Eaters got One-Eye and his family in his cave. They built a fire in the mouth and smoked him out, like we smoked out the bear there to-day. Then they went after Six-Fingers, up his tree, and while they were killing him and his grown son, the rest of us ran away. They caught some of our women, and killed two old men who could not run fast and several children. The women they carried away with them to the Big Valley.

"After that the rest of us crept back, and somehow, perhaps because we were in fear and felt the need for one another, we talked the thing over. It was our first council—our first real council. And in that council we formed our first tribe. For we had learned the lesson. Of the ten Meat-Eaters, each man had had the strength of ten, for the ten had fought as one man. They had added their strength together. But of the thirty families and the sixty men of us, we had had the strength of but one man, for each had fought alone.

"It was a great talk we had, and it was hard talk, for we did not have the words then as now with which to talk. The Bug made some of the words long afterwards, and so did others of us make words from time to time. But in the end we agreed to add our strength together and to be as one man when the Meat-Eaters came over the divide to steal our women. And that was the tribe.

"We set two men on the divide, one for the day and one for the night, to watch if the Meat-Eaters came. These were the eyes of the tribe. Then, also, day and night, there were to be ten men awake with their clubs and spears and arrows in their hands, ready to fight. Before, when a man went after fish or clams or gull eggs, he carried his weapons with him and half the time he was getting food and half the time watching for fear some other man would get him. Now that was all changed. The men went out without their weapons and spent all their time getting food. Likewise, when the women went into the mountains after roots and berries, five of the ten men went with them to guard them, while all the time, day and night, the eyes of the tribe watched from the top of the divide.

"But troubles came. As usual, it was about the women. Men without wives wanted other men's wives, and there was much fighting between men, and now and again one got his head smashed or a spear through his body. While one of the watchers was on the top of the divide another man stole his wife, and he came down to fight. Then the other watcher was in fear that some one would take his wife, and he came down likewise. Also, there was trouble among the ten men who carried always their weapons, and they fought five against five, till some ran away down the coast and the others ran after them.

"So it was that the tribe was left without eyes or guards. We had not the strength of sixty. We had no strength at all. So we held a council and made our first laws. I was but a cub at the time, but I remember. We said that in order to be strong we must not fight one another, and we made a law that when a man killed another, him would the tribe kill. We made another law that whoso stole another man's wife, him would the tribe kill. We said that whatever man had too great strength, and by that strength hurt his brothers in the tribe, him would we kill that his strength might hurt no more. For if we let his strength hurt, the brothers would become afraid and the tribe would fall apart, and we would be as weak as when the Meat-Eaters first came upon us and killed Boo-oogh.

"Knuckle-Bone was a strong man, a very strong man, and he knew not law. He knew only his own strength, and in the fullness thereof he went forth and took the wife of Three-

Clams. Three-Clams tried to fight, but Knuckle-Bone clubbed out his brains. Yet had Knuckle-Bone forgotten that all the men of us had added our strength to keep the law among us, and him we killed, at the foot of his tree, and hung his body on a branch as a warning that the law was stronger than any man. For we were the law, all of us, and no man was greater than the law.

"Then there were other troubles, for know, O Deer-Runner and Yellow-Head and Afraid-of-the-Dark, that it is not easy to make a tribe. There were many things, little things, that it was a great trouble to call all the men together to have a council about. We were having councils morning, noon and night, and in the middle of the night. We could find little time to go out and get food, what of the councils, for there was always some little thing to be settled, such as naming two new watchers to take the place of the old ones on the hill, or naming how much food should fall to the share of the men who kept their weapons always in their hands and got no food for themselves.

"We stood in need of a chief man to do these things, who would be the voice of the council and who would account to the council for the things he did. So we named Fith-Fith the chief man. He was a strong man, too, and very cunning, and when he was angry he made noises just like that, *fith-fith*, like a wildcat.

"The ten men who guarded the tribe were set to work making a wall of stones across the narrow part of the valley. The women and large children helped, as did other men, until the wall was strong. After that, all the families came down out of their caves and trees and built grass houses behind the shelter of the wall. These houses were large and much better than the caves and trees, and everybody had a better time of it because the men had added their strength together and become a tribe. Because of the wall and the guards and the watchers, there was more time to hunt and fish and pick roots and berries; there was more food, and better food, and no one went hungry. And Three-Legs, so named because his legs had been smashed when a boy and he walked with a stick, Three-Legs got the seed of the wild corn and planted it in the ground in the valley near his house. Also, he tried planting fat roots and other things he found in the mountain valleys.

"Because of the safety in the Sea Valley, which was because of the wall and the watchers and the guards, and because there was food in plenty for all without having to fight for it, many families came in from the coast valleys on both sides and from the high back mountains where they had lived more like wild animals than men. And it was not long before the Sea Valley filled up, and in it were countless families. But before this happened the land, which had been free to all and belonged to all, was divided up. Three-Legs began it when he planted corn. But most of us did not care about the land. We thought the marking of the boundaries with fences of stone was a foolishness. We had plenty to eat, and what more did we want? I remember that my father and I built stone fences for Three-Legs and were given corn in return.

"So only a few got all the land, and Three-Legs got most of it. Also, others that had taken land gave it to the few that held on, being paid in return with corn and fat roots and bearskins and fishes which the farmers got from the fishermen in exchange for corn. And the first thing we knew, all the land was gone.

"It was about this time that Fith-Fith died, and Dog-Tooth, his son, was made chief. He demanded to be made chief anyway, because his father had been chief before him. Also, he looked upon himself as a greater chief than his father. He was a good chief at first, and worked hard, so that the council had less and less to do. Then arose a new voice in the Sea Valley. It was Twisted-Lip. We had never thought much of him, until he began to talk with the spirits of the dead. Later we called him Big-Fat, because he ate overmuch and did no work and grew round and large. One day Big-Fat told us that the secrets of the dead were his, and that he was the voice of God. He became great friends with Dog-Tooth, who commanded that we build Big-Fat a grass house. And Big-Fat put taboos all around this house and kept God inside.

"More and more Dog-Tooth became greater than the council, and when the council grumbled and said it would name a new chief, Big-Fat spoke with the voice of God and said no. Also, Three-Legs and the others who held the land stood behind Dog-Tooth. Moreover, the strongest man in the council was Sea-Lion, and him the landowners gave land to secretly, along with many bearskins and baskets of corn. So Sea-Lion said that Big-Fat's voice was truly the voice of God and must be obeyed. And soon afterwards Sea-Lion was named the voice of Dog-Tooth and did most of his talking for him.

"Then there was Little-Belly, a little man, so thin in the middle that he looked as if he never had had enough to eat. Inside the mouth of the river, after the sand-bar had combed the strength of the breakers, he built a big fish trap. No man had ever seen or dreamed of a fish trap before. He worked weeks on it, with his son and his wife, while the rest of us laughed at their labors. But when it was done, the first day he caught more fish in it than could the whole tribe in a week, whereat there was great rejoicing. There was only one other place in the river for a fish trap; but when my father and I and a dozen other men started to make a very large trap, the guards came from the big grass house we had built for Dog-Tooth. And the guards poked us with their spears and told us begone, because Little-Belly was going to build a trap there himself on the word of Sea-Lion, who was the voice of Dog-Tooth.

"There was much grumbling, and my father called a council. But when he rose to speak, him the Sea-Lion thrust through the throat with a spear, and he died. And Dog-Tooth and Little-Belly and Three-Legs and all that held land said it was good. And Big-Fat said it was the will of God. And after that all men were afraid to stand up in the council, and there was no more council.

"Another man, Pig-Jaw, began to keep goats. He had

heard about it among the Meat-Eaters, and it was not long before he had many flocks. Other men, who had no land and no fish traps and who else would have gone hungry were glad to work for Pig-Jaw, caring for his goats, guarding them from wild dogs and tigers and driving them to the feeding pastures in the mountains. In return Pig-Jaw gave them goat meat to eat, and goatskins to wear, and sometimes they traded the goat meat for fish and corn and fat roots.

"It was this time that money came to be. Sea-Lion was the man who first thought of it, and he talked it over with Dog-Tooth and Big-Fat. You see, these three were the ones that got a share of everything in the Sea Valley. One basket out of every three of corn was theirs, one fish out of every three, one goat out of every three. In return, they fed the guards and the watchers, and kept the rest for themselves. Sometimes, when a big haul of fish was made, they did not know what to do with all their share. So Sea-Lion set the women to making money out of shell—little round pieces, with a hole in each one, and all made smooth and fine. These were strung on strings, and the strings were called money.

"Each string was of the value of thirty fish, or forty fish, but the women who made a string a day were given two fish each. The fish came out of the shares of Dog-Tooth, Big-Fat and Sea-Lion, which they three did not eat. So all the money belonged to them. Then they told Three-Legs and the other landowners that they would take their share of corn and roots in money, Little-Belly that they would take their share of fish in money, and Pig-Jaw that they would take their share of goat and cheese in money. Thus, a man who had nothing worked for one who had and was paid in money. With this money he bought corn and fish and meat and cheese. And Three-Legs and all owners of things paid Dog-Tooth and Sea-Lion and Big-Fat their share in money. And they paid the guards and watchers in money, and the guards and watchers bought their food with the money. And because money was cheap, Dog-Tooth made many more men into guards. And because money was cheap to make, a number of men began to make money out of shells themselves. But the guards stuck spears in them and shot them full of arrows, because they were trying to break up the tribe. It was bad to break up the tribe, for then the Meat-Eaters would come over the divide and kill them all.

"Big-Fat was the voice of God, but he took Broken-Rib and made him into a priest, so that he became the voice of Big-Fat and did most of his talking for him. And both had other men to be servants to them. So also did Little-Belly and Three-Legs and Pig-Jaw have other men to lie in the sun about their grass houses and carry messages for them and give commands. And more and more were men taken away from work, so that those that were left worked harder than ever before. It seemed that men desired to do no work and strove to seek out other ways whereby men should work for them. Crooked-Eyes found such a way. He made the first firebrew out of corn. And thereafter he worked no more, for he talked secretly with Dog-Tooth and Big-Fat and the other masters, and it was agreed that he should be the only one to make firebrew. But Crooked-Eyes did no work himself. Men made the brew for him, and he paid them in money. Then he sold the firebrew for money, and all men bought. And many strings of money did he give Dog-Tooth and Sea-Lion and all of them.

"Big-Fat and Broken-Rib stood by Dog-Tooth when he took his second wife, and his third wife. They said Dog-Tooth was different from other men and second only to God that Big-Fat kept in his taboo house, and Dog-Tooth said so, too, and wanted to know who were they to grumble about how many wives he took. Dog-Tooth had a big canoe made, and many more men he took from work, who did nothing and lay in the sun save only when Dog-Tooth went in the canoe when they paddled for him. And he made Tiger-Face head man over all the guards, so that Tiger-Face became his right arm, and when he did not like a man Tiger-Face killed that man for him. And Tiger-Face, also, made another man to be his right arm, and to give commands and to kill for him.

"But this was the strange thing: as the days went by, we who were left worked harder and harder and yet did we get less and less to eat."

"But what of the goats and the corn and the fat roots and the fish trap?" spoke up Afraid-of-the-Dark. "What of all this? Was there not more food to be gained by a man's work?"

"It is so," Long-Beard agreed. "Three men on the fish trap got more fish than the whole tribe before there was a fish trap. But have I not said we were fools? The more food we were able to get, the less food did we have to eat."

"But was it not plain that the many men who did not work ate it all up?" Yellow-Head demanded.

Long-Beard nodded his head sadly. "Dog-Tooth's dogs were stuffed with meat, and the men who lay in the sun and did no work were rolling in fat, and at the same time there were little children crying themselves to sleep with hunger biting them with every wail."

Deer-Runner was spurred by the recital of famine to tear out a chunk of bear meat and broil it on a stick over the coals. This he devoured with smacking lips while Long-Beard went on.

"When we grumbled, Big-Fat arose and with the voice of God said that God had chosen the wise men to own the land and the goats and the fish trap and the firebrew and that without these wise men we would all be animals as in the days when we lived in trees.

"And there arose one who became a singer of songs for the king. Him they called the Bug, because he was small and ungainly of face and limb and excelled not in work or deed. He loved the fattest marrowbones, the choicest fish, the milk warm from the goats, the first corn that was ripe, and the snug place by the fire. And thus, becoming singer of songs to the king, he found a way to do nothing and be fat. And when the people grumbled more and more, and some threw stones at the king's big grass house, the Bug sang a song of how good it was to be a Fish-Eater. In his song he told that the Fish-

Eaters were the chosen of God and the finest men God had made. He sang of the Meat-Eaters as pigs and crows, and sang how fine and good it was for the Fish-Eaters to fight and die doing God's work, which was the killing of Meat-Eaters. The words of his song were like fire in us, and we clamored to be led against the Meat-Eaters. And we forgot that we were hungry and why we had grumbled, and were glad to be led by Tiger-Face over the divide where we killed many Meat-Eaters and were content.

"But things were no better in the Sea Valley. The only way to get food was to work for Three-Legs or Little-Belly or Pig-Jaw; for there was no land that a man might plant with corn for himself. And often there were more men than Three-Legs and the others had work for. So these men went hungry, and so did their wives and children and their old mothers. Tiger-Face said they could become guards if they wanted to, and many of them did; and thereafter they did no work except to poke spears in the men who did work and who grumbled at feeding so many idlers.

"And when we grumbled, ever the Bug sang new songs. He said that Three-Legs and Pig-Jaw and the rest were strong men, and that that was why they had so much. He said that we should be glad to have strong men with us, else would we perish of our own worthlessness and the Meat-Eaters. Therefore we should be glad to let such strong men have all they could lay hands on. And Big-Fat and Pig-Jaw and Tiger-Face and all the rest said it was true.

" 'All right,' said Long-Fang, 'then will I, too, be a strong man.' And he got himself corn and began to make firebrew and sell it for strings of money. And when Crooked-Eyes complained, Long-Fang said that he was himself a strong man, and that if Crooked-Eyes made any more noise he would dash his brains out for him. Whereat Crooked-Eyes was afraid and went and talked with Three-Legs and Pig-Jaw. And all three went and talked to Dog-Tooth. And Dog-Tooth spoke to Sea-Lion, and Sea-Lion sent a runner with a message to Tiger-Face. And Tiger-Face sent his guards, who burned Long-Fang's house along with the firebrew he had made. Also, they killed him and all his family. And Big-Fat said it was good, and the Bug sang another song about how good it was to observe the law, and what a fine land the Sea Valley was, and how every man who loved the Sea Valley should go forth and kill the bad Meat-Eaters. And again his song was as fire to us, and we forgot to grumble.

"It was very strange. When Little-Belly caught too many fish, so that it took a great many to sell for a little money, he threw many of the fish back into the sea so that more money would be paid for what was left. And Three-Legs often let many large fields lie idle so as to get more money for his corn. And the women, making so much money out of shell that much money was needed to buy with, Dog-Tooth stopped the making of money. And the women had no work, so they took the places of the men. I worked on the fish trap, getting a string of money every five days. But my sister now did my work, getting a string of money for every ten days. The women worked cheaper, and there was less food, and Tiger-Face said for us to become guards. Only I could not become a guard, because I was lame of one leg and Tiger-Face would not have me. And there were many like me. We were broken men and only fit to beg for work or to take care of the babies while the women worked."

Yellow-Head, too, was made hungry by the recital, and broiled a piece of bear meat on the coals.

"But why didn't you rise up, all of you, and kill Three-Legs and Pig-Jaw and Big-Fat and the rest, and get enough to eat?" Afraid-of-the-Dark demanded.

"Because we could not understand," Long-Beard answered. "There was too much to think about, and also there were the guards sticking spears into us, and Big-Fat talking about God, and the Bug singing new songs. And when any man did think right, and said so, Tiger-Face and the guards got him and he was tied out to the rocks at low tide so that the rising waters drowned him.

"It was a strange thing—the money. It was like the Bug's

songs. It seemed all right, but it wasn't, and we were slow to understand. Dog-Tooth began to gather the money in. He put it in a big pile, in a grass house, with guards to watch it day and night. And the more money he piled in the house, the dearer money became, so that a man worked a longer time for a string of money than before. Then, too, there was always talk of war with the Meat-Eaters, and Dog-Tooth and Tiger-Face filled many houses with corn and dried fish and smoked goat meat and cheese. And with the food piled there in mountains, the people had not enough to eat. But what did it matter? Whenever the people grumbled too loudly, the Bug sang a new song, and Big-Fat said it was God's word that we should kill Meat-Eaters, and Tiger-Face led us over the divide to kill and be killed. I was not good enough to be a guard and lie fat in the sun, but when we made war Tiger-Face was glad to take me along. And when we had eaten all the food stored in the houses we stopped fighting and went back to work to pile up more food."

"Then were you all crazy," commented Deer-Runner.

"Then were we indeed all crazy," Long-Beard agreed. "It was strange, all of it. There was Split-Nose. He said everything was wrong. He said it was true that we grew strong by adding our strength together. And he said that when we first formed the tribe it was right that the men whose strength hurt the tribe should be shorn of their strength—men who bashed their brothers' heads and stole their brothers' wives. And now, he said, the tribe was not getting stronger but was getting weaker, because there were men with another kind of strength that were hurting the tribe—men who had the strength of the land, like Three-Legs; who had the strength of the fish trap, like Little-Belly; who had the strength of all the goat meat, like Pig-Jaw. The thing to do, Split-Nose said, was to shear these men of their evil strength; to make them go to work, all of them, and to let no man eat who did not work.

"And the Bug sang another song about men like Split-Nose, who wanted to go back and live in trees.

"Yet Split-Nose said no; that he did not want to go back

but ahead; that they grew strong only as they added their strength together; and that if the Fish-Eaters would add their strength to the Meat-Eaters, there would be no more fighting and no more watchers and no more guards, and that with all men working there would be so much food that each man would have to work not more than two hours a day.

"Then the Bug sang again, and he sang that Split-Nose was lazy, and he sang also the 'Song of the Bees.' It was a strange song, and those who listened were made mad as from the drinking of strong firebrew. The song was of a swarm of bees, and of a robber wasp who had come in to live with the bees, and who was stealing all their honey. The wasp was lazy and told them there was no need to work; also, he told them to make friends with the bears who were not honey stealers but only very good friends. And the Bug sang in crooked words, so that those who listened knew that the swarm was the Sea Valley tribe, that the bears were the Meat-Eaters, and that the lazy wasp was Split-Nose. And when the Bug sang that the bees listened to the wasp till the swarm was near to perishing, the people growled and snarled; and when the Bug sang that at last the good bees arose and stung the wasp to death, the people picked up stones from the ground and stoned Split-Nose to death till there was naught to be seen of him but the heap of stones they had flung on top of him. And there were many poor people who worked long and hard and had not enough to eat that helped throw the stones on Split-Nose.

"And after the death of Split-Nose there was but one other man that dared rise up and speak his mind, and that man was Hair-Face. 'Where is the strength of the strong?' he asked. 'We are the strong, all of us, and we are stronger than Dog-Tooth and Tiger-Face and Three-Legs and Pig-Jaw and all the rest who do nothing and eat much and weaken us by the hurt of their strength, which is bad strength. Men who are slaves are not strong. If the man who first found the virtue and use of fire had used his strength, we would have been his slaves, as we are the slaves to-day of Little-Belly who found the virtue and use of the fish trap, and of the men who found the virtue and use of the land and the goats and the firebrew. Before, we lived in trees, my brothers, and no man was safe. But we fight no more with one another. We have added our strength together. Then let us fight no more with the Meat-Eaters. Let us add our strength and their strength together. Then will we be indeed strong. And then we will go out together, the Fish-Eaters and the Meat-Eaters, and we will kill the tigers and the lions and the wolves and the wild dogs, and we will pasture our goats on all the hillsides and plant our corn and fat roots in all the high mountain valleys.

" 'In that day we will be so strong that all the wild animals will flee before us and perish. And nothing will withstand us, for the strength of each man will be the strength of all men in the world.'

"So said Hair-Face, and they killed him, because they said he was a wild man and wanted to go back and live in a tree. It was very strange. Whenever a man arose and wanted to go forward all those that stood still said he went backward and should be killed. And the poor people helped stone him, and were fools. We were all fools, except those who were fat and did no work. The fools were called wise, and the wise were stoned. Men who worked did not get enough to eat, and the men who did not work ate too much.

"And the tribe went on losing strength. The children were weak and sickly. And because we ate not enough, strange sicknesses came among us and we died like flies. And then the Meat-Eaters came upon us. We had followed Tiger-Face too often over the divide and killed them. And now they came to repay in blood. We were too weak and sick to man the big wall. And they killed us, all of us, except some of the women which they took away with them. The Bug and I escaped, and I hid in the wildest places, and became a hunter of meat and went hungry no more. I stole a wife from among the Meat-Eaters, and went to live in the caves of the high mountains where they could not find me. And we had three sons, and each son stole a wife from the Meat-Eaters. And the rest you know, for are you not the sons of my sons?"

"But the Bug?" queried Deer-Runner. "What became of him?"

"He went to live with the Meat-Eaters and to be a singer of songs to the king. He is an old man now, but he sings the same old songs; and when a man rises up to go forward he sings that that man is walking backward to live in a tree."

Long-Beard dipped into the bear carcass and sucked with toothless gums at a fist of suet.

"Someday," he said, wiping his hands on his sides, "all the fools will be dead, and then all live men will go forward. The secret of the strength of the strong will be theirs, and they will add their strength together, so that of all the men in the world not one will fight with another. There will be no guards nor watchers on the walls. And all the hunting animals will be killed, and, as Hair-Face said, all the hillsides will be pastured with goats, and all the high mountain valleys will be planted with corn and fat roots. And all men will be brothers, and no man will lie idle in the sun and be fed by his fellows. And all that will come to pass in the time when the fools are dead, and when there will be no more singers to stand still and sing the 'Song of the Bees.' Bees are not men."

Paul Laurence Dunbar

Paul Laurence Dunbar *(1872–1906) was born in Dayton, Ohio. The son of ex-slaves, he was a novelist, short story writer, and poet, best known for his book* Lyrics of Lowly Life.

THE SCAPEGOAT

The law is usually supposed to be a stern mistress, not to be lightly wooed, and yielding only to the most ardent pursuit. But even law, like love, sits more easily on some natures than on others.

This was the case with Mr. Robinson Asbury. Mr. Asbury had started life as a bootblack in the growing town of Cadgers. From this he had risen one step and become porter and messenger in a barbershop. This rise fired his ambition, and he was not content until he had learned to use the shears and the razor and had a chair of his own. From this, in a man of Robinson's temperament, it was only a step to a shop of his own, and he placed it where it would do the most good.

Fully one-half of the population of Cadgers was composed of Negroes, and with their usual tendency to colonize, a tendency encouraged, and in fact compelled, by circumstances, they had gathered into one part of the town. Here in alleys, and streets as dirty and hardly wider, they thronged like ants.

It was in this place that Mr. Asbury set up his shop, and he won the hearts of his prospective customers by putting up the significant sign, "Equal Rights Barbershop." This legend was quite unnecessary, because there was only one race about, to patronize the place. But it was a delicate sop to the people's vanity, and it served its purpose.

Asbury came to be known as a clever fellow, and his business grew. The shop really became a sort of club and, on Saturday nights especially, was the gathering-place of the men of the whole Negro quarter. He kept the illustrated and race journals there, and those who cared neither to talk nor listen to someone else might see pictured the doings of high society in very short skirts or read in the Negro papers how Miss Boston had entertained Miss Blueford to tea on such and such an afternoon. Also, he kept the policy returns, which was wise, if not moral.

It was his wisdom rather more than his morality that made the party managers after a while cast their glances towards him as a man who might be useful to their interests. It would be well to have a man—a shrewd, powerful man—down in that part of the town who could carry his people's vote in his vest pocket, and who at any time its delivery might be needed, could hand it over without hesitation. Asbury seemed that man, and they settled upon him. They gave him money, and they gave him power and patronage. He took it all silently and he carried out his bargain faithfully. His hands and his lips alike closed tightly when there was anything within them. It was not long before he found himself the big Negro of the district and, of necessity, of the town. The time came when, at a critical moment, the managers saw that they had not reckoned without their host in choosing this barber of the black district as the leader of his people.

Now, so much success must have satisfied any other man. But in many ways Mr. Asbury was unique. For a long time he himself had done very little shaving—except of notes, to keep his hand in. His time had been otherwise employed. In the evening hours he had been wooing the coquettish Dame Law, and wonderful to say, she had yielded easily to his advances.

It was against the advice of his friends that he asked for

admission to the bar. They felt that he could do more good in the place where he was.

"You see, Robinson," said old Judge Davis, "it's just like this: If you're not admitted, it'll hurt you with the people; if you are admitted, you'll move uptown to an office and get out of touch with them."

Asbury smiled an inscrutable smile. Then he whispered something into the judge's ear that made the old man wrinkle from his neck up with appreciative smiles.

"Asbury," he said, "you are—you are—well, you ought to be white, that's all. When we find a black man like you we send him to State's prison. If you were white, you'd go to the Senate."

The Negro laughed confidently.

He was admitted to the bar soon after, whether by merit or by connivance is not to be told.

"Now he will move uptown," said the black community. "Well, that's the way with a colored man when he gets a start."

But they did not know Robinson Asbury yet. He was a man of surprises, and they were destined to disappointment. He did not move uptown. He built an office in a small open space next to his shop, and there hung out his shingle.

"I will never desert the people who have done so much to elevate me," said Mr. Asbury. "I will live among them and I will die among them."

This was a strong card for the barber-lawyer. The people seized upon the statement as expressing a nobility of an altogether unique brand.

They held a mass meeting and endorsed him. They made resolutions that extolled him, and the Negro band came around and serenaded him, playing various things in varied time.

All this was very sweet to Mr. Asbury, and the party managers chuckled with satisfaction and said, "That Asbury, that Asbury!"

Now there is a fable extant of a man who tried to please

everybody, and his failure is a matter of record. Robinson Asbury was not more successful. But be it said that his ill success was due to no fault or shortcoming of his.

For a long time his growing power had been looked upon with disfavor by the colored law firm of Bingo & Latchett. Both Mr. Bingo and Mr. Latchett themselves aspired to be Negro leaders in Cadgers, and they were delivering Emancipation Day orations and riding at the head of processions when Mr. Asbury was blacking boots. Is it any wonder, then, that they viewed with alarm his sudden rise? They kept their counsel, however, and treated with him, for it was best. They allowed him his scope without open revolt until the day upon which he hung out his shingle. This was the last straw. They could stand no more. Asbury had stolen their other chances from them, and now he was poaching upon the last of their preserves. So Mr. Bingo and Mr. Latchett put their heads together to plan the downfall of their common enemy.

The plot was deep and embraced the formation of an opposing faction made up of the best Negroes of the town. It would have looked too much like what it was for the gentlemen to show themselves in the matter, and so they took into their confidence Mr. Isaac Morton, the principal of the colored school, and it was under his ostensible leadership that the new faction finally came into being.

Mr. Morton was really an innocent young man, and he had ideals which should never have been exposed to the air. When the wily confederates came to him with their plan he believed that his worth had been recognized, and at last he was to be what nature destined him for—a leader.

The better class of Negroes—by that is meant those who were particularly envious of Asbury's success—flocked to the new man's standard. But whether the race be white or black, political virtue is always in a minority, so Asbury could afford to smile at the force arrayed against him.

The new faction met together and resolved. They resolved, among other things, that Mr. Asbury was an enemy to his race and a menace to civilization. They decided that he should be abolished; but as they couldn't get out an injunction against him, and as he had the whole undignified but still voting black belt behind him, he went serenely on his way.

"They're after you hot and heavy, Asbury," said one of his friends to him.

"Oh, yes," was the reply, "they're after me, but after a while I'll get so far away that they'll be running in front."

"It's all the best people, they say."

"Yes. Well, it's good to be one of the best people, but your vote only counts one just the same."

The time came, however, when Mr. Asbury's theory was put to the test. The Cadgerites celebrated the first of January as Emancipation Day. On this day there was a large procession, with speechmaking in the afternoon and fireworks at night. It was the custom to concede the leadership of the colored people of the town to the man who managed to lead the procession. For two years past this honor had fallen, of course, to Robinson Asbury, and there had been no disposition on the part of anybody to try conclusions with him.

Mr. Morton's faction changed all this. When Asbury went to work to solicit contributions for the celebration, he suddenly became aware that he had a fight upon his hands. All the better-class Negroes were staying out of it. The next thing he knew was that plans were on foot for a rival demonstration.

"Oh," he said to himself, "that's it, is it? Well, if they want a fight they can have it."

He had a talk with the party managers, and he had another with Judge Davis.

"All I want is a little lift, Judge," he said, "and I'll make 'em think the sky has turned loose and is vomiting niggers."

The judge believed that he could do it. So did the party managers. Asbury got his lift. Emancipation Day came.

There were two parades. At least, there was one parade and the shadow of another. Asbury's, however, was not the shadow. There was a great deal of substance about it—substance made up of many people, many banners, and numerous bands. He did not have the best people. Indeed among his cohorts there were a good many of the pronounced ragtag and bobtail. But he had noise and numbers. In such cases, nothing more is needed. The success of Asbury's side of the affair did everything to confirm his friends in their good opinion of him.

When he found himself defeated, Mr. Silas Bingo saw that it would be policy to placate his rival's just anger against him. He called upon him at his office the day after the celebration.

"Well, Asbury," he said, "you beat us, didn't you?"

"It wasn't a question of beating," said the other calmly. "It was only an inquiry as to who were the people—the few or the many."

"Well, it was well done, and you've shown that you are a manager. I confess that I haven't always thought that you were doing the wisest thing in living down here and catering to this class of people when you might, with your ability, be much more to the better class."

"What do they base their claims of being better on?"

"Oh, there ain't any use discussing that. We can't get along without you, we see that. So I, for one, have decided to work with you for harmony."

"Harmony. Yes, that's what we want."

"If I can do anything to help you at any time, why you have only to command me."

"I am glad to find such a friend in you. Be sure, if I ever need you, Bingo, I'll call on you."

"And I'll be ready to serve you."

Asbury smiled when his visitor was gone. He smiled, and knitted his brow. "I wonder what Bingo's got up his sleeve," he said. "He'll bear watching."

It may have been pride at his triumph, it may have been gratitude at his helpers, but Asbury went into the ensuing campaign with reckless enthusiasm. He did the most daring things for the party's sake. Bingo, true to his promise, was ever at his side ready to serve him. Finally, association and immunity made danger less fearsome; the rival no longer appeared a menace.

With the generosity born of obstacles overcome, Asbury determined to forgive Bingo and give him a chance. He let him in on a deal, and from that time they worked amicably together until the election came and passed.

It was a close election and many things had had to be done, but there were men there ready and waiting to do them. They were successful, and then the first cry of the defeated party was, as usual, "Fraud! Fraud!" The cry was taken up by the jealous, the disgruntled, and the virtuous.

Someone remembered how two years ago the registration books had been stolen. It was known upon good authority that money had been freely used. Men held up their hands in horror at the suggestion that the Negro vote had been juggled with, as if that were a new thing. From their pulpits ministers denounced the machine and bade their hearers rise and throw off the yoke of a corrupt municipal government. One of those sudden fevers of reform had taken possession of the town and threatened to destroy the successful party.

They began to look around them. They must purify themselves. They must give the people some tangible evidence of their own yearnings after purity. They looked around them for a sacrifice to lay upon the altar of municipal reform. Their eyes fell upon Mr. Bingo. No, he was not big enough. His blood was too scant to wash the political stains. Then they looked into each other's eyes and turned their gaze away to let it fall upon Mr. Asbury. They really hated to do it. But there must be a scapegoat. The god from the Machine commanded them to slay him.

Robinson Asbury was charged with many crimes—with all that he had committed and some that he had not. When Mr. Bingo saw what was afoot he threw himself heart and soul into the work of his old rival's enemies. He was of incalculable use to them.

Judge Davis refused to have anything to do with the matter. But in spite of his disapproval it went on. Asbury was indicted and tried. The evidence was all against him, and no one gave more damaging testimony than his friend Mr. Bingo. The judge's charge was favorable to the defendant, but the current of popular opinion could not be entirely stemmed. The jury brought in a verdict of guilty.

"Before I am sentenced, Judge, I have a statement to make to the court. It will take less than ten minutes."

"Go on, Robinson," said the judge kindly.

Asbury started, in a monotonous tone, a recital that brought the prosecuting attorney to his feet in a minute. The judge waved him down, and sat transfixed by a sort of fascinated horror as the convicted man went on. The before-mentioned attorney drew a knife and started for the prisoner's dock. With difficulty he was restrained. A dozen faces in the courtroom were red and pale by turns.

"He ought to be killed," whispered Mr. Bingo audibly.

Robinson Asbury looked at him and smiled, and then he told a few things of him. He gave the ins and outs of some of the misdemeanors of which he stood accused. He showed who were the men behind the throne. And still, pale and transfixed, Judge Davis waited for his own sentence.

Never were ten minutes so well taken up. It was a tale of rottenness and corruption in high places told simply and with the stamp of truth upon it.

He did not mention the judge's name. But he had torn the mask from the face of every other man who had been concerned in his downfall. They had shorn him of his strength, but they had forgotten that he was yet able to bring the roof and pillars tumbling about their heads.

The judge's voice shook as he pronounced sentence upon his old ally—a year in State's prison.

Some people said it was too light, but the judge knew what it was to wait for the sentence of doom, and he was grateful and sympathetic.

When the sheriff led Asbury away the judge hastened to have a short talk with him.

"I'm sorry, Robinson," he said, "and I want to tell you that you were no more guilty than the rest of us. But why did you spare me?"

"Because I knew you were my friend," answered the convict.

"I tried to be, but you were the first man that I've ever known since I've been in politics who ever gave me any decent return for friendship."

"I reckon you're about right, Judge."

In politics, party reform usually lies in making a scapegoat of someone who is only as criminal as the rest, but a little weaker. Asbury's friends and enemies had succeeded in making him bear the burden of all the party's crimes, but their reform was hardly a success, and their protestations of a change of heart were received with doubt. Already there were those who began to pity the victim and to say that he had been hardly dealt with.

Mr. Bingo was not of these; but he found, strange to say, that his opposition to the idea went but a little way, and that even with Asbury out of his path he was a smaller man than he was before. Fate was strong against him. His poor, prosperous humanity could not enter the lists against a martyr. Robinson Asbury was now a martyr.

II

A year is not a long time. It was short enough to prevent people from forgetting Robinson, and yet long enough for their pity to grow strong as they remembered. Indeed, he was not gone a year. Good behavior cut two months off the time of his sentence, and by the time people had come around to the notion that he was really the greatest and smartest man in Cadgers he was at home again.

He came back with no flourish of trumpets, but quietly, humbly. He went back again into the heart of the black district. His business had deteriorated during his absence, but he put new blood and new life into it. He did not go to work in the shop himself but, taking down the shingle that had swung idly before his office door during his imprisonment, he opened the little room as a news- and cigar-stand.

Here anxious, pitying customers came to him and he prospered again. He was very quiet. Uptown hardly knew that he was again in Cadgers, and it knew nothing whatever of his doings.

"I wonder why Asbury is so quiet," they said to one another. "It isn't like him to be quiet." And they felt vaguely uneasy about him.

So many people had begun to say, "Well, he was a mighty good fellow after all."

Mr. Bingo expressed the opinion that Asbury was quiet because he was crushed, but others expressed doubt as to this. There are calms and calms, some after and some before the storm. Which was this?

They waited a while, and, as no storm came, concluded that this must be the afterquiet. Bingo, reassured, volunteered to go and seek confirmation of this conclusion.

He went, and Asbury received him with an indifferent, not to say impolite, demeanor.

"Well, we're glad to see you back, Asbury," said Bingo patronizingly. He had variously demonstrated his inability to lead during his rival's absence and was proud of it. "What are you going to do?"

"I'm going to work."

"That's right. I reckon you'll stay out of politics."

"What could I do even if I went in?"

"Nothing now, of course; but I didn't know—"

He did not see the gleam in Asbury's half-shut eyes. He only marked his humility, and he went back swelling with the news.

"Completely crushed—all the run taken out of him," was his report.

The black district believed this, too, and a sullen, smouldering anger took possession of them. Here was a good man ruined. Some of the people whom he had helped in his former days—some of the rude, coarse people of the low quarter who were still sufficiently unenlightened to be grateful—talked among themselves and offered to get up a demonstration for him. But he denied them. No, he wanted nothing of the kind. It would only bring him into unfavorable notice. All he wanted was that they would always be his friends and would stick by him.

They would to the death.

There were again two factions in Cadgers. The schoolmaster could not forget how once on a time he had been made a tool of by Mr. Bingo. So he revolted against his rule and set himself up as the leader of an opposing clique. The fight had been long and strong, but had ended with odds slightly in Bingo's favor.

But Mr. Morton did not despair. As the first of January and Emancipation Day approached, he arrayed his hosts, and the fight for supremacy became fiercer than ever. The schoolteacher brought the schoolchildren in for chorus singing, secured an able orator, and the best essayist in town. With all this, he was formidable.

Mr. Bingo knew that he had the fight of his life on his hands, and he entered with fear as well as zest. He, too, found an orator, but he was not sure that he was good as Morton's. There was no doubt but that his essayist was not. He secured a band, but still he felt unsatisfied. He had hardly done enough, and for the schoolmaster to beat him now meant his political destruction.

It was in this state of mind that he was surprised to receive a visit from Mr. Asbury.

"I reckon you're surprised to see me here," said Asbury, smiling.

"I am pleased, I know." Bingo was astute.

"Well, I just dropped in on our business."

"To be sure, to be sure, Asbury. What can I do for you?"

"It's more what I can do for you that I came to talk about," was the reply.

"I don't believe I understand you."

"Well, it's plain enough. They say that the schoolteacher is giving you a pretty hard fight."

"Oh, not so hard."

"No man can be too sure of winning though. Mr. Morton once did me a mean turn when he started the faction against me."

Bingo's heart gave a great leap, and then stopped for the fraction of a second.

"You were in it, of course," pursued Asbury, "but I can look over your part in it in order to get even with the man who started it."

It was true, then, thought Bingo gladly. He did not know. He wanted revenge for his wrongs and upon the wrong man. How well the schemer had covered his tracks! Asbury should have his revenge and Morton would be the sufferer.

"Of course, Asbury, you know that I did what I did innocently."

"Oh, yes, in politics we are all lambs and the wolves are only to be found in the other party. We'll pass that, though. What I want to say is that I can help you to make your celebration an overwhelming success. I still have some influence down in my district."

"Certainly, and very justly, too. Why I should be delighted with your aid. I could give you a prominent position in the procession."

"I don't want it; I don't want to appear in this at all. All I want is revenge. You can have all the credit, but let me down my enemy."

Bingo was perfectly willing, and with their heads close together, they had a long and close consultation. When Asbury was gone, Mr. Bingo lay back in his chair and laughed. "I'm a slick duck," he said.

From that hour Mr. Bingo's cause began to take on the appearance of something very like a boom. More bands were hired. The interior of the State was called upon a more eloquent orator secured. The crowd hastened to array itself on the growing side.

With surprised eyes, the schoolmaster beheld the wonder of it, but he kept to his own purpose with dogged insistence, even when he saw that he could not turn aside the overwhelming defeat that threatened him. But in spite of his obstinacy, his hours were dark and bitter. Asbury worked like a mole, all underground, but he was indefatigable. Two days before the celebration time everything was perfected for the biggest demonstration that Cadgers had ever known. All the next day and night he was busy among his allies.

On the morning of the great day, Mr. Bingo, wonderfully caparisoned, rode down to the hall where the parade was to form. He was early. No one had yet come. In an hour a score of men all told had collected. Another hour passed, and no more had come. Then there smote upon his ear the sound of music. They were coming at last. Bringing his sword to his shoulder, he rode forward to the middle of the street. Ah, there they were. But—but—could he believe his eyes? They were going in another direction, and at their head rode—Morton! He gnashed his teeth in fury. He had been led into a trap and betrayed. The procession passing had been his—all his. He heard them cheering, and then, oh! climax of infidelity, he saw his own orator go past in a carriage, bowing and smiling to the crowd.

There was no doubting who had done this thing. The hand of Asbury was apparent in it. He must have known the truth all along, thought Bingo. His allies left him one by one for the other hall, and he rode home in a humiliation deeper than he had ever known before.

Asbury did not appear at the celebration. He was at his little newsstand all day.

In a day or two the defeated aspirant had further cause to curse his false friend. He found that not only had the people defected from him, but that the thing had been so adroitly managed that he appeared to be in fault, and three-fourths of those who knew him were angry at some supposed grievance. His cup of bitterness was full when his partner, a quietly ambitious man, suggested that they dissolve their relations.

His ruin was complete.

The lawyer was not alone in seeing Asbury's hand in his downfall. The party managers saw it too, and they met together to discuss the dangerous factor which, while it appeared to slumber, was so terribly awake. They decided that he must be appeased, and they visited him.

He was still busy at his newsstand. They talked to him adroitly, while he sorted papers and kept an impassive face. When they were all done, he looked up for a moment and replied, "You know, gentlemen, as an ex-convict I am not in politics."

Some of them had the grace to flush.

"But you can use your influence," they said.

"I am not in politics," was his only reply.

And the spring elections were coming on. Well, they worked hard, and he showed no sign. He treated with neither one party nor the other. "Perhaps," thought the managers, "he is out of politics," and they grew more confident.

It was nearing eleven o'clock on the morning of election when a cloud no bigger than a man's hand appeared upon the horizon. It came from the direction of the black district. It grew, and the managers of the party in power looked at it, fascinated by an ominous dread. Finally it began to rain Negro voters, and as one man they voted against their former candidates. Their organization was perfect. They simply came, voted, and left, but they overwhelmed everything. Not one of the party that had damned Robinson Asbury was left in power save old Judge Davis. His majority was overwhelming.

The generalship that had engineered the thing was perfect. There were loud threats against the newsdealer. But no one bothered him except a reporter. The reporter called to see just how it was done. He found Asbury very busy sorting papers. To the newspaperman's questions he had only this reply, "I am not in politics, sir."

But Cadgers had learned its lesson.

Theodore Dreiser

Theodore Dreiser (1871–1945) was born in Terre Haute, Indiana. He began his career as a journalist, later becoming one of the most renowned novelists in the United States, the author of works such as An American Tragedy *and* Sister Carrie. *"A Mayor and His People" was published in 1919, although an earlier version appeared in 1903.*

A MAYOR
AND HIS PEOPLE

Here is the story of an individual whose political and social example, if such things are ever worth anything (the moralists to the contrary notwithstanding), should have been, at the time, of the greatest importance to every citizen of the United States. Only it was not. Or was it? Who really knows? Anyway, he and his career are entirely forgotten by now, and have been these many years.

He was the mayor of one of those dreary New England mill towns in northern Massachusetts—a bleak, pleasureless realm of about forty thousand, where, from the time he was born until he finally left at the age of thirty-six to seek his fortune elsewhere, he had resided without change. During that time he had worked in various of the local mills, which in one way and another involved nearly all of the population. He was a mill shoe-maker by trade, or, in other words, a factory shoehand, knowing only a part of all the processes necessary to make a shoe in that fashion. Still, he was a fair workman, and earned as much as fifteen or eighteen dollars a week at times—rather good pay for that region. By temperament a humanitarian, or possibly because of his own humble state one who was compelled to take cognizance of the difficulties of others, he finally expressed his mental unrest by organizing a club for the study and propagation of socialism, and later, when it became powerful enough to have a candidate and look for political expression of some kind, he was its first, and thereafter for a number of years, its regular candidate for mayor. For a long time, or until its membership became sufficient to attract some slight political attention, its members (following our regular American, unintellectual custom) were looked upon by the rest of the people as a body of harmless kickers, filled with fool notions about a man's duty to his fellowman, some silly dream about an honest and economical administration of public affairs—their city's affairs, to be exact. We are so wise in America, so interested in our fellowman, so regardful of his welfare. They were so small in number, however, that they were little more than an object of pleasant jest, useful for that purpose alone.

This club, however, continued to put up its candidate until about 1895, when suddenly it succeeded in polling the very modest number of fifty-four votes—double the number it had succeeded in polling any previous year. A year later one hundred and thirty-six were registered, and the next year six hundred. Then suddenly the mayor who won that year's battle died, and a special election was called. Here the club polled six hundred and one, a total and astonishing gain of one. In 1898 the perennial candidate was again nominated and received fifteen hundred, and in 1899, when he ran again, twenty-three hundred votes, which elected him.

If this fact be registered casually here, it was not so regarded in that typically New England mill town. Ever study New England—its Puritan, self-defensive, but unintellectual and selfish psychology? Although this poor little snip of a mayor was only elected for one year, men paused astounded, those who had not voted for him, and several of the older conventional political and religious order, wedded to their church and all the routine of the average puritanic mill town, actually cried. No one knew, of course, who the new mayor was, or what he stood for. There were open assertions that the club behind him was anarchistic—that ever-ready charge against anything new in America—and that the courts should be called upon to prevent his being seated. And this from people who were as poorly "off" commercially and socially as any might well be. It was stated, as proving the worst, that he was, or had been, a mill worker!—and, before that a grocery clerk—both at twelve a week, or less!! Immediate division of property, the forcing of all employers to pay as much as five a day to every laborer (an unheard-of sum in New England), and general constraint and subversion of individual rights (things then unknown in America, of course), loomed in the minds of these conventional Americans as the natural and immediate result of so modest a victory. The old-time politicians and corporations who understood much better what the point was, the significance of this straw, were more or less disgruntled, but satisfied that it could be undone later.

An actual conversation which occurred on one of the outlying street corners one evening about dusk will best illustrate the entire situation.

"Who is the man, anyway?" asked one citizen of a total stranger whom he had chanced to meet.

"Oh, no one in particular, I think. A grocery clerk, they say."

"Astonishing, isn't it? Why, I never thought those people would get anything. Why, they didn't even figure last year."

"Seems to be considerable doubt as to just what he'll do."

"That's what I've been wondering. I don't take much stock in all their talk about anarchy. A man hasn't so very much power as mayor."

"No," said the other.

"We ought to give him a trial, anyway. He's won a big fight. I should like to see him, see what he looks like."

"Oh, nothing startling. I know him."

"Rather young, ain't he?"

"Yes."

"Where did he come from?"

"Oh, right around here."

"Was he a mill-hand?"

"Yes."

The stranger made inquiry as to other facts and then turned off at a corner.

"Well," he observed at parting, "I don't know. I'm inclined to believe in the man. I should like to see him myself. Good-night."

"Good-night," said the other, waving his hand. "When you see me again you will know that you are looking at the mayor."

The inquirer stared after him and saw a six-foot citizen, of otherwise medium proportions, whose long, youthful face and mild gray eyes, with just a suggestion of washed-out blue in them, were hardly what was to be expected of a notorious and otherwise astounding political figure.

"He is too young," was the earliest comments, when the public once became aware of his personality.

"Why, he is nothing but a grocery clerk," was another, the skeptical and condemnatory possibilities of which need not be dilated upon here.

And he was, in his way—nothing much of a genius, as such things go in politics, but an interesting figure. Without much taste (or its cultivated shadow) or great vision of any kind, he was still a man who sensed the evils of great and often unnecessary social inequalities and the need of reorganizing influences, which would tend to narrow the vast gulf between the unorganized and ignorant poor, and the huge beneficiaries of unearned (yes, and not even understood) increment. For what does the economic wisdom of the average capitalist amount to, after all: the narrow, gourmandizing hunger of the average multi-millionaire?

At any rate, people watched him as he went to and fro between his office and his home, and reached the general conclusion after the first excitement had died down that he did not amount to much.

When introduced into his office in the small but pleasant city hall, he came into contact with a "ring," and a fixed condition, which nobody imagined a lone young mayor could change. Old-time politicians sat there giving out contracts for street-cleaning, lighting, improvements and supplies of all kinds, and a bond of mutual profit bound them closely together.

"I don't think he can do much to hurt us," these individuals said one to another. "He don't amount to much."

The mayor was not of a talkative or confiding turn. Neither was he cold or wanting in good and natural manners. He was, however, of a preoccupied turn of mind, "up in the air," some called it, and smoked a good many cigars.

"I think we ought to get together and have some sort of a conference about the letting of contracts," said the president of the city council to him one morning shortly after he had been installed. "You will find these gentlemen ready to meet you half-way in these matters."

"I'm very glad to hear that," he replied. "I've something to say in my message to the council, which I'll send over in the morning."

The old-time politician eyed him curiously, and he eyed the old-time politician in turn, not aggressively, but as if they might come to a very pleasant understanding if they wanted to, and then went back to his office.

The next day his message was made public, and this was its key-note:

"All contract work for the city should be let with a proviso, that the workmen employed receive not less than two dollars a day."

The dissatisfied roar that followed was not long in making itself heard all over the city.

"Stuff and nonsense," yelled the office jobbers in a chorus. "Socialism!" "Anarchy!" "This thing must be put down!" "The city would be bankrupt in a year." "No contractor could afford to pay his ordinary day laborers two a day. The city could not afford to pay any contractor enough to do it."

"The prosperity of the city is not greater than the prosperity of the largest number of its component individuals," replied the mayor, in a somewhat altruistic and economically abstruse argument on the floor of the council hall. "We must find contractors."

"We'll see about that," said the members of the opposition. "Why, the man's crazy. If he thinks he can run this town on a goody-good basis and make everybody rich and happy, he's going to get badly fooled, that's all there is to that."

Fortunately for him three of the eight council members were fellows of the mayor's own economic beliefs, individuals elected on the same ticket with him. These men could not carry a resolution, but they could stop one from being carried over the mayor's veto. Hence it was found that if the contracts could not be given to men satisfactory to the mayor they could not be given at all, and he stood in a fair way to win.

"What the hell's the use of us sitting here day after day!" were the actual words of the leading members of the opposition in the council some weeks later, when the fight became wearisome. "We can't pass the contracts over his veto. I say let 'em go."

So the proviso was tacked on, that two a day was the minimum wage to be allowed, and the contracts passed.

The mayor's followers were exceedingly jubilant at this, more so than he, who was of a more cautious and less hopeful temperament.

"Not out of the woods yet, gentlemen," he remarked to a group of his adherents at the reform club. "We have to do a great many things sensibly if we expect to keep the people's confidence and 'win again.' "

Under the old system of letting contracts, whenever there was a wage rate stipulated, men were paid little or nothing, and the work was not done. There was no pretense of doing it. Garbage and ashes accumulated, and papers littered the streets. The old contractor who had pocketed the appropriated sum thought to do so again.

"I hear the citizens are complaining as much as ever," said the mayor to this individual one morning. "You will have to keep the streets clean."

The contractor, a robust, thick-necked, heavy-jawed Irishman, of just so much refinement as the sudden acquisition of a comfortable fortune would allow, looked him quizzically over, wondering whether he was "out" for a portion of the appropriation or whether he was really serious.

"We can fix that between us," he said.

"There's nothing to fix," replied the mayor. "All I want you to do is to clean the streets."

The contractor went away and for a few days after the streets were really clean, but it was only for a few days.

In his walks about the city the mayor himself found garbage and paper uncollected, and then called upon his new acquaintance again.

"I'm mentioning this for the last time, Mr. M——," he said. "You will have to fulfill your contract, or resign in favor of someone who will."

"Oh, I'll clean them, well enough," said this individual, after five minutes of rapid fire explanation. "Two dollars a day for men is high, but I'll see that they're clean."

Again he went away, and again the mayor sauntered about, and then one morning sought out the contractor in his own office.

"This is the end," he said, removing a cigar from his mouth and holding it before him with his elbow at right angles. "You are discharged from this work. I'll notify you officially tomorrow."

"It can't be done the way you want it," the contractor exclaimed with an oath. "There's no money in it at two dollars. Hell, anybody can see that."

"Very well," said the mayor in a kindly well-modulated tone. "Let another man try, then."

The next day he appointed a new contractor, and with a schedule before him showing how many men should be employed and how much profit he might expect, the latter succeeded. The garbage was daily removed, and the streets carefully cleaned.

Then there was a new manual training school about to be added to the public school system at this time, and the contract for building was to be let, when the mayor threw a bomb into the midst of the old-time jobbers at the city council. A contractor had already been chosen by them and the members were figuring out their profits, when at one of the public discussions of the subject the mayor said:

"Why shouldn't the city build it, gentlemen?"

"How can it?" exclaimed the councilmen. "The city isn't an individual; it can't watch carefully."

"It can hire its own architect, as well as any contractor. Let's try it."

There were sullen tempers in the council chamber after this, but the mayor was insistent. He called an architect who made a ridiculously low estimate. Never had a public building been estimated so cheaply before.

"See here," said one of the councilmen when the plans were presented to the chamber. "This isn't doing this city right, and the gentlemen of the council ought to put their feet down on any such venture as this. You're going to waste the city's money on some cheap thing in order to catch votes."

"I'll publish the cost of the goods as delivered," said the mayor. "Then the people can look at the building when it's built. We'll see how cheap it looks then."

To head off political trickery on the part of the enemy he secured bills for material as delivered, and publicly compared them with prices paid for similar amounts of the same material used in other buildings. So the public was kept aware of what was going on and the cry of cheapness for political purposes set at naught. It was the first public structure erected by the city, and by all means the cheapest and best of all the city's buildings.

Excellent as these services were in their way, the mayor realized later that a powerful opposition was being generated and that if he were to retain the interest of his constituents he would have to set about something which would endear him and his cause to the public.

"I may be honest," he told one of his friends, "but honesty will play a lone hand with these people. The public isn't interested in its own welfare very much. It can't be bothered or hasn't the time. What I need is something that will impress it and still be worth while. I can't be reëlected on promises, or on my looks, either."

When he looked about him, however, he found the possibility of independent municipal action pretty well hampered by mandatory legislation. He had promised, for instance, to do all he could to lower the exorbitant gas rate and to abolish grade crossings, but the law said that no municipality could do either of these things without first voting to do so three years in succession—a little precaution taken by the corporation representing such things long before he came into power. Each vote must be for such contemplated action, or it could not become a law.

"I know well enough that promises are all right," he said to one of his friends, "and that these laws are good enough excuses, but the public won't take excuses from me for three years. If I want to be mayor again I want to be doing something, and doing it quick."

In the city was a gas corporation, originally capitalized at $45,000, and subsequently increased to $75,000, which was earning that year the actual sum of $58,000 over and above all expenses. It was getting ready to inflate the capitalization, as usual, and water its stock to the extent of $500,000, when it occurred to the mayor that if the corporation was making such enormous profits out of a $75,000 investment as to be able to offer to pay six per cent on $500,000 to investors, and put the money it would get for such stocks into its pocket, perhaps it could reduce the price of gas from one dollar and nineteen cents to a more reasonable figure. There was the three years' voting law, however, behind which, as behind an entrenchment, the very luxurious corporation lay comfortable and indifferent.

The mayor sent for his corporation counsel, and studied gas law for a while. He found that at the State capital there was a State board, or commission, which had been created to look after gas companies in general, and to hear the complaints of municipalities which considered themselves unjustly treated.

"This is the thing for me," he said.

Lacking the municipal authority himself, he decided to present the facts in the case and appeal to this commission for a reduction of the gas rate.

When he came to talk about it he found that the opposition he would generate would be something much more than local. Back of the local reduction idea was the whole system of extortionate gas rates of the State and of the nation; hundreds of fat, luxurious gas corporations whose dividends would be threatened by any agitation on this question.

"You mean to proceed with this scheme of yours?" asked a prominent member of the local bar who called one morning to interview him. "I represent the gentlemen who are interested in our local gas company."

"I certainly do," replied the mayor.

"Well," replied the uncredentialed representative of private interests, after expostulating a long time and offering various "reasons" why it would be more profitable and politically advantageous for the new mayor not to proceed, "I've said all I can say. Now I want to tell you that you are going up against a combination that will be your ruin. You're not dealing with this town now; you're dealing with the State, the whole nation. These corporations can't afford to let you win,

147

and they won't. You're not the one to do it; you're not big enough."

The mayor smiled and replied that of course he could not say as to that.

The lawyer went away, and that next day the mayor had his legal counsel look up the annual reports of the company for the consecutive years of its existence, as well as a bulletin issued by a firm of brokers, into whose hands the matter of selling a vast amount of watered stock it proposed to issue had been placed. He also sent for a gas expert and set him to figuring out a case for the people.

It was found by this gentleman that since the company was first organized it had paid dividends on its capital stock at the rate of ten per cent per annum, for the first thirty years; had made vast improvements in the last ten, and notwithstanding this fact, had paid twenty per cent, and even twenty-five per cent per annum in dividends. All the details of cost and expenditure were figured out, and then the mayor with his counsel took the train for the State capitol.

Never was there more excitement in political circles than when this young representative of no important political organization whatsoever arrived at the State capitol and walked, at the appointed time, into the private audience room of the commission. Every gas company, as well as every newspaper and every other representative of the people, had curiously enough become interested in the fight he was making, and there was a band of reporters at the hotel where he was stopping, as well as in the commission chambers in the State capitol where the hearing was to be. They wanted to know about him—why he was doing this, whether it wasn't a "strike" or the work of some rival corporation. The fact that he might foolishly be sincere was hard to believe.

"Gentlemen," said the mayor, as he took his stand in front of an august array of legal talent which was waiting to pick his argument to pieces in the commission chambers at the capitol, "I miscalculated but one thing in this case which I am about to lay before you, and that is the extent of public interest. I came here prepared to make a private argument, but now I want to ask the privilege of making it public. I see the public itself is interested, or should be. I will ask leave to postpone my argument until the day after tomorrow."

There was considerable hemming and hawing over this, since from the point of view of the corporation it was most undesirable, but the commission was practically powerless to do aught but grant his request. And meanwhile the interest created by the newspapers added power to his cause. Hunting up the several representatives and senators from his district, he compelled them to take cognizance of the cause for which he was battling, and when the morning of the public hearing arrived a large audience was assembled in the chamber of representatives.

When the final moment arrived the young mayor came forward, and after making a very simple statement of the cause which led him to request a public hearing and the local condition which he considered unfair begged leave to introduce an expert, a national examiner of gas plants and lighting facilities, for whom he had sent, and whose twenty years of experience in this line had enabled him to prepare a paper on the condition of the gas-payers in the mayor's city.

The commission was not a little surprised by this, but signified its willingness to hear the expert as counsel for the city, and as his statement was read a very clear light was thrown upon the situation.

Counsel for the various gas corporations interrupted freely. The mayor himself was constantly drawn into the argument, but his replies were so simple and convincing that there was not much satisfaction to be had in stirring him. Instead, the various counsel took refuge in long-winded discussions about the methods of conducting gas plants in other cities, the cost of machinery, labor and the like, which took days and days, and threatened to extend into weeks. The astounding facts concerning large profits and the present intentions of not only this but every other company in the State could not be dismissed. In fact the revelation of huge corporation profits everywhere became so disturbing that after the committee had considered and re-considered, it finally, when threatened with political extermination, voted to reduce the price of gas to eighty cents.

It is needless to suggest the local influence of this decision. When the mayor came home he received an ovation, and that at the hands of many of the people who had once been so fearful of him, but he knew that this enthusiasm would not last long. Many disgruntled elements were warring against him, and others were being more and more stirred up. His home life was looked into as well as his past, his least childish or private actions. It was a case of finding other opportunities for public usefulness, or falling into the innocuous peace which would result in his defeat.

In the platform on which he had been elected was a plank which declared that it was the intention of this party, if elected, to abolish local grade crossings, the maintenance of which had been the cause of numerous accidents and much public complaint. With this plank he now proposed to deal.

In this of course he was hampered by the law before mentioned, which declared that no city could abolish its grade crossings without having first submitted the matter to the people during three successive years and obtained their approval each time. Behind this law was not now, however, as in the case of the gas company, a small $500,000 corporation, but all the railroads which controlled New England, and to which brains and legislators, courts and juries, were mere adjuncts. Furthermore, the question would have to be voted on at the same time as his candidacy, and this would have deterred many another more ambitious politician. The mayor was not to be deterred, however. He began his agitation, and the enemy began theirs, but in the midst of what seemed to be a fair battle the great railway company endeavored to steal a march. There was suddenly and secretly introduced into the lower house of the State legislature a bill which in deceptive phraseology declared that the law which allowed all cities, by three successive votes, to abolish grade crossings in three years, was, in the case of a particular city mentioned, hereby abrogated for a term of four years. The question might not even be discussed politically.

When the news of this attempt reached the mayor, he took the first train for the State capitol and arrived there just in time to come upon the floor of the house when the bill was being taken up for discussion. He asked leave to make a statement. Great excitement was aroused by his timely arrival. Those who secretly favored the bill endeavored to have the matter referred to a committee, but this was not to be. One member moved to go on with the consideration of the bill, and after a close vote the motion carried.

The mayor was then introduced.

After a few moments, in which the silent self-communing with which he introduced himself impressed everyone with his sincerity, he said:

"I am accused of objecting to this measure because its enactment will remove, as a political issue, the one cause upon which I base my hope for reëlection. If there are no elevated crossings to vote for, there will be no excuse for voting for me. Gentlemen, you mistake the temper and the intellect of the people of our city. It is you who see political significance in this thing, but let me assure you that it is of a far different kind from that which you conceive. If the passing of this measure had any significance to me other than the apparent wrong of it, I would get down on my knees and urge its immediate acceptance. Nothing could elect me quicker. Nothing could bury the opposition further from view. If you wish above all things to accomplish my triumph you will only need to interfere with the rights of our city in this arbitrary manner, and you will have the thing done. I could absolutely ask nothing more."

The gentlemen who had this measure in charge weighed well these assertions and trifled for weeks with the matter, trying to make up their minds.

Meanwhile election time approached, and amid the growing interest of politics it was thought unwise to deal with it. A great fight was arranged for locally, in which every conceivable element of opposition was beautifully harmonized by forces and conceptions which it is almost impossible to explain. Democrats, republicans, prohibitionists, saloon men and religious circles, all were gathered into one harmonious body and inspired with a single idea, that of defeating the mayor. From some quarter, not exactly identified, was issued a call for a civic committee of fifty, which should take into its hands the duty of rescuing the city from what was termed a "throttling policy of commercial oppression and anarchy." Democrats, republicans, liquor and anti-liquorites, were invited to the same central meeting place, and came. Money was not lacking, nor able minds, to prepare campaign literature. It was openly charged that a blank check was handed in to the chairman of this body by the railway whose crossings were in danger, to be filled out for any amount necessary to the destruction of the official upstart who was seeking to revolutionize old methods and conditions.

As may be expected, this opposition did not lack daring in making assertions contrary to facts. Charges were now made that the mayor was in league with the railroad to foist upon the city a great burden of expense, because the law under which cities could compel railroads to elevate their tracks declared that one-fifth of the burden of expense must be borne by the city and the remaining four-fifths by the railroad. It would saddle a debt of $250,000 upon the taxpayers, they said, and give them little in return. All the advantage would be with the railroad. "Postpone this action until the railroad can be forced to bear the entire expense, as it justly should," declared handbill writers, whose services were readily rendered to those who could afford to pay for them.

The mayor and his committee, although poor, answered with handbills and street corner speeches, in which he showed that even with the extravagantly estimated debt of $250,000, the city's tax-rate would not be increased by quite six cents to the individual. The cry that each man would have to pay five dollars more each year for ten years and thus wholesomely disposed of, and the campaign proceeded.

Now came every conceivable sort of charge. If he were not defeated, all reputable merchants would surely leave the city. Capital was certainly being scared off. There would be idle factories and empty stomachs. Look out for hard times. No one but a fool would invest in a city thus hampered.

In reply the mayor preached a fair return by corporations for benefits received. He, or rather his organization, took a door-to-door census of his following, and discovered a very considerable increase in the number of those intending to vote for him. The closest calculations of the enemy were discovered, the actual number they had fixed upon as sufficient to defeat him. This proved to the mayor that he must have three hundred more votes if he wished to be absolutely sure. These he hunted out from among the enemy, and had them pledged before the eventual morning came.

The night preceding election ended the campaign, for the enemy at least, in a blaze of glory, so to speak. Dozens of speakers for both causes were about the street corners and in the city meeting room.

Oratory poured forth in streams, and gasoline-lighted bandwagons rattled from street to street, emitting song and invective. Even a great parade was arranged by the anti-mayoral forces, in which horses and men to the number of hundreds were brought in from nearby cities and palmed off as enthusiastic citizens.

"Horses don't vote," a watchword handed out by the mayor, took the edge off the extreme ardor of this invading throng, and set to laughing the hundreds of his partisans, who needed such encouragement.

Next day came the vote, and then for once, anyhow, he was justified. Not only was a much larger vote cast than ever, but he thrashed the enemy with a tail of two hundred votes to spare. It was an inspiring victory from one point of view, but rather doleful for the enemy. The latter had imported a carload of fireworks, which now stood sadly unused upon the very tracks which, apparently, must in the future be raised. The crowning insult was offered when the successful forces offered to take them off their hands at half price.

For a year thereafter (a mayor was elected yearly there), less was heard of the commercial destruction of the city. Gas stood, as decided, at eighty cents a thousand. A new manual training school, built at a very nominal cost, a monument to municipal honesty, was also in evidence. The public water-works had also been enlarged and the rates reduced. The streets were clean.

Then the mayor made another innovation. During his first term of office there had been a weekly meeting of the reform club, at which he appeared and talked freely of his plans and difficulties. These meetings he now proposed to make public.

Every Wednesday evening for a year thereafter a spectacle of municipal self-consciousness was witnessed, which those who saw it felt sure would redound to the greater strength and popularity of the mayor. In a large hall, devoted to public gatherings, a municipal meeting was held. Every one was invited. The mayor was both host and guest, an individual who chose to explain his conduct and his difficulties and to ask advice. There his constituents gathered, not only to hear but to offer counsel.

"Gentlemen," so ran the gist of his remarks on various of these occasions, "the present week has proved a most trying one. I am confronted by a number of difficult problems, which I will now try to explain to you. In the first place, you know my limitations as to power in the council. But three members now vote for me, and it is only by mutual concessions that we move forward at all."

Then would follow a detailed statement of the difficulties, and a general discussion. The commonest laborer was free to offer his advice. Every question was answered in the broadest spirit of fellowship. An inquiry as to "what to do" frequently brought the most helpful advice. Weak and impossible solutions were met as such, and shown to be what they were. Radicals were assuaged, conservatives urged forward. The whole political situation was so detailed and explained that no intelligent person could leave, it was thought, with a false impression of the mayor's position or intent.

With five thousand or more such associated citizens abroad each day explaining, defending, approving the official conduct of the mayor, because they understood it, no misleading conceptions, it was thought, could arise. Men said that his purpose and current leaning in any matter was always clear. He was thought to be closer to his constituency than any other official within the whole range of the Americas and that there could be nothing but unreasoning partisan opposition to his rule.

After one year of such service a presidential campaign drew near, and the mayor's campaign for reëlection had to be contested at the same time. No gas monopoly evil was now a subject of contention. Streets were clean, contracts fairly executed; the general municipal interests as satisfactorily attended to as could be expected. Only the grade crossing war remained as an issue, and that would require still another vote after this. His record was the only available campaign argument.

On the other side, however, were the two organizations of the locally defeated great parties, and the railroad. The latter, insistent in its bitterness, now organized these two bodies into a powerful opposition. Newspapers were subsidized; the national significance of the campaign magnified; a large number of railroad-hands colonized. When the final weeks of the campaign arrived a bitter contest was waged, and money triumphed. Five thousand four hundred votes were cast for the mayor. Five thousand four hundred and fifty for the opposing candidate, who was of the same party as the successful presidential nominee.

It was a bitter blow, but still one easily borne by the mayor, who was considerable of a philosopher. With simple, undisturbed grace he retired, and three days later applied to one of the principal shoe factories for work at his trade.

"What? You're not looking for a job, are you?" exclaimed the astonished foreman.

"I am," said the mayor.

"You can go to work, all right, but I should think you could get into something better now."

"I suppose I can later," he replied, "when I complete my law studies. Just now I want to do this for a change, to see how things are with the rank and file." And donning the apron he had brought with him he went to work.

It was not long, however, before he was discharged, largely because of partisan influence anxious to drive him out of that region. It was said that this move of seeking a job in so simple a way was a bit of "grand standing"—insincere—that he didn't need to do it, and that he was trying to pile up political capital against the future. A little later a local grocery man of his social faith offered him a position as clerk, and for some odd reason—humanitarian and sectarian, possibly—he accepted this. At any rate, here he labored for a little while. Again many said he was attempting to make political capital out of this simple life in order to further his political interests later, and this possibly, even probably, was true. All men have methods of fighting for that which they believe. So here he worked for a time, while a large number of agencies pro and con continued to denounce or praise him, to ridicule or extol his so-called Jeffersonian simplicity. It was at this time that I encountered him—a tall, spare, capable and interesting individual, who willingly took me into his confidence and explained all that had hitherto befallen him. He was most interesting, really, a figure to commemorate in this fashion.

In one of the rooms of his very humble home—a kind of office or den, in a small house such as any clerk or workingman might occupy—was a collection of clippings, laudatory, inquiring, and abusive, which would have done credit to a candidate for the highest office in the land. One would have judged by the scrap-books and envelopes stuffed to overflowing with long newspaper articles and editorials that had been cut from papers all over the country from Florida to Oregon, that his every movement at this time and earlier was all-essential to the people. Plainly, he had been watched, spied upon, and ignored by one class, while being hailed, praised and invited by another. Magazine editors had called upon him for contributions, journalists from the large cities had sought him out to obtain his actual views, citizens' leagues in various parts of the nation had invited him to come and speak, and yet he was still a very young man in years, not over-intelligent politically or philosophically, the ex-mayor of a small city, and the representative of no great organization of any sort.

In his retirement he was now comforted, if one can be so comforted, by these memories, still fresh in his mind and by the hope possibly for his own future, as well as by a droll humor with which he was wont to select the sharpest and most willful slur upon his unimpeachable conduct as an offering to public curiosity.

"Do you really want to know what people think of me?" he said to me on one occasion. "Well, here's something. Read this." And then he would hand me a bunch of the bitterest attacks possible, attacks which pictured him as a sly and treacherous enemy of the people—or worse yet a bounding anarchistic ignoramus. Personally I could not help admiring his stoic mood. It was superior to that of his detractors. Apparent falsehoods did not anger him. Evident misunderstandings could not, seemingly, disturb him.

"What do you expect?" he once said to me, after I had made a very careful study of his career for a current magazine, which, curiously, was never published. I was trying to get him to admit that he believed that his example might be fruitful of results agreeable to him in the future. I could not conclude that he really agreed with me. "People do not remember; they forget. They remember so long as you are directly before them with something that interests them. That may be a lower gas-rate, or a band that plays good music. People like strong people, and only strong people, characters of that sort —good, bad or indifferent—I've found that out. If a man or a corporation is stronger than I am, comes along and denounces me, or spends more money than I do (or can), buys more beers, makes larger promises, it is "all day" for me. What has happened in my case is that, for the present, anyhow, I have come up against a strong corporation, stronger than I am. What I now need to do is to go out somewhere and get some more strength in some way, it doesn't matter much how. People are not so much interested in me or you, or your or my ideals in their behalf, as they are in strength, an interesting spectacle. And they are easily deceived. These big fighting corporations with their attorneys and politicians and newspapers make me look weak—puny. So the people forget me. If I could get out, raise one million or five hundred thousand dollars and give the corporations a good drubbing, they would adore me—for awhile. Then I would have to go out and get another five hundred thousand somewhere, or do something else."

"Quite so," I replied. "Yet *Vox populi, vox dei.*"

Sitting upon his own doorstep one evening, in a very modest quarter of the city, I said:

"Were you very much depressed by your defeat the last time?"

"Not at all," he replied. "Action, reaction, that's the law. All these things right themselves in time, I suppose, or, anyhow, they ought to. Maybe they don't. Some man who can hand the people what they really need or ought to have will triumph, I suppose, some time. I don't know, I'm sure. I hope so. I think the world is moving on, all right."

In his serene and youthful face, the pale blue, philosophical eyes, was no evidence of dissatisfaction with the strange experiences through which he had passed.

"You're entirely philosophical, are you?"

"As much as any one can be, I suppose. They seem to think that all my work was an evidence of my worthlessness," he said. "Well, maybe it was. Self-interest may be the true law, and the best force. I haven't quite made up my mind yet. My sympathies of course are all the other way. 'He ought to be sewing shoes in the penitentiary,' one paper once said of me. Another advised me to try something that was not above my intelligence, such as breaking rock or shoveling dirt. Most of them agreed, however," he added with a humorous twitch of his large, expressive mouth, "that I'll do very well if I will only stay where I am, or, better yet, get out of here. They want me to leave. That's the best solution for them."

He seemed to repress a smile that was hovering on his lips.

"The voice of the enemy," I commented.

"Yes, sir, the voice of the enemy," he added. "But don't think that I think I'm done for. Not at all. I have just returned to my old ways in order to think this thing out. In a year or two I'll have solved my problem, I hope. I may have to leave here, and I may not. Anyhow, I'll turn up somewhere, with something."

He did have to leave, however, public opinion never being allowed to revert to him again, and five years later, in a fairly comfortable managerial position in New York, he died. He had made a fight, well enough, but the time, the place, the stars, perhaps, were not quite right. He had no guiding genius, possibly, to pull him through. Adherents did not flock to him and save him. Possibly he wasn't magnetic enough—that pagan, non-moral, non-propagandistic quality, anyhow. The fates did not fight for him as they do for some, those fates that ignore the billions and billions of others who fail. Yet are not all lives more or less failures, however successful they may appear to be at one time or another, contrasted, let us say, with what they hoped for? We compromise so much with everything—our dreams and all.

As for his reforms, they may be coming fast enough, or they may not. *In medias res.*

But as for him . . . ?

Isaac Babel

Isaac Babel *(1894–1940?) was born in Odessa. His best known works are* Benya Krik the Gangster *and* Red Cavalry. *Despite the world-wide reputation of this Russian Jewish writer, he was arrested in 1939 by direct order of Lavrenti Beria, Stalin's terror chief. For many years it was believed that he died in a concentration camp in 1941, but in 1989 a Soviet periodical revealed that he was tried in Beria's own office on trumped-up charges ("counter-revolutionary Trotskyite activity" and spying for Austria and France) and shot in Moscow on January 27, 1940.*

GEDALI

On Sabbath eves I am oppressed by the dense melancholy of memories. In bygone days on these occasions my grandfather would stroke the volumes of Ibn Ezra with his yellow beard. His old woman in her lace cap would trace fortunes with her knotty fingers over the Sabbath candles, and sob softly to herself. On those evenings my child's heart was rocked like a little ship upon enchanted waves. O the rotted Talmuds of my childhood! O the dense melancholy of memories!

I roam through Zhitomir in search of a shy star. By the ancient synagogue, by its yellow and indifferent walls, old Jews with prophets' beards and passionate rags on their sunken chests sell chalk and wicks and bluing.

Here before me is the market, and the death of the market. Gone is the fat soul of plenty. Dumb padlocks hang upon the booths, and the granite paving is as clean as a skull. My shy star blinks, and fades from sight.

Success came to me later on; success came just before sunset. Gedali's little shop was hidden away in a row of others, all hermetically closed. Where was your kindly shade that evening, Dickens? In that little old curiosity shop you would have seen gilt slippers, ship's cables, an ancient compass, a stuffed eagle, a Winchester with the date 1810 engraved upon it, a broken saucepan.

Old Gedali, the little proprietor in smoked glasses and a green frock coat down to the ground, meandered around his treasures in the roseate void of evening. He rubbed his small white hands, plucked at his little gray beard, and listened, head bent, to the mysterious voices wafting down to him.

The shop was like the box of an important and knowledge-loving little boy who will grow up to be a professor of botany. There were buttons in it, and a dead butterfly, and its small owner went by the name of Gedali. All had abandoned the market; but Gedali had remained. He wound in and out of a labyrinth of globes, skulls, and dead flowers, waving a bright feather duster of cock's plumes and blowing dust from the dead flowers.

And so we sat upon small beer-barrels, Gedali twisting and untwisting his narrow beard. Like a little black tower, his hat swayed above us. Warm air flowed past. The sky changed color. Blood, delicate-hued, poured down from an overturned bottle up there, and a vague odor of corruption enfolded me.

"The Revolution—we will say 'yes' to it, but are we to say 'no' to the Sabbath?" began Gedali, winding about me the straps of his smoke-hidden eyes. "Yes, I cry to the Revolution. Yes, I cry to it, but it hides its face from Gedali and sends out on front nought but shooting . . ."

"The sunlight doesn't enter eyes that are closed," I answered the old man. "But we will cut open those closed eyes . . ."

"A Pole closed my eyes," whispered the old man, in a voice that was barely audible. "The Poles are bad-tempered dogs.

They take the Jew and pluck out his beard, the curs! And now they are being beaten, the bad-tempered dogs. That is splendid, that is the Revolution. And then those who have beaten the Poles say to me: 'Hand your phonograph over to the State, Gedali . . .' 'I am fond of music, Pani,' I say to the Revolution. 'You don't know what you are fond of, Gedali. I'll shoot you and then you'll know. I cannot do without shooting, because I am the Revolution.' "

"She cannot do without shooting, Gedali," I told the old man, "because she is the Revolution."

"But the Poles, kind sir, shot because they were the Counter-Revolution. You shoot because you are the Revolution. But surely the Revolution means joy. And joy does not like orphans in the house. Good men do good deeds. The Revolution is the good deed of good men. But good men do not kill. So it is bad people that are making the Revolution. But the Poles are bad people too. Then how is Gedali to tell which is Revolution and which is Counter-Revolution? I used to study the Talmud, I love Rashi's Commentaries and the books of Maimonides. And there are yet other understanding folk in Zhitomir. And here we are, all of us learned people, falling on our faces and crying out in a loud voice: 'Woe unto us, where is the joy-giving Revolution?' "

The old man fell silent. And we saw the first star pierce through the Milky Way.

"The Sabbath has begun," Gedali stated solemnly; "Jews should be going to the synagogue. Pan comrade," he said, rising, his top hat like a little black tower swaying on his head, "bring a few good people to Zhitomir. Oh, there's a scarcity of good people in our town. Oh, what a scarcity! Bring them along and we will hand over all our phonographs to them. We are not ignoramuses. The International—we know what the International is. And I want an International of good people. I would like every soul to be listed and given first-category rations. There, soul, please eat and enjoy life's pleasures. Pan comrade, you don't know what the International is eaten with . . ."

"It is eaten with gunpowder," I answered the old man, "and spiced with best-quality blood."

And then, from out of the blue gloom, the young Sabbath came to take her seat of honor.

"Gedali," I said, "today is Friday, and it's already evening. Where are Jewish biscuits to be got, and a Jewish glass of tea, and a little of that pensioned-off God in a glass of tea?"

"Not to be had," Gedali replied, hanging the padlock on his little booth. "Not to be had. Next door is a tavern, and they were good people who served in it; but nobody eats there now, people weep there."

He buttoned his green frock coat on three bone buttons, flicked himself with the cock's feathers, sprinkled a little water on his soft palms, and departed, a tiny, lonely visionary in a black top hat, carrying a big prayerbook under his arm.

The Sabbath is coming. Gedali, the founder of an impossible International, has gone to the synagogue to pray.

Joseph Roth

Joseph Roth (1894–1939) was born in Brody, Galicia (in the eastern part of the Austro-Hungarian Empire). He was a journalist in Vienna and Berlin before fleeing the Nazis to Paris, where he played a leading role among exiled anti-Nazi intellectuals. His fiction is especially concerned with the decline of the Hapsburg Empire. His most celebrated works include The Radetsky March *and* Job.

THE BUST
OF THE EMPEROR

I

In what used to be Eastern Galicia, and today is Poland, far indeed from the solitary railway line which links Przemysl with Brody, lies the small village of Lopatyny, about which I intend to tell a remarkable tale.

Will readers be so kind as to forgive the narrator for prefacing the facts which he has to impart by a historicopolitical explanation. The unnatural moods which world history has recently exhibited compel him to this explanation, since younger readers may wish, perhaps need, to have it pointed out to them that a part of the eastern territories, which today belong to the Polish Republic, formed a part of the many Crown Lands of the old Austro-Hungarian monarchy until the end of the Great War which is now called the World War.

Thus, in the village of Lopatyny, there lived the Count

Franz Xaver Morstin, the scion of an old Polish family, a family which (in parenthesis) originated in Italy and came to Poland in the sixteenth century. Count Morstin had, in his youth, served in the Ninth Dragoons. He thought of himself neither as a Polish aristocrat nor as an aristocrat of Italian origin. No: like so many of his peers in the former Crown Lands of the Austro-Hungarian monarchy, he was one of the noblest and purest sort of Austrian, plain and simple. That is, a man above nationality, and therefore of true nobility. Had anyone asked him, for example—but to whom would such a senseless question have occurred?—to which "nationality" or race he felt he belonged, the Count would have felt rather bewildered, baffled even, by his questioner, and probably bored and somewhat indignant. And on what indications might he have based his membership of this or that race? He spoke almost all European languages equally well, he was at home in almost all the countries of Europe. His friends and relations were scattered about the wide colourful world. Indeed the Imperial and Royal monarchy was itself a microcosm of this colourful world, and for this reason the Count's only home. One of his brothers-in-law was District Commandant in Sarajevo, another was Counsellor to the Governor in Prague; one of his brothers was serving as an *Oberleutnant* of artillery in Bosnia, one of his cousins was Counsellor of Embassy in Paris, another was a landowner in the Hungarian Banat, a third was in the Italian diplomatic service and a fourth, from sheer love of the Far East, had for years lived in Peking.

From time to time it was Franz Xaver's custom to visit his relations; more frequently, of course, those who lived within the monarchy. They were, as he used to say, his "tours of inspection." These tours were not only mindful of his relatives, but also of his friends, certain former pupils at the *Theresianische Akademie* who lived in Vienna. Here Count Morstin would settle twice a year, winter and summer (for a fortnight or longer).

As he travelled backwards and forwards and through the

centre of his many-faceted fatherland he would derive a quite particular pleasure from certain distinguishing marks which were to be picked out, unvarying but gay, on all the railway stations, kiosks, public buildings, schools and churches of the old Crown Lands throughout the Empire. Everywhere the gendarmes wore the same cap with a feather or the same mud-coloured helmet with a golden knob and the gleaming double eagle of the Habsburgs; everywhere the doors of the Imperial tobacco monopoly's shops were painted with black and yellow diagonal stripes; in every part of the country the revenue officers carried the same green (almost flowering) pommels above their naked swords; in every garrison town one saw the same blue uniform blouses and black formal trousers of the infantry officers sauntering down the Corso, the same coffee-coloured jackets of the artillery, the same scarlet trousers of the cavalry; everywhere in that great and many-coloured Empire, and at the same moment every evening, as the clocks in the church towers struck nine, the same retreat was sounded, consisting of cheerfully questioning calls and melancholy answers.

Everywhere were to be found the same coffee-houses, with their smoky vaulted ceilings and their dark alcoves where the chess-players sat hunched like strange birds, with their sideboards heavy with coloured bottles and shining glasses, presided over by golden-blonde, full-bosomed cashiers. Almost everywhere, in all the coffee-houses of the Empire, there crept with a knee already a little shaky, feet turning outwards, a napkin across his arm, the whiskered waiter, the distant humble image of an old servitor of His Majesty, that mighty whiskered gentleman to whom all Crown Lands, gendarmes, revenue officers, tobacconists, turnpikes, railways, and all his peoples belonged.

And in each Crown Land different songs were sung; peasants wore different clothes; people spoke a different tongue or, in some instances, several different tongues. And what so pleased the Count was the solemn and yet cheerful black-and-yellow that shone with such familiar light amidst so many different colours; the equally solemn and happy *Gott erhalte, God Save the Emperor,* which was native among all the songs of all the peoples, and that particular, nasal, drawling, gentle German of the Austrians, reminding one of the Middle Ages which was always to be picked out again among the varying idioms and dialects of the peoples. Like every Austrian of his day, he loved what was permanent in the midst of constant change, what was familiar amid the unfamiliar. So that things which were alien became native to him without losing their colour, and his native land had the eternal magic of the alien.

In his village of Lopatyny the Count was more powerful than any of the administrative branches known to, and feared by, the peasants and the Jews, more powerful than the circuit judge in the nearest small town, more so than the local town mayor himself and more so than any of the senior officers who commanded the troops at the annual manoeuvres, requisitioning huts and houses for billets, and generally representing that warlike might which is so much more impressive than actual military power in wartime. It seemed to the people of Lopatyny that "Count" was not only a title of nobility but also quite a high position in local government. In practice they were not far wrong. Thanks to his generally accepted standing, Count Morstin was able to moderate taxes, relieve the sickly sons of Jews from military service, forward requests for favours, relieve punishments meted out to the innocent, reduce punishments which were unduly severe, obtain reductions in railway fares for poor people, secure just retribution for gendarmes, policemen and civil servants who overstepped their position, obtain assistant masterships at the *Gymnasium* for teaching candidates, find jobs as tobacconists, deliverers of registered letters and telegraphists for time-expired NCOs and find "bursaries" for the student sons of poor peasants and Jews.

How happy he was to attend to it all! In order to keep abreast of his duties, he employed two secretaries and three writers. On top of this, true to the tradition of his house, he practised "seigneurial charity," as it was known in the village.

For more than a century the tramps and beggars of the neighbourhood had gathered every Friday beneath the balcony of the Morstin manor and received from the footmen copper coins in twists of paper. Usually, the Count would appear on the balcony and greet the poor, and it was as if he were giving thanks to the beggars who thanked him: as if giver and receiver exchanged gifts.

In parenthesis, it was not always goodness of heart which produced all these good works, but one of those unwritten laws common to so many families of the nobility. Their far distant forebears might indeed, centuries before, have practised charity, help and support of their people out of pure love. Gradually, though, as the blood altered, this goodness of heart had to some extent become frozen and petrified into duty and tradition. Furthermore, Count Morstin's busy willingness to be helpful formed his only activity and distraction. It lent to his somewhat idle life as a *grand seigneur* who, unlike his peers and neighbours, took no interest even in hunting, an object and an aim, a constantly beneficent confirmation of his power. If he had arranged a tobacconist's business for one person, a licence for another, a job for a third, an interview for a fourth, he felt at ease not only in his conscience but in his pride. If, however, he proved unsuccessful in his good offices on behalf of one or another of his *protégés,* then his conscience was uneasy and his pride was wounded. And he never gave up; he invariably went to appeal, until his wish—that is, the wish of his *protégés*—had been fulfilled. For this reason the people loved and respected him. For ordinary folk have no real conception of the motives which induce a man of power to help the powerless and the unimportant. People just wish to see a "good master"; and people are often more magnanimous in their childlike trust in a powerful man than is the very man whose magnaminity they credulously assume. It is the deepest and noblest wish of ordinary folk to believe that the powerful must be just and noble.

This sort of consideration was certainly not present in Count Morstin's mind as he dispensed protection, beneficence and justice. But these considerations, which may have led an ancestor here and an ancestor there to the practice of generosity, pity and justice, were still alive and working, in the blood or, as they say today, the "subconscious" of this descendant. And just as he felt himself in duty bound to help those who were weaker than himself, so he exhibited duty, respect and obedience towards those who were higher placed than himself. The person of His Royal and Imperial Majesty was to him for ever a quite uniquely remarkable phenomenon. It would, for example, have been impossible for the Count to consider the Emperor simply as a person. Belief in the hereditary hierarchy was so deep-seated and so strong in Franz Xaver's soul that he loved the Emperor because of his Imperial, not his human, attributes. He severed all connection with friends, acquaintances or relations if they let fall what he considered a disrespectful word about the Emperor. Perhaps he sensed even then, long before the fall of the monarchy, that frivolous witticisms can be far more deadly than criminal attempts at assassination and the solemn speeches of ambitious and rebellious world reformers; in which case world history would have borne out Count Morstin's suspicions. For the old Austro-Hungarian monarchy died, not through the empty verbiage of its revolutionaries, but through the ironical disbelief of those who should have believed in, and supported, it.

II

One fine day—it was a couple of years before the Great War, which people now call the World War—Count Morstin was told in confidence that the next Imperial manoeuvres were to take place in Lopatyny and the adjacent territory. The Emperor planned to spend a day or two, or a week, or longer in his house. And Morstin flew into a real taking, drove to the town mayor, dealt with the civil police authorities and the urban district council of the neighbouring market town, arranged for the policemen and night-watchmen of the entire

district to have new uniforms and swords, spoke with the
priests of all three confessions, Greek Catholics, Roman
Catholics, and the Jewish Rabbi, wrote out a speech for the
Ruthenian mayor of the town (which he could not read but
had to learn by heart with the help of the school-teacher),
bought white dresses for the little girls of the village and
alerted the commanding officers of every regiment in the
area. All this so much "in confidence" that in early spring,
long before the manoeuvres, it was known far and wide in the
neighbourhood that the Emperor himself would be attending
the manoeuvres.

At that time Count Morstin was no longer young, but hag-
gard and prematurely grey. He was a bachelor and a myso-
gynist, considered somewhat peculiar by his more robust
equals, a trifle "comic" and "from a different planet." Nobody in the district had seen a woman near him, nor had he
ever made any attempt to marry. None had seen him drink,
gamble or make love. His solitary passion was combating "the
problem of nationalities." Indeed it was at this time that the
so-called "problem of nationalities" began to arouse the passions. Everybody like himself—whether he wished to, or felt
impelled to act as if he wished to—concerned himself with
one or other of the many nations which occupied the territory
of the old Monarchy. It had been discovered and brought to
people's attention in the course of the nineteenth century
that in order to possess individuality as a citizen every person
must belong to a definite nationality or race. "From humanity, via nationalism to bestiality," the Austrian poet
Grillparzer had said. It was just at this time that nationalism
was beginning, the stage before the bestiality which we are
experiencing today. One could see clearly then that national
sentiment sprang from the vulgar turn of mind of all the people who derived from, and corresponded with, the most com-
monplace attitudes of a modern country. They were generally
photographers with a sideline in the volunteer fire brigade,
self-styled artists who for lack of talent had found no home in
the art academy and in consequence had ended up as sign-

painters and paper-hangers, discontented teachers in primary schools who would have liked to teach in secondary schools, apothecaries' assistants who wanted to be doctors, tooth pullers who could not become dentists, junior employees in the Post Office and the railways, bank clerks, woodmen and, generally speaking, anyone with any of the Austrian nationalities who had an unjustifiable claim to a limitless horizon within that bourgeois society. And all these people who had never been anything but Austrians, in Tarnopol, Sarajevo, Brünn, Prague, Czernowitz, Oderburg or Troppau; all these who had never been anything but Austrian, began in accordance with the "Spirit of the Age" to look upon themselves as members of the Polish, Czech, Ukrainian, German, Roumanian, Slovenian and Croatian "nations," and so on and so forth.

At about this time "universal, secret and direct suffrage" was introduced in the Monarchy. Count Morstin detested this as much as he did the concept of "nation."

He used to say to the Jewish publican Solomon Piniowsky, the only person for miles around in whose company he had some sort of confidence, "Listen to me, Solomon! This dreadful Darwin, who says men are descended from apes, seems to be right. It is no longer enough for people to be divided into races, far from it! They want to belong to particular nations. Nationalism; do you hear Solomon?! Even the apes never hit on an idea like that. Darwin's theory still seems to me incomplete. Perhaps the apes are descended from the nationalists since they are certainly a step forward. You know your Bible, Solomon, and you know that it is written there that on the sixth day God created man, not nationalist man. Isn't that so, Solomon?"

"Quite right, *Herr Graf!*" said the Jew, Solomon.

"But," the Count went on, "to change the subject: we are expecting the Emperor this summer. I will give you some money. You will clean up and decorate this place and light up the window. You will dust off the Emperor's picture and put it in the window. I will make you a present of a black and yellow flag with the double eagle on it, and you will fly it from the roof. Is that understood?"

Indeed, the Jew Piniowsky understood, as, moreover, did everybody else with whom the Count had discussed the arrival of the Emperor.

III

That summer the Imperial manoeuvres took place, and His Imperial, Royal and Apostolic Majesty took up residence in Count Morstin's castle. The Emperor was to be seen every morning as he rode out to watch the exercises, and the peasants and Jewish merchants of the neighbourhood would gather to see him, this old man who was their ruler. And as soon as he and his suite appeared they would shout *hoch* and *hurra* and *niech zyje,* each in his own tongue. A few days after the Kaiser's departure, the son of a local peasant called upon Count Morstin. This young man, whose ambition was to become a sculptor, had prepared a bust of the Emperor in sandstone. Count Morstin was enchanted. He promised the young sculptor a free place at the Academy of Arts in Vienna.

He had the bust of the Emperor mounted at the entrance to his little castle.

Here it remained, year in, year out, until the outbreak of the Great War which became known as the World War.

Before he reported for duty as a volunteer, elderly, drawn, bald and hollow-eyed as he had become with the passage of years, Count Morstin had the Emperor's bust taken down, packed in straw and hidden in the cellar.

And there it rested until the end of the war and of the Monarchy, until Count Morstin returned home, until the constitution of the new Polish Republic.

IV

Count Franz Xaver Morstin had thus come home. But could one call this a homecoming? Certainly, there were the same fields, the same woods, the same cottages and the same sort of peasants—the same *sort,* let it be said advisedly—for many of the ones whom the Count had known had fallen in battle.

It was winter, and one could already feel Christmas approaching. As usual at this time of year, and as it had been in days long before the war, the Lopatinka was frozen, crows crouched motionless on the bare branches of the chestnut trees and the eternal leisurely wind of the Eastern winter blew across the fields onto which the western windows of the house gave.

As the result of the war, there were widows and orphans in the villages: enough material for the returning Count's beneficence to work upon. But instead of greeting his native Lopatyny as a home regained, Count Morstin began to indulge in problematical and unusual meditations on the question of home generally. Now, thought he, since this village belongs to Poland and not to Austria, is it still my home? What, in fact, is home? Is not the distinctive uniform of gendarmes and customs officers, familiar to us since childhood, just as much "home" as the fir and the pine, the pond and the meadow, the cloud and the brook? But if the gendarmes and customs officers are different and fir, pine, brook and pond remain the same, is that still home? Was I not therefore at home in this spot—continued the Count enquiringly—only because it belonged to an overlord to whom there also belonged countless other places of different kinds, all of which I loved? No doubt about it! This unnatural whim of history has also destroyed my private pleasure in what I used to know as home. Nowadays they are talking hereabouts and everywhere else of this new fatherland. In their eyes I am a so-called Lackland. I have always been one. Ah! but there was once a fatherland, a real one, for the Lacklands, the only possible fatherland. That was the old Monarchy. Now I am homeless and have lost the true home of the eternal wanderer.

In the false hope that he could forget the situation if he were outside the country, the Count decided to go abroad. But he discovered to his astonishment that he needed a passport and a number of so-called visas before he could reach those countries which he had chosen for his journey. He was quite old enough to consider as fantastically childish and dreamlike such things as passports, visas and all the formalities which the brazen laws of traffic between man and man had imposed after the war. However, since Fate had decreed that he was to spend the rest of his days in a desolate dream, and because he hoped to find abroad, in other countries, some part of that old reality in which he had lived before the war, he bowed to the requirements of this ghostly world, took a passport, procured visas and proceeded first to Switzerland, the one country in which he believed he might find the old peace, simply because it had not been involved in the war.

He had known the city of Zurich for many years, but had not seen it for the better part of twelve. He supposed that it would make no particular impact on him, for better or for worse. His impression coincided with the not altogether unjustified opinion of the world, both rather more pampered and rather more adventurous, on the subject of the worthy cities of the worthy Swiss. What, after all, could be expected to happen there? Nevertheless, for a man who had come out of the war and out of the eastern marches of the former Austrian Monarchy, the peace of a city which even before that war had harboured refugees, was almost equivalent to an adventure. Franz Xaver Morstin gave himself up in those first days to the pursuit of long-lost peace. He ate, drank and slept.

One day, however, there occurred a disgusting incident in a Zurich night club, as the result of which Count Morstin was forced to leave the country at once.

At that time there was often common gossip in the newspapers of every country about some wealthy banker who was supposed to have taken in pawn, against a loan to the Austrian royal family, not only the Habsburg Crown Jewels, but also the old Habsburg Crown itself. No doubt about it that these stories came from the tongues and pens of those irresponsible customers known as journalists and even if it were true that a certain portion of the Imperial family's heritage had found its way into the hands of some conscienceless banker, there was still no question of the old Habsburg crown coming into it, or so Franz Xaver Morstin felt that he knew.

So he arrived one night in one of the few bars, known only to the select, which are open at night in the moral city of Zurich where, as is well known, prostitution is illegal, immorality is taboo, the city in which to sin is as boring as it is costly. Not for a moment that the Count was seeking this out! Far from it: perfect peace had begun to bore him and to give him insomnia and he had decided to pass the night-time away wherever he best could.

He began his drink. He was sitting in one of the few quiet corners of the establishment. It is true that he was put out by the newfangled American style of the little red table lamps, by the hygienic white of the barman's coat which reminded him of an assistant in an operating theatre and by the dyed blonde hair of the waitress which awoke associations with apothecaries; but to what had he not already accustomed himself, this poor old Austrian? Even so, he was startled out of the peace which he had with some trouble arranged for himself in these surroundings by a harsh voice announcing: "And here, ladies and gentlemen, is the crown of the Habsburgs!"

Franz Xaver stood up. In the middle of the long bar he observed a fairly large and animated party. His first glance informed him that every type of person he hated—although until then he had no close contact with them—was represented at that table: women with dyed blonde hair in short dresses which shamelessly revealed ugly knees; slender, willowy young men of olive complexion, baring as they smiled sets of flawless teeth such as are to be seen in dental advertisements, disposable little dancing men, cowardly, elegant, watchful, looking like cunning hairdressers; elderly gentlemen who assiduously but vainly attempted to disguise their paunches and their bald pates, good-humoured, lecherous, jovial and bow-legged; in short a selection from that portion of humanity which was for the time being the inheritor of the vanished world, only to yield it a few years later, at a profit, to even more modern and murderous heirs.

One of the elderly gentlemen now rose from the table. First he twirled a crown in his hand, then placed it on his bald head, walked round the table, proceeded to the middle of the bar, danced a little jig, waggled his head and with it the crown, and sang a popular hit of the day, "The sacred crown is worn like this!"

At first Franz Xaver could not make head nor tail of this lamentable exhibition. It seemed to him that the party consisted of decaying old gentlemen with grey hair (made fools of by mannequins in short skirts); chambermaids celebrating their day off; female barflies who would share with the waitresses the profits from the sale of champagne and their own bodies; a lot of good-for-nothing pimps who dealt in women and foreign exchange, wore wide padded shoulders and wide flapping trousers that looked more like women's clothes; and dreadful-looking middlemen who dealt in houses, shops, citizenships, passports, concessions, good marriages, birth certificates, religious beliefs, titles of nobility, adoptions, brothels and smuggled cigarettes. This was the section of society which was relentlessly commited, in every capital city of a Europe which had, as a whole continent, been defeated, to live off its corpse, slandering the past, exploiting the present, promoting the future, sated but insatiable. These were the Lords of Creation after the Great War. Count Morstin had the impression of being his own corpse, and that these people were dancing on his grave. Hundreds and thousands had died in agony to prepare the victory of people like these, and hundreds of thoroughly respectable moralists had prepared the collapse of the old Monarchy, had longed for its fall and for the liberation of the nation-states! And now, pray observe, over the grave of the old world and about the cradles of the newborn nations, there danced the spectres of the night from American bars.

Morstin came closer, so as to have a better view. The shadowy nature of these well-covered, living spectres aroused his interest. And upon the bald pate of this bow-legged, jigging man he recognised a fascimile—for fascimile it must surely be —of the crown of St Stephen. The waiter, who was obsequious in drawing the attention of his customers to anything noteworthy, came to Franz Xaver and said, "That is Walakin the banker, a Russian. He claims to own the crowns of all the dethroned monarchies. He brings a different one here every evening. Last night it was the Tsars' crown; tonight it is the crown of St Stephen."

Count Morstin felt his heart stop beating, just for a second. But during this one second—which seemed to him later to have lasted for at least an hour—he experienced a complete transformation of his own personality. It was as if an unknown, frightening, alien Morstin were growing within him, rising, growing, developing and taking possession not only of his familiar body but, further, of the entire space occupied by the American bar. Never in his life, never since his childhood had Franz Xaver Morstin experienced a fury like this. He had a gentle disposition and the sanctuary which had been vouchsafed him by his position, his comfortable circumstances and the brilliance of his name had until then shielded him from the grossness of the world and from any contact with its meanness. Otherwise, no doubt, he would have learned anger sooner. It was as if he sensed, during that single second that changed him, that the world had changed long before. It was as if he now felt that the change in himself was in fact a necessary consequence of universal change. That much greater than this unknown anger, which now rose up in him, grew and overflowed the bounds of his personality, must have been the growth of meanness in this world, the growth of that baseness which had so long hidden behind the skirts of fawning "loyalty" and slavish servility. It seemed to him, who had always assumed without a second thought that everyone was by nature honourable, that at this instant he had discovered a lifetime of error, the error of any generous heart, that he had given credit, limitless credit. And this sudden recognition filled him with the honest shame which is sister to honest anger. An honest man is doubly shamed at the sight of meanness, first because the very existence of it is shameful, second because he sees at once that he has been deceived in his heart. He sees himself betrayed and his pride rebels against the fact that people have betrayed his heart.

It was no longer possible for him to weigh, to measure, to consider. It seemed to him that hardly any kind of violence could be bestial enough to punish and wreak vengeance on the baseness of the man who danced with a crown on his bald whoremongering head; every night a different crown. A gramophone was blaring out the song from *Hans, who does things with his knee;* the barmaids were shrilling; the young men clapped their hands; the barman, white as a surgeon, rattled among his glasses, spoons and bottles, shook and mixed, brewed and concocted in metal shakers the secret and magical potions of the modern age. He clinked and rattled, from time to time turning a benevolent but calculating eye on the banker's performance. The little red lamps trembled every time the bald man stamped. The light, the gramophone, the noise of the mixer, the cooing and giggling of the women drove Count Morstin into a marvellous rage. The unbelievable happened: for the first time in his life he became laughable and childish. He armed himself with a half-empty bottle of champagne and a blue soda-siphon, then approached the strangers. With his left hand he squirted soda water over the company at the table and with his right hand struck the dancer over the head with the bottle. The banker fell to the ground. The crown fell from his head. And as the Count stooped to pick it up, as it were to rescue the real crown and all that was associated with it, waiters, girls and pimps all rushed at him. Numbed by the powerful scent of the women and the blows of the young men, Count Morstin was finally brought out into the street. There, at the door of the American bar, the obsequious waiter presented the bill, on a silver tray, under the wide heavens and, in a manner of speaking, in the presence of every distant and indifferent star; for it was a crisp winter night.

The next day Count Morstin returned to Lopatyny.

V

Why—said he to himself during the journey—should I not go back to Lopatyny? Since my world seems to have met with final defeat and I no longer have a proper home it is better that I should seek out the wreckage of my old one!

He thought of the bust of the Emperor Franz Josef which lay in his cellar, and he thought of this, his Emperor's corpse, which had long lain in the Kapuzinergruft.

I was always odd man out, thought he to himself, both in my village and in the neighbourhood. I shall remain odd man out.

He sent a telegram to his steward announcing the day of his arrival.

And when he arrived they were waiting for him, as always, as in the old days, as if there had been no war, no dissolution of the Monarchy, no new Polish Republic.

For it is one of the greatest mistakes made by the new—or as they like to call themselves, modern—statesmen that the people (the "nation") share their own passionate interest in world politics. The people in no way lives by world politics, and is thereby agreeably distinguishable from politicians. The people lives by the land, which it works, by the trade which it exercises and by the craft which it understands. (It nevertheless votes at free elections, dies in wars and pays taxes to the Ministry of Finance.) Anyway, this is the way things were in Count Morstin's village of Lopatyny, and the whole of the World War and the complete redrawing of the map of Europe had not altered the opinions of the people of Lopatyny. Why and how? The sound, human sense of the Jewish publicans and the Polish and Ruthenian peasants resented the incomprehensible whims of world history. These whims are abstract: but the likes and dislikes of the people are concrete.

The people of Lopatyny, for instance, had for years known the Counts Morstin, those representatives of the Emperor and the house of Habsburg. New gendarmes appeared, and a tax-levy is a tax-levy, and Count Morstin is Count Morstin. Under the rule of the Habsburgs the people of Lopatyny had been happy or unhappy—each according to the will of God. Independent of all the changes in world history, in spite of republics and monarchies, and what are known as national self-determination or suppression, their life was determined by a good or bad harvest, healthy or rotten fruit, productive or sickly cattle, rich pasture or thin, rain at the right or the wrong season, a sun to bring forth fruit or drought and disaster. The world of the Jewish merchant consisted of good or bad customers; for the publican in feeble or reliable drinkers and for the craftsman it was important whether people did or did not require new roofs, new boots, new trousers, new stoves, new chimneys or new barrels. This was the case, at least in Lopatyny. And in our prejudiced view the whole wide world is not so different from the village of Lopatyny as popular leaders and politicians would like to believe. When they have read the newspapers, listened to speeches, elected officials and talked over the doings of the world with their friends, these worthy peasants, craftsmen and shopkeepers—and in big cities the workmen as well—go back to their houses and their places of work. And at home they find worry or happiness; healthy children or sick children, discontented or peaceable wives, customers who pay well or pay slowly, pressing or patient creditors, a good meal or a bad one, a clean or a dirty bed. It is our firm conviction that ordinary folk do not trouble their heads over world events, however much they may rant and rave about them on Sundays. But this may, of course, be a personal conviction. We have in fact only to report on the village of Lopatyny. These things were as we have described them.

No sooner was Count Morstin home than he repaired at once to Solomon Piniowsky, that Jew in whom innocence and shrewdness went hand in hand, as if they were brother and sister. And the Count asked the Jew, "Solomon, what do you count on in this world?"

"Herr Graf," said Piniowsky, "I no longer count on anything at all. The world has perished, there is no Emperor any more, people choose presidents, and that is the same thing as when I pick a clever lawyer for a lawsuit. So the whole people picks a lawyer to defend it. But, I ask myself, *Herr Graf,* before what tribunal? Just a tribunal of other lawyers. And supposing the people have no lawsuit and therefore no need to be defended, we all know just the same that the very existence of these lawyers will land us up to the neck in a lawsuit. And so there will be constant lawsuits. I still have the black and yellow flag, *Herr Graf,* which you gave me as a present. What am I to do with it? It is lying on the floor of my attic. I still have the picture of the old Emperor. What about that, now? I read the newspapers, I attend a bit to business, and a bit to the world. I know the stupid things that are being done. But our peasants have no idea. They simply believe that the old Emperor has introduced new uniforms and set Poland free, that he no longer has his Residence in Vienna, but in Warsaw."

"Let them go on thinking that," said Count Morstin.

And he went home and had the bust of the Emperor Franz Joseph brought up from the cellar. He stood it at the entrance to his house.

And from the following day forward, as though there had been no war and no Polish Republic; as though the old Emperor had not been long laid to rest in the Kapuzinergruft; as though this village still belonged to the territory of the old Monarchy; every peasant who passed by doffed his cap to the sandstone bust of the old Emperor and every Jew who passed by with his bundle murmured the prayer which a pious Jew will say on seeing an Emperor. And this improbable bust—presented in cheap sandstone from the unaided hand of a peasant lad, this bust in the uniform jacket of the dead Emperor, with stars and insignia and the Golden Fleece, all preserved in stone, just as the youthful eye of the lad had seen the Emperor and loved him—won with the passing of time a quite special and particular artistic merit, even in the eyes of Count Morstin. It was as if the passing of time ennobled and improved the work which represented this exalted subject. Wind and weather worked as if with artistic consciousness upon the simple stone. It was as if respect and remembrance also worked upon this portrait, as if every salute from a peasant, every prayer from a believing Jew, had ennobled the unconscious work of the young peasant's hands.

And so the bust stood for years outside Count Morstin's house, the only memorial which had ever existed in the village of Lopatyny and of which all its inhabitants were rightly proud.

The bust meant even more, however, to the Count, who in those days no longer left the village any more. It gave him the impression, whenever he left his house, that nothing had altered. Gradually, for he had aged prematurely, he would stumble upon quite foolish ideas. He would persuade himself for hours at a time, although he had fought through the whole of the greatest of all wars, that this had just been a bad dream, and that all the changes which had followed it were also bad dreams. This in spite of the fact that he saw almost every week how his appeals to officials and judges no longer helped his *protégés* and that these officials indeed made fun of him. He was more infuriated than insulted. It was already well known in the neighbouring small town, as in the district, that "old Morstin was half crazy." The story circulated that at home he wore the uniform of a *Rittmeister* of Dragoons, with all his old orders and decorations. One day a neighbouring landowner, a certain Count, asked him straight out if this were true.

"Not as yet," replied Morstin, "but you've given me a good idea. I shall put on my uniform and wear it not only at home but out and about."

And so it happened.

From that time on Count Morstin was to be seen in the uniform of an Austrian *Rittmeister* of Dragoons, and the inhabitants of Lopatyny never gave the matter a second thought. Whenever the *Rittmeister* left his house he saluted his Supreme Commander, the bust of the dead Emperor Franz Josef. He would then take his usual route between two little pinewoods along the sandy road which led to the neighbouring small town. The peasants who met him would take off their hats and say: "Jesus Christ be praised!", adding *"Herr Graf!"* as if they believed the Count to be some sort of close relative of the Redeemer's, and that two titles were better than one. Alas, for a long time past he had been powerless to help them as he had in the old days. Admittedly the peasants were unable to help themselves. But he, the Count, was no longer a power in the land! And like all those who have been powerful once, he now counted even less than those who had always been powerless: in the eyes of officialdom he almost belonged among the ridiculous. But the people of Lopatyny and its surroundings still believed in him, just as they believed in the Emperor Franz Josef whose bust it was their custom to salute. Count Morstin seemed in no way laughable to the peasants and Jews of Lopatyny; venerable, rather. They revered his lean, thin figure, his grey hair, his ashen, sunken countenance, and his eyes which seemed to stare into the boundless distance; small wonder, for they were staring into the buried past.

It happened one day that the regional commissioner for Lwow, which used to be called Lemberg, undertook a tour of inspection and for some reason had to stop in Lopatyny. Count Morstin's house was pointed out to him and he at once made for it. To his astonishment he caught sight of the bust of the Emperor Franz Josef in front of the house, in the midst of a little shrubbery. He looked at it for a long while and finally decided to enter the house and ask the Count himself about the significance of this memorial. But he was even more astonished, not to say startled, at the sight of Count Morstin coming towards him in the uniform of a *Rittmeister* of Dragoons. The regional commissioner was himself a "Little Pole"; which means he came from what was formerly Galicia.

He had himself served in the Austrian Army. Count Morstin appeared to him like a ghost from a chapter of history long forgotten by the regional commissioner.

He restrained himself and at first asked no questions. As they sat down to table, however, he began cautiously to enquire about the Emperor's memorial.

"Ah, yes," said the Count, as if no new world had been born, "His late Majesty of blessed memory spent eight days in this house. A very gifted peasant lad made the bust. It has always stood here and will do so as long as I live."

The commissioner stifled the decision which he had just taken and said with a smile, as it were quite casually, "You still wear the old uniform?"

"Yes," said Morstin, "I am too old to have a new one made. In civilian clothes, do you know, I don't feel altogether at ease since circumstances became so altered. I'm afraid I might be confused with a lot of other people. Your good health," continued the Count, raising his glass and toasting his guest.

The regional commissioner sat on for a while, and then left the Count and the village of Lopatyny to continue his tour of inspection. When he returned to his Residence he issued orders that the bust should be removed from before Count Morstin's house.

These orders finally reached the mayor (termed *Wojt*) of the village of Lopatyny and therefore, inevitably, were brought to the attention of Count Morstin.

For the first time, therefore, the Count now found himself in open conflict with the new power, of whose existence he had previously hardly taken cognizance. He realised that he was too weak to oppose it. He recalled the scene at night in the American bar in Zurich. Alas, there was no point any more in shutting one's eyes to these new bankers and wearers of crowns, to the new ladies and gentlemen who ruled the world. One must bury the old world, but one must give it a decent burial.

So Count Morstin summoned ten of the oldest inhabitants

of the village of Lopatyny to his house—among them the clever and yet innocent Jew, Solomon Piniowsky. There also attended the Greek Catholic priest, the Roman Catholic priest and the Rabbi.

When they were all assembled Count Morstin began the following speech,

"My dear fellow-citizens, you have all known the old Monarchy, your old fatherland. It has been dead for years, and I have come to realise that there is no point in not seeing that it is dead. Perhaps it will rise again, but old people like us will hardly live to see it. We have received orders to remove, as soon as possible, the bust of the dead Emperor, of blessed memory, Franz Josef the First.

"We have no intention of removing it, my friends!

"If the old days are to be dead we will deal with them as one does deal with the dead: we will bury them.

"Consequently I ask you, my dear friends, to help me bury the dead Emperor, that is to say his bust, with all the ceremony and respect that are due to an Emperor, in three days' time, in the cemetery."

VI

The Ukranian joiner, Nikita Koldin, made a magnificent sarcophagus of oak. Three dead Emperors could have found accomodation in it.

The Polish blacksmith, Jarowslaw Wojciechowski, forged a mighty double eagle in brass which was firmly nailed to the coffin's lid.

The Jewish Thorah scribe, Nuchin Kapturak, inscribed with a goose quill upon a small roll of parchment the blessing which believing Jews must pronounce at the sight of a crowned head, cased it in hammered tin and laid it in the coffin.

Early in the morning—it was a hot summer day, countless invisible larks were trilling away in the heavens and countless invisible crickets were replying from the meadows—the inhabitants of Lopatyny gathered at the memorial to Franz Josef the First. Count Morstin and the mayor laid the bust to rest in its magnificent great sarcophagus. At this moment the bells of the church on the hill began to toll. All three pastors placed themselves at the head of the procession. Four strong old peasants bore the coffin on their shoulders. Behind them, his drawn sabre in his hand, his dragoon helmet draped in field grey, went Count Franz Xaver Morstin, the closest person in the village to the dead Emperor, quite lonely and alone, as becomes a mourner. Behind him, wearing a little round black cap upon his silver hair, came the Jew, Solomon Piniowsky, carrying in his left hand his round velvet hat and raised in his right the black and yellow flag with the double eagle. And behind him the whole village, men and women.

The church bells tolled, the larks trilled and the crickets sang unceasingly.

The grave was prepared. The coffin was lowered with the flag draped over it, and for the last time Franz Xaver Morstin raised his sabre in salute to his Emperor.

The crowd began to sob as though the Emperor Franz Josef and with him the old Monarchy and their own old home had only then been buried. The three pastors prayed.

So the old Emperor was laid to rest a second time, in the village of Lopatyny, in what had once been Galicia.

A few weeks later the news of this episode reached the papers. They published a few witticisms about it, under the heading, "Notes from all over."

VII

Count Morstin, however, left the country. He now lives on the Riviera, an old man and worn out, spending his evenings playing chess and *skat* with ancient Russian generals. He spends an hour or two every day writing his memoirs. They will probably possess no significant literary value, for Count Morstin has no experience as a literary man, and no ambition as a writer. Since, however, he is a man of singular grace and style he delivers himself of a few memorable phrases, such as the following for example, which I reproduce with his permission: "It has been my experience that the clever are capable of stupidity, that the wise can be foolish, that true prophets can lie and that those who love truth can deny it. No human virtue can endure in this world, save only one: true piety. Belief can cause us no disappointment since it promises us nothing in this world. The true believer does not fail us, for he seeks no recompense on earth. If one uses the same yardstick for peoples, it implies that they seek in vain for national virtues, so-called, and that these are even more questionable than human virtues. For this reason I hate nationalism and nation states. My old home, the Monarchy, alone, was a great mansion with many doors and many chambers, for every condition of men. This mansion has been divided, split up, splintered. I have nothing more to seek for, there. I am used to living in a home, not in cabins."

So, proudly and sadly, writes the old Count. Peaceful, self-possessed, he waits on death. Probably he longs for it. For he has laid down in his will that he is to be buried in the village of Lopatyny; not, indeed, in the family vault, but alongside the grave of the Emperor Franz Josef, beside the bust of the Emperor.

Aleksander Wat

Alexander Wat *(1900–1967) was born to Jewish parents in Warsaw. In the 1920s he was a leader of the Polish literary "futurists" and then a Communist. After fleeing the Nazi invasion of Poland he was imprisoned by the Soviets and converted to Christianity. Following World War II he returned to Poland, only to find himself in conflict with the new Communist government there. He eventually settled in Paris. This story comes from his volume* Lucifer Unemployed *(1927). His memoirs, taped in dialogue with Nobel laureate Czeslaw Milosz, have also appeared in English as* My Century—The Odyssey of a Polish Intellectual.

KINGS IN EXILE

I

The first mate of the English ship *Cromwell* peered at the horizon, ragged as an envelope ripped open by an impatient hand, at the dry landscape of the Arkhangel'sk coast, at the fisherwoman nursing her baby under her striped fustian, at the sky—that great mirror, where from under the fustian of clouds and fog emerged the milky breast of the sun.

Fog, he thought, and turned around, hearing steps behind him. Two natives walked onto the deck: an old man with a long gray beard dressed in a bourgeois frock coat, fatigue cap, and tree-bark moccasins, and a short, frail young man, barefoot, in a red tunic, with a thick rope around his waist. The first mate couldn't stand barbarians. He looked with equal contempt upon the smelly, dirty, slant-eyed Melanesians with curly hair and decorations of shells and straws who swarmed the eastern shores of the Pacific, and the light-eyed, blond Slavs from the White Sea. How astonished he was, therefore, when the gray-bearded newcomer spoke to him with the purest London accent: "I would like to speak with the captain."

A few hours later the *Cromwell* was sailing on the open seas. And in the evening the telegraph machines clattered from Vologda to Arkhangel'sk and from Arkhangel'sk to Moscow, to the Red fleet. A thick fog facilitated the escape of the English ship. It eluded the wandering tentacle-spotlights of the cruisers and torpedo ships propelled by the rhythmic effort of the steel muscles of the machines and the twisted muscles of the proletariat of the sea. After five weeks of sailing the *Cromwell* was hauled into the Thames at night. But only two people left the ship that night: the graybearded old man and the frail youth from Arkhangel'sk, both dressed as officers of the English Navy. On the boulevard a large mud-spattered taxi with drawn windows awaited them. Inside sat the director of the London Police. He was so tall that to bow he had to fold himself in half. "Your Majesty," he lisped in a voice full of homage.

II

Thomas Clark was a pillar of the Chicago *Tribune*. He had an unsurpassed nose for sniffing out what was happening, a splendid gift for anticipating the course of events, and the skill to integrate his daily experiences into fascinating short paragraphs, serving them up to the citizen with his morning coffee in the form of a simplified image of the world that stimulated digestion—in other words, all the qualities that make a model journalist. During the war he was tossed from one front to another, he flew over enemy countries as if he were spat from the jaws of the fronts and astride cannonballs, like Baron von Münchhausen. On the shores of the Aduga he shouted "Avanti!" along with swarthy Italians; on the banks of the Marne he offered cigars to the brave *voyous*. He retreated from the Carpathian mountains with Russian muzhiks; valiantly served the allies, the Hapsburgs, and the bankers from Wall Street; tore through Siberia to the Pacific Ocean along with the Czechs, fought in Kolchak's ranks, transported valuable documents to the English in Baku, was taken prisoner by the Bolsheviks, was imprisoned by the Cheka, escaped to Mongolia, spoke with Chutuchta in Urga, after which, sated with adventure, he returned home.

His philosophy of history was amazingly simple. He knew that a watermark showed through the pages of history: Cleopatra's nose and Newton's apple. ("If Cleopatra's nose had been a millimeter longer, the history of the world would have taken a different turn." "Newton was sitting under an apple tree one evening, meditating, when all of a sudden a falling apple revealed the law of gravity to him.") Thomas Clark knew all too well the importance of the minute detail and the role of chance. Chance governed the fate of Balkanized Europe. The firing of a telephone operator, who had diverted the pay of a girlfriend (who had broken solidarity) into the union till, unleashed a social revolution in Bulgaria. Thomas Clark was alert to the significance of facts: hence his ease in jumping from one trampoline of opinion to another and his skill at reading historical upheavals from insignificant events, qualities that made him the augur and Madame de Thebes of journalism.

III

Another of Thomas's strengths was an intimate acquaintance with Europe. He knew its cities and nationalities, markets and churches, its politicians, jazz bands, monarchs, criminals, restaurants, scholars, prisons, church hierarchy, revolutionaries, brothels (he was the anonymous author of a deluxe edition of a catalog of bordellos in postwar Europe intended for the use of American millionaires), its ministers, adventurers, inventors, journalists, fashion designers, industrialists, dancers, poets, financiers, aristocrats, spies, theaters, and doctors. He knew all the luminaries of his day and collected their photographs in albums, similar to those containing pictures of wanted criminals.

Yet only his closest friends knew the real reason for his drive. Only they knew that an especially pathological passion —the completely unbridled desire to possess women of all nations and tribes—had made Thomas an indefatigable Ahasuerus of the press. When he was thirty-five, Thomas could boast of intimate ties with almost a hundred tribes. His political pessimism derived from a limited number of ethnic groups. In order to possess the stinking female dwarf of a Pygmy tribe or the enormous Matabele gardener, he did not hesitate to travel to the Kaffirs. He arrived in England in pursuit of the last red-skinned woman of the Sioux-Oglala tribe appearing in a London music hall, and here he got wind of the secret of the *Cromwell*.

IV

A few days later the *Chicago Tribune, Times, Temps,* and *Corriere della Serra* simultaneously published the extraordinary supplements. The commotion spread by newsboys screaming: Czar Nicholas II lives! The Secret of the *Cromwell!* Such was the overture to the monarchic opera buffa which constitutes the plot of our story.

V

News of the survival of Nicholas II, the heir to Alexander's throne, evoked an eruption of monarchic activity, fortified the impetus of the dreams and hopes of bankrupt courtiers, Junkers, students, *rentiers,* restorationists and panderers. In all the countries of Europe, aristocratic counterfeiters, assuming that only monarchs had the right to coin money and following the brilliant example set by the Prince Windisch-grätz, started to compete with the mints of republican states, often surpassing them in precision of execution. In Italy, Mussolini recognized the moment as one appropriate to proclaiming the Holy Roman Empire. In Poland the blue generals, landholders, clergy, student fraternities and guild masters dragged out and dusted off lithographic portraits of the czar's family and felt a rising tide of nostalgia for savings account books, gold braid, samovars, the czarist police and kopecks, the sunshine of bygone days. Wilhelm II published a letter threatening to unleash civil war in Germany in the name of saving civilization, authority, and religion. Entire anthills of German kinglings and princes and Russian exiles dusted off their uniforms, decorations, and banners. The former Persian shah organized an army of marauders, Parisian pimps, and slender sutlers from la place Pigalle. The information about the survival of the czar was the fuse that ignited the musty dynamite of monarchic sentiment.

VI

Thomas Clark trotted back and forth between Paris, Berlin, Budapest, Doorm, and Rome, devising and hatching a great plan under the rallying cry: "Monarchs of the World Unite!" His small cat eyes bereft of a steady point—when he looked at an object, he seemed to strip it of color and shape—ran over the agitated landscapes of an agitated continent from the air, or from the windows of speeding limousines or lightning-swift trains. During the day he was oppressed by the revolting alienness of their masks—Thomas hated nature and knew it best because he knew it from the windows of a train car. (It was with amazement that he discovered the possibility of something that was not urban civilization. Through the windows of a speeding train he was able to see for himself the enormous expanses of nature, of which cities are but a tiny, insignificant fraction. Each time he observed with involuntary amazement that trees are not houses crawling with people, that, in fact, man does not have to be a part of the tormenting, bothersome, disintegrating process of a collectivity.)

VII

A Congress of dethroned monarchs convened in Geneva in December 192-. . .

The list of participants would fill a hefty volume of the Gotha Almanac.* Let us add the dethroned Turkish sultan, the Chinese bodhi khan, the Persian shah, the Abyssinian negus and their courts. In Geneva, there was a plague of aristocrats, cinema operators, diplomats, cocaine sellers, discharged generals, correspondents, women—every inch of whose bodies was loved into discoloration—swindlers, traveling salesmen, Negroes, American girls, and an enormous number of secret agents mobilized from around the entire world. The creased pants and faces of Englishmen; the scarred and ruddy faces of Germans; the full feminine shapes of the Italians, Romanians, Brazilians, with hair that gleamed like ads for shoe polish; Yankees on wide rubber soles, with Rolls-Royces in their heads and skyscrapers in their vest pockets; slithering Russians; the lace of titles woven for centuries, the chasubles of clerics, stars, decorations, and the zodiacs of heraldic shields.

At five o'clock in the evening in the hotels of Geneva the Bourbons, Hohenzollerns, Hapsburgs, Romanovs, and Zamojskis danced the Charleston with the daughters of watchmakers, Swiss hotelkeepers, kings of grease, crude, and preserves from Dolarika.

Thomas Clark moved around in this throng and looked with pride at his work. He was let in on all the backstage secrets, he reconciled the feuding, was a go-between, the author of many ideas and resolutions. It was his doing to implement the principle of dynastic seniority and seniority for pretenders, on the basis of which the descendants of Bona-

* A yearbook of European aristocracy and dynastic genealogy.—Ed.

parte had to resign their claim to the throne and concede to the Bourbons. It was he who brought about the election of an executive committee, made up of the crown prince, Albert Hapsburg, Rupert Wittelsbach and Nicholas Nikolayevich. And wasn't he the author of a proclamation to the peoples of Europe, a call to arms, in which Hermes Trismegista, the Apocalypse, Professor Teufelsdreck and many other authorities were cited:

Monarchy is the sole refuge of culture and progress, the sole rock of authority, morality, the scale of the classes.

Monarchy alone corresponds to the spirit and intellect of man with his aspirations to unity and his instinct for decorativeness.

Monarchy is the symbol of the collectivity, the personification of the unification and power of the people, it is the root of mysticism, it is the spinal column of history. Monarchy is the sash of tradition, continuity, majesty, religion. Monarchy is the only basis for justice. Monarchy is the only just system of distribution of material goods.

Monarchy is the sole defender of the proletariat, a representation of the battle and harmony of the classes.

Monarchy is the reduction of complex problems to simplicity, the order of hierarchy.

Monarchy is the rebirth of prosperity.

Only monarchy is able to defend European culture from an onslaught of Bolshevik barbarianism, from soulless American mechanization, from the anger of awakening Asiatic nationalisms.

Monarchy is the only panacea for our economic, political, social, moral, and philosophical ills.

Only the kings of peoples are capable of liberating Europe from the destructive yoke of the American kingpins of production.

Europe can choose: annihilation or monarchy.

The congress of monarchs, anticipating the senseless resistance and blindness of the peoples, poisoned with the venom of republican anarchy, resolves, sacrificing its pride, to nevertheless repay evil with good. It resolves therefore to resurrect monarchy wherever it does not exist, despite the momentary opposition of its subjects, for it assumes that the continuity of the monarchic tradition cannot be subject to interruption. In the meantime, far from their homelands, in exile, the anointed of all the nations will continue to exercise their complete powers, just as they had received them from their fathers and God, in order that the peoples, when they realize what they have done, will have a ready and efficient apparatus of power and authority without which they would face certain death in the dregs of anarchy. The sole just republic, the republic of kings in exile, will be a convincing model of the beneficence of the monarchic order.

VIII

The first and most important goal of the Executive Committee was to organize and secure a place for the republic of kings. This was an inordinately difficult task. A separate proclamation was issued to the League of Nations, in which, among other things, the Committee demanded that one of the countries of Central Europe be turned over to the kings. Ramsay MacDonald,* who together with the car given to him by his friend the confectioner had just moved into Downing Street for the second time, chaired the meeting of the League. (For in England each election brought victory to the Labour and Conservative Party, in its turn. The wise, far-sighted gentility of English politicians resulted in each government's continuing the undertakings of its predecessors. Thanks to this the conservative government was socialist in essence, and by the same token the socialist was conservative.) After the proclamation was read, MacDonald gave a

---

* James Ramsay MacDonald (1866–1937) formed the first Labour government in England's history.—TRANS.

beautiful speech. He spoke about King Arthur and about the Knights of the Round Table, about the spirit of early Christianity, socialism, humanity, the attachment of the English people to the Prince of Wales, the frock coat, the New Jerusalem, the dawn of freedom, the dawn of peace, the hill of wisdom, the beneficial effect of sport on cultivation of the intellect, Monsalvat, and he ended with an enthusiastic paean to international brotherhood. The enraptured Geneva audience, that Olympics of oratory showmanship, that international Academy of Eloquence, showered him with applause. Then the delegate from North Africa, John Smith, an ex-ship's boy, currently the owner of tens of thousands of acres of pasture and farm lands, a coarse man oblivious to subtle European diplomatic arcana, steered the discussion onto completely different tracks. Alas, to the dissatisfaction of the dignified gathering, he dragged the matter under discussion out into the open in all of its nakedness and proposed that Paris be ceded to the kings.

IX

In those days Paris was the City of Delight for the Anglo-Saxon race. Journey by air from England to Paris took a couple of hours. After a day of work enormous fleets of planes plied La Manche. Especially on Saturday afternoons masses of mechanical birds swarmed over the Channel like fish at spawning time. Lean, toothy Englishwomen would point out the few native French (hiding in the narrow rotting rooms of their houses and darting surreptitiously across streets) and would then peer into their Baedekers: "Frenchman: usually dark-haired, short, dirty weakling, hermit, etc." The virtuous sons and daughters of Old England, self-made men, gentlemen and sportsmen, leaving their phlegm, Bible, and Ten Commandments at home, dragged out their hidden instincts, eviscerated the stale, swollen-with-desire dregs of their subconscious, made animals of themselves and wallowed in open-air orgies in the Bois de Boulogne, in the musty caves of

debauchery. Big-bellied native Americans fondled frail, Tana-
gra-shaped girls. Sadistic American women tormented Russians, those professional masochists. The French were cooped
up between brothels under cover of ancient cathedrals and
churches. In the summer, at dawn, pious processions—looked
at with amazement by libertines returning from a long night
out—emerged from over a hundred chapels and churches
and quickly crossed the streets proclaiming their tender ado-
ration of the Divine Mother in rapt canticles.

X

John Smith's proposal was laughed down. Instead, Councilor
Seipel offered Vienna as the seat of the kings. But his proposal met with lively protest from the Little Entente and the
perfidious Italians. The newspapers reported that Chicherin
proposed the forming of a soviet of kings in the Crimea for
the sum of two hundred million pounds.

XI

At about the same time the papers reported the appearance
of a new island in the Indian Ocean. Located east of Mada-
gascar (between longitude 82–83° and latitude 12–15°) far
from sea routes, it measured about 3,000 square kilometers.
Surrounded by coral reefs, it constituted an almost inaccessi-
ble volcanic plateau, twelve hundred meters above sea level.
Lying in the path of trade winds, the island possessed a wonderful, healthy climate and luxurious flora, and lent itself well
to colonization. On the south side it was jagged, on the remaining three sides straight, so that it resembled a crown.
The head of the scientific expedition that first landed on the
island, a confirmed German monarchist, called it the Isle of
the Kings.

Thomas Clark, who usually drew his inspiration and ideas
from chance analogies, saw the finger of destiny in the name.

XII

The exodus of the dethroned monarchs to the Isle of the Kings began in July of the following year. Multidecked steamers furrowed the Indian Ocean and delivered gold, old furniture, mistresses, architects, portraits of ancestors, music hall troupes, faithful butlers, counselors of state, officers, genealogical charts, tourists, film directors, aristocrats from all over the world, tailors, racehorses, engineers, exquisite chefs, automobiles, and land surveyors. The first thing the monarchs did was to divide the island into individual kingdoms in proportion to their prewar possessions. Thus Bourbon France gave up Alsace-Lorraine to Hohenzollern Germany. Borders were delineated; border checkpoints were set up and manned with gendarmes and banners. A standing army of young blue bloods and imported globetrotters was created. The monarchs also built palaces—miniature imitations of capitals and courts, Parises, Berlins, Viennas, Versailles, Schönbrunns —with great creative enthusiasm and lightning speed. Military decorations and prewar constitutions were restored and parliaments and senates were called into session. And thus began a feast of life that had long been missing from human history: tottering, overflowing with delight, pleasure, and an excess of all things.

Impoverished Republican Europe looked with envy upon the cornucopia of the Isle of Kings.

XIII

In spite of the difficult access, contact with the island to the year 193- was unusually lively. From Europe came the marauders and argonauts of the aristocracy, dethroned kings, antique dealers, doctors who treated venereal disease, officers stripped of their rank, prostitutes, racers and cannons— everything that Europe had to dispose of. From America came morganatic wives of dethroned monarchs together with their dowries, canned goods, currency, wheat, meat, and surplus goods. In this way a few years passed imperceptibly—it was anticipated that exile would last but a few months. But the peoples of Europe did not see the error of their ways. On the contrary, the Isle of Kings welcomed more and more of the anointed: Italy's King Alphonse XIII; Yugoslavia's King Alexander; the Prince of Monaco; the Romanian King; the Sultans of Morocco; and Faisul, King of Iraq. Each additional invasion brought nothing but confusion and conflict to peaceful relations on the island. The land had to be redivided, which caused border disputes and even armed skirmishes.

War—guardian angel of the thrones—accompanied a party of English emigrants on the steamship *Old England,* which brought the English court.

XIV

This was the last ruling dynasty on the continent and the last batch of emigrants. The gigantic steamship Old England delivered its passengers but never returned to its native harbors. It was smashed in a terrible cyclone that ravaged the Indian Ocean. It was also at this time that dangerous reefs and underwater cliffs surfaced around the Isle of the Kings, cutting it off from the world and eliminating all access to it for centuries. But this was not the only cause of the long isolation of the Island. The defeats and upheavals taking place all over the world were the focus of universal emotions and drew attention away from the remote island in the Indian Ocean. When, after ten years, calm was restored and someone recalled the lost exile of the kings, it was decided to forgo the search and let the whole matter be forgotten, so that new generations would remain ignorant of the concept and idea of monarchy.

It is only now that the real history of this out-of-the-way place, cut off from the world for centuries and harnassed irrevocably to the twilight of the history of monarchy, begins.

XV

The history of the Isle of the Kings can barely be recreated in its most rudimentary outlines from the few surviving documents. As we have mentioned, the arrival of the English court dealt a profound blow to international relations on the island. The German Emperor Wilhelm II, fearing his role as leader would be undermined, concluded an anti-English alliance with the Hapsburgs. Wilhelm II acknowledged England's right only to land equaling the European territory of Great Britain, without taking into consideration its colonial possessions. He based his position on the fact that during the first division of the island the colonies of Germany, France, and Italy were not considered. The war which erupted as a result of the conflict between England, France and Russia, and Germany and Austria was almost a continuation of the Great War of 1914–18. In spite of the fact that it was shorter, it brought about profound losses in human life and in material and cultural acquisitions.

Peace, owing to the skill of English diplomacy (and most of all to the indefatigable efforts of Lloyd George), brought partial appeasement of England's demands, and in international politics, victory for a system that balanced the great powers.

XVI

One of the consequences of the war was a transformation in the system of governing the states. Owing to their isolation, the monarchs were liberated from having to espouse democracy, from having to set an example, from all administration and institutions which had been created as showpieces for distrustful peoples. The first strike at the constitution and parliamentary system, dealt by Czar Aleksey on the day of his coronation, had a detrimental effect on the remainder of the rulers.

Constitutional monarchy was transformed into absolutist monarchy.

XVII

Years, decades, centuries passed. The Isle of the Kings, cut off from the world, was plummeting into poverty; its culture and civilization were gradually disappearing. Poverty, absolutism, and militarism increased wars, and wars increased poverty and decline. Forced to satisfy their needs, the people began to specialize and differentiate themselves more and more and so broke down into three strata: the working folk, the army, and the court. The cities fell into disrepair, the palaces crumbled. The last remnants of knowledge slowly disappeared while superstitions and a militantly religious government took their place.

And just as at the close of the Middle Ages the discovery of new markets, revival of international relations, birth of capital, growing power of the cities, renaissance of humanistic culture, and development of lay science had transformed a feudal monarchy into an absolutist one; so now, in reverse, the isolation of the lost Isle of the Kings, its being cut off from the world for so many centuries, and the accompanying decline in its cities, capital, and science and reduction to a natural economy transformed an absolutist government into a feudal one.

XVIII

The histories of the individual monarchies are difficult to reconstruct because of the small number and poor scientific value of the surviving historical documents. An example of this might be the biography of the French King Ludwig XXV (dated the end of the twenty-first century) which was written by a court historian in a strange, mangled French.

From it we learn that Ludwig XXV was a patron of the fine arts. He built a stable, whose beauty the chronicler sings in a lengthy panegyric, praising it as the eighth wonder of the world, a most beautiful work of architecture. The years of this monarch's reign, in the words of this court sycophant, constituted the golden age of French history. By all accounts, this illustrious period boasted victorious wars, which—as a result of the malice of the king's enemies—ended in defeat; wise governance, just courts, religiosity and mercy, gay court pageants, and beautiful women. Much space is devoted to this obsequious historian's descriptions of the great hunts, in which Ludwig XXV was an ardent participant, as well as the amorous jousts and feasts, of which he was a discriminating gourmet.

XIX

Relatively few of these documents have survived. We would find out very little that was interesting from the monotonous histories of the lives of the various Ludwigs, Karols, Fredericks, Richards, Alphonses, Emanuels, Johns, Wilhelms, Nicholases; or the history of the various war expeditions, plunderings, fratricides, treasons, murders, plots, violence, pageants, celebrations, hunts, invasions, superstitions, jousts, deaths, or plagues.

We are familiar with these things; a precise description can be found in any handbook of medieval history, if we read it backward.

XX

Of the later documents, let us mention, for the sake of curiosity, a map which will give a concrete image of the disappearance of culture and tradition on the Isle of the Kings. It depicts the world as a circle of water with the Isle of the Kings, the only land, in the very center.

XXI

In the year 2431, Anarchasis Hualalai, a professor of history at the University of Hilo (Hawaii), ferreted out a reference to a vanished island that had appeared in the Indian Ocean in the twentieth century and was subsequently occupied by kings. According to the entry, the island had vanished in waves of oblivion in the aftermath of various oceanic and social cataclysms. That is why it was noted on only a few maps published at the time of its discovery and unknown until rediscovered this year by a professor digging around in old archives.

Professor Anarchasis organized a scientific expedition, made up chiefly of learned representatives of the black race (the professor was distinguished by an especially lustrous blackness and deep in his heart was extremely proud of it).

XXII

They set out in an enormous airship. After searching for a long time with no success, they suddenly came upon the island they were seeking. And when the black participants of the expedition trained their binoculars on the land stretched before them, they saw something quite out of the ordinary. Here on the naked plain stood several hundred whites gathered in a circle, clothed in animal skins and armed with long spears and shields. In the center a contest was underway between two hairy giants distinguished by an abundance and wealth of ornament and steel crowns on splendid red manes of hair. The shield of one of the wrestlers bore an insignia in which one could discern the crude outline of a lily, while the other shield bore the picture of a black eagle. In their hands the opponents held enormous javelins, which they manipulated and dodged with amazing agility.

Professor Anarchasis Hualalai watched them closely and then said to his black colleagues with characteristic solemnity:

"This is a typical scene in the life of barbarians: the outcome of the struggle between the chiefs resolves the dispute between the two tribes. From the emblems on the shields I would conclude that the King of the Franks is doing battle with the King of the Germans. Incidentally, now, as I watch them, I do not know how the whites could ever have prided themselves on the universality of their civilization, in contrast to us, blacks. If we were to rummage through every last corner of the earth, would we find even one black who was not basking in all the blessings of technology and culture? Never! Alas, these are observations out of their time. *We* know that not the color of one's skin, but the color of one's heart makes the man and that differences of race have long been obliterated. Now, gentlemen, the wearisome task of civilizing our civilizers awaits us."

Frank O'Connor

Frank O'Connor *(1903–1966) was born Michael Francis O'Donovan in Cork. He was a celebrated Irish practitioner and theorist of the short story, and the author of numerous collections of short fiction.*

ETERNAL TRIANGLE

Revolutions? I never had any interest in them. A man in my position have to mind his job and not bother about what other people are doing. Besides, I never could see what good they did anybody, and I see more of that kind of thing than most people. A watchman have to be out at all hours in all kinds of weather. He have to keep his eyes open. All I ever seen out of things like that was the damage. And who pays for the damage? You and me and people like us, so that one set of jackeens can get in instead of another set of jackeens. What is it to me who's in or out? All I know is that I have to pay for the damage they do.

I remember well the first one I saw. It was a holiday, and when I turned up to the depot, I was told there was a tram after breaking down in town, and I was to go in and keep an eye on it. A lot of the staff was at the races, and it might be a couple of hours before they could get a breakdown gang. So I took my lunch and away with me into town. It was a nice spring day and I thought I might as well walk.

Mind you, I noticed nothing strange, only that the streets were a bit empty, but it struck me that a lot of people were away for the day. Then, all at once, just as I got to town, I noticed a handful of them Volunteer boys in the street. Some of them had green uniforms with slouch hats; more of them had nothing only belts and bandoliers. All of them had guns of one sort or another. I paid no attention. Seeing that it was a holiday, I thought they might be on some sort of manoeuvre. They were a crowd I never had anything to do with. As I say, I'm a man that minds his own business.

Suddenly, one of them raises his gun and halts me.

"Halt!" says he. "Where are you bound for, mate?"

"Just down here, to keep an eye on a tram," I said, taking it in good parts.

"A tram?" says he. "That's the very thing we want for a barricade. Could you drive it?"

"Ah, is it to have the union after me?" says I.

"Ah, to hell with the union," says a second fellow. "If you'll drive it we'll rig it up as an armored train."

Now, I did not like the tone them fellows took. They were making too free altogether, and it struck me as peculiar that there wouldn't be a bobby there to send them about their business. I went on a couple of hundred yards, and what did I see only a second party. These fellows were wearing khaki, and I recognized them as cadets from the college. They were standing on the steps of the big hotel overlooking the tram, and the young fellow that was supposed to be their officer was very excited.

"That tram is in the direct line of fire," he says. "It's not a safe place."

"Ah, well," I said, "in my job there's a lot of things aren't safe. I hope if anything happens me you'll put in a good word for me with the tramway company."

Mind you, I was still not taking them seriously. I didn't know what I was after walking into. And the first thing I did was to go over the tram to see was there anything missing. The world is full of light-fingered people, and a thing like that, if you only left it for five minutes, you wouldn't know what would be gone. I was shocked when I seen the upstairs. The glass was all broken and the upholstery ripped.

Then the shooting began, and I had to lie on the floor, but after a while it eased off, and I sat up and ate my lunch and read the daily paper. There was no one around, because whenever anyone showed himself at the end of the road, there was a bang and he ran for his life. Coming on to dusk, I began to worry a bit about whether I was going to be relieved at all that day. I knew Danny Delea, the foreman, was a conscientious sort of man, and if he couldn't get a relief, he'd send me word what to do, but no one came, and I was beginning to get a bit hungry. I don't mind admitting that a couple of times I got up to go home. I didn't like sitting there with the darkness coming on, not knowing was I going to be relieved that night or the next week. But each time I sat down again. That is the sort I am. I knew the light-fingered gentry, and I knew that, firing or no firing, they were on the look-out and I wouldn't be out of that tram before one of them would be along to see what could he pick up. I would not give it to say to the rest of the men that I would leave a valuable thing like a tram.

Then, all at once, the firing got hot again, and when I looked out, what did I see in the dusk only a girl coming from behind the railings in the park and running this way and that in an aimless sort of way. She looked as if she was out of her mind with fright, and I could see the fright was more a danger to her than anything else. Mind, I had no wish for her company! I saw what she was, and they are a sort of woman I would never have much to do with. They are always trying to make friends with watchmen, because we are out at all hours. At the same time, I saw if I didn't do something quick, she'd be killed under my eyes, so I stood on the platform and shouted to her to come in. She was a woman I didn't know by sight; a woman of about thirty-five. Cummins her name was. The family was from Waterford. She was a good-looking piece too, considering. I made her lie on the floor to get out of the shooting, but she was nearly hysterical, lifting her head to look at me and lowering it not to see what was going on.

"But who in hell is it, mister?" she says. "God Almighty, I only came out for a bit of sugar for me tea, and look at the capers I'm after walking into! . . . Sacred Heart of Jesus, they're off again. . . . You'd think I was something at a fair, the way they were banging their bloody bullets all round me. Who is it at all?"

"It's the cadets in the hotel here, shooting at the other fellows beyond the park," I said.

"But why don't someone send for the police? Damn soon them fellows would be along if it was only me talking to a fellow!"

"'Twould take a lot of police to stop this," says I.

"But what are they shooting for, mister?" says she. "Is it for Ireland?"

"Ireland?" says I. "A fat lot Ireland have to hope for from little whipper-snappers like them."

"Still and all," says she, "if 'twas for Ireland, you wouldn't mind so much."

And I declare to God but she had a tear in her eye. That is the kind of women they are. They'll steal the false teeth from a corpse, but let them lay eyes on a green flag or a child in his First Communion suit, and you'd think patriotism and religion were the only two things ever in their minds.

"That sort of blackguarding isn't going to do any good to Ireland or anyone else," says I. "What I want to know is who is going to pay for the damage? Not them. They never did an honest day's work in their lives, most of them. We're going to pay for it, the way we always do."

"I'd pay them every bloody penny I have in the world this minute if only they'd shut up and go away," she says. "For God's sake, will you listen to them!"

Things were getting hotter again. What was after happening was that some of the Volunteer fellows were after crossing the park behind the shrubbery and were firing up at the hotel. They might as well be firing at the moon. The cadets were after knocking out every pane of glass and barricading the windows. One of the Volunteers jumped from a branch of a tree over the railings and ran across the road to the tram. He was an insignificant little article with a saucy air. You could tell by his accent he wasn't from Dublin. I took him to be from somewhere in the North. I didn't like him much. I never did like them Northerners anyway.

"What are ye doing here?" he says in surprise when he seen us lying on the floor.

"I'm the watchman," says I, cutting him short.

"Begor, a watchman ought to be able to watch himself better than that," he says, and without as much as "By your leave" he up with the rifle butt and knocked out every pane of glass in the side of the tram. It went to my heart to see it go. Any other time I'd have taken him and wrung his neck, but, you see, I was lying on the floor and couldn't get up to him with the firing. I pretended not to mind, but I looked at the glass and then I looked at him.

"And who," I said, "is going to pay for that?"

"Och, Mick MacQuaid to be sure," says he.

"Ah, the gentleman is right," says the woman. "Only for him we might all be kilt."

The way she about-faced and started to soft-solder that fellow got on my nerves. It is always the same with that sort of woman. They are people you can't trust.

"And what the hell is it to anyone whether you're killed or not?" I said. "No one asked you to stop. This is the tramway company's property, and if you don't like it you can leave it. You have no claim."

"We'll see whose property this is when it's all over," says the man, and he began shooting up at the windows of the hotel.

"Hey, mister," says the woman, "is that the English you're shooting at?"

"Who else do you think 'twould be?" says he.

"Ah, I was only saying when you came in that I'd never

mind if 'twas against the English. I suppose 'twill be in the history books, mister, like Robert Emmet?"

"Robert Emmet!" I said. "I'd like to know where you and the likes of you would be only for the English."

"Well, do you know," she says, as innocent as you please, "'tis a funny thing about me, but I never cared much for the English soldiers. Of course, mind you, you'd meet nice fellows everywhere, but you'd never know where you were with the English. They haven't the same nature as our own somehow."

Then someone blew a whistle in the park, and your man dropped his rifle and looked out to see how he was going to get back.

"You're going to get your nose shot off if you go out in that, mister," says the woman. "If you'll take my advice, you'll wait till 'tis dark."

"I'm after getting into a tight corner all right," says he.

"Oh, you'll never cross that street alive, mister," she says as if she was delighted with it. "The best thing you could do now would be to wait till after dark and come round to my little place for a cup of tea. You'd be safe there anyway."

"Och, to hell with it," says he. "I have only to take a chance," and he crept down the steps and made for the railings. They spotted him, because they all began to blaze together. The woman got on her hands and knees to look after him.

"Aha, he's away!" says she, clapping her hands like a child. "Good man you are, me bold fellow. . . . I wouldn't wish for a pound that anything would happen that young man," says she to me.

"The shooting on both sides is remarkably wide," says I. "That fellow should have more sense."

"Ah, we won't know till we're dead who have the sense and who haven't," says she. "Some people might get a proper suck-in. God, wouldn't I laugh."

"Some people are going to get a suck-in long before that," says I. "The impudence of that fellow, talking about the tramway company. He thinks they're going to hand it over to him. Whoever is in, he's not going to see much of it."

"Ah, what matter?" she said. "'Tis only youth. Youth is lovely, I always think. And 'tis awful to think of young fellows being kilt, whoever they are. Like in France. God, 'twould go to your heart. And what is it all for? Ireland! Holy Moses, what did Ireland ever do for us? Bread and dripping and a kick in the ass is all we ever got out of it. You're right about the English, though. You'd meet some very genuine English chaps. Very sincere, in their own way."

"Oh, they have their good points," says I. "I never saw much to criticize in them, only they're given too much liberty."

"Ah, what harm did a bit of liberty ever do anyone, though?" says she.

"Now, it does do harm," says I. "Too much liberty is bad. People ought to mind themselves. Look at me! I'm on this job the best part of my life, and I have more opportunities than most, but thanks be to God, I can say I never took twopenceworth belonging to my employers nor never had anything to do with a woman outside my own door."

"And a hell of a lot of thanks you'll get for it in the heel of the hunt," says she. "Five bob a week pension and the old woman stealing it out of your pocket while you're asleep. Don't I know all about it? Oh, God, I wish I was back in me own little room. I'd give all the countries that ever was this minute for a cup of tea with sugar in it. I'd never mind the rations only for the bit of sugar. Hi, mister, would you ever see me home to the doss? I wouldn't be afraid if I had you with me."

"But I have to mind this tram," says I.

"You have what?" says she, cocking her head. "Who do you think is going to run away with it?"

"Now, you'd be surprised," says I.

"Surprised?" says she. "I'd be enchanted."

"Well," I said, "the way I look at it, I'm paid to look after it, and this is my place till I'm relieved."

"But how the hell could you be relieved with this merry-go-round?"

"That is a matter for my employers to decide," says I.

"God," says she, "I may be bad but you're looney," and then she looked at me and she giggled. She started giggling, and she went on giggling, just as if she couldn't stop. That is what I say about them women. There is a sort of childishness in them all, just as if they couldn't be serious about anything. That is what has them the way they are.

So the night came on, and the stars came out, and the shooting only got louder. We were sitting there in the tram, saying nothing, when all at once I looked out and saw the red light over the houses.

"That's a fire," says I.

"If it is, 'tis a mighty big fire," says she.

And then we saw another one to the left of it, and another and another till the whole sky seemed to be lit up, and the smoke pouring away out to sea as if it was the whole sky was moving.

"That's the whole city on fire," says I.

"And 'tis getting mighty close to us," says she. "God send they don't burn this place as well. 'Tis bad enough to be starved and frozen without being roasted alive as well."

I was too mesmerized to speak. I knew what 'twas worth. Millions of pounds' worth of property burning, and no one to pour a drop of water on it. That is what revolutions are like. People talk about poverty, and then it all goes up in smoke—enough to keep thousands comfortable.

Then, all at once, the shooting got nearer, and when I looked out I saw a man coming up the road. The first impression I got of him was that he was badly wounded, for he was staggering from one side of the road to the other with his hands in the air. "I surrender, I surrender," he was shouting, and the more he shouted, the harder they fired. He staggered out into the middle of the road again, stood there for a minute, and then went down like a sack of meal.

"Oh, the poor misfortunate man!" says the woman, putting

her hands to her face. "Did you ever see such barbarity? Killing him like that in cold blood?"

But he wasn't killed yet, for he began to bawl all over again, and when he got tired of holding up his hands, he stuck his feet in the air instead.

"Cruel, bloody, barbarous brutes!" says the woman. "They ought to be ashamed of themselves. He told them he surrendered, and they won't let him." And without another word, away with her off down the street to him, bawling: "Here, mister, come on in here and you'll be safe."

A wonder we weren't all killed with her. He got up and started running towards the tram with his hands still in the air. When she grabbed him and pushed him up on the platform, he still had them there. I seen then by his appearance that he wasn't wounded but drunk. He was a thin-looking scrawny man with a cloth cap.

"I surrender," he bawls. *"Kamerad."*

"Hi, mister," says the woman, "would you for the love of the suffering God stop surrendering and lie down."

"But they won't let me lie down," says he. "That's all I want is to lie down, but every time I do they makes a cockshot of me. What in hell is it?"

"Oh, this is the Rising, mister," she says.

"The what?" says he.

"The Rising," says she. "Like they said in the papers there would be."

"Who's rising?" says he, grabbing his head. "What paper said that? I want to know is this the D.T.'s I have or isn't it?"

"Oh, 'tisn't the D.T.'s at all, mister," she says, delighted to be able to spread the good news. "This is all real, what you see. 'Tis the Irish rising. Our own boys, don't you know? Like in Robert Emmet's time. The Irish are on that side and the English are on this. 'Twas the English was firing at you, the low scuts!"

"Bugger them!" he says. "They're after giving me a splitting head. There's no justice in this bloody world." Then he sat on the inside step of the tram and put his head between his knees. "Like an engine," he says. "Have you e'er a drop of water?"

"Ah, where would we get it, man?" says the woman, brightening up when she seen him take the half pint of whiskey out of his hip pocket. 'Tis a mystery to me still it wasn't broken. "Is that whiskey you have, mister?"

"No water?" says he, and then he began to shudder all over and put his hand over his face. "Where am I?" says he.

"Where should you be?" says she.

"How the hell do I know and the trams not running?" says he. "Tell me, am I alive or dead?"

"Well, you're alive for the time being," says the woman. "How long we're all going to be that way is another matter entirely."

"Well, are you alive, ma'am?" says he. "You'll excuse me being personal?"

"Oh, no offense, mister," says she. "I'm still in the queue."

"And do you see what I see?" says he.

"What's that, mister?"

"All them fires."

"Oh," says she, "don't let a little thing like that worry you, mister. That's not Hell, if that's what you're afraid of. That's only the city burning."

"The what burning?" says he.

"The city burning," says she. "That's it, there."

"There's more than the bloody city burning," says he. "Haven't you e'er a drop of water at all?"

"Ah, we can spare it," she says. "I think it must be the Almighty God sent you, mister. I declare to you, with all the goings-on, I hadn't a mouthful to eat the whole day, not as much as a cup of tea."

So she took a swig of the bottle and passed it to me. It is stuff I would never much care for, the whiskey, but having nothing to eat, I was feeling in the want of something.

"Who's that fellow in there?" says he, noticing me for the first time.

"That's only the watchman," says she.

"Is he Irish or English?" says the drunk.

"Ah, what the hell would he be only Irish?"

"Because if he's English, he's getting none of my whiskey," says the drunk, beginning to throw his arms about. "I'd cut the throat of any bloody Englishman."

Oh, pure, unadulterated patriotism! Leave it to a boozer.

"Now, don't be attracting attention, like a good man," she says. "We all have our principles but we don't want to be overheard. We're in trouble enough, God knows."

"I'm not afraid of anyone," says he, staggering to his feet. "I'm not afraid to tell the truth. A bloody Englishman that would shoot a misfortunate man and he on the ground, I despise him. I despise the English."

Then there was a couple of bangs, and he threw up his hands and down with him like a scarecrow in a high wind.

"I declare to me God," says the woman with an ugly glance at the hotel, "them fellows in there are wound up. Are you hit, mister?" says she, giving him a shake. "Oh, begod, I'm afraid his number's up."

"Open his collar and give us a look at him," says I. By this time I was sick of the pair of them.

"God help us, and not a priest nor doctor to be had," says she. "Could you say the prayers for the dying?"

"How would I know the prayers for the dying?" says I.

"Say an act of contrition so," says she.

Well, I began, but I was so upset that I started the Creed instead.

"That's not the act of contrition," says she.

"Say it yourself as you're so smart," says I, and she began, but before she was finished, the drunk shook his fist in the air and said: "I'll cut the living lights out of any Englishman," and then he began to snore.

"Some people have the gift," says she.

Gift was no word for it. We sat there the whole night, shivering and not able to get more than a snooze, and that fellow never stirred, only for the roar of the snoring. He never woke at all until it was coming on to dawn, and then he put his head in his hands again and began complaining of the headache.

"Bad whiskey is the ruination of the world," says he.

"Everyone's trouble is their own," says the woman.

And at that moment a lot of cadets came out of the hotel and over to the tram.

"Will you look at them?" says the woman. "Didn't I tell you they were wound up?"

"You'll have to get out of this now," says the officer, swinging his gun.

"And where are we going to go?" says she.

"The city is all yours," says he.

"And so is the Bank of Ireland," says she. "If I was only in my own little room this minute, you could have the rest of the city—with my compliments. Where are you off to?" she asked the drunk.

"I'll have to get the Phibsboro tram," says he.

"You could order two while you're about it," she says. "The best thing the pair of ye can do is come along to my little place and wait till this jigmareel is over."

"I have to stop here," says I.

"You can't," says the officer.

"But I must stop till I'm relieved, man," says I, getting angry with him.

"You're relieved," he says. "I'm relieving you."

And, of course, I had to do what he said. All the same, before I went, I gave him a piece of my mind.

"There's no need for this sort of thing at all," I says. "There's nothing to be gained by destroying valuable property. If people would only do what they were told and mind their own business, there would be no need for any of this blackguarding."

The woman wanted me to come into her room for a cup of tea, but I wouldn't. I was too disgusted. Away with me across the bridge, and the fellows that were guarding it never halted me or anything, and I never stopped till I got home to my own place. Then I went to bed, and I didn't get up for a week, till the whole thing was over. They had prisoners going in by droves, and I never as much as looked out at them. I was never so disgusted with anything in my life.

E. M. Forster

E. M. Forster *(1879–1970) was born in London and is the author of* A Room With a View, Howard's End, *and* A Passage to India, *among other works. This story, post-humously published in his collection* The Life to Come and Other Stories *was probably written in the 1930s, according to his editors.*

WHAT DOES IT MATTER?
A MORALITY

Before the civil war, Pottibakia was a normal member of the Comity of Nations. She erected tariff walls, broke treaties, persecuted minorities, obstructed at conferences unless she was convinced there was no danger of a satisfactory solution; then she strained every nerve in the cause of peace. She had an unknown warrior, a national salvo, commemorative post-age-stamps, a characteristic peasantry, arterial roads; her emblem was a bee on a bonnet, her uniform plum-grey. In all this she was in line with her neighbours, and her capital city could easily be mistaken for Bucharest or Warsaw, and often was. Her president (for she was a republic) was Dr Bonifaz Schpiltz; Count Waghaghren (for she retained her aristocracy) being head of the police, and Mme Sonia Rodoconduco being Dr Schpiltz's mistress (for he was only human).

Could it be this liaison which heralded the amazing change —a change which has led to the complete isolation of a sovereign state? Presidents so often have mistresses, it is part of the constitution they have inherited from Paris, and Dr Schpiltz was an ideal president, with a long thin brown beard flecked with grey, and a small protuberant stomach. Mme Rodoconduco, as an actress and a bad one, also filled her part. She was extravagant, high-minded and hysterical, and kept Bopp (for thus all the ladies called him) on tenterhooks lest she did anything temperamental. She lived in a lovely villa on the shores of Lake Lago.

Now Count Waghaghren desired the President's downfall, and what the Count desired always came about, for he was powerful and unscrupulous. He desired it for certain reasons of *haute politique* which have been obscured by subsequent events—perhaps he was a royalist, perhaps a traitor or patriot, perhaps he was an emissary of that sinister worldwide Blue Elk organization which is said to hold its sessions in the Azores. It is hopeless to inquire. Enough that he decided, as part of his scheme, to sow dissension between husband and wife. Mme Schpiltz's relatives were financiers, and a scandal was likely to start fluctuations on the exchange.

His plot was easily laid. He forged a letter from Mme Rodoconduco to Mme Schpiltz, inviting her to visit the lovely Villa Lago at a certain hour upon a certain day, he intercepted the reply of Mme Schpiltz accepting the invitation, and he arranged that the President and his mistress should be found in a compromising position at the moment of her call. All worked to perfection. The gendarme outside the villa omitted (under instructions) the national salvo when the President's wife drove up, the servants (bribed) conducted her as if by mistake to the Aphrodite bedroom, and there she found her husband in a pair of peach-blush pyjamas supported by Mme Rodoconduco in a lilac negligée.

Mme Rodoconduco went into hysterics, hoping they would gain her the upper hand. She shrieked and raved, while Count Waghaghren's microphone concealed under the lace pillows transmitted every tremor to his private cabinet. The President also played up. At first he pretended he was not there, then he rebuked his wife for interfering and his mistress for licentiousness, whereas he—he was a man, with a morality of his own. "I am a man, ha ha!" and he tried folding his arms. Smack! He got one over the ear from Mme Rodoconduco for that. All was going perfectly except for the lack of cooperation on the part of Mme Schpiltz, who had started on entering the room and had said "Bopp Bopp Bopp," but had then said no more. She watched the lovers without animosity and without amusement, occasionally showing concern when they struck one another but not caring to intervene. When there was a pause she said rather shyly, "Madame—madame, j'ai faim," and since the only reply was a stare she added, "Vous m'avez invitée pour le goûter, n'est-ce-pas?"

"Certainly not, out of my house!" shrieked Mme Rodoconduco, but seeing a genuine look of disappointment on her visitor's face she said, "Oh, very well, if you must eat you must."

The servants now took Mme Schpiltz into another apartment, where *goûter* for two was already in evidence. She fell upon it, and Mme Rodoconduco followed her and sulkily did the honours. No allusion was made to the Aphrodite bedroom, the President had slipped away, and though the hostess was very nervous and therefore very rude she became easier in the presence of so much apathy, and they chatted on subjects of intellectual interest for quite a time.

The Count was unaccustomed to incidents without consequence and expected one lady or the other to come round to him in tears, or it might be the President himself asking him, as man to man, for advice in a little private difficulty. Then they would have fallen into his toils. But nothing happened. A few more officials and lackeys were in the know, but that was all. He must devise some other means of starting the ball rolling.

It may be remembered that there was a gendarme on duty that afternoon outside the Villa Lago. He, in the course of his usual dossier, reported that the President winked at him before driving away.

"Did you wink back?"

"Oh no, sir."

The Count docked him a week's pay, and an order went out to all ranks that when the President of the Republic winked at them they were to wink back.

The order had no effect because it was based on a misconception. It is true that the President had winked as he drove away, but only because some dust blew in his eye. His thoughts were with the ladies at their *goûter*, not of gendarmes at all. Defeated by the subsequent steadiness of his gaze, Count Waghaghren reissued the order in a more drastic form: all ranks were to wink without waiting. This again had no effect. We do not see what we do not seek, and Dr Schpiltz, though a stickler for uniforms, was oblivious to all that passes inside them. It was his wife who enlightened him. "Oh Bopp, how the poor policemen's eyes do twitch," she remarked at a review. His attention once drawn, he observed that a twitch seemed to have become part of the national salvo. He did not like innovations about which he had not been consulted, and was about to issue a memorandum, when he noticed that the twitch was accompanied in some cases with a roguish smile. This put him on the right track. He had seen the same combination on the faces of little milliners and modistes of easy virtue, and he came to the only possible conclusion: the police were giving him the glad eye.

This called for a reprimand. But before drafting it he waited to make sure. There was no hurry—he could play cat and mouse if he liked, and he did get amusement at watching the forces of law and order playing futile tricks. He never winked back, oh no, he was always impassive and correct, besides, "I am a man, aha, no danger in that quarter for *me!*" and he pulled at his thin brown beard. His drives through his capital city became more vivid, and he began to contrast the methods of superior and subordinate ranks. The way in which a peasant lad, fresh inside his uniform, would be half afraid to move his eyelid, and yet move it as if he could have moved much more, was indescribably droll. He became more and more entertained by his discovery, which not even his wife shared now, for she had a mind like a sieve and completely forgot the whole matter.

One day he happened to take a short constitutional in the Victory Park. This splendid park is a favourite resort of Pottibakians of all types, and it was his duty, as first citizen in the state, to walk there now and then. "Look," the people would say, "there is the President walking round the bandstand! He is holding a newspaper in his hand, just as if he were you or me! Marvellous!" But it was in a quieter part of the park that he suddenly encountered an incredibly goodlooking mounted gendarme, and before he could stop himself had winked back. The man, who was very young, smiled charmingly, and pretended to have trouble with his horse. This led to a short conversation. There was not time for much, since the Bessarabian Minister was expected, but it included some presidential patting of the horse's neck, and a slight leaning forward on the part of its rider. "Mirko, Your Excellency, Mirko Bolnovitch. Yes." Which was all very well, but where? Not in the park, for God's sake, and he could not risk more tension with his wife. It is the pride of the Republic to house its president in prehistoric discomfort, and No. 100, Browning Street does not even possess a tradesman's entrance. The parlour is on the left of the door, the schoolroom on the right, and Mme Schpiltz or the young ladies see everyone who comes in. Not there, nor indeed anywhere. He withdrew hurriedly.

After his interview with the Bessarabian Minister he received a letter from Mme Rodoconduco. They had scarcely met since she boxed his ears, but it was tacitly understood that they were not to break. She wrote now on the deepest of black-edged paper, to make him part of the death of her brother, a realistic novelist to whom she was greatly attached. She must instantly repair to his estate, in case her nephews took a wrong view of the will. This, and the funeral, would detain her for at least a week, but as soon as she got back she much hoped to see her Bopp, and to apologize for her unfortunate warmth. On the whole not a bad letter. The woman wanted money—still, he had faced that long ago. She spoke of good taste and restraint—oh that she possessed them to the extent Mme Schpiltz did!—and she implied that though her mourning would be in good taste it could not be restrained. A *ménage à trois:* is it impossible when all three are rather exceptional? Finally she asked him a favour. All the servants at the Villa Lago had been dismissed owing to their treachery, and she wanted someone to keep an eye on the new set in her absence. Would he be so very good as to pay a surprise visit one afternoon—Friday, say?

He replied pleasantly, condoled, enclosed a cheque, said he would look in at the villa next Friday at 3.0 on the pretext of having a bathe, hoped too for the possibilities of a *ménage à trois.* She replied to this from her family estate. His note had caught her just before starting, she said, she was deeply appreciative also for the enclosure, though the loss of a brother could never be repaired, and if only Mme Schpiltz could feel it possible to receive her some time . . . Then she spoke of the grief of the tenantry and the conduct of her nephews, correct hitherto, the arrangements in the little upland church, the hearse, the wreaths of Alpine flowers . . .

The Bessarabian affair still occupying him, he thought no more of Friday till his secretary reminded him. Then, punctually at 3.0, he drove up to the deserted villa. By chance his gendarme friend from the park was on guard. He had hardly given him a thought from that moment to this, but now it was as if he had been thinking of him all the time. He wanted to greet him, but it was impossible with the new major-domo bowing and inquiring whether he had done right in Madame la Baronne's absence to cover the sconces with brown holland. Turning away, he inspected the villa peevishly. He had never liked it less, and the Aphrodite bedroom was repellent. Was all this frou-frou and expense really necessary, as Sonia said it was, for love? She was always talking about love and sending in bills. He went out on to a balcony to get another glimpse of the mounted beauty, but the fellow looked in every direction but upwards, most exasperating, and the President dared not cough. Would Madame la Baronne desire the dining-room suite re-upholstered in banana beige? Yes, if he knew her, she would. Then he said he must re-examine the hydrangeas in the porch. The gendarme kept absolutely still, a model of Pottibakian manhood, not winking now, all glorious in plum-grey. How grandly he sat his horse! Cheerful chatter, meant to embrace him, brought no smile to the strong lips. Alarmed by the fluting quality in his own voice, Dr Schpiltz withdrew, sharper set than ever. Now he would never know what happens when two men . . . and it might have been such a lesson with such a teacher . . . Well, well, he must just have his bathe and go, perhaps all's for the best.

Now the bathing-room at the Villa Lago is a veritable triumph of Lido art. Divans and gymnastic apparatus mingle inseparably. It is accessible from the house and also on the lake side, where great sliding doors give access to marble steps leading down to Mme Rodoconduco's private beach. The view is beyond all description—poets have hymned it: rhododendrons, azaleas, bougainvillaeas, the blue waters of the lake, and on the farther side of it, just visible through the summer haze, the great rock of Praz, where the Pottibakians used to sacrifice their domestic animals before the introduction of Christianity. But the prospect gave the President no pleasure, not even when an aeroplane passed over it. Everything seemed worth just nothing at all. Holding up his swimming-suit he prepared to step into it, when there was the sound of crunched pebbles, and the gendarme rode round the corner of the little bay, dismounted, strode clanging up the steps, took a gauntlet off, and shook hands.

The President frowned—often a sign of joy in the middle-aged, and it was thus understood. "Your Excellency—at your service. Now . . . My inspector has gone back to the city: he is a fool." He pulled the sliding doors together and latched them. "Excuse me . . ." He hung up his spiked helmet next to Mme Rodoconduco's hat. "Excuse me again . . ." He un-buckled his holster. Sitting down on a settee, which was so soft that it made him laugh, he took his gaiters and boots off. "Oh, I say, what a lovely room—better than the Victory Park."

Dr Schpiltz could not speak. His mouth opened and shut like a bird's.

"Have you thought of me since?"

"Ye . . . yes."

"I don't believe you. What is my name?"

The President could not remember.

"Mirko. Mirko Bolnovitch. Oh, I say!" He had noticed the parallel bars. "That shall be my horse in here. Oh, I say!" He had seen the trapeze. Dr Schpiltz locked the door leading into the house. "I'll do that, Your Excellency, don't you trouble." And with a movement too rapid to follow he unlocked it. "Now I'm in your power."

"I think I'm in yours," said the President, admiring him more boldly.

"I'm only eighteen. Shall we see?"

"You come from beyond Praz, don't you, Mirko?"

"Yes. How did you know? By my speech? Or by something else?" He continued to undress. The uniform lay neatly folded, official property. "My singlet." He drew it over his head. "My shorts . . ."

"Well?"

"Well? Never content?" He stepped out of them smiling and sprang on to the trapeze. "Do you like me up here?"

"You are much too far off!"

"Oh, but come up here, Your Excellency, join me!"

"No, thank you, Mirko, not at my age!"

"See, it's so easy, catch hold of whatever you like, only swinging." The light filtered through high orange curtains on to loins and back. "It is cooler with no clothes on," he said. It did not seem to be. "Now I have exercised all my muscles except . . ." He was sitting astride the parallel bars.

The President of the Republic approached his doom.

225

Deftly, as he did so, was his pince-nez twitched off his nose. "Now you can't see how ugly I am."

"Mirko, you ugly . . ." He tottered into the trap and it closed on him.

"Aie, you're in too much of a hurry," laughed the young man. "Come up and do exercises with me first. Business before pleasure."

"I'd rather not, I shall fall, my dear boy."

"Oh no you won't, dearest boyest."

Contrary to his better judgement, Dr Schpiltz now ascended the parallel bars. He became more and more involved. Heaven knew what he had to pass through, how he was twisted about and pinched. He felt like a baby monkey, scratched and mismanaged on the top of a lofty tree. The science of the barrackroom, the passions of the stables, the primitive instincts of the peasantry, the accident of the parallel bars and Dr Schpiltz's quaint physique—all combined into something quite out of the way, and as it did so the door opened and Mme Rodoconduco came into the room, followed by the Bessarabian Minister.

"We have here . . ." she was saying.

Neither of them heard her.

"We have here . . . we have . . ."

The Bessarabian Minister withdrew. Mirko, alerted, relaxed a grip and they fell off the bars on to a mattress. Mme Rodoconduco was so thunderstruck that she could not even scream. She remained in a sort of frenzied equilibrium, and when she did speak it was in ordinary tones. She said, "Bopp, oh Bopp, Bopp!"

He heard that, and raised a lamentable goatee. "You Jezebel! Why aren't you at the funeral?" he hissed.

"Whose funeral?" cried she in flame-coloured taffeta, Titian-cut.

"Your brother's."

"Alekko's? He's alive."

"How dare you contradict me? He's dead. Oh, oh . . . You've written to me about his funeral twice."

"I never did, Bopp, never." Distracted, she picked up a bath-towel and threw it over the pair. They looked better as a heap.

"Disgraceful! Incredible! And I wrote back and sent you a cheque for the mourning."

"I have received no cheque," she cried. "Here's something gravely amiss."

"Yes, all you think of is cheques! What are you here for now?"

"Why, your telephone call," she replied with tears in her eyes. "You rang me up this morning to be here at 3.30 in case the Bessarabian Minister called."

"I never rang you up. More lies."

"You did, dear, you did really, I answered the call myself, and the Minister said you had rung him up also."

"The Minister? Good God! When is he coming?"

"He has come and has gone."

"Not—oh Sonia, not—"

"Yes, and his wife was with him, to see the view, and this is the view they saw. My villa. My Villa Lago. Well, this is the end of my career, such as it is. I can never go back to the stage."

"I am likely never to leave it," said Dr Schpiltz slowly. "I shall go down to history as the president who—oh, what can even the historians say? I shall resign tomorrow, but that will be the beginning, not the end. Could I get over the frontier? Would an aeroplane . . . ? How ever did you open the door?"

"It was unlocked."

"Unlocked? I locked it myself!"

"I think we must both be bewitched," she said, shading her eyes. She was behaving wonderfully well, she was one of those women who behave alternately well and badly. The President began to be convinced of her sincerity and to feel ashamed.

"I know that *I* have been. Whatever has possessed me? When I look round"—and he thrust his head out of the towel—"when I think what I was an hour ago, I begin to wonder,

Sonia, whether those old fairytales you used to recite may not be true, whether men cannot be changed into beasts . . ."

"Ah!" she interrupted, catching sight of the spiked helmet hanging beside her hat, "I've seen the whole thing! We've got Waghaghren here!"

"Well, hardly," he demurred.

"It's one of his traps."

"Trap? But how should he set one?"

"Who knows how or why the Count does things? We only know he does them. Now are you absolutely sure you locked the door into the villa?"

"Absolutely, because this lad—because he—" He broke off and cried, "Mirko! You're not here under orders, are you?"

Mirko lay on the mattress half a-dreaming, drowsy with delight. He had carried out the instructions of his superior officer, gratified a nice old gentleman and had a lovely time himself. He could not understand why, when the President's question was repeated, he should get a kick. He laughed and made the reply on which the whole history of Pottibakia turns. If he had said "Yes, I am here under orders," or if, acting under orders, he had said "No," his country would still be part of the Comity of Nations. But he made the reply which is now engraved on his statue. He said: "What does it matter?"

"You will soon learn whether it matters," said the President. "Sonia, please ring the bell." Mme Rodoconduco stopped him: "No, do not ring. We suffer too much from distant communications. I must question him myself, I see." She raised her eyes to the trapeze. "You! You down on the floor, you have admitted to His Excellency that you are an *agent provocateur?*"

Propping his chin on his fists, Mirko answered: "Gracious lady, I am. But His Excellency acts provokingly too. When I netted him in the park I thought to myself, 'This will mean fun.' And I am a peasant, and we peasants never think a little fun matters. You and His Excellency and the head of the police know better, but we peasants have a proverb: 'Poking doesn't count.' "

"And pray what does that mean?"

"Oh, never mind, Sonia, don't question him. You belong to such different worlds."

"You should know what poking means, lady, if half the tales about you are true. Anyhow, it is a religious story. It is about the Last Judgement."

"We are freethinkers, religion means nothing to us," said the President, but Mirko continued:

"At the Last Judgement the Pottibakians were in a terrible fright, because they had all done something which all three of us have done and hope to do again. There they were going up in a long line, the nobility like you going first, the people of my sort waiting far behind. We waited and waited and presently heard a loud cheering up at the Gate. So we sent a messenger to find out what had happened, and he came back shouting all down the line, 'Hooray! Hooray! Poking doesn't count.' And why should it? Do you understand now?"

"I understand that you are the lowest of the low, or the Count would not employ you," said she. "Will you be so good as to insert that remark of mine into your report?"

"No need, gracious lady, a microphone is already installed."

"Where?" gasped the President.

"These new servants would know. That major-domo is a government electrician."

"Then has all I said been heard?"

"Yes, and all the strange noises you made. Still, what does it matter? It was fun. Oh, some things matter, of course, the crops, and the vintage matters very much, and our glorious Army, Navy and Air Force, and fighting for our friends, and baiting the Jews, but isn't that all? Why, in my village where everyone knows one another and the priest is worst . . . Why, when my uncle needed a goat . . ."

But here the door opened again and Mme Schpiltz entered the room. Dressed in alpaca and a home-made toque, she presented an equal contrast to her husband's bath-towel, to Mme Rodoconduco's Venetian splendours, and to the naked gendarme. As on her previous visit, she was greeted with torrents of talk and knew not how to reply. "Madame, madame," wailed her hostess, "we are ruined," and beneath her full-bosomed lamentations could be heard the President's plaintive pipe: "Oh Charlotte, I have been fatally indiscreet. Why did you come?"

"Because you telephoned to me."

"I telephoned to you? Never!"

"But what has happened? You have only been bathing."

"Madame, madame, do not ask him further, it is something too awful, something he could never explain, something which even I . . . and which you with your fine old-world outlook, your nobility, your strictness of standard . . . Oh madame . . . and in my villa too, after all your previous goodness to me . . . my Villa Lago . . . But you have influence in high financial circles, use it at once before it is too late, let us fly to a cottage *à trois* before the Count—what am I saying? The Count not only heard but he hears! Count Waghaghren!" She whirled her arms in every direction. "Somewhere, a microphone!"

"But I like the wireless so much as long as I have something to do at the same time," said Mme Schpiltz.

"Charlotte! We have reason to believe that a microphone has been secretly installed here, and that the Count can hear everything in his private cabinet."

"But why shouldn't he hear everything? I think that's such a nice idea. He is such a clever man, I knew his poor grandmother well. I remember him saying when he was quite a tiny tot, 'Me want to hear evvyfing,' and we saying 'No, baby dear, baby can't ever do that,' but he knew and we didn't, for thanks to this wonderful invention he can. How like him!"

"He has probably installed television too."

"How like him again! He always used to say, 'Me peepy-weep,' and now he can. Really I do think science . . . But can no one tell me what has happened?"

"I could," said Mirko.

"Charlotte, don't speak to that man! I forbid it!"

"Excuse me, Bopp, I shall speak to him; besides, judging by those clothes over on the divan, he seems to be a policeman, and so the proper person. Well, my man?"

"Lady, do you in God's name know what poking is?"

"But of course. There would be no babies without it. But naturally."

"Thank heaven for that! Well, His Excellency wanted to poke me but did not know how, so I showed him."

"And is that the whole story?"

"Yes."

"Young man, you didn't hurt my husband with rough jokes, I hope?"

"Only in ways he enjoyed."

"And are you yourself satisfied?"

"Not yet. I want to show him again."

"For that you will have to wait. Thank you." She dismissed him and turned to the others. "Well, there we are at last. I thought that someone had been hurt, and it's simply that two people—yes, one doesn't talk about these things of course, but really—what do they matter?"

"Ah!" cried Mirko, "here is someone at last who says what I do. What does it matter?" And he shouted out the cry which was soon to rend the nation asunder, shouted it with such force and, as it happened, so close to the microphone that Count Waghaghren fell senseless.

"What does it matter? Well, that's one way of looking at it, I suppose," said Mme Rodoconduco, examining her fingernails.

"It's the only way," pronounced the President. "It's essential to a stable society. But no government has ever thought of it, and we've learned it too late."

They were not too late, because the Count remained unconscious for the rest of the day. A master plotter, he left no one to carry on his plans, and by the time he came to himself the famous Manifesto had been drafted and affixed to the principal public buildings in the capital. Its wording was as follows:

> Fellow Citizens! Since all of you are interested in the private lives of the great, we desire to inform you that we have all three of us had carnal intercourse with the President of the Republic, and are hoping to repeat it.
>
> Charlotte Schpiltz (housewife)
> Sonia Rodoconduco (artiste)
> Mirko Bolnovitch (gendarme)

There was some discussion as to the wording of the Manifesto. Mme Rodoconduco wanted some reference to the overmastering and ennobling power of love, Mirko something more popular. Both were overruled. The Manifesto appeared in the evening papers, and led to questions both in the Senate and the Chamber of Deputies. The Ministry could not answer the questions and resigned. The President then drove down in state and addressed both houses. He began by paying a glowing tribute to Count Waghaghren, whose organization had now reached such a pitch that not only the private actions of each citizen but even his or her thoughts would soon be recorded automatically. "I intend therefore," he went on, "to form a Ministry of all the Morals, which can alone survive such scrutiny, and as soon as it is in office its first duty will be to depose me. Once deposed, I shall be liable to arrest and to prosecution under our Criminal Code, the most admirable, as we often agreed, in Eastern Europe. Or it may be that I shall not be prosecuted at all, but dealt with summarily, like one of the signatories to the Manifesto, who has been sent for six years to the mines, on the charge of deserting his horse. The other two signatories are at large for the moment, but should not long remain so."

The scenes at the conclusion of his speech were indescribable, particularly in the Senate, where old men got up and poured out their confessions for hours, and could not be stopped. The Chamber of Deputies kept a stiffer upper lip, and there were cries of "Flogging's too good!" and faint counter-cries of "Flog me!" No one dared to take office, owing to the President's unmeasured eulogy of the police, and he continued to govern as dictator until the outbreak of the civil war.

He is now dictator again, but since all the states, led by Bessarabia, have broken off diplomatic relations it is extremely difficult to get Pottibakian news. Visas are refused, and the international express traverses the territory behind frosted glass. Now and then a postcard of the Bolnovitch Monument falls out of an aeroplane, but unlike most patriotic people the Pottibakians appear to be self-contained. They till the earth and have become artistic, and are said to have developed a fine literature which deals very little with sex. This is puzzling, as is the indissolubility of marriage—a measure for which the Church has vainly striven elsewhere. Gratified by her triumph, she is now heart and soul with the nation, and the Archimandrite of Praz has reinterpreted certain passages of scripture, or has pronounced them corrupt. Much here is obscure, links in the argument have been denied to us, nor, since we cannot have access to the novels of Alekko, can we trace the steps by which natural impulses were converted into national assets. There seem, however, to have been three stages: first the Pottibakians were ashamed of doing what they liked, then they were aggressive over it, and now they do as they like. There I must leave them. We shall hear little of them in the future, for the surrounding powers dare not make war. They hold—and perhaps rightly—that the country has become so infectious that if it were annexed it would merely get larger.

And what of the Count? Some rumours have come through. He fought in the civil war, was taken prisoner, and his punishment had to be decided. Mirko wanted him sent to the mines, Sonia flogged, the President banished, but Mme Schpiltz was the cruellest of all. "Poor man, I can't see what he has done," she said. "Do let him keep on doing it." Her advice was taken, and the Count was reinstated in his former office, which has been renamed the Lunatic Asylum, and of which he is the sole inmate. Here he sits all alone amid the latest apparatus, hearing, seeing, tasting and smelling through his fellow citizens, and indexing the results. On public holidays his private cabinet (now his cell) is thrown open, and is visited by an endless queue of smiling Pottibakians, who try to imagine the old days when that sort of thing mattered, and emerge laughing.

Thomas Mann

Thomas Mann (1875–1955) was born in Lübeck, Germany. He is one of the great figures of twentieth-century literature and won the Nobel prize for literature in 1929. Among his works are The Magic Mountain, Tonio Kröger, Buddenbrooks, *and* Doctor Faustus. *"Mario and the Magician" is his fictional exploration of the dynamics of fascism in Mussolini's Italy.*

MARIO AND
THE MAGICIAN

The atmosphere of Torre di Venere remains unpleasant in the memory. From the first moment the air of the place made us uneasy, we felt irritable, on edge; then at the end came the shocking business of Cipolla, that dreadful being who seemed to incorporate, in so fateful and so humanly impressive a way, all the peculiar evilness of the situation as a whole. Looking back, we had the feeling that the horrible end of the affair had been preordained and lay in the nature of things; that the children had to be present at it was an added impropriety, due to the false colours in which the weird creature presented himself. Luckily for them, they did not know where the comedy left off and the tragedy began; and we let them remain in their happy belief that the whole thing had been a play up till the end.

Torre di Venere lies some fifteen kilometres from Portocle-

mente, one of the most popular summer resorts on the Tyr-
rhenian Sea. Portoclemente is urban and elegant and full to
overflowing for months on end. Its gay and busy main street
of shops and hotels runs down to a wide sandy beach covered
with tents and pennanted sand-castles and sunburnt humanity, where at all times a lively social bustle reigns, and much
noise. But this same spacious and inviting fine-sanded beach,
this same border of pine grove and near, presiding mountains, continues all the way along the coast. No wonder then
that some competition of a quiet kind should have sprung up
further on. Torre di Venere—the tower that gave the town its
name is gone long since, one looks for it in vain—is an off-
shoot of the larger resort, and for some years remained an
idyll for the few, a refuge for more unworldly spirits. But the
usual history of such places repeated itself: peace has had to
retire further along the coast, to Marina Petriera and dear
knows where else. We all know how the world at once seeks
peace and puts her to flight—rushing upon her in the fond
idea that they two will wed, and where she is, there it can be
at home. It will even set up its Vanity Fair in a spot and be
capable of thinking that peace is still by its side. Thus Torre—
though its atmosphere so far is more modest and contempla-
tive than that of Portoclemente—has been quite taken up, by
both Italians and foreigners. It is no longer the thing to go to
Portoclemente—though still so much the thing that it is as
noisy and crowded as ever. One goes next door, so to speak:
to Torre. So much more refined, even, and cheaper to boot.
And the attractiveness of these qualities persists, though the
qualities themselves long ago ceased to be evident. Torre has
got a Grand Hotel. Numerous pensions have sprung up, some
modest, some pretentious. The people who own or rent the
villas and pinetas overlooking the sea no longer have it all
their own way on the beach. In July and August it looks just
like the beach at Portoclemente: it swarms with a screaming,
squabbling, merrymaking crowd, and the sun, blazing down
like mad, peels the skin off their necks. Garish little flat-
bottomed boats rock on the glittering blue, manned by chil-

dren, whose mothers hover afar and fill the air with anxious cries of Nino! and Sandro! and Bice! and Maria! Pedlars step across the legs of recumbent sun-bathers, selling flowers and corals, oysters, lemonade, and *cornetti al burro,* and crying their wares in the breathy, full-throated southern voice.

Such was the scene that greeted our arrival in Torre: pleasant enough, but after all, we thought, we had come too soon. It was the middle of August, the Italian season was still at its height, scarcely the moment for strangers to learn to love the special charms of the place. What an afternoon crowd in the cafés on the front! For instance, in the Esquisito, where we sometimes sat and were served by Mario, that very Mario of whom I shall have presently to tell. It is well-nigh impossible to find a table; and the various orchestras contend together in the midst of one's conversation with bewildering effect. Of course, it is in the afternoon that people come over from Portoclemente. The excursion is a favourite one for the restless denizens of that pleasure resort, and a Fiat motor-bus plies to and fro, coating inch-thick with dust the oleander and laurel hedges along the highroad—a notable if repulsive sight.

Yes, decidedly one should go to Torre in September, when the great public has left. Or else in May, before the water is warm enough to tempt the Southerner to bathe. Even in the before and after seasons Torre is not empty, but life is less national and more subdued. English, French, and German prevail under the tent-awnings and in the pension dining-rooms; whereas in August—in the Grand Hotel, at least, where, in default of private addresses, we had engaged rooms —the stranger finds the field so occupied by Florentine and Roman society that he feels quite isolated and even temporarily *déclassé.*

We had, rather to our annoyance, this experience on the evening we arrived, when we went in to dinner and were shown to our table by the waiter in charge. As a table, it had nothing against it, save that we had already fixed our eyes upon those on the veranda beyond, built out over the water, where little red-shaded lamps glowed—and there were still some tables empty, though it was as full as the dining-room within. The children went into raptures at the festive sight, and without more ado we announced our intention to take our meals by preference in the veranda. Our words, it appeared, were prompted by ignorance; for we were informed, with somewhat embarrassed politeness, that the cosy nook outside was reserved for the clients of the hotel: *ai nostri clienti*. Their clients? But we were their clients. We were not tourists or trippers, but boarders for a stay of some three or four weeks. However, we forbore to press for an explanation of the difference between the likes of us and that clientèle to whom it was vouchsafed to eat out there in the glow of the red lamps, and took our dinner by the prosaic common light of the dining-room chandelier—a thoroughly ordinary and monotonous hotel bill of fare, be it said. In Pensione Eleonora, a few steps landward, the table, as we were to discover, was much better.

And thither it was that we moved, three or four days later, before we had had time to settle in properly at the Grand Hotel. Not on account of the veranda and the lamps. The children, straightway on the best of terms with waiters and pages, absorbed in the joys of life on the beach, promptly forgot those colourful seductions. But now there arose, between ourselves and the veranda clientèle—or perhaps more correctly with the compliant management—one of those little unpleasantnesses which can quite spoil the pleasure of a holiday. Among the guests were some high Roman aristocracy, a Principe X and his family. These grand folk occupied rooms close to our own, and the Principessa, a great and a passionately maternal lady, was thrown into a panic by the vestiges of a whooping-cough which our little ones had lately got over, but which now and then still faintly troubled the unshatterable slumbers of our youngest-born. The nature of this illness is not clear, leaving some play for the imagination. So we took no offence at our elegant neighbour for clinging to the widely held view that whooping-cough is acoustically contagious and quite simply fearing lest her children yield to the bad example set by ours. In the fullness of her feminine self-confidence she protested to the management, which then, in the person of the proverbial frock-coated manager, hastened to represent to us, with many expressions of regret, that under the circumstances they were obliged to transfer us to the annexe. We did our best to assure him that the disease was in its very last stages, that it was actually over, and presented no danger of infection to anybody. All that we gained was permission to bring the case before the hotel physician—not one chosen by us—by whose verdict we must then abide. We agreed, convinced that thus we should at once pacify the Princess and escape the trouble of moving. The doctor appeared, and behaved like a faithful and honest servant of science. He examined the child and gave his opinion: the disease was quite over, no danger of contagion was present. We drew a long breath and considered the incident closed—until the manager announced that despite the doctor's verdict it would still be necessary for us to give up our rooms and retire to the *dépendance*. Byzantinism like this outraged us. It is not likely that the Principessa was responsible for the wilful breach of faith. Very likely the fawning management had not even dared to tell her what the physician said. Anyhow, we made it clear to his understanding that we preferred to leave the hotel altogether and at once—and packed our trunks. We could do so with a light heart, having already set up casual friendly relations with Casa Eleonora. We had noticed its pleasant exterior and formed the acquaintance of its proprietor, Signora Angiolieri, and her husband: she slender and black-haired, Tuscan in type, probably at the beginning of the thirties, with the dead ivory complexion of the southern woman, he quiet and bald and carefully dressed. They owned a larger establishment in Florence and presided only in summer and early autumn over the branch in Torre di Venere. But earlier, before her marriage, our new landlady had been companion, fellow-traveller, wardrobe mistress, yes, friend, of Eleonora Duse and manifestly regarded that period as the crown of her career. Even at our first visit she spoke of it with animation. Numerous photographs of the great actress, with affectionate inscriptions, were displayed about the drawing-room, and other souvenirs of their life together adorned the little tables and étagères. This cult of a so interesting past was calculated, of course, to heighten the advantages of the signora's present business. Nevertheless our pleasure and interest were quite genuine as we were conducted through the house by its owner and listened to her sonorous and staccato Tuscan voice relating anecdotes of that immortal mistress, depicting her suffering saintliness, her genius, her profound delicacy of feeling.

Thither, then, we moved our effects, to the dismay of the staff of the Grand Hotel, who, like all Italians, were very good to children. Our new quarters were retired and pleasant, we were within easy reach of the sea through the avenue of young plane trees that ran down to the esplanade. In the clean, cool dining-room Signora Angiolieri daily served the soup with her own hands, the service was attentive and good, the table capital. We even discovered some Viennese acquaintances, and enjoyed chatting with them after luncheon, in front of the house. They, in their turn, were the means of our finding others—in short, all seemed for the best, and we were heartily glad of the change we had made. Nothing was now wanting to a holiday of the most gratifying kind.

And yet no proper gratification ensued. Perhaps the stupid occasion of our change of quarters pursued us to the new ones we had found. Personally, I admit that I do not easily forget these collisions with ordinary humanity, the naïve misuse of power, the injustice, the sycophantic corruption. I dwelt upon the incident too much, it irritated me in retrospect—quite futilely, of course, since such phenomena are only all too natural and all too much the rule. And we had not broken off relations with the Grand Hotel. The children were as friendly as ever there, the porter mended their toys, and we sometimes took tea in the garden. We even saw the Principessa. She would come out, with her firm and delicate tread, her lips emphatically corallined, to look after her children, playing under the supervision of their English governess. She did not dream that we were anywhere near, for so soon as she appeared in the offing we sternly forbade our little one even to clear his throat.

The heat—if I may bring it in evidence—was extreme. It was African. The power of the sun, directly one left the border of the indigo-blue wave, was so frightful, so relentless, that the mere thought of the few steps between the beach and luncheon was a burden, clad though one might be only in pyjamas. Do you care for that sort of thing? Weeks on end? Yes, of course, it is proper to the south, it is classic weather, the sun of Homer, the climate wherein human culture came to flower—and all the rest of it. But after a while it is too much for me, I reach a point where I begin to find it dull. The burning void of the sky, day after day, weighs one down; the high coloration, the enormous naïveté of the unrefracted light—they do, I dare say, induce light-heartedness, a carefree mood born of immunity from downpours and other meteorological caprices. But slowly, slowly, there makes itself felt a lack: the deeper, more complex needs of the northern soul remain unsatisfied. You are left barren—even it may be, in time, a little contemptuous. True without that stupid business of the whooping-cough I might not have been feeling these things. I was annoyed, very likely I wanted to feel them and so half-unconsciously seized upon an idea lying ready to hand to induce, or if not to induce, at least to justify and strengthen, my attitude. Up to this point, then, if you like, let us grant some ill will on our part. But the sea; and the mornings spent extended upon the fine sand in face of its eternal splendours—no, the sea could not conceivably induce such feelings. Yet it was none the less true that, despite all previous experience, we were not at home on the beach, we were not happy.

It was too soon, too soon. The beach, as I have said, was still in the hands of the middle-class native. It is a pleasing breed to look at, and among the young we saw much shapeliness and charm. Still, we were necessarily surrounded by a great deal of very average humanity—a middle-class mob, which, you will admit, is not more charming under this sun than under one's own native sky. The voices these women have! It was sometimes hard to believe that we were in the land which is the western cradle of the art of song. *"Fuggièro!"* I can still hear that cry, as for twenty mornings long I heard it close behind me, breathy, full-throated, hideously stressed, with a harsh open *e,* uttered in accents of mechanical despair. *"Fuggièro! Rispondi almeno!"* Answer when I call you! The *sp* in *rispondi* was pronounced like *shp,* as Germans pronounce it; and this, on top of what I felt already, vexed my sensitive soul. The cry was addressed to a repulsive youngster whose sunburn had made disgusting raw sores on his shoulders. He outdid anything I have ever seen for ill-breeding, refractoriness, and temper and was a great coward to boot, putting the whole beach in an uproar, one day, because of his outrageous sensitiveness to the slightest pain. A sand-crab had pinched his toe in the water, and the minute injury made him set up a cry of heroic proportions—the shout of an antique hero in his agony—that pierced one to the marrow and called up visions of some frightful tragedy. Evidently he considered himself not only wounded, but poisoned as well; he crawled out on the sand and lay in apparently intolerable anguish, groaning *"Ohi!"* and *"Ohimè!"* and threshing about with arms and legs to ward off his mother's tragic appeals and the questions of the bystanders. An audience gathered round. A doctor was fetched—the same who had pronounced objective judgment on our whooping-cough—and here again acquitted himself like a man of science. Good-naturedly he reassured the boy, telling him that he was not hurt at all, he should simply go into the water again to relieve the smart. Instead of which, Fuggièro was borne off the beach, followed by a concourse of people. But he did not fail to appear next morning, nor did he leave off spoiling our children's sandcastles. Of course, always by accident. In short, a perfect terror.

And this twelve-year-old lad was prominent among the influences that, imperceptibly at first, combined to spoil our holiday and render it unwholesome. Somehow or other, there was a stiffness, a lack of innocent enjoyment. These people stood on their dignity—just why, and in what spirit, it was not easy at first to tell. They displayed much self-respectingness; towards each other and towards the foreigner their bearing was that of a person newly conscious of a sense of honour. And wherefore? Gradually we realized the political implications and understood that we were in the presence of a national ideal. The beach, in fact, was alive with patriotic children—a phenomenon as unnatural as it was depressing. Children are a human species and a society apart, a nation of their own, so to speak. On the basis of their common form of life, they find each other out with the greatest ease, no matter how different their small vocabularies. Ours soon played with natives and foreigners alike. Yet they were plainly both puzzled and disappointed at times. There were wounded sensibilities, displays of assertiveness—or rather hardly assertiveness, for it was too self-conscious and too didactic to deserve the name. There were quarrels over flags, disputes about authority and precedence. Grownups joined in, not so much to pacify as to render judgment and enunciate principles. Phrases were dropped about the greatness and dignity of Italy, solemn phrases that spoilt the fun. We saw our two little ones retreat, puzzled and hurt, and were put to it to explain the situation. These people, we told them, were just passing through a certain stage, something rather like an illness, perhaps; not very pleasant, but probably unavoidable.

We had only our own carelessness to thank that we came to blows in the end with this "stage"—which, after all, we had seen and sized up long before now. Yes, it came to another "cross-purposes," so evidently the earlier ones had not been sheer accident. In a word, we became an offence to the public morals. Our small daughter—eight years old, but in physical development a good year younger and thin as a chicken—had had a good long bathe and gone playing in the warm sun in her wet costume. We told her that she might take off her bathing-suit, which was stiff with sand, rinse it in the sea, and put it on again, after which she must take care to keep it cleaner. Off goes the costume and she runs down naked to the sea, rinses her little jersey, and comes back. Ought we to have foreseen the outburst of anger and resentment which her conduct, and thus our conduct, called forth? Without delivering a homily on the subject, I may say that in the last decade our attitude towards the nude body and our feelings regarding it have undergone, all over the world, a fundamental change. There are things we "never think about" any more, and among them is the freedom we had permitted to this by no means provocative little childish body. But in these parts it was taken as a challenge. The patriotic children hooted. Fuggièro whistled on his fingers. The sudden buzz of conversation among the grown people in our neighbourhood boded no good. A gentleman in city togs, with a not very apropos bowler hat on the back of his head, was assuring his outraged womenfolk that he proposed to take punitive measures; he stepped up to us, and a philippic descended on our unworthy heads, in which all the emotionalism of the sense-loving south spoke in the service of morality and discipline. The offence against decency of which we had been guilty was, he said, the more to be condemned because it was also a gross ingratitude and an insulting breach of his country's hospitality. We had criminally injured not only the letter and spirit of the public bathing regulations, but also the honour of Italy; he, the gentleman in the city togs, knew how to defend that honour and proposed to see to it that our offence against the national dignity should not go unpunished.

We did our best, bowing respectfully, to give ear to this eloquence. To contradict the man, overheated as he was, would probably be to fall from one error into another. On the tips of our tongues we had various answers: as, that the word "hospitality," in its strictest sense, was not quite the right one, taking all the circumstances into consideration. We were not literally the guests of Italy, but of Signora Angiolieri, who had assumed the rôle of dispenser of hospitality some years ago on laying down that of familiar friend to Eleonora Duse. We longed to say that surely this beautiful country had not sunk so low as to be reduced to a state of hypersensitive prudishness. But we confined ourselves to assuring the gentleman that any lack of respect, any provocation on our parts, had been the furthest from our thoughts. And as a mitigating circumstance we pointed out the tender age and physical slightness of the little culprit. In vain. Our protests were waved away, he did not believe in them; our defence would not hold water. We must be made an example of. The authorities were notified, by telephone, I believe, and their representatives appeared on the beach. He said the case was *"molto grave."* We had to go with him to the Municipio up in the Piazza, where a higher official confirmed the previous verdict of *"molto grave,"* launched into a stream of the usual didactic phrases—the selfsame tune and words as the man in the bowler hat—and levied a fine and ransom of fifty lire. We felt that the adventure must willy-nilly be worth to us this much of a contribution to the economy of the Italian government; paid, and left. Ought we not at this point to have left Torre as well?

If we only had! We should thus have escaped that fatal Cipolla. But circumstances combined to prevent us from making up our minds to a change. A certain poet says that it is indolence that makes us endure uncomfortable situations. The *aperçu* may serve as an explanation for our inaction. Anyhow, one dislikes voiding the field immediately upon such an event. Especially if sympathy from other quarters encourages one to defy it. And in the Villa Eleonora they pronounced as with one voice upon the injustice of our punishment. Some Italian after-dinner acquaintances found that the episode put their country in a very bad light, and proposed taking the man in the bowler hat to task, as one fellow-citizen to another. But the next day he and his party had vanished from the beach. Not on our account, of course. Though it might be that the consciousness of his impending departure had added energy to his rebuke; in any case his going was a relief. And, furthermore, we stayed because our stay had by now become remarkable in our own eyes, which is worth something in itself, quite apart from the comfort or discomfort involved. Shall we strike sail, avoid a certain experience so soon as it seems not expressly calculated to increase our enjoyment or our self-esteem? Shall we go away whenever life looks like turning in the slightest uncanny, or not quite normal, or even rather painful and mortifying? No, surely not. Rather stay and look matters in the face, brave them out; perhaps precisely in so doing lies a lesson for us to learn. We stayed on and reaped as the awful reward of our constancy the unholy and staggering experience with Cipolla.

I have not mentioned that the after season had begun, almost on the very day we were disciplined by the city authorities. The worshipful gentleman in the bowler hat, our denouncer, was not the only person to leave the resort. There was a regular exodus, on every hand you saw luggage-carts on their way to the station. The beach denationalized itself. Life in Torre, in the cafés and the pinetas, became more homelike and more European. Very likely we might even have eaten at a table in the glass veranda, but we refrained, being content at Signora Angiolieri's—as content, that is, as our evil star would let us be. But at the same time with this turn for the better came a change in the weather: almost to an hour it showed itself in harmony with the holiday calendar of the general public. The sky was overcast; not that it grew any cooler, but the unclouded heat of the entire eighteen days since our arrival, and probably long before that, gave place to a stifling sirocco air, while from time to time a little ineffectual rain sprinkled the velvety surface of the beach. Add to which, that two-thirds of our intended stay at Torre had passed. The colourless, lazy sea, with sluggish jellyfish floating in its shallows, was at least a change. And it would have been silly to feel retrospective longings after a sun that had caused us so many sighs when it burned down in all its arrogant power.

At this juncture, then, it was that Cipolla announced himself. Cavaliere Cipolla he was called on the posters that appeared one day stuck up everywhere, even in the dining-room of Pensione Eleonora. A travelling virtuoso, an entertainer, *"forzatore, illusionista, prestidigatore,"* as he called himself, who proposed to wait upon the highly respectable population of Torre di Venere with a display of extraordinary phenomena of a mysterious and staggering kind. A conjuror! The bare announcement was enough to turn our children's heads. They had never seen anything of the sort, and now our present holiday was to afford them this new excitement. From that moment on they besieged us with prayers to take tickets for the performance. We had doubts, from the first, on the score of the lateness of the hour, nine o'clock; but gave way, in the idea that we might see a little of what Cipolla had to offer, probably no great matter, and then go home. Besides, of course, the children could sleep late next day. We bought four tickets of Signora Angiolieri herself, she having taken a number of the stalls on commission to sell them to her guests. She could not vouch for the man's performance, and we had no great expectations. But we were conscious of a need for diversion, and the children's violent curiosity proved catching.

The Cavaliere's performance was to take place in a hall where during the season there had been a cinema with a weekly programme. We had never been there. You reached it by following the main street under the wall of the *"palazzo,"* a ruin with a "For sale" sign, that suggested a castle and had obviously been built in lordlier days. In the same street were the chemist, the hairdresser, and all the better shops; it led, so to speak, from the feudal past the bourgeois into the proletarian, for it ended off between two rows of poor fishing-huts, where old women sat mending nets before the doors. And here, among the proletariat, was the hall, not much more, actually than a wooden shed, though a large one, with a turreted entrance, plastered on either side with layers of gay placards. Some while after dinner, then, on the appointed evening, we wended our way thither in the dark, the children dressed in their best and blissful with the sense of so much irregularity. It was sultry, as it had been for days; there was heat lightning now and then, and a little rain; we proceeded under umbrellas. It took us a quarter of an hour.

Our tickets were collected at the entrance, our places we had to find ourselves. They were in the third row left, and as we sat down we saw that, late though the hour was for the performance, it was to be interpreted with even more laxity. Only very slowly did an audience—who seemed to be relied upon to come late—begin to fill the stalls. These comprised the whole auditorium; there were no boxes. This tardiness gave us some concern. The children's cheeks were already flushed as much with fatigue as with excitement. But even when we entered, the standing-room at the back and in the side aisles was already well occupied. There stood the manhood of Torre di Venere, all and sundry, fisherfolk, rough-and-ready youths with bare forearms crossed over their striped jerseys. We were well pleased with the presence of this native assemblage, which always adds colour and animation to occasions like the present; and the children were frankly delighted. For they had friends among these people—acquaintances picked up on afternoon strolls to the further ends of the beach. We would be turning homeward, at the hour when the sun dropped into the sea, spent with the huge effort it had made and gilding with reddish gold the oncoming surf; and we would come upon bare-legged fisherfolk standing in rows, bracing and hauling with long-drawn cries as they drew in the nets and harvested in dripping baskets their catch, often so scanty, of *frutto di mare*. The children looked on, helped to pull, brought out their little stock of Italian words, made friends. So now they exchanged nods with the "standing-room" clientèle; there was Guiscardo, there Antonio, they knew them by name and waved and called across in half-whispers, getting answering nods and smiles that displayed rows of healthy white teeth. Look, there is even Mario, Mario from the Esquisito, who brings us the chocolate. He wants to see the conjuror, too, and he must have come early, for he is almost in front; but he does not see us, he is not paying attention; that is a way he has, even though he is a waiter. So we wave instead to the man who lets out the little boats on the beach; he is there too, standing at the back.

It had got to a quarter past nine, it got to almost half past. It was natural that we should be nervous. When would the children get to bed? It had been a mistake to bring them, for now it would be very hard to suggest breaking off their enjoyment before it had got well under way. The stalls had filled in time; all Torre, apparently, was there: the guests of the Grand Hotel, the guests of Villa Eleonora, familiar faces from the beach. We heard English and German and the sort of French that Rumanians speak with Italians. Madame Angiolieri herself sat two rows behind us, with her quiet, bald-headed spouse, who kept stroking his moustache with the two middle fingers of his right hand. Everybody had come late, but nobody too late. Cipolla made us wait for him.

He made us wait. That is probably the way to put it. He heightened the suspense by his delay in appearing. And we could see the point of this, too—only not when it was carried to extremes. Towards half past nine the audience began to clap—an amiable way of expressing justifiable impatience, evincing as it does an eagerness to applaud. For the little ones, this was a joy in itself—all children love to clap. From the popular sphere came loud cries of *"Pronti!"* *"Cominciamo!"* And lo, it seemed now as easy to begin as before it had been hard. A gong sounded, greeted by the standing rows with a many-voiced "Ah-h!" and the curtains parted. They revealed a platform furnished more like a schoolroom than like the theatre of a conjuring performance —largely because of the blackboard in the left foreground. There was a common yellow hat-stand, a few ordinary straw-bottomed chairs, and further back a little round table holding a water carafe and glass, also a tray with a liqueur glass and a flask of pale yellow liquid. We had still a few seconds of time to let these things sink in. Then, with no darkening of the house, Cavaliere Cipolla made his entry.

He came forward with a rapid step that expressed his eagerness to appear before his public and gave rise to the illusion that he had already come a long way to put himself at their service—whereas, of course, he had only been standing in the wings. His costume supported the fiction. A man of an age hard to determine, but by no means young; with a sharp, ravaged face, piercing eyes, compressed lips, small black waxed moustache, and a so-called imperial in the curve between mouth and chin. He was dressed for the street with a sort of complicated evening elegance, in a wide black pelerine with velvet collar and satin lining; which, in the hampered state of his arms, he held together in front with his white-gloved hands. He had a white scarf round his neck; a top hat with a curving brim sat far back on his head. Perhaps more than anywhere else the eighteenth century is still alive in Italy, and with it the charlatan and mountebank type so characteristic of the period. Only there, at any rate, does one still encounter really well-preserved specimens. Cipolla had in his whole appearance much of the historic type; his very clothes helped to conjure up the traditional figure with its blatantly, fantastically foppish air. His pretentious costume sat upon him, or rather hung upon him, most curiously, being in one place drawn too tight, in another a mass of awkward folds. There was something not quite in order about his figure, both front and back—that was plain later on. But I must emphasize the fact that there was not a trace of personal jocularity or clownishness in his pose, manner, or behaviour. On the contrary, there was complete seriousness, an absence of any humorous appeal; occasionally even a cross-grained pride, along with that curious, self-satisfied air so characteristic of the deformed. None of all this, however, prevented his appearance from being greeted with laughter from more than one quarter of the hall.

All the eagerness had left his manner. The swift entry had been merely an expression of energy, not of zeal. Standing at the footlights he negligently drew off his gloves, to display long yellow hands, one of them adorned with a seal ring with

a lapis-lazuli in a high setting. As he stood there, his small
hard eyes, with flabby pouches beneath them, roved apprais-
ingly about the hall, not quickly, rather in a considered exam-
ination, pausing here and there upon a face with his lips
clipped together, not speaking a word. Then with a display of
skill as surprising as it was casual, he rolled his gloves into a
ball and tossed them across a considerable distance into the
glass on the table. Next from an inner pocket he drew forth a
packet of cigarettes; you could see by the wrapper that they
were the cheapest sort the government sells. With his fingertips he pulled out a cigarette and lighted it, without looking,
from a quick-firing benzine lighter. He drew the smoke deep
into his lungs and let it out again, tapping his foot, with both
lips drawn in an arrogant grimace and the grey smoke stream-
ing out between broken and saw-edged teeth.

With a keenness equal to his own his audience eyed him.
The youths at the rear scowled as they peered at this cocksure
creature to search out his secret weaknesses. He betrayed
none. In fetching out and putting back the cigarettes his
clothes got in his way. He had to turn back his pelerine, and
in so doing revealed a riding-whip with a silver claw-handle
that hung by a leather thong from his left forearm and looked
decidedly out of place. You could see that he had on not
evening clothes but a frock-coat, and under this, as he lifted it
to get at his pocket, could be seen a striped sash worn about
the body. Somebody behind me whispered that this sash went
with his title of Cavaliere. I give the information for what it
may be worth—personally, I never heard that the title carried
such insignia with it. Perhaps the sash was sheer pose, like the
way he stood there, without a word, casually and arrogantly
puffing smoke into his audience's face.

People laughed, as I said. The merriment had become almost general when somebody in the "standing seats," in a
loud, dry voice, remarked: *"Buona sera."*

Cipolla cocked his head. "Who was that?" asked he, as
though he had been dared. "Who was that just spoke? Well?
First so bold and now so modest? *Paura*, eh?" He spoke with

a rather high, asthmatic voice, which yet had a metallic quality. He waited.

"That was me," a youth at the rear broke into the stillness, seeing himself thus challenged. He was not far from us, a handsome fellow in a woollen shirt, with his coat hanging over one shoulder. He wore his surly, wiry hair in a high, dishevelled mop, the style affected by the youth of the awakened Fatherland; it gave him an African appearance that rather spoiled his looks. *"Bè!* That was me. It was your business to say it first, but I was trying to be friendly."

More laughter. The chap had a tongue in his head. *"Ha sciolto la scilinguágnolo,"* I heard near me. After all, the retort was deserved.

"Ah, bravo!" answered Cipolla. "I like you, *giovanotto.* Trust me, I've had my eye on you for some time. People like you are just in my line. I can use them. And you are the pick of the lot, that's plain to see. You do what you like. Or is it possible you have ever not done what you liked—or even, maybe, what you didn't like? What somebody else liked, in short? Hark ye, my friend, that might be a pleasant change for you, to divide up the willing and the doing and stop tackling both jobs at once. Division of labour, *sistema americano, sa!* For instance, suppose you were to show your tongue to this select and honourable audience here—your whole tongue, right down to the roots?"

"No, I won't," said the youth, hostilely. "Sticking out your tongue shows a bad bringing-up."

"Nothing of the sort," retorted Cipolla. "You would only be *doing* it. With all due respect to your bringing-up, I suggest that before I count ten, you will perform a right turn and stick out your tongue at the company here further than you knew yourself that you could stick it out."

He gazed at the youth, and his piercing eyes seemed to sink deeper into their sockets. *"Uno!"* said he. He had let his riding-whip slide down his arm and made it whistle once through the air. The boy faced about and put out his tongue, so long, so extendedly, that you could see it was the very uttermost in tongue which he had to offer. Then turned back, stony-faced, to his former position.

"That was me," mocked Cipolla, with a jerk of his head towards the youth. *"Bè!* That was me." Leaving the audience to enjoy its sensations, he turned towards the little round table, lifted the bottle, poured out a small glass of what was obviously cognac, and tipped it up with a practised hand.

The children laughed with all their hearts. They had understood practically nothing of what had been said, but it pleased them hugely that something so funny should happen, straightaway, between that queer man up there and somebody out of the audience. They had no preconception of what an "evening" would be like and were quite ready to find this a priceless beginning. As for us, we exchanged a glance and I remember that involuntarily I made with my lips the sound that Cipolla's whip had made when it cut the air. For the rest, it was plain that people did not know what to make of a preposterous beginning like this to a sleight-of-hand performance. They could not see why the *giovanotto*, who after all in a way had been their spokesman, should suddenly have turned on them to vent his incivility. They felt that he had behaved like a silly ass and withdrew their countenances from him in favour of the artist, who now came back from his refreshment table and addressed them as follows:

"Ladies and gentlemen," said he, in his wheezing, metallic voice, "you saw just now that I was rather sensitive on the score of the rebuke this hopeful young linguist saw fit to give me"—*"questo linguista di belle speranze"* was what he said, and we all laughed at the pun. "I am a man who sets some store by himself, you may take it from me. And I see no point in being wished a good-evening unless it is done courteously and in all seriousness. For anything else there is no occasion. When a man wishes me a good-evening he wishes himself one, for the audience will have one only if I do. So this ladykiller of Torre di Venere" (another thrust) "did well to testify that I have one tonight and that I can dispense with any wishes of his in the matter. I can boast of having good evenings almost without exception. One not so good does come my way now and again, but very seldom. My calling is hard and my health not of the best. I have a little physical defect which prevented me from doing my bit in the war for the greater glory of the Fatherland. It is perforce with my mental and spiritual parts that I conquer life—which after all only means conquering oneself. And I flatter myself that my achievements have aroused interest and respect among the educated public. The leading newspapers have lauded me, the *Corriere della Sera* did me the courtesy of calling me a phenomenon, and in Rome the brother of the *Duce* honoured me by his presence at one of my evenings. I should not have thought that in a relatively less important place" (laughter here, at the expense of poor little Torre) "I should have to give up the small personal habits which brilliant and elevated audiences had been ready to overlook. Nor did I think I had to stand being heckled by a person who seems to have been rather spoilt by the favours of the fair sex." All this of course at the expense of the youth whom Cipolla never tired of presenting in the guise of *donnaiuolo* and rustic Don Juan. His persistent thin-skinnedness and animosity were in striking contrast to the self-confidence and the worldly success he boasted of. One might have assumed that the *giovanotto* was merely the chosen butt of Cipolla's customary professional sallies, had not the very pointed witticisms betrayed a genuine antagonism. No one looking at the physical parts of the two men need have been at a loss for the explanation, even if the deformed man had not constantly played on the other's supposed success with the fair sex. "Well," Cipolla went on, "before beginning our entertainment this evening, perhaps you will permit me to make myself comfortable."

And he went towards the hat-stand to take off his things.

"Parla benissimo," asserted somebody in our neighbourhood. So far, the man had done nothing; but what he had said was accepted as an achievement, by means of that he had made an impression. Among southern peoples speech is a constituent part of the pleasure of living, it enjoys far livelier

social esteem than in the north. That national cement, the mother tongue, is paid symbolic honours down here, and there is something blithely symbolical in the pleasure people take in their respect for its forms and phonetics. They enjoy speaking, they enjoy listening; and they listen with discrimination. For the way a man speaks serves as a measure of his personal rank; carelessness and clumsiness are greeted with scorn, elegance and mastery are rewarded with social éclat. Wherefore the small man too, where it is a question of getting his effect, chooses his phrase nicely and turns it with care. On this count, then, at least, Cipolla had won his audience; though he by no means belonged to the class of men which the Italian, in a singular mixture of moral and aesthetic judgments, labels *"simpatico."*

After removing his hat, scarf, and mantle he came to the front of the stage, settling his coat, pulling down his cuffs with their large cuff-buttons, adjusting his absurd sash. He had very ugly hair; the top of his head, that is, was almost bald, while a narrow, black-varnished frizz of curls ran from front to back as though stuck on; the side hair, likewise blackened, was brushed forward to the corners of the eyes—it was, in short, the hairdressing of an old-fashioned circus-director, fantastic, but entirely suited to his outmoded personal type and worn with so much assurance as to take the edge off the public's sense of humour. The little physical defect of which he had warned us was now all too visible, though the nature of it was even now not very clear; the chest was too high, as is usual in such cases, but the corresponding malformation of the back did not sit between the shoulders, it took the form of a sort of hips or buttocks hump, which did not indeed hinder his movements but gave him a grotesque and dipping stride at every step he took. However, by mentioning his deformity beforehand he had broken the shock of it, and a delicate propriety of feeling appeared to reign throughout the hall.

"At your service," said Cipolla. "With your kind permission, we will begin the evening with some arithmetical tests."

Arithmetic? That did not sound much like sleight-of-hand.

We began to have our suspicions that the man was sailing under a false flag, only we did not yet know which was the right one. I felt sorry on the children's account; but for the moment they were content simply to be there.

The numerical test which Cipolla now introduced was as simple as it was baffling. He began by fastening a piece of paper to the upper right-hand corner of the blackboard; then lifting it up, he wrote something underneath. He talked all the while, relieving the dryness of his offering by a constant flow of words, and showed himself a practised speaker, never at a loss for conversational turns of phrase. It was in keeping with the nature of his performance, and at the same time vastly entertained the children, that he went on to eliminate the gap between stage and audience, which had already been bridged over by the curious skirmish with the fisher lad; he had representatives from the audience mount the stage, and himself descended the wooden steps to seek personal contact with his public. And again, with individuals, he fell into his former taunting tone. I do not know how far that was a deliberate feature of his system; he preserved a serious, even a peevish air, but his audience, at least the more popular section, seemed convinced that that was all part of the game. So then, after he had written something and covered the writing by the paper, he desired that two persons should come up on the platform and help to perform the calculations. They would not be difficult, even for people not clever at figures. As usual, nobody volunteered, and Cipolla took care not to molest the more select portion of his audience. He kept to the populace. Turning to two sturdy young louts standing behind us, he beckoned them to the front, encouraging and scolding by turns. They should not stand there gaping, he said, unwilling to oblige the company. Actually he got them in motion; with clumsy tread they came down the middle aisle, climbed the steps, and stood in front of the blackboard, grinning sheepishly at their comrades' shouts and applause. Cipolla joked with them for a few minutes, praised their heroic firmness of limb and the size of their hands, so well calculated to do this service for the public. Then he handed one of them the chalk and told him to write down the numbers as they were called out. But now the creature declared that he could not write! *"Non so scrivere,"* said he in his gruff voice, and his companion added that neither did he.

God knows whether they told the truth or whether they wanted to make game of Cipolla. Anyhow, the latter was far from sharing the general merriment which their confession aroused. He was insulted and disgusted. He sat there on a straw-bottomed chair in the centre of the stage with his legs crossed, smoking a fresh cigarette out of his cheap packet; obviously it tasted the better for the cognac he had indulged in while the yokels were stumping up the steps. Again he inhaled the smoke and let it stream out between curling lips. Swinging his leg, with his gaze sternly averted from the two shamelessly chuckling creatures and from the audience as well, he stared into space as one who withdraws himself and his dignity from the contemplation of an utterly despicable phenomenon.

"Scandalous," said he, in a sort of icy snarl. "Go back to your places! In Italy everybody can write—in all her greatness there is no room for ignorance and unenlightenment. To accuse her of them, in the hearing of this international company, is a cheap joke, in which you yourselves cut a very poor figure and humiliate the government and the whole country as well. If it is true that Torre di Venere is indeed the last refuge of such ignorance, then I must blush to have visited the place—being, as I already was, aware of its inferiority to Rome in more than one respect—"

Here Cipolla was interrupted by the youth with the Nubian coiffure and his jacket across his shoulder. His fighting spirit, as we now saw, had only abdicated temporarily, and he now flung himself into the breach in defence of his native heath. "That will do," said he loudly. "That's enough jokes about Torre. We all come from the place and we won't stand strangers making fun of it. These two chaps are our friends. Maybe they are no scholars, but even so they may be straighter than some folks in the room who are so free with their boasts about Rome, though they did not build it either."

That was capital. The young man had certainly cut his eye-teeth. And this sort of spectacle was good fun, even though it still further delayed the regular performance. It is always fascinating to listen to an altercation. Some people it simply amuses, they take a sort of kill-joy pleasure in not being principals. Others feel upset and uneasy, and my sympathies are with these latter, although on the present occasion I was under the impression that all this was part of the show—the analphabetic yokels no less than the *giovanotto* with the jacket. The children listened well pleased. They understood not at all, but the sound of the voices made them hold their breath. So this was a "magic evening"—at least it was the kind they have in Italy. They expressly found it "lovely." Cipolla had stood up and with two of his scooping strides was at the footlights.

"Well, well, see who's here!" said he with grim cordiality. "An old acquaintance! A young man with his heart at the end of his tongue" (he used the word *linguaccia*, which means a coated tongue, and gave rise to much hilarity). "That will do, my friends," he turned to the yokels. "I do not need you now, I have business with this deserving young man here, *con questo torregiano di Venere,* this tower of Venus, who no doubt expects the gratitude of the fair as a reward for his prowess—"

"Ah, non scherziamo! We're talking earnest," cried out the youth. His eyes flashed, and he actually made as though to pull off his jacket and proceed to direct methods of settlement.

Cipolla did not take him too seriously. We had exchanged apprehensive glances; but he was dealing with a fellow-countryman and had his native soil beneath his feet. He kept quite cool and showed complete mastery of the situation. He looked at his audience, smiled, and made a sideways motion of the head towards the young cockerel as though calling the public to witness how the man's bumptiousness only served to betray the simplicity of his mind. And then, for the second time, something strange happened, which set Cipolla's calm superiority in an uncanny light, and in some mysterious and irritating way turned all the explosiveness latent in the air into matter for laughter.

Cipolla drew still nearer to the fellow, looking him in the eye with a peculiar gaze. He even came half-way down the steps that led into the auditorium on our left, so that he stood directly in front of the trouble-maker, on slightly higher ground. The riding-whip hung from his arm.

"My son, you do not feel much like joking," he said. "It is only too natural, for anyone can see that you are not feeling too well. Even your tongue, which leaves something to be desired on the score of cleanliness, indicates acute disorder of the gastric system. An evening entertainment is no place for people in your state; you yourself, I can tell, were of several minds whether you would not do better to put on a flannel bandage and go to bed. It was not good judgment to drink so much of that very sour white wine this afternoon. Now you have such a colic you would like to double up with the pain. Go ahead, don't be embarrassed. There is a distinct relief that comes from bending over, in cases of intestinal cramp."

He spoke thus, word for word, with quiet impressiveness and a kind of stern sympathy, and his eyes, plunged the while deep in the young man's, seemed to grow very tired and at the same time burning above their enlarged tearducts—they were the strangest eyes, you could tell that not manly pride alone was preventing the young adversary from withdrawing his gaze. And presently, indeed, all trace of its former arrogance was gone from the bronzed young face. He looked open-mouthed at the Cavaliere and the open mouth was drawn in a rueful smile.

"Double over," repeated Cipolla. "What else can you do? With a colic like that you *must* bend. Surely you will not struggle against the performance of a perfectly natural action just because somebody suggests it to you?"

Slowly the youth lifted his forearms, folded and squeezed

them across his body; it turned a little sideways, then bent, lower and lower, the feet shifted, the knees turned inward, until he had become a picture of writhing pain, until he all but grovelled upon the ground. Cipolla let him stand for some seconds thus, then made a short cut through the air with his whip and went with his scooping stride back to the little table, where he poured himself out a cognac.

"Il boit beaucoup," asserted a lady behind us. Was that the only thing that struck her? We could not tell how far the audience grasped the situation. The fellow was standing upright again, with a sheepish grin—he looked as though he scarcely knew how it had all happened. The scene had been followed with tense interest and applauded at the end; there were shouts of *"Bravo, Cipolla!"* and *"Bravo, giovanotto!"* Apparently the issue of the duel was not looked upon as a personal defeat for the young man. Rather the audience encouraged him as one does an actor who succeeds in an unsympathetic rôle. Certainly his way of screwing himself up with cramp had been highly picturesque, its appeal was directly calculated to impress the gallery—in short, a fine dramatic performance. But I am not sure how far the audience were moved by that natural tactfulness in which the south excels, or how far it penetrated into the nature of what was going on.

The Cavaliere, refreshed, had lighted another cigarette. The numerical tests might now proceed. A young man was easily found in the back row who was willing to write down on the blackboard the numbers as they were dictated to him. Him too we knew; the whole entertainment had taken on an intimate character through our acquaintance with so many of the actors. This was the man who worked at the greengrocer's in the main street; he had served us several times, with neatness and dispatch. He wielded the chalk with clerkly confidence, while Cipolla descended to our level and walked with his deformed gait through the audience, collecting numbers as they were given, in two, three, and four places, and calling them out to the grocer's assistant, who wrote them down in a column. In all this, everything on both sides was calculated to amuse, with its jokes and its oratorical asides. The artist could not fail to hit on foreigners, who were not ready with their figures, and with them he was elaborately patient and chivalrous, to the great amusement of the natives, whom he reduced to confusion in their turn, by making them translate numbers that were given in English or French. Some people gave dates concerned with great events in Italian history. Cipolla took them up at once and made patriotic comments. Somebody shouted "Number one!" The Cavaliere, incensed at this as at every attempt to make game of him, retorted over his shoulder that he could not take less than two-place figures. Whereupon another joker cried out "Number two!" and was greeted with the applause and laughter which every reference to natural functions is sure to win among southerners.

When fifteen numbers stood in a long straggling row on the board, Cipolla called for a general adding-match. Ready reckoners might add in their heads, but pencil and paper were not forbidden. Cipolla, while the work went on, sat on his chair near the blackboard, smoked and grimaced, with the complacent, pompous air cripples so often have. The five-place addition was soon done. Somebody announced the answer, somebody else confirmed it, a third had arrived at a slightly different result, but the fourth agreed with the first and second. Cipolla got up, tapped some ash from his coat, and lifted the paper at the upper right-hand corner of the board to display the writing. The correct answer, a sum close on a million, stood there; he had written it down beforehand.

Astonishment, and loud applause. The children were overwhelmed. How had he done that, they wanted to know. We told them it was a trick, not easily explainable offhand. In short, the man was a conjuror. This was what a sleight-of-hand evening was like, so now they knew. First the fisherman had cramp, and then the right answer was written down beforehand—it was all simply glorious, and we saw with dismay that despite the hot eyes and the hand of the clock at almost half past ten, it would be very hard to get them away. There would be tears. And yet it was plain that this magician did not "magick"—at least not in the accepted sense, of manual dexterity—and that the entertainment was not at all suitable for children. Again, I do not know, either, what the audience really thought. Obviously there was grave doubt whether its answers had been given of "free choice"; here and there an individual might have answered of his own motion, but on the whole Cipolla certainly selected his people and thus kept the whole procedure in his own hands and directed it towards the given result. Even so, one had to admire the quickness of his calculations, however much one felt disinclined to admire anything else about the performance. Then his patriotism, his irritable sense of dignity—the Cavaliere's own countrymen might feel in their element with all that and continue in a laughing mood; but the combination certainly gave us outsiders food for thought.

Cipolla himself saw to it—though without giving them a name—that the nature of his powers should be clear beyond a doubt to even the least-instructed person. He alluded to them, of course, in his talk—and he talked without stopping —but only in vague, boastful, self-advertising phrases. He went on awhile with experiments on the same lines as the first, merely making them more complicated by introducing operations in multiplying, subtracting, and dividing; then he simplified them to the last degree in order to bring out the method. He simply had numbers "guessed" which were previously written under the paper; and the guess was nearly always right. One guesser admitted that he had had in mind to give a certain number, when Cipolla's whip went whistling through the air, and a quite different one slipped out, which proved to be the "right" one. Cipolla's shoulders shook. He pretended admiration for the powers of the people he questioned. But in all his compliments there was something fleering and derogatory; the victims could scarcely have relished them much, although they smiled, and although they might easily have set down some part of the applause to their own credit. Moreover, I had not the impression that the artist was popular with his public. A certain ill will and reluctance were in the air, but courtesy kept such feelings in check, as did Cipolla's competency and his stern self-confidence. Even the riding-whip, I think, did much to keep rebellion from becoming overt.

From tricks with numbers he passed to tricks with cards. There were two packs, which he drew out of his pockets, and so much I still remember, that the basis of the tricks he played with them was as follows: from the first pack he drew three cards and thrust them without looking at them inside his coat. Another person then drew three out of the second pack, and these turned out to be the same as the first three—not invariably all the three, for it did happen that only two were the same. But in the majority of cases Cipolla triumphed, showing his three cards with a little bow in acknowledgment of the applause with which his audience conceded his possession of strange powers—strange whether for good or evil. A young man in the front row, to our right, an Italian, with proud, finely chiselled features, rose up and said that he intended to assert his own will in his choice and consciously to resist any influence, of whatever sort. Under these circumstances, what did Cipolla think would be the result? "You will," answered the Cavaliere, "make my task somewhat more difficult thereby. As for the result, your resistance will not alter it in the least. Freedom exists, and also the will exists; but freedom of the will does not exist, for a will that aims at its own freedom aims at the unknown. You are free to draw or not to draw. But if you draw, you will draw the right cards—the more certainly, the more wilfully obstinate your behaviour."

One must admit that he could not have chosen his words better, to trouble the waters and confuse the mind. The refractory youth hesitated before drawing. Then he pulled out a card and at once demanded to see if it was among the chosen three. "But why?" queried Cipolla. "Why do things by halves?" Then, as the other defiantly insisted, *"E servito,"* said the juggler, with a gesture of exaggerated servility; and held out the three cards fanwise, without looking at them himself. The left-hand card was the one drawn.

Amid general applause, the apostle of freedom sat down. How far Cipolla employed small tricks and manual dexterity to help out his natural talents, the deuce only knew. But even without them the result would have been the same: the curiosity of the entire audience was unbounded and universal, everybody both enjoyed the amazing character of the entertainment and unanimously conceded the professional skill of the performer. *"Lavora bene,"* we heard, here and there in our neighbourhood; it signified the triumph of objective judgment over antipathy and repressed resentment.

After his last, incomplete, yet so much the more telling success, Cipolla had at once fortified himself with another cognac. Truly he did "drink a lot," and the fact made a bad impression. But obviously he needed the liquor and the cigarettes for the replenishment of his energy, upon which, as he himself said, heavy demands were made in all directions. Certainly in the intervals he looked very ill, exhausted and hollow-eyed. Then the little glassful would redress the balance, and the flow of lively, self-confident chatter run on, while the smoke he inhaled gushed out grey from his lungs. I clearly recall that he passed from the card-tricks to parlour games— the kind based on certain powers which in human nature are higher or else lower than human reason: on intuition and "magnetic" transmission; in short, upon a low type of manifestation. What I do not remember is the precise order things came in. And I will not bore you with a description of these experiments; everybody knows them, everybody has at one time or another taken part in this finding of hidden articles, this blind carrying out of a series of acts, directed by a force that proceeds from organism to organism by unexplored paths. Everybody has had his little glimpse into the equivocal, impure, inexplicable nature of the occult, has been conscious of both curiosity and contempt, has shaken his head over the human tendency of those who deal in it to help themselves out with humbuggery, though, after all, the humbuggery is no disproof whatever of the genuineness of the other elements in the dubious amalgam. I can only say here that each single circumstance gains in weight and the whole greatly in impressiveness when it is a man like Cipolla who is the chief actor and guiding spirit in the sinister business. He sat smoking at the rear of the stage, his back to the audience while they conferred. The object passed from hand to hand which it was his task to find, with which he was to perform some action agreed upon beforehand. Then he would start to move zigzag through the hall, with his head thrown back and one hand outstretched, the other clasped in that of a guide who was in the secret but enjoined to keep himself perfectly passive, with his thoughts directed upon the agreed goal. Cipolla moved with the bearing typical in these experiments: now groping upon a false start, now with a quick forward thrust, now pausing as though to listen and by sudden inspiration correcting his course. The rôles seemed reversed, the stream of influence was moving in the contrary direction, as the artist himself pointed out, in his ceaseless flow of discourse. The suffering, receptive, performing part was now his, the will he had before imposed on others was shut out, he acted in obedience to a voiceless common will which was in the air. But he made it perfectly clear that it all came to the same thing. The capacity for self-surrender, he said, for becoming a tool, for the most unconditional and utter self-abnegation, was but the reverse side of that other power to will and to command. Commanding and obeying formed together one single principle, one indissoluble unity; he who knew how to obey knew also how to command, and conversely; the one idea was comprehended in the other, as people and leader were comprehended in one another. But that which was *done,* the highly exacting and exhausting performance, was in every case his, the leader's and mover's, in whom the will became obedience, the obedience will, whose person was the cradle and womb of both, and who thus suffered enormous hardship. Repeatedly he emphasized the fact that his lot was a hard one—presumably to account for his need of stimulant and his frequent recourse to the little glass.

Thus he groped his way forward, like a blind seer, led and sustained by the mysterious common will. He drew a pin set with a stone out of its hiding-place in an English-woman's shoe, carried it, halting and pressing on by turns, to another lady—Signora Angiolieri—and handed it to her on bended knee, with the words it had been agreed he was to utter. "I present you with this in token of my respect," was the sentence. Their sense was obvious, but the words themselves not easy to hit upon, for the reason that they had been agreed on in French; the language complication seemed to us a little malicious, implying as it did a conflict between the audience's natural interest in the success of the miracle, and their desire to witness the humiliation of this presumptuous man. It was a strange sight: Cipolla on his knees before the signora, wrestling, amid efforts at speech, after knowledge of the pre-ordained words. "I must say something," he said, "and I feel clearly what it is I must say. But I also feel that if it passed my lips it would be wrong. Be careful not to help me unintentionally!" he cried out, though very likely that was precisely what he was hoping for. *"Pensez très fort,"* he cried all at once, in bad French, and then burst out with the required words—in Italian, indeed, but with the final substantive pronounced in the sister tongue, in which he was probably far from fluent: he said *vénération* instead of *venerazione,* with an impossible nasal. And this partial success, after the complete success before it, the finding of the pin, the presentation of it on his knees to the right person—was almost more impressive than if he had got the sentence exactly right, and evoked bursts of admiring applause.

Cipolla got up from his knees and wiped the perspiration from his brow. You understand that this experiment with the pin was a single case, which I describe because it sticks in my memory. But he changed his method several times and improvised a number of variations suggested by his contact with his audience; a good deal of time thus went by. He seemed to get particular inspiration from the person of our landlady; she drew him on to the most extraordinary displays of clairvoyance. "It does not escape me, madame," he said to her, "that there is something unusual about you, some special and honourable distinction. He who has eyes to see descries about your lovely brow an aureola—if I mistake not, it once was stronger than now—a slowly paling radiance . . . hush, not a word! Don't help me. Beside you sits your husband—yes?" He turned towards the silent Signor Angiolieri. "You are the husband of this lady, and your happiness is complete. But in the midst of this happiness memories rise . . . the past, signora, so it seems to me, plays an important part in your present. You knew a king . . . has not a king crossed your path in bygone days?"

"No," breathed the dispenser of our midday soup, her golden-brown eyes gleaming in the noble pallor of her face.

"No? No, not a king; I meant that generally, I did not mean literally a king. Not a king, not a prince, and a prince after all, a king of a loftier realm; it was a great artist, at whose side you once—you would contradict me, and yet I am not wholly wrong. Well, then! It was a woman, a great, a world-renowned woman artist, whose friendship you enjoyed in your tender years, whose sacred memory overshadows and transfigures your whole existence. Her name? Need I utter it, whose fame has long been bound up with the Fatherland's, immortal as its own? Eleonora Duse," he finished, softly and with much solemnity.

The little woman bowed her head, overcome. The applause was like a patriotic demonstration. Nearly everyone there knew about Signora Angiolieri's wonderful past; they were all able to confirm the Cavaliere's intuition—not least the present guests of Casa Eleonora. But we wondered how much of the truth he had learned as the result of professional inquiries made on his arrival. Yet I see no reason at all to cast doubt, on rational grounds, upon powers which, before our very eyes, became fatal to their possessor.

At this point there was an intermission. Our lord and master withdrew. Now I confess that almost ever since the beginning of my tale I have looked forward with dread to this moment in it. The thoughts of men are mostly not hard to read; in this case they are very easy. You are sure to ask why we did not choose this moment to go away—and I must continue to owe you an answer. I do not know why. I cannot defend myself. By this time it was certainly eleven, probably later. The children were asleep. The last series of tests had been too long, nature had had her way. They were sleeping in our laps, the little one on mine, the boy on his mother's. That was, in a way, a consolation; but at the same time it was also ground for compassion and a clear leading to take them home to bed. And I give you my word that we wanted to obey this touching admonition, we seriously wanted to. We roused the poor things and told them it was now high time to go. But they were no sooner conscious than they began to resist and implore—you know how horrified children are at the thought of leaving before the end of a thing. No cajoling has any effect, you have to use force. It was so lovely, they wailed. How did we know what was coming next? Surely we could not leave until after the intermission; they liked a little nap now and again—only not go home, only not go to bed, while the beautiful evening was still going on!

We yielded, but only for the moment, of course—so far as we knew—only for a little while, just a few minutes longer. I cannot excuse our staying, scarcely can I even understand it. Did we think, having once said A, we had to say B—having once brought the children hither we had to let them stay? No, it is not good enough. Were we ourselves so highly entertained? Yes, and no. Our feelings for Cavaliere Cipolla were of a very mixed kind, but so were the feelings of the whole audience, if I mistake not, and nobody left. Were we under the sway of a fascination which emanated from this man who took so strange a way to earn his bread; a fascination which he gave out independently of the programme and even between the tricks and which paralysed our resolve? Again, sheer curiosity may account for something. One was curious to know how such an evening turned out; Cipolla in his remarks having all along hinted that he had tricks in his bag stranger than any he had yet produced.

But all that is not it—or at least it is not all of it. More correct it would be to answer the first question with another. Why had we not left Torre di Venere itself before now? To me the two questions are one and the same, and in order to get out of the impasse I might simply say that I had answered it already. For, as things had been in Torre in general: queer, uncomfortable, troublesome, tense, oppressive, so precisely they were here in this hall tonight. Yes, more than precisely. For it seemed to be the fountainhead of all the uncanniness and all the strained feelings which had oppressed the atmosphere of our holiday. This man whose return to the stage we were awaiting was the personification of all that; and, as we had not gone away in general, so to speak, it would have been inconsistent to do it in the particular case. You may call this an explanation, you may call it inertia, as you see fit. Any argument more to the purpose I simply do not know how to adduce.

Well, there was an interval of ten minutes, which grew into nearly twenty. The children remained awake. They were enchanted by our compliance, and filled the break to their own satisfaction by renewing relations with the popular sphere, with Antonio, Guiscardo, and the canoe man. They put their hands to their mouths and called messages across, appealing to us for the Italian words. "Hope you have a good catch tomorrow, a whole netful!" They called to Mario, Esquisto Mario: *"Mario, una cioccolata e biscotti!"* And this time he heeded and answered with a smile: *"Subito, signorini!"* Later we had reason to recall this kindly, if rather absent and pensive smile.

Thus the interval passed, the gong sounded. The audience, which had scattered in conversation, took their places again, the children sat up straight in their chairs with their hands in their laps. The curtain had not been dropped. Cipolla came

forward again, with his dipping stride, and began to introduce
the second half of the programme with a lecture.

Let me state once for all that this self-confident cripple was
the most powerful hypnotist I have ever seen in my life. It was
pretty plain now that he threw dust in the public eye and
advertised himself as a prestidigitator on account of police
regulations which would have prevented him from making his
living by the exercise of his powers. Perhaps this eye-wash is
the usual thing in Italy; it may be permitted or even connived
at by the authorities. Certainly the man had from the beginning made little concealment of the actual nature of his operations; and this second half of the programme was quite
frankly and exclusively devoted to one sort of experiment.
While he still practised some rhetorical circumlocutions, the
tests themselves were one long series of attacks upon the willpower, the loss or compulsion of volition. Comic, exciting,
amazing by turns, by midnight they were still in full swing; we
ran the gamut of all the phenomena this natural-unnatural
field has to show, from the unimpressive at one end of the
scale to the monstrous at the other. The audience laughed
and applauded as they followed the grotesque details; shook
their heads, clapped their knees, fell very frankly under the
spell of this stern, self-assured personality. At the same time I
saw signs that they were not quite complacent, not quite unconscious of the peculiar ignominy which lay, for the individual and for the general, in Cipolla's triumphs.

Two main features were constant in all the experiments: the
liquor glass and the claw-handled riding-whip. The first was
always invoked to add fuel to his demoniac fires; without it,
apparently, they might have burned out. On this score we
might even have felt pity for the man; but the whistle of his
scourge, the insulting symbol of his domination, before which
we all cowered, drowned out every sensation save a dazed
and outbraved submission to his power. Did he then lay claim
to our sympathy to boot? I was struck by a remark he made—
it suggested no less. At the climax of his experiments, by
stroking and breathing upon a certain young man who had

offered himself as a subject and already proved himself a particularly susceptible one, he had not only put him into the condition known as deep trance and extended his insensible body by neck and feet across the backs of two chairs, but had actually sat down on the rigid form as on a bench, without making it yield. The sight of this unholy figure in a frock-coat squatted on the stiff body was horrible and incredible; the audience, convinced that the victim of this scientific diversion must be suffering, expressed its sympathy: *"Ah, poveretto!"* Poor soul, poor soul! *"Poor soul!"* Cipolla mocked them, with some bitterness. "Ladies and gentlemen, you are barking up the wrong tree. *Sono io il poveretto.* I am the person who is suffering, I am the one to be pitied." We pocketed the information. Very good. Maybe the experiment was at his expense, maybe it was he who had suffered the cramp when the *giovanotto* over there had made the faces. But appearances were all against it; and one does not feel like saying *poveretto* to a man who is suffering to bring about the humiliation of others.

I have got ahead of my story and lost sight of the sequence of events. To this day my mind is full of the Cavaliere's feats of endurance; only I do not recall them in their order—which does not matter. So much I do know: that the longer and more circumstantial tests, which got the most applause, impressed me less than some of the small ones which passed quickly over. I remember the young man whose body Cipolla converted into a board, only because of the accompanying remarks which I have quoted. An elderly lady in a cane-seated chair was lulled by Cipolla in the delusion that she was on a voyage to India and gave a voluble account of her adventures by land and sea. But I found this phenomenon less impressive than one which followed immediately after the intermission. A tall, well-built, soldierly man was unable to lift his arm, after the hunchback had told him that he could not and given a cut through the air with his whip. I can still see the face of that stately, mustachioed colonel smiling and clenching his teeth as he struggled to regain his lost freedom of action. A staggering performance! He seemed to be exerting his will, and in vain; the trouble, however, was probably simply that he could not will. There was involved here that recoil of the will upon itself which paralyses choice—as our tyrant had previously explained to the Roman gentleman.

Still less can I forget the touching scene, at once comic and horrible, with Signora Angiolieri. The Cavaliere, probably in his first bold survey of the room, had spied out her ethereal lack of resistance to his power. For actually he bewitched her, literally drew her out of her seat, out of her row, and away with him whither he willed. And in order to enhance his effect, he bade Signor Angiolieri call upon his wife by her name, to throw, as it were, all the weight of his existence and his rights in her into the scale, to rouse by the voice of her husband everything in his spouse's soul which could shield her virtue against the evil assaults of magic. And how vain it all was! Cipolla was standing at some distance from the couple, when he made a single cut with his whip through the air. It caused our landlady to shudder violently and turn her face towards him. "Sofronia!" cried Signor Angiolieri—we had not known that Signora Angiolieri's name was Sofronia. And he did well to call, everybody saw that there was no time to lose. His wife kept her face turned in the direction of the diabolical Cavaliere, who with his ten long yellow fingers was making passes at his victim, moving backwards as he did so, step by step. Then Signora Angiolieri, her pale face gleaming, rose up from her seat, turned right round, and began to glide after him. Fatal and forbidding sight! Her face as though moonstruck, stiff-armed, her lovely hands lifted a little at the wrists, the feet as it were together, she seemed to float slowly out of her row and after the tempter. "Call her, sir, keep on calling," prompted the redoubtable man. And Signor Angiolieri, in a weak voice, called: "Sofronia!" Ah, again and again he called; as his wife went further off he even curved one hand round his lips and beckoned with the other as he called. But the poor voice of love and duty echoed unheard, in vain, behind the lost one's back; the signora swayed along, moonstruck, deaf, enslaved; she glided into the middle aisle and down it towards the fingering hunchback, towards the door. We were driven to the conviction, that she would have followed her master, had he so willed it, to the ends of the earth.

"Accidente!" cried out Signor Angiolieri, in genuine affright, springing up as the exit was reached. But at the same moment the Cavaliere put aside, as it were, the triumphal crown and broke off. "Enough, signora, I thank you," he said, and offered his arm to lead her back to her husband. "Signor," he greeted the latter, "here is your wife. Unharmed, with my compliments, I give her into your hands. Cherish with all the strength of your manhood a treasure which is so wholly yours, and let your zeal be quickened by knowing that there are powers stronger than reason or virtue, and not always so magnanimously ready to relinquish their prey!"

Poor Signor Angiolieri, so quiet, so bald! He did not look as though he would know how to defend his happiness, even against powers much less demoniac than these which were now adding mockery to frightfulness. Solemnly and pompously the Cavaliere retired to the stage, amid applause to which his eloquence gave double strength. It was this particular episode, I feel sure, that set the seal upon his ascendancy. For now he made them dance, yes, literally; and the dancing lent a dissolute, abandoned, topsy-turvy air to the scene, a drunken abdication of the critical spirit which had so long resisted the spell of this man. Yes, he had had to fight to get the upper hand—for instance against the animosity of the young Roman gentleman, whose rebellious spirit threatened to serve others as a rallying-point. But it was precisely upon the importance of example that the Cavaliere was so strong. He had the wit to make his attack at the weakest point and to choose as his first victim that feeble, ecstatic youth whom he had previously made into a board. The master had but to look at him, when this young man would fling himself back as though struck by lightning, place his hands rigidly at his sides, and fall into a state of military somnambulism, in which it was plain to any eye that he was open to the most absurd suggestion that might be made to him. He seemed quite content in his abject state, quite pleased to be relieved of the burden of voluntary choice. Again and again he offered himself as a subject and gloried in the model facility he had in losing consciousness. So now he mounted the platform, and a single cut of the whip was enough to make him dance to the Cavaliere's orders, in a kind of complacent ecstasy, eyes closed, head nodding, lank limbs flying in all directions.

It looked unmistakably like enjoyment, and other recruits were not long in coming forward: two other young men, one humbly and one well dressed, were soon jigging alongside the first. But now the gentleman from Rome bobbed up again, asking defiantly if the Cavaliere would engage to make him dance too, even against his will.

"Even against your will," answered Cipolla, in unforgettable accents. That frightful *"anche se non vuole"* still rings in my ears. The struggle began. After Cipolla had taken another little glass and lighted a fresh cigarette he stationed the Roman at a point in the middle aisle and himself took up a position some distance behind, making his whip whistle through the air as he gave the order: *"Balla!"* His opponent did not stir. *"Balla!"* repeated the Cavaliere incisively, and snapped his whip. You saw the young man move his neck round in his collar; at the same time one hand lifted slightly at the wrist, one ankle turned outward. But that was all, for the time at least; merely a tendency to twitch, now sternly repressed, now seeming about to get the upper hand. It escaped nobody that here a heroic obstinacy, a fixed resolve to resist, must needs be conquered; we were beholding a gallant effort to strike out and save the honour of the human race. He twitched but danced not; and the struggle was so prolonged that the Cavaliere had to divide his attention between it and the stage, turning now and then to make his riding-whip whistle in the direction of the dancers, as it were to keep them in leash. At the same time he advised the audience that no fatigue was involved in such activities, however long they went on, since it was not the automatons up there who danced, but himself. Then once more his eye would bore itself into the back of the Roman's neck and lay siege to the strength of purpose which defied him.

One saw it waver, that strength of purpose, beneath the repeated summons and whip-crackings. Saw with an objective interest which yet was not quite free from traces of sympathetic emotion—from pity, even from a cruel kind of pleasure. If I understand what was going on, it was the negative character of the young man's fighting position which was his undoing. It is likely that not willing is not a practicable state of mind; *not* to want to do something may be in the long run a mental content impossible to subsist on. Between not willing a certain thing and not willing at all—in other words, yielding to another person's will—there may lie too small a space for the idea of freedom to squeeze into. Again, there were the Cavaliere's persuasive words, woven in among the whip-crackings and commands, as he mingled effects that were his own secret with others of a bewilderingly psychological kind. *"Balla!"* said he. "Who wants to torture himself like that? Is forcing yourself your idea of freedom? *Una ballatina!* Why, your arms and legs are aching for it. What a relief to give way to them—there, you are dancing already! That is no struggle any more, it is a pleasure!" And so it was. The jerking and twitching of the refractory youth's limbs had at last got the upper hand; he lifted his arms, then his knees, his joints quite suddenly relaxed, he flung his legs and danced, and amid bursts of applause the Cavaliere led him to join the row of puppets on the stage. Up there we could see his face as he "enjoyed" himself; it was clothed in a broad grin and the eyes were half-shut. In a way, it was consoling to see that he was having a better time than he had had in the hour of his pride.

His "fall" was, I may say, an epoch. The ice was completely broken, Cipolla's triumph had reached its height. The Circe's wand, that whistling leather whip with the claw handle, held absolute sway. At one time—it must have been well after midnight—not only were there eight or ten persons dancing on the little stage, but in the hall below a varied animation reigned, and a long-toothed Anglo-Saxoness in a pince-nez left her seat of her own motion to perform a tarantella in the centre aisle. Cipolla was lounging in a cane-seated chair at the left of the stage, gulping down the smoke of a cigarette and breathing it impudently out through his bad teeth. He tapped his foot and shrugged his shoulders, looking down upon the abandoned scene in the hall; now and then he snapped his whip backwards at a laggard upon the stage. The children were awake at the moment. With shame I speak of them. For it was not good to be here, least of all for them; that we had not taken them away can only be explained by saying that we had caught the general devil-may-careness of the hour. By that time it was all one. Anyhow, thank goodness, they lacked understanding for the disreputable side of the entertainment, and in their innocence were perpetually charmed by the unheard-of indulgence which permitted them to be present at such a thing as a magician's "evening." Whole quarter-hours at a time they drowsed on our laps, waking refreshed and rosy-cheeked, with sleep-drunken eyes, to laugh to bursting at the leaps and jumps the magician made those people up there make. They had not thought it would be so jolly; they joined with their clumsy little hands in every round of applause. And jumped for joy upon their chairs, as was their wont, when Cipolla beckoned to their friend Mario from the Esquisito, beckoned to him just like a picture in a book, holding his hand in front of his nose and bending and straightening the forefinger by turns.

Mario obeyed. I can see him now going up the stairs to Cipolla, who continued to beckon him, in that droll, picture-book sort of way. He hesitated for a moment at first; that, too, I recall quite clearly. During the whole evening he had lounged against a wooden pillar at the side entrance, with his arms folded, or else with his hands thrust into his jacket pockets. He was on our left, near the youth with the militant hair, and had followed the performance attentively, so far as we had seen, if with no particular animation and God knows how much comprehension. He could not much relish being summoned thus, at the end of the evening. But it was only too easy to see why he obeyed. After all, obedience was his calling in life; and then, how should a simple lad like him find it within his human capacity to refuse compliance to a man so throned and crowned as Cipolla at that hour? Willy-nilly he left his column and with a word of thanks to those making way for him he mounted the steps with a doubtful smile on his full lips.

Picture a thickset youth of twenty years, with clipt hair, a low forehead, and heavy-lidded eyes of an indefinite grey, shot with green and yellow. These things I knew from having spoken with him, as we often had. There was a saddle of freckles on the flat nose, the whole upper half of the face retreated behind the lower, and that again was dominated by thick lips that parted to show the salivated teeth. These thick lips and the veiled look of the eyes lent the whole face a primitive melancholy—it was that which had drawn us to him from the first. In it was not the faintest trace of brutality—indeed, his hands would have given the lie to such an idea, being unusually slender and delicate even for a southerner. They were hands by which one liked being served.

We knew him humanly without knowing him personally, if I may make that distinction. We saw him nearly every day, and felt a certain kindness for his dreamy ways, which might at times be actual inattentiveness, suddenly transformed into a redeeming zeal to serve. His mien was serious, only the children could bring a smile to his face. It was not sulky, but uningratiating, without intentional effort to please—or, rather, it seemed to give up being pleasant in the conviction that it could not succeed. We should have remembered Mario in any case, as one of those homely recollections of travel which often stick in the mind better than more important ones. But of his circumstances we knew no more than that his father was a petty clerk in the Municipio and his mother took in washing.

His white waiter's-coat became him better than the faded striped suit he wore, with a gay coloured scarf instead of a collar, the ends tucked into his jacket. He neared Cipolla, who however did not leave off that motion of his finger before his nose, so that Mario had to come still closer, right up to the chair-seat and the master's legs. Whereupon the latter spread out his elbows and seized the lad, turning him so that we had a view of his face. Then gazed him briskly up and down, with a careless, commanding eye.

"Well, *ragazzo mio,* how comes it we make acquaintance so late in the day? But believe me, I made yours long ago. Yes, yes, I've had you in my eye this long while and known what good stuff you were made of. How could I go and forget you again? Well, I've had a good deal to think about. . . . Now tell me, what is your name? The first name, that's all I want."

"My name is Mario," the young man answered, in a low voice.

"Ah, Mario. Very good. Yes, yes, there is such a name, quite a common name, a classic name too, one of those which preserve the heroic traditions of the Fatherland. *Bravo! Salve!*" And he flung up his arm slantingly above his crooked shoulder, palm outward, in the Roman salute. He may have been slightly tipsy by now, and no wonder; but he spoke as before, clearly, fluently, and with emphasis. Though about this time there had crept into his voice a gross, autocratic note, and a kind of arrogance was in his sprawl.

"Well, now, Mario *mio,*" he went on, "it's a good thing you came this evening, and that's a pretty scarf you've got on; it is becoming to your style of beauty. It must stand you in good stead with the girls, the pretty pretty girls of Torre—"

From the row of youths, close by the place where Mario had been standing, sounded a laugh. It came from the youth with the militant hair. He stood there, his jacket over his shoulder, and laughed outright, rudely and scornfully.

Mario gave a start. I think it was a shrug, but he may have started and then hastened to cover the movement by shrugging his shoulders, as much as to say that the neckerchief and the fair sex were matters of equal indifference to him.

The Cavaliere gave a downward glance.

"We needn't trouble about him," he said. "He is jealous, because your scarf is so popular with the girls, maybe partly because you and I are so friendly up here. Perhaps he'd like me to put him in mind of his colic—I could do it free of charge. Tell me, Mario. You've come here this evening for a bit of fun—and in the daytime you work in an ironmonger's shop?"

"In a café," corrected the youth.

"Oh, in a café. That's where Cipolla nearly came a cropper! What you are is a cup-bearer, a Ganymede—I like that, it is another classical allusion—*Salvietta!*" Again the Cavaliere saluted, to the huge gratification of his audience.

Mario smiled too. "But before that," he interpolated, in the interest of accuracy, "I worked for a while in a shop in Portoclemente." He seemed visited by a natural desire to assist the prophecy by dredging out its essential features.

"There, didn't I say so? In an ironmonger's shop?"

"They kept combs and brushes," Mario got round it.

"Didn't I say that you were not always a Ganymede? Not always at the sign of the serviette? Even when Cipolla makes a mistake, it is a kind that makes you believe in him. Now tell me: Do you believe in me?"

An indefinite gesture.

"A half-way answer," commented the Cavaliere. "Probably it is not easy to win your confidence. Even for me, I can see, it is not so easy. I see in your features a reserve, a sadness, *un tratto di malinconia* . . . tell me" (he seized Mario's hand persuasively) "have you troubles?"

"*Nossignore,*" answered Mario, promptly and decidedly.

"You *have* troubles," insisted the Cavaliere, bearing down the denial by the weight of his authority. "Can't I see? Trying to pull the wool over Cipolla's eyes, are you? Of course, about the girls—it is a girl, isn't it? You have love troubles?"

Mario gave a vigorous head-shake. And again the *giovanotto*'s brutal laugh rang out. The Cavaliere gave heed. His eyes were roving about somewhere in the air: but he cocked an ear to the sound, then swung his whip backwards, as he had once or twice before in his conversation with Mario, that none of his puppets might flag in their zeal. The gesture had nearly cost him his new prey: Mario gave a sudden start in the direction of the steps. But Cipolla had him in his clutch.

"Not so fast," said he. "That would be fine, wouldn't it? So you want to skip, do you, Ganymede, right in the middle of the fun, or, rather, when it is just beginning? Stay with me, I'll show you something nice. I'll convince you. You have no reason to worry, I promise you. This girl—you know her and others know her too—what's her name? Wait! I read the name in your eyes, it is on the tip of my tongue and yours too—"

"Silvestra!" shouted the *giovanotto* from below.

The Cavaliere's face did not change.

"Aren't there the forward people?" he asked, not looking down, more as in undisturbed converse with Mario. "Aren't there the young fighting-cocks that crow in season and out? Takes the word out of your mouth, the conceited fool, and seems to think he has some special right to it. Let him be. But Silvestra, your ilvestra—ah, what a girl that is! What a prize! Brings your heart into your mouth to see her walk or laugh or breathe, she is so lovely. And her round arms when she washes, and tosses her head back to get the hair out of her eyes! An angel from paradise!"

Mario started at him, his head thrust forward. He seemed to have forgotten the audience, forgotten where he was. The red rings round his eyes had got larger, they looked as though they were painted on. His thick lips parted.

"And she makes you suffer, this angel," went on Cipolla, "or, rather, you make yourself suffer for her—there is a difference, my lad, a most important difference, let me tell you. There are misunderstandings in love, maybe nowhere else in the world are there so many. I know what you are thinking: what does this Cipolla, with his little physical defect, know about love? Wrong, all wrong, he knows a lot. He has a wide and powerful understanding of its workings, and it pays to listen to his advice. But let's leave Cipolla out, cut him out

altogether and think only of Silvestra, your peerless Silvestra!
What! Is she to give any young gamecock the preference, so
that he can laugh while you cry? To prefer him to a chap like
you, so full of feeling and so sympathetic? Not very likely, is
it? It is impossible—we know better, Cipolla and she. If I
were to put myself in her place and choose between the two
of you, a tarry lout like that—a codfish, a sea-urchin—and a
Mario, a knight of the serviette, who moves among gentlefolk
and hands round refreshments with an air—my word, but my
heart would speak in no uncertain tones—it knows to whom I
gave it long ago. It is time that he should see and understand,
my chosen one! It is time that you see me and recognize me,
Mario, my beloved! Tell me, who am I?"

It was grisly, the way the betrayer made himself irresistible,
wreathed and coquetted with his crooked shoulder, lan-
guished with the puffy eyes, and showed his splintered teeth
in a sickly smile. And alas, at his beguiling words, what was
come of our Mario? It is hard for me to tell, hard as it was for
me to see; for here was nothing less than an utter abandon-
ment of the inmost soul, a public exposure of timid and de-
luded passion and rapture. He put his hands across his
mouth, his shoulders rose and fell with his pantings. He could
not, it was plain, trust his eyes and ears for joy, and the one
thing he forgot was precisely that he could not trust them.
"Silvestra!" he breathed, from the very depths of his van-
quished heart.

"Kiss me!" said the hunchback. "Trust me, I love thee. Kiss
me here." And with the tip of his index finger, hand, arm, and
little finger outspread, he pointed to his cheek, near the
mouth. And Mario bent and kissed him.

It had grown very still in the room. That was a monstrous
moment, grotesque and thrilling, the moment of Mario's
bliss. In that evil span of time, crowded with a sense of the
illusiveness of all joy, one sound became audible, and that not
quite at once, but on the instant of the melancholy and ribald
meeting between Mario's lips and the repulsive flesh which
thrust itself forward for his caress. It was the sound of a

laugh, from the *giovanotto* on our left. It broke into the dramatic suspense of the moment, coarse, mocking, and yet—or I must have been grossly mistaken—with an undertone of compassion for the poor bewildered, victimized creature. It had a faint ring of that *"Poveretto"* which Cipolla had declared was wasted on the wrong person, when he claimed the pity for his own.

The laugh still rang in the air when the recipient of the caress gave his whip a little swish, low down, close to his chair-leg, and Mario started up and flung himself back. He stood in that posture staring, his hands one over the other on those desecrated lips. Then he beat his temples with his clenched fists, over and over; turned and staggered down the steps, while the audience applauded, and Cipolla sat there with his hands in his lap, his shoulders shaking. Once below, and even while in full retreat, Mario hurled himself round with legs flung wide apart; one arm flew up, and two flat shattering detonations crashed through applause and laughter.

There was instant silence. Even the dancers came to a full stop and stared about, struck dumb. Cipolla bounded from his seat. He stood with his arms spread out, slanting as though to ward everybody off, as though next moment he would cry out: "Stop! Keep back! Silence! What was that?" Then, in that instant, he sank back in his seat, his head rolling on his chest; in the next he had fallen sideways to the floor, where he lay motionless, a huddled heap of clothing, with limbs awry.

The commotion was indescribable. Ladies hid their faces, shuddering, on the breasts of their escorts. There were shouts for a doctor, for the police. People flung themselves on Mario in a mob, to disarm him, to take away the weapon that hung from his fingers—that small, dull-metal, scarcely pistol-shaped tool with hardly any barrel—in how strange and unexpected a direction had fate levelled it!

And now—now finally, at last—we took the children and led them towards the exit, past the pair of *carabinieri* just entering. Was that the end, they wanted to know, that they might go in peace? Yes, we assured them, that was the end. An end of horror, a fatal end. And yet a liberation—for I could not, and I cannot, but find it so!

Ignazio Silone

Ignazio Silone (1900–1978) was born Secondo Tranquilli in Pescina, Italy. He is the author of two twentieth-century classics in political fiction, Fontamara *and* Bread and Wine. *In the 1920s Silone became a Communist and a leader of the resistance to fascism in Italy. He traveled to Moscow, meeting many of the leading figures of the Soviet Union. His disenchantment and break with communism in 1931 is recounted in his acclaimed essay in* The God That Failed, *an anthology of former Communists. After World War II he became a member of Italy's National Assembly for the Socialist Party.*

SIMPLICIO

The first alarm was given by a washerwoman. Through the open door of his carpenter's shop, Simplicio could hear her shouting:

"Quick! Run! Run! Hide! Quick!"

The washerwoman's words, which held no meaning for Simplicio, were accompanied by gesticulations implying that he should flee, hide himself, run for his life. Still shouting at him, the woman disappeared behind a building in course of construction.

"What's the matter with her?" said Simplicio to himself. "Is she crazy? Can it be the heat's gone to her head?"

Simplicio had been at work all day long in his carpenter's shop. He had not left the shop for a single moment; he had not quit his work for a single moment. He had seen no one, spoken to no one. He had attended strictly to his own business.

A goatherd appeared shortly after, making the same crazy gestures as the washerwoman and shouting the same meaningless words:

"Run! Run! What are you waiting for? For Christ's sake and the Madonna's, why don't you hide?"

The goatherd seemed very excited, and he too kept on shouting as he disappeared. It was as if a big storm were approaching. But the heavens were as bright and calm as they are at the end of May. Simplicio had worked all day long in his carpenter's shop. All day long he had attended to his own affairs. He had spent the entire day in finishing a kneading-trough which had been ordered by Rosa, the dye-woman, for her daughter who was about to be married.

"Can that goatherd be crazy, too?" Simplicio asked himself. "Can it be that, up there all alone with his flocks, he's lost his reason?"

He now noticed that the masons and laborers on the building that was under construction near by had left off work and were holding whispered consultations. It couldn't be more than four o'clock in the afternoon. It wasn't time to stop work. Yet the masons and the laborers had left off work, and stood there whispering. One of the workmen now came running over to Simplicio.

"Is that the signal?" he shouted as he came. "Is it starting now? Holy Mother of God, why don't you answer? Is that the signal? Is it starting?"

Simplicio made no response. He had worked all day in his shop. All day long he had worked on that kneading-trough for Rosa, the dye-woman. He had attended strictly to his own business.

"Are those masons out of their wits?" he wondered now. "Can it be the June sun has gone to their heads?"

He now saw the stone-diggers leaving the quarry and making for the village. It couldn't be more than four o'clock in the afternoon. It wasn't yet time to stop work. But there the quarrymen were, scampering down from the mountainside, talking and gesticulating with great animation. In the little provincial road which runs along the riverside at the foot of the hill, Simplicio could see groups of peasants on their way to the town. It certainly was not any later than four o'clock, and it was not time to stop work. Yet there were the peasants, hastening along, urging on with blows and kicks their donkeys, laden with bags.

It was then that Simplicio began to be scared. He had worked all day long in his carpenter's shop. He had minded his own affairs, being concerned with nothing other than that kneading-trough for Rosa, the dye-woman. But in the meantime, something undreamed of must have happened. Something he had not seen. Something terrible—

It was then he began to be scared.

An elderly mason, surrounded by his fellow masons and the workmen, as they stood there among the building material for the dock that was going up near by, now called out to Simplicio.

"Is that the signal? Does that mean it's starting? Saints alive, man, why don't you answer!"

"Signal? What signal?" was the question Simplicio put to himself. He had not left his carpenter's shop for a moment. All day long, he had not given a thought to anything but that trough for Rosa, the dye-woman. Why couldn't they leave him in peace?

The men whom Simplicio had seen coming down from the stone-quarry a short while before now went past the shop. They appeared astonished at seeing him there, going quietly about his business.

"Is it starting?" they shouted at him. "Is it starting at last? It was about time for it to start!"

It was at this moment that Simplicio beheld, rising from the center of the town, an enormous column of smoke and flame. The town hall was on fire! The town hall was burning! It was then that Simplicio understood what it was all about. He could see a group of carabineers, with bayonets fixed, making for his carpenter's shop from the center of the village. It was then that Simplicio understood what it was all about.

"They are coming to get me!" he said.

He did not take time to close his shop door, nor even to snatch up his hat and coat. He did not lose an instant, but ran for the mountain for dear life.

The conflagration was in the middle of New Town, which was situated at the foot of the hill and inhabited almost exclusively by merchants, land-owners and artisans. On the top of the hill was the Old Town, known as Purgatory. It was made up of a hundred or more hovels and stables where only peasants dwelt. About the flaming municipal building, the inhabitants of New Town were now swarming like ants, when an anthill has been kicked over. The peasants, on the other hand, were enjoying the spectacle from every point of vantage that Purgatory afforded. From down in New Town, those who were in charge of the work of putting out the fire, would from time to time shout up and gesticulate to the residents of the upper town, by way of signifying that they ought to lend a hand.

"Come down! Come on down!"

But the peasants pretended not to understand.

"What's the matter?" they shouted back. "Fire? What fire? Where's the fire?"

Now, the New Town residents were a little more thin-skinned than the Purgatory peasants, and those among the artisans, merchants, and land-owners who ventured to draw near the flames speedily drew back again, finding the atmosphere a little too hot for them. It was for this reason that the constables and carabineers were urging those up in Purgatory to come down, but the latter did not get their meaning. It could now be seen how fierce and relentless was that hatred which for years had been piling up between Purgatory and New Town. The former place was now transformed into a sort of grandstand. In those spots from which the view was best, the peasants could be seen squatting about on the ground, smoking their pipes and telling funny stories as they watched the fire. Round about, the young lads were cutting capers out of sheer exuberance.

The fire in the town hall had started on the top floor where the offices of the civilian authorities were.

"Just think," said Donato Frascone, in a half-jesting tone, "of all the birth certificates, marriage certificates, and death certificates that are going up in smoke down there! It's terrible, I tell you! Why, it means that the dead are no longer dead, those that are born have not yet been born, and those that are married are unmarried—it's terrible! It means that we no longer exist!"

The fire by this time had got down to the second floor, where the office of the bureau of grazing rights was.

"That means," remarked the Ortonese, "that there's no grass left! There are no mountains any more. All the records are burned. What are the poor sheep going to do?"

But it was as the fire reached the first floor, where the tax offices were, that the peasants' mourning took on a lyric quality.

"What are we going to do if we can't pay taxes any more? How's a body to go on living if he doesn't get his little notice from the assessor at the end of the month?" And old lady Continenza sobbed and tore at her hair.

"And to think that this very evening I was going down to pay up my back taxes!" Old Geremia turned his empty pockets inside out. "Yes, sir, this very evening—and now, the office is burned! Oh, what have I done that the Lord should punish me like this?"

Each of them had his say, and their lamentations were accompanied by the chorus of lads: "Oh, what are we going to do! What are we going to do!"

The peasants stayed there until late at night, their eyes on the smoldering town hall. They stayed until the last rafter had dropped. And then, the show being over, the lanes of Purgatory were once more deserted.

"Good night! Pleasant dreams!" the peasants said to one

another with an understanding smile on their lips. There was no need of saying anything more. But Sabbatino, the frog-catcher, had to have his say: "As a beginning, it wasn't bad." All were agreed on this but felt there was no need of saying so. "As a beginning, it wasn't bad," Sabbatino, the frog-catcher, repeated. "No, of course not! Of course not!" the others replied, feeling that there was no need of all this talk.

"What I mean to say," Sabbatino insisted, "is that a beginning is one thing, and keeping it up is another."

"That's right! That's right!" the other replied. What was the use, anyway, of putting it into words?

"Do you think for a minute," the Ortonese asked Sabbatino, "that Simplicio needs any advice from you?"

Sabbatino dropped to his knees, bent his bearded face to the ground, and kissed the earth.

"May the Heavenly Father be his guide!" he said.

Simplicio eluded the search of carabineers and peasants alike. The former had received orders to fire on him, in case he should be found and should refuse to surrender or should attempt to escape. The peasants, on the contrary, were endeavoring to get into touch with him, in order to furnish him with food and ammunition.

"If he's started the thing, he'll certainly see it through," they assured one another. In many of the mountain villages of southern Italy the only history that the peasant knows is that having to do with bandits. That is the only political experience he has had. The ownership of a small piece of land or a vineyard commonly serves to sever any bond of solidarity. The wrongs and injustices inflicted by employers are almost always looked upon as individual calamities, calamities which the peasant, if he has a stout heart, must face as an individual. The bandit tales which each learns at his mother's knee invariably have to do with the fate of one of his kind who has been wrongfully persecuted, and who, by way of "taking justice into his own hands," has committed some crime or other. In order to flee arrest, the hero is thereupon constrained to take to the mountains. And in order to throw the carabineers off the track, punish the defection of his false friends, and procure for himself something to eat, he is thereafter forced to certain other "acts of justice," until the total number of crimes chalked up against him mounts so high that there is no longer hope of a reconciliation between him and society. Every peasant is aware of all this, but the thing he never forgets is that initial cause which spurred the bandit on to "take justice into his own hands"; and inasmuch as "there was no other way," everything that the outlaw afterwards is led to do not only is not regarded as blameworthy but is even admired as heroism. And so, inspired by this tradition, the Purgatory peasants now began making preparations to aid and succor Simplicio.

"Before starting out," they said to one another, "Simplicio must have made his calculations. The first act of justice has been accomplished; the others will follow."

The peasants are acquainted with many stories of brigands, but what above all aroused their admiration in this case, was the calm manner in which Simplicio had kept his revolutionary plans concealed. It was for this reason that the carabineers had always been suspicious of him.

When he was a young man, Simplicio had been an anarchist; he had let his hair and beard grow, and had dreamed of the equality of all beings.

"Man is good," he would preach to the peasants; "man has no need of carabineers."

Simplicio was good, he had no need of carabineers; but the carabineers had need of him. Carabineers exist for the purpose of defending institutions, and against whom would they defend them, if not against the enemies of institutions? Simplicio accordingly had been placed upon the list of such enemies; and on the eve of every patriotic celebration, he was regularly put in jail by way of avoiding possible conspiracies and disorders. After the celebration was over, he was given his freedom again. Free institutions had been saved.

"The business of carabineers is to prevent trouble, so that they won't have to put it down," the marshal in charge of the carabineers would always explain to Simplicio on the eve of patriotic events, when he repaired to the carpenter's shop with a warrant for arrest.

"Man is good," Simplicio would reply; but he did not venture to add that, in order to be good and remain good, man had no need of carabineers; for the marshal might have taken offense at this. In those days the peasants still could emigrate, still could go to try their luck in Argentine or Brazil; and for this reason they did not pay very much attention to Simplicio.

"If it wasn't for the carabineers," they would object to him, "where would we go for our passports when we want to leave the country?"

"Man is good," Simplicio still would say, "and has no need of a passport when he wants to travel."

"But without a passport, they'll put you in jail!" was the peasants' irrefutable logic.

Simplicio himself would very much have liked to go overseas, but he had given up this idea so that he would not be forced to ask the carabineers for a passport. What is more, he was the one anarchist of the region, the one avowed enemy of institutions; and the carabineers, whose business it is to defend institutions, would not have liked very well to see him go. He was good, he had no need of carabineers, but the carabineers had need of him. The result was, he had stayed on in his native village, always kind and gentle, always ready to do anyone a favor, always sympathetic, with advice for each of life's emergencies and with a good word for all who came his way. Many of the peasants had taken advantage of him, and had carpenter work done for which they had not paid. With the approach of age, however, Simplicio had become a little more prudent.

"Man is almost always good," was now as far as he would go. Or, "Man could be good." Or, more prudently still: "They say that man once upon a time was good."

Yes, with the approach of age, Simplicio had become a

little more wary; he no longer talked anarchism, nor committed himself as to the innate goodness of mankind. He worked from morning to evening in his carpenter's shop and minded his own business. He had never married, but looked after his own household needs; and this had left a certain mild, timid, feminine imprint upon his character. Nevertheless, by reason of his youthful opinions, he remained a marked man; he was down in the police books as the dangerous element of the community. Just before each big patriotic festival the village carabineers would receive a telegram from Aquila, ordering Simplicio's arrest as a preventive measure. The marshal would personally attend to this little ceremony, and the courteousness he displayed in executing it appeared to grow with the years.

"It's a formality," he would say to Simplicio, "a mere formality."

"I understand, I understand," Simplicio would reply; "your duty is your duty."

He would then go to spend, without remonstrance, a few days behind bars. This happened three or four times a year, his detention lasting, according to circumstance, from three to five days. When the celebration was over, he was set at liberty, and free institutions once again were saved. Those institutions, in the course of time, came to be altered; but Simplicio's periodic arrest as a preventive measure continued. It even happened more frequently than ever now, since a new government naturally means new anniversaries to celebrate. The taking of Simplicio into temporary custody was, it might be said, the sole echo which reached the village of the patriotic celebrations in the metropolis.

"There must be big doings in the city," the peasants would remark when word ran around that the marshal had come for Simplicio.

But Simplicio had no complaints to make. "Your duty is your duty," was all he would say, when shown the telegram from Aquila. In the jail he was treated with respect. The jailer's wife would sometimes slip a tomato into his soup, and he in turn would promise to mend her chairs for her.

"Man could be good," he would observe on such occasions.

"If I had a daughter, I'd give her to you for a wife," the jailer's spouse once said to him in a moment of compassion. As it happened, she had no daughter. Simplicio thought he would catch the ball on the bounce.

"Couldn't you," he ventured to ask, "give me another tomato?"

The good dame looked at him in amazement.

"Another tomato! Have you any idea what tomatoes are worth?"

The price of tomatoes had gone up. Everything had gone up. The peasants could no longer leave the country, and with the new government, poverty had increased to a point where it had become utterly unbearable. Wages were low, land rents were high. The famous Southland Law, absolving the poverty-stricken small-farmers from certain taxes, had been abolished.

It was at this time that something happened which was to have a great influence on Simplicio's life. At Sulmona there was an uprising of the peasants against the local authorities. It was put down by force in two or three days, but the feeling of excitement remained and spread round about Sulmona, all the way to the villages of Marsica. In the watercloset of the railway station of Simplicio's village, there was found a bundle of smuggled leaflets containing an appeal to the peasants. All efforts to find out where these leaflets came from were in vain, and it was likewise impossible to determine the individual of the locality to whom they had been sent. The carabineers knew only one man who had ever taken a hand in politics, and that was Simplicio. They arrested him.

"Is it some new anniversary?" he asked the marshal. This time the marshal was not alone but had with him four carabineers. No, this was once when it wasn't a case of some new anniversary. Simplicio at the time was busy making a table for Crescenza Noce.

"I only have a few hours more work on this," he said to the armed men who stood in front of him. "Just wait till I finish this table, and I'll go wherever you like."

The marshal, however, was shortspoken on this occasion.

"Grab your coat and a pair of pocket-handkerchiefs and come along," he said. Simplicio was handcuffed and taken off to Aquila.

This occurrence made a new man of him in the eyes of all the peasants of Marsica; he became an exalted figure.

"He was just playing the goody-goody," they said when they spoke of him; "he was just playing possum, and all the while he was stirring up a revolution at Sulmona."

"But why did he have to begin at Sulmona?" was the question that Sabbatino, the frog-catcher, put to everyone he met. "Why couldn't he have started it here?"

"If he started it at Sulmona," the other peasants answered him, "he had his own reasons for it."

"The powder magazine is at Sulmona," was Raffaele Piunzo's afterthought one day, "every revolution begins with taking the munitions supply."

They did not keep Simplicio in prison but deported him to a small island near Tripoli. The poverty of the peasants, meanwhile, increased from day to day, now that the outlet provided by emigration had been cut off. The gentry were treating them worse and worse all the time, and there was no way of getting justice.

"If Simplicio were only here!"

"That fellow will be back one of these days," the peasants kept saying to themselves.

After a year spent in repairing the tables, windows, doors, and chairs on the little island to which he had been deported, Simplicio had been paroled "for good conduct," and was sent back to his native village. He got off at the station, crossed the village and went straight to his shop; and since it was still daylight, he took off his coat, just as if he had never been out of the shop, and at once fell to work finishing Crescenza

Noce's table. He was rather pale and coughed a little but was as calm and gentle as ever in aspect.

"He hasn't a word to say, not a word," Sabbatino, the frog-catcher, informed his acquaintance from house to house. "It's no use to try to talk to him, it's no use to be getting him into trouble with foolish chatter."

"Did you have a good look at him?" Raffaele Piunzo went around saying. "Did you notice that way he has of smiling to himself? He's got something up his sleeve, you can bank on that!"

Simplicio went back to work. He worked in his shop from morning to night. He minded his business. He saw no one. He was sober, mild, and gentle. Under pretext of asking him for some sticks of wood for the fire, some of the women folk from time to time would go around to his shop, in order to tell him what was happening in the town and the neighboring locality; they told him of the widespread poverty and how insolent the gentry were. It was no use appealing to the authorities, since those who were guilty of these injustices had themselves become the ones in power. What were they to do, then? Simplicio let them tell him what was on their minds; he listened with a compassionate smile upon his lips but made no reply, although once or twice his eyes filled with tears; and after that he would accompany them to the door. It was not only the peasants without land, but sometimes the small land-holders, or even occasionally a well-to-do farmer who would come like this, stealthily, to Simplicio.

"There's no use getting him into trouble with a lot of fool woman's talk!" Sabbatino, the frog-catcher, became angry on the subject. "He's only biding his time."

Simplicio's tranquillity and apparent indifference merely served to strengthen this supposition on the part of the peasants. He worked from morning to night and saw no one outside his shop. Why should anyone want to lead a life like that unless he had some hidden purpose? The carabineers for their part did not let him out of their sight and made it a point to pass his shop at frequent intervals, but they saw nothing which might arouse their suspicions. Several months went by, and when at last the fire broke out in the town hall, there was no longer any doubt.

"It's Simplicio beginning again!" was the thought that went through every peasant's mind. "That's his signal!"

The young fellows and the women marveled greatly at the fact that, a week after the firing of the town hall, Simplicio had as yet committed no further "act of justice"; but this was no cause for wonderment to the old men.

"It's a good method," they would say. "He's now getting ready his base of operations and his hiding places. That's the way real bandits always do. There's no need to be too hasty about it."

And indeed, after about a week, reports began to come that Simplicio had been seen in this place or that. Along the road from Luco to Trasacco, he had stopped to ask for a drink, and a woman had recognized him, despite the fact that he was disguised in a monk's hood. At Celano, he had been glimpsed at the entrance of the town dressed as a beggar. At Lecce, by way of contrast, he had been sighted in a soldier's uniform. The fact of the matter is, Simplicio was beginning to be seen just about everywhere at once.

"He's reconnoitering, that's what he's doing," the old peasants would shake their heads and say.

These appearances of Simplicio were not always peaceful ones; they sometimes left damage in their wake. In the neighborhood of Ortucchio, one night, he set fire to the wheat field of a landowner whom the peasants loathed. A couple of days later he made his way into the shrine of the Madonna of Venere and carried off all the treasury, including the ciborium from the tabernacle. The women folk were a little put out over this.

"If the Madonna lets herself be robbed, it means that she wants to be robbed," Sabbatino, the frog-catcher, took it on himself to explain. "Otherwise, she would have worked a miracle to protect her treasure."

Another night Simplicio poisoned four cows belonging to a doctor of Trasacco. The nerve that he displayed won the peasants' admiration.

"He was only playing the goody-goody; he was playing possum," they said. It got to the point where the gentry did not dare leave their houses any more of an evening. And every day brought them threatening letters of this sort: "You had better lower your rents, or you'll have Simplicio to deal with." "Fifty per cent interest is disgraceful. Is Simplicio going to have to take a hand?" "The time has come now for an accounting, you old skinflint."

A dozen carabineers were sent down from Sulmona as a reënforcement, but Simplicio remained uncaptured. Nor were the peasants any more successful in their attempt to establish relations with him. A number of young fellows would have liked to find him, in order to ask him if he would consent to take them as his armed followers; but they were unable to secure a bonafide contact. Among these were two or three who felt like taking to the mountains as a means of avoiding a deserved prison sentence for thefts which they had committed, but others were really spurred on by a hatred of their employers and the authorities.

Simplicio kept on making his appearance in regions far and wide, but all the efforts of his well-wishers to track him down proved unavailing.

"Why does he treat us that way?" the village lads demanded; "why doesn't he send for us?"

"You can never be too cautious in such matters," their elders reminded them. "Simplicio knows his history, and history is clear on the subject: bandits have always been betrayed by some one of their own followers."

"Does he think we're going to betray him?" asked the indignant youths. But their elders were firm: "History is clear on the subject."

The weapons on which the youths might count, in case Simplicio did send for them, were not many in number. Fernando Perzica had at his disposition the knives that he used in sticking pigs in winter time; Peppino Cicerchia could supply a pistol without any ammunition; Giacinto Barile and Antonio Lenticchia could each furnish a hunting rifle, with powder and shot, which they used in hunting wolves. That was about all.

"But once you take to the mountains, you can always disarm a constable or two," was Antonio Carrito's pat observation.

Taking to the mountains, however, without knowing where Simplicio was to be found, was out of the question. Mountain life is hard, and the brigand's trade is a difficult one and not to be thought of without a leader.

"Supposing Simplicio doesn't want us?" said Raffaele Piunzo.

"The thing to do is to ask him; we've simply got to get a message to him," Antonio Carrito insisted.

Simplicio's appearances kept up; he was seen by many here and there, especially at night, but not by any of those who wanted a word with him, that they might enroll as his followers.

"It would be better to think about getting some victuals to him," said Sabbatino, the frog-catcher. "If he's out of victuals, he'll be obliged to come in too close, and the carabineers will get him."

"But how are we going to do it," said the youths, "if we don't know where he is?"

"What do you mean, where he is? Do you think a bandit has a house to live in?" replied Sabbatino. "A bandit never stays two hours in the same spot. He has certain places that he operates from and visits occasionally, but he keeps an eye out and changes them from week to week, depending on what the carabineers are up to. So there's no use asking 'where is he?' The thing to do is find out those places that he visits or might visit."

Tales of the past were then recalled, and the oldest inhabitants were consulted, those who knew the story of Viola, of Marco Sciarra, and of Sciabolone, the brigand of Santa Fede.

The larger part of the guesses hit upon a certain grotto which was situated on the road from Pescina to Pescasseroli. Seeing that Simplicio had paid a visit one night to the shrine of Our Lady of Venere, it was more than likely that the famous grotto, which is on the same highway, was one of his bases of operation. In any event, all they could do was to try an experiment. Antonio Carrito volunteered to put it into execution. Leaving Purgatory one night with a basket of provisions, he set out along the road to Pescasseroli.

When he came to the place in question, he saw a large vertical cleft in the side of the mountain. He thereupon left the wagon-road and began clambering up a small rocky foot-path, which led him to a point at about the center of the opening, where there was a large pile of flint-stone. This concealed from the sight of anyone passing along the road the entrance of a deep cave. It was the famous Brigands' Cave. There was no one inside, but the burnt branches lying about showed that someone had been there recently.

Antonio set his basket down at the entrance; it contained some corn bread, a few onions, and a little honey, accompanied by a pencil-scrawled note which said, simply: "Do you need us?"

Two days later Antonio went back to the cave, to see what had happened. The bread, the onions, and the honey had disappeared! Weighted down by a stone was a piece of paper with these words: "Thanks, but I didn't care for the onions." This was the first time that Simplicio had communicated with the peasants of his village. Not a word as to whether he needed any help or not. The piece of paper with his message was handed about like a religious relic. Everyone felt a little hurt by that remark about the onions.

"Onions!" exclaimed the young fellows. "To think of our sending onions to a man like Simplicio! To a fellow who lives up on the mountain and sleeps on the bare ground—we send onions!"

"Simplicio knows very well that we are not rich," the women folk answered.

Nevertheless, sou by sou, a few lire were scraped together, and with them Antonio Carrito bought a salame. The following night the sausage, with a box of honey and a long loaf of corn bread, was deposited at the entrance of the cave, and beside it a note was left, saying: "Please excuse the onions. But do you need US?" The US was underlined three times.

Two days again went by, and Antonio returned to investigate. Once more, the food was gone, and under the usual stone was found a note: "Couldn't you send me wheat bread in place of corn bread?"

There was general mortification over this, as over the preceding communication.

"Corn bread!" said the village lads. "To think of our sending corn bread to a man like Simplicio!"

"Has Simplicio forgotten how poor we are?" the women wanted to know.

But for all of that, sou by sou, they got together the money to buy a little white bread and a fresh sausage, and to it they added another box of honey. Antonio took the packet to the entrance of the cave, and beside it left the penciled lines: "When are you coming back to town?" Upon his return visit, in two days, Antonio found the food gone, and the answer waiting for him under the stone: "On St. Louis' Day."

So that was that; on St. Louis' Day, Simplicio would be back.

This news produced the greatest excitement imaginable among the peasants.

"And now," remarked Sabbatino, the frog-catcher, "we've got to settle that business about the wages for the next harvest. The bosses had better come straight out and say what they mean to do, and not be waiting till the last day—"

Harvest-time was, indeed, drawing near, and it was not as yet known whether the peasants would receive the same wages as they had the year before, or whether those wages were to be increased or diminished. The excitement occasioned by the announcement that Simplicio was about to put in an appearance in the town, led to the feeling that this was a good time to bring up the question. And so, on the night of June 20th, on the eve of the feast of St. Louis, Sabbatino and the Ortonese and Donato Frascone and one or two others proceeded to call on a few of the landowners, with the object of finding out what the latter intended paying in the harvest field. They received the same answer all around.

"This year everything depends on the Corporation."

"We don't fix the wages any more; it's the Corporate Committee that does that."

"Better go make inquiries of the Corporation."

The peasants did not understand a word of all this.

"What is the Corporation?" they asked.

"Why," replied the owners, "there's been talk of it all these years, and you mean to say you haven't heard of it?"

This was not a very clear explanation; but the chief thing was, the peasants were glad to learn that it was not the bosses who were to fix the harvest scale.

"That's Simplicio's doings!" Sabbatino went about telling everybody.

This was around Hail Mary time. At one o'clock that night the word spread that the wages for the harvest had been posted up, and the peasants at once started making for the center of the town. On the door of the prefecture, opposite the carabineers' barracks, and on the door of the bureau of salt and tobacco, there was a small notice, put up by the Corporation, which stated that the wages for the coming harvest, "by common agreement between peasants, owners, and the authorities, and in the interest of the national economy," were to be reduced by three lire. Wherever one of these notices was posted, a group of peasants gathered, protesting loudly.

"So they are cutting us again, are they? What do they expect us to do, starve to death?"

"Better let the grain rot in the fields than take another cut in wages!" others said.

"Talk doesn't get you anywhere," Antonio Carrito reminded them. "Don't you think it might be better to wait and hear what Simplicio has to say about it?"

The very mention of Simplicio's name brought a feeling of calm and trust.

"But I'd like to know what that Corporation is, anyway," Sabbatino insisted. "And what's the national economy? What's it got to do with the harvest?"

Accompanied by Geremia, by the Ortonese, by Frascone, and some others, Sabbatino set out to look up one Peppino Cicerchia, who was known to have served several months in the Fascist militia, and who had been expelled for insubordination.

"Can you tell us what the Corporation or the national economy is?" was the question they put to him.

"Oh, that's only a new-fangled way of talking," was Cicerchia's reply.

"What do you mean, a new-fangled way of talking?" Sabbatino was bent on knowing.

"Why," Cicerchia tried to explain, "you know very well that there are new ways of saying things. Instead of saying 'Good-by,' for instance, you can say 'So long,' but it amounts to the same thing. It's just as if, instead of saying 'Tighten up your belt,' you was to say, 'Better take the horse in and give the grass a chance to grow.' The Corporation, you see, is a new word."

This explanation did not satisfy them.

"We know it's a new word," said Donato Frascone, "but what does it mean?"

"I tell you what," suggested Cicerchia, "let's go see Niccodemo. Niccodemo's been in the Fascist militia, too; he was discharged 'for absolute failure to grasp the new corporative spirit'; so he certainly ought to know what's what."

They accordingly hunted up Niccodemo.

"I wish," said Cicerchia, "that you would tell these fellows what the Corporation is."

"The Corporation is the bosses," Niccodemo answered.

"There have always been bosses," said the Ortonese, "but this Corporation is a new word."

"The Corporation is the bosses," was Niccodemo's curt rejoinder. "When there's any dirty work to be done, the bosses don't do it individually any more; individualism is a thing of the past; nowadays, when there's dirty work, it's like this: three of the bosses get together; one represents the peasants, another the Super-Class Authority, and a third boss represents the bosses, and the three of them are the Corporation—"

"Then," spoke up Geremia, "it's just like Holy Friday in the Cathedral at Pescina when they're putting on the Passion Play; one priest is Pilate, another is Caiaphas, another is Barabbas, one is Christ, and one is the howling mob; yet they're all five of them priests, and everybody knows how the story's going to end."

"But isn't there at least one peasant in the Corporation— one from the militia, anyway?" Sabbatino asked.

"Well," said Niccodemo, "I'll tell you how it was. When the Corporation met last year, it was winter time, and so they sent for me. They sent for me to keep the stove going and to serve the wine while the gentlemen talked—"

"But what's the national economy?" Sabbatino broke in on him. Niccodemo racked his brain.

"If I'm not mistaken," he began, "the national economy must be the demijohn; because when the Corporation met, in a little room next to the one where the meeting was held, there was a demijohn of red wine, and on it were the words CORPORATIVE ECONOMY. Tending the stove the way I was, I naturally got thirsty oftener than the gentlemen did, and so I kept going back and forth to the demijohn, until the first thing I knew it was empty. When the three gentlemen on the Corporation found this out, there was one devil of a stink. The one who was hotter under the collar about it than anybody else was the Super-Class Authority. He gave me a kick in the belly that knocked the wind out of me and sent me over into one corner of the room.

" 'You wretch!' the Super-Class Authority shouted at me, 'you traitor! The only thing that keeps me from killing you outright is the fact you are too ignorant to know what you were doing! You worm of the earth! You miserable peasant! So you'd dare to drink up the CORPORATIVE ECONOMY, would you?'

"The result was, I was discharged from the militia 'for absolute failure to grasp the new corporative spirit.' "

"That's all the explanation we need!" Sabbatino decided.

Meanwhile, the news that harvest wages were to be cut was evoking loud protests, even from the ranks of the Fascist militia, which had been called out by the authorities to reënforce the carabineers, in case that Simplicio should come back to town the next day. No sooner was it mobilized than the squad was at once drawn up behind the carabineers' barracks with Loreto Ciccuzzo, a corporal, at the head. The marshal in charge of the carabineers then came out to read the men the orders of the day.

"For some weeks past," he began, "a bloodthirsty bandit has been terrorizing the entire population—"

"Nobody but the bosses!" one of the soldiers, Gaudenzio del Pinto, interrupted him. The marshal tried to go on.

"A dangerous criminal, a desperado—"

"Why not talk about the harvest wages?" It was Gaudenzio again.

"That's right! Let's talk about the harvest!" the other militiamen chimed in.

"If that's the way you feel about it," the marshal replied, "the mobilization orders for this squad are revoked. You may go home. I shall report to my superiors at once!"

Two hours later three truckloads of carabineers arrived from Avezzano, to take the place of the militia squad.

From Purgatory the peasants followed the movements of the carabineers in the new part of the town, about the barracks, the prefecture, and what once had been the town hall. They were too excited to go to bed, but stood about discussing the cut in harvest wages and speculating as to what would happen when Simplicio came and took a hand. Numerous clusters were to be seen here and there, wherever there was a good view of what was going on below. The largest group of all was seated on the ground about Sabbatino, the frog-catcher, at a point directly opposite Simplicio's closed shop. They were discussing what was to be done the next day, a question as to which there was some disagreement. They fell silent when someone drew attention to a couple of carabineers who were making their way up to Purgatory.

"What are you doing here at this hour?" the carabineers asked as they came up.

"Tomorrow is a feast day," Rosa, the dye-woman, replied, "and we're just sitting around here telling stories."

There was a prolonged silence. The peasants were waiting for the carabineers to go away, but the latter showed no signs of doing so.

"Go ahead and tell that one about the Bandit and the King's Daughter," Giacinto Barile said to Rosa.

"No bandit stories allowed!" said one of the carabineers.

"Then I," said Geremia, "will tell the one that's called 'Troubles aren't always troubles.'" Inasmuch as the carabineers made no objection to this, the old fellow began, as all sat listening intently:

> *"The postman came*
> *and said to the folks:*
> *'A terrible thing*
> *has happened at Rome;*
> *the post-office flag*
> *they've put at half-mast!'*
>
> *The poor peasant*
> *was not excited,*
> *but the hen in the belfry*
> *rang the bells,*

the mouse in the key-hole
whistled a tune,
the ass in the stable
strummed the guitar,
the ox in his stall
played the two-stringed lute,
and the sheep at the fountain
grew a star on their foreheads.

The postman came back
and said to the folks:
'What's the meaning of all
this jubilee?
A terrible thing
has happened at Rome;
the post-office flag
they've put at half-mast!'

But the poor peasant
was unexcited still,
to hear the same story again.
The she-goat on the mountain
played the trumpet,
as the pig kept time
with bagpipe and grunt;
the dogs in the kennel
beat on the drum;
and the porcupine
down in the wheat
laughed to himself:
'That's very neat.'

The postman came back
and said to the folks:
'What's the meaning of all
this jubilee?'

> *And the animals answered*
> *in a chorus:*
> *'A terrible thing*
> *has happened at Rome.' "*

"That will be enough of that!" said one of the carabineers to old Geremia. What's all this about a 'terrible thing'?"

"History is history," the old man answered him; "he who has understanding will understand."

"Tell the story about the true miracle that happened to St. Bernard," Peppino Cicerchia said to Geremia.

"No discussion of miracles allowed!" a carabineer warned them.

"Well, then," said Donato Frascone, "maybe you won't mind if I tell the story, 'One and one don't always make two'?"

"What's it about?" the carabineers asked; for they had not the faintest idea.

"Here's what it's about," said Frascone:

> *"One, two and three,*
> *the Pope's not a king,*
> *the king's not a Pope,*
> *the bee is not a wasp,*
> *the wasp is not a bee,*
> *the cat is not a rabbit,*
> *the rabbit is not a cat,*
> *the umbrella is not a cane,*
> *the cane is not an umbrella,*
> *the worker is not boss,*
> *the boss is not a worker.*
> *One, two and three,*
> *the Pope's been made king,*
> *but the king's not a pope,*
> *the bee stings like the wasp,*

but the wasp gives no honey like the bee,
the cat often plays the rabbit,
but the rabbit never plays the cat,
an umbrella may serve as a cane,
but a cane cannot serve as an umbrella,
the worker can be a boss,
but the boss cannot be a worker.
One and one do not always make two,
but one and two are always three."

"That will do!" shouted the carabineers. "What's the meaning of all this?"

"History is history," Frascone replied; "he who has understanding will understand."

"Do you mind if I tell the one about the Three Friars who went a-hunting?" asked old Sabina.

"What's it about?"

"Listen," said Sabina; and there was a hush:

"There were three friars,
one naked and two stripped,
who went a-hunting without a gun
and knocked on a house without a door:
'We are three friars,
one naked and two stripped,
we are a-hunting without a gun,
and we have caught three rabbits;
two got away and the other escaped.'
'Come in, come in,'
from behind the door
answered the one
who was not there,
'to cook your rabbits,
there's a burnt-out fire,
and here are three pots,
one broken and two of them smashed.'"

They all burst into a laugh, which tended to make the carabineers more suspicious than ever, since they had not been able to make head or tail of it all.

"Clear out of here! Get out!" they now began shouting. "You're making light of the law and of religion. If you don't go home at once, every last one of you, we'll send down below for help!"

"That's fair enough," said Sabbatino approvingly; "let's go to bed. The sweetest stories are those that are never told."

And they all got to their feet and went off home.

On the morning of St. Louis' Day all the Purgatory peasants were out in the street and on their way to church. It was the first time they had ever shown so heartfelt a devotion to this particular saint. For it should be stated that St. Louis Gonzaga is the patron saint of the young and, more especially, of the chaste; and the peasants accordingly have always been inclined to make light of him. This turnout on the part of the inhabitants of the upper town had been anticipated by the authorities, who had taken strict measures to prevent any trouble. On every corner in New Town carabineers were standing sentry. The peasants, however, pretended not to notice this, but acted just as if it were a daily and normal occurrence. Liberato Boccella, the butcher, in front of his shop, was the only one to make a fool of himself, as if he did not know what it was all about.

"You old fox, you," he called to Sabbatino, as he caught sight of the frog-catcher among the other churchward-bound peasants, "you don't mean to tell me you've got religion on St. Louis' Day?"

Sabbatino, to tell the truth, did not look any too devout. He had on the rags that he wore to work, he had not shaved, and there were circles under his eyes, as if he had not slept all night, but he had an answer for the butcher:

"Better late than never, you old robber, you!"

With Sabbatino were Antonio Carrito, Niccodemo, Peppino Cicerchia, and some of the other lads. They were going quietly to church, as if they knew perfectly well what they were up to. The butcher turned to a group of carabineers and started orating:

"There ought to be a law against all these devotions to St. Louis, if the government is as interested as it pretends to be in having children—"

Some of the carabineers laughed at this; for St. Louis' name was often used as a popular synonym for that vice which is called after Onan, the second son of Judah, who, according to the Bible, refusing Tamar, his brother's widow, spilled his seed on the ground, which brought down on him Jehovah's wrath and led to his death. St. Louis Gonzaga, when he was alive, not only had nothing to do with his sisters-in-law, for he had none, but kept away from women in general and died a virgin; and for this, being more fortunate than Onan, he was made a saint, and is held up by the Church as a model for the young.

When the services began, the New Town church was unusually packed. Upon the great altar was St. Louis' image, which appeared bent upon lending confirmation to what the people commonly said, the Saint being represented as a tall, skinny youth with deep eye-sockets and with his eyes constantly fixed on the ground. In the first rows, up against the railing of the great altar, were the so-called "Little Brothers of St. Louis," lads between the ages of eight and fourteen, who had recently made their first communion, or who were getting ready to make it. Next came a few rows of the Daughters of Mary, young girls of the same age as the boys, or a trifle older. In behind them was a throng of kneeling women, while at the back of the church, near the door, and about the Holy Water fonts, were the men folk, a few stone-masons, and the rest, peasants. Sabbatino with his following was standing near the baptismal fount. The sound of the bell which marked the beginning of the Mass was drowned out by the buzz of voices and almost unnoticed. In the churches of southern Italy, while services are going on, the faithful—and especially the women—are in the habit of chattering as if they were at market; and it would have been a strange thing indeed if, on this particular day, when so great an event was looked forward to, the women had seen fit to remain silent. None uttered *his* name, but all spoke of *him;* some told of having seen *him* in a dream, while others had seen *him* in real life the day before, not far from the town.

The only group to remain silent was the one about Sabbatino. He must have organized something in the nature of a liaison service; for every so often a young lad would come into the church and come running up to him, would whisper something in his ear, and then would leave. The messages could not have been very important, for Sabbatino stuck to his post, motionless and unperturbed. Once only was there an alarm. That was when Donato Frascone's son, who had been on guard up in the belfry, came bursting in.

"A man disguised as a monk has just come into town!"

The frog-catcher had Carrito and Niccodemo go out at once to make sure; and in the meantime, Peppino Cicerchia silently made the rounds of the church, going to all the corners where the men from Purgatory were stationed.

"Be ready!" was the whispered word he gave them.

The stir that followed Cicerchia's announcement served to make plain in what manner it was the residents of Purgatory meant to be ready; everything they had been able to find at home which had a sharp point or was capable of dealing a heavy blow—old knives, hedgebills, sickles, razors, hammers, mallets—they had brought with them to church, concealing these weapons under their clothes. Upon Cicerchia's announcement, each one now brought out whatever it was he had with him, or at least saw to it that he had it within arm's reach. The Mass went on, but no one, not even the lay-sisters, was any longer paying the least bit of attention, and the women's voices rose to a shrill pitch. Carrito and Niccodemo now came back into the church.

"He's a real monk; it's the preacher from Luco."

Cicerchia once more made the rounds of the church.

"It's a false alarm," he said.

It was, as a matter of fact, the preacher of the day, who at this moment came in and made straight for the sacristy. Inasmuch as the Mass had already got along as far as the Gospel, he reappeared at once in his surplice and went up into the pulpit for the sermon. He certainly did not look the least bit like Simplicio. He was a real Capuchin, and a tall, lean one with a white beard. Once in the pulpit, he did not at once begin preaching, but stood for a long while gazing about him from right to left, in astonishment at the unexpected size of the congregation. He was smiling and almost weeping. It was as if he could not believe his eyes. This pause on the part of the preacher impressed everybody. A woman who had been kneeling directly under the pulpit now rose and was on the point of screaming: "That's who it is!" when the Capuchin suddenly began.

Addressing himself to the peasants, he started in by confessing that the sermon he had prepared was one for children, while on the other hand his heart was rejoiced at seeing that, though there were so few children present, there were so very many adults.

"This is a great day in Heaven," the preacher continued, raising his voice and his arms at one and the same time. "I can see from your eyes what it is that brings you to St. Louis and to purity; it is out of disgust for the sins of the flesh that you have come here. The flesh—that is the enemy that we have to fight!"

At this moment, Donato Frascone's son came back from the belfry.

"A man is coming to town from the direction of the cemetery!" he told Sabbatino. The latter at once dispatched Carrito and Niccodemo to find out if it was *the one;* and in the interim, Cicerchia slowly circled the church for a third time, by way of giving the signal to all those from Purgatory: "Be ready!"

"Heretofore," the Capuchin was droning on, "you have yielded to the Devil's temptings, you have yielded to all the temptations of the flesh, you have wallowed in the sin of gluttony, the sin of impurity and of lust; and now, listen to what St. Louis has to say to you—"

The peasants, following Cicerchia's warning signal, had again produced or placed within arm's reach, those weapons which they had concealed in coat or trousers. Carrito and Niccodemo were slow in returning, and Sabbatino grew impatient.

"The pleasures of the body are a deception and a snare. Stop and think, what have you left to show for all these pleasures in the past? What is left you of all the succulent meals and banquets at which you have sat, what of all those luxurious garments by which your hearts set so great a store—?"

Carrito and Niccodemo came in.

"It's a beggar from Celano," they announced; "he's come here to beg during the procession."

Cicerchia went around again saying: "It's a false alarm!"

"The flesh—the flesh is our enemy!" The Capuchin was concluding his sermon.

"Right you are," was Sabbatino's comment, "the butcher sure wants enough for his."

The sermon over, the Mass went on. When the Mass was finished, St. Louis' image was brought down from the altar, the main door of the church was opened, and the procession started. First of all came a young lad bearing the Cross; after him, by twos, came the "Little Brothers of St. Louis," then the Daughters of Mary, and after them the image of St. Louis, borne on the shoulders of four young fellows; behind the Saint came the priest with the sacristan, and a crowd of men and women brought up the rear. As the procession emerged into the square, it could be seen that the carabineers were there in force. The "Little Brothers," with their childish voices, were singing:

> Thy glance bend on me,
> Louis on high;
> One of the angel choir to be,
> Here at thy feet I lie.

And from the tail end of the procession, bellowing horribly, the peasants responded:

> Let thy soul's light, O Louis,
> Shine down on me.

The Daughters of Mary, in their turn, wailed:

> A fragrant wreath we bring thee,
> The Lily and the Rose,
> Whose beauty doth disclose
> Thy purity.

And once again from the end of the procession, came the bovine rumble:

> Let thy contempt of the world,
> O Louis, come to me.

The procession sprawled down the streets of New Town and struck off in the direction of Purgatory, without anything untoward happening. From the elevation afforded by Purgatory, squads of carabineers could be seen, scouring the countryside; they were obviously on the lookout for Simplicio before he could enter the town. But there were to be seen also a number of strapping lads, whose duty it probably was to pass the word along to Sabbatino. For it was to be expected that, even in case he should be arrested, Simplicio would put up a resistance while they were engaged in taking him down the street to the barracks, and this would give the peasants time to come in on it. The important thing was to be there at the right time.

The procession made its way through Purgatory and started back down to New Town. The priest was chanting the litany of the saints, and after the name of each saint, the women would respond with a "Pray for us." The men, restless and impatient, were scanning the landscape round about, but could see nothing which would indicate Simplicio's presence. Slowly, the procession came back to New Town and entered the square. At this moment Donato Frascone's son, who had remained on watch in the belfry, began gesticulating violently. At one end of the square was the church, and to the right of it was the carabineers' barracks. That was all the peasants, who were bringing up the end of the procession, were able to see. But Frascone's boy was still waving his arms like a crazy man.

"Where? Where is he? Which direction?" they all shouted at once.

The lad replied by pointing toward the square; but in the square there was only the procession and a few carabineers. At the other end of the square was the church, its main door open to let the procession come in again, and to the right was the barracks. No sign of Simplicio. Yet Frascone's boy kept on waving his arms.

The cross-bearer, who led the procession, and the "Little Brothers" were already in the church, when out of the main street, which ran along directly beneath the belfry, there appeared a man riding a small ass and dressed like a beggar. Instantly the procession broke up.

"Simplicio! Simplicio! He's here! He's here!" cried the peasants from the far end of the square, bringing out their hidden weapons from their trousers and their coats, and brandishing them in the air. The Daughters of Mary ran into the church as fast as their legs would carry them, like hens in a hail storm. St. Louis' image, which had been abandoned by the four young fellows who had borne it on their shoulders, was now swaying perilously and ended by flopping over on one side, its plaster head striking against Liberato Boccella's butcher shop sign, as the priest and lay-sisters screamed: "Sacrilege! Sacrilege!"

The man on the ass had been by this time surrounded by carabineers, and he and his ass along with him were dragged into the barracks a few feet away. Instead of running at once to Simplicio's rescue, Sabbatino and his lads made a dive for St. Louis' image, which in falling had lost its head and the

Saint's lily; they proceeded to strip off the robe and from the papier-maché body they extracted four large pistols and a hunting rifle. At sight of these weapons the priest and lay-sisters, frightened out of their wits, ran into the church and closed the door behind them. In the square there were now left only the men from Purgatory, who were clustered about Sabbatino; there were something like a hundred of them in all.

"If anyone is afraid, let him get out of here!" cried Sabbatino, turning to the other peasants; but no one stirred. Then Sabbatino, hunting rifle in hand, made for the barracks, with his followers a few steps behind him. He went all the way up to the door and knocked the butt of his rifle against it.

"Bring that man out!" he called.

The door immediately opened and out came the man with the ass. It was not Simplicio. It was a blind man. It was the blind man of Trasacco. He had come to beg during the procession.

"Alms," he said, throwing back his tattered hood, "for the love of St. Louis, give me alms!"

"Back to Purgatory!" Sabbatino ordered his men. "Back to Purgatory, before the other carabineers get here!"

The peasants left New Town on the run and sought refuge in the cluster of huts and stables that went to make up Purgatory. They had abandoned all hope of Simplicio's coming for that day. While Simplicio had given them his word that he would come, he quite possibly had not foreseen such a show of force on the part of the authorities; and so, even supposing that he had approached the town, it was possible that he had gone away without trying to enter. It was not Simplicio's coming that the peasants were thinking of now, but of a possible attack on Purgatory by the carabineers.

"After that tom-foolishness that Sabbatino got us into down there in the square, with weapons and everything, they'll certainly be here!" said the Ortonese.

"If only Simplicio were here," said Fernando Perzica, "we

would know how to set about defending ourselves; but without Simplicio, who is there who knows what's to be done?"

Without Simplicio, no one knew. The majority of the peasants were angry with Sabbatino.

"And Simplicio, when he hears of it," said Geremia, "will be angrier than anybody else. Bandits do everything by acting quick and taking the other fellow by surprise; they've always done that."

"To go to jail just when the harvest's beginning wouldn't be so sweet," reflected Donato Frascone.

Niccodemo carried all this back to Sabbatino, and the latter was very downcast about it. The afternoon went by and evening came, and still the carabineers had launched no attack on Purgatory. Each one had quickly seen to hiding away his improvised weapons; and each kept telling himself that the carabineers would not come after all, while in case they did come, everyone must have a good story ready to prove he had not been in the square.

"To go to jail in winter, that's not so bad; but in the month of June, just as the harvest is about to begin, that's terrible!" the peasants kept saying to one another.

The next day was a work day; and with such thoughts as these, everybody went to bed early; but this was more of an excuse to get away from the others than anything else. It was by no means impossible that the carabineers would come during the night, and the mere thought of such a thing was sufficient to keep everyone awake. The roosters crowed three times, and the carabineers had not come. At daybreak, Purgatory was deserted within a shorter space of time than usual. One by one, and being careful not to go through New Town, the peasants went out into the country. For most of the men from Purgatory, this was one work day that was all too short. Sabbatino had gone to sprinkle disinfectant in a little vineyard which he had behind the cemetery. He had no sooner filled his pump, than four carabineers stood before him.

"Please come with us," they said; "the marshal wants to talk to you."

Sabbatino offered no resistance. In the street they were overtaken by a truck into which the Ortonese, Niccodemo, Donato Frascone and his son, Peppino Cicerchia and others already had been put. They had all been picked up, one by one, on their way to work. Sabbatino had to climb up on the truck, and they were all driven away to the barracks. As soon as the door had closed on them, the truck was off again to pick up the rest.

The next day the carabineers succeeded in discovering Simplicio's hiding place. He was found dead near a shepherd's hut at a point near the Forca Caruso Pass in a valley between Mt. Treppa and Mt. Ventrino. He had died there on the night of St. Louis' Day in the company of only a few shepherds of the vicinity. As soon as he had breathed his last, a shepherd had gone down to Collarmele to notify the carabineers. The man told how Simplicio had arrived in the neighborhood of Forca Caruso at the end of May, on St. Augustine's Day, and had stayed on until the day of his death, on the evening of St. Louis' Day. He had a high fever at the time he arrived and was coughing much; and after two or three days he had begun to spit blood and was too weak to stand on his feet.

When the news of Simplicio's death spread abroad, a large number of carabineers came to Forca Caruso from Pescina, Collarmele and Castelvecchio Subequo, to take possession of the much feared bandit's remains and to verify the story of the shepherd who had notified the authorities, and who had immediately been placed under arrest.

Simplicio was lying on the ground with his arms and legs sprawled out, like one who has dropped exhausted after having made his way through a forest of bramble bushes. His shirt and trousers were in shreds; and through the tatters there could be seen, upon both arms and legs, the red and blue marks left by dogs' teeth. His head was as devoid of flesh as that of a skeleton and was a frightful object to behold. His beard had grown, and was matted with dirt and blood. His mouth was half open, as if he were suffering from a desperate thirst. The eyelids were not entirely closed over the huge, empty sockets; it was as if he were still keeping an eye on what was going on about him and waiting, perhaps, for the moment to escape.

The authorities came and proceeded to divide up the work between them. Four carabineers with rifles on their shoulders were stationed about the corpse, as if to say, "If you try to get away, we'll shoot!" But Simplicio had no thought of trying to get away. In the presence of the body the officials opened an inquest concerned with Simplicio's residence at Forca Caruso. One by one, the shepherds, all of whom had been taken into custody, came up for questioning. Each of them told the same story. The principal witness was Carmine Massaro, the shepherd at whose place Simplicio had died.

"On the evening of St. Augustine's Day," his story ran, "I heard the loud barking of dogs down in the valley and a man's cries. When I got there, I found a man in his shirt sleeves, surrounded by large dogs that were leaping on him from all sides and which had bitten him on the legs and arms—"

"By the way, when is St. Augustine's Day?" inquired a sergeant of carabineers.

"The day after the Feast of the Holy Trinity," replied Carmine Massaro.

"And when is Trinity Day?"

"Trinity Day is Trinity Day," stoutly asserted Carmine, marveling that an educated person could ask such a question.

With the aid of a country constable who was present, it was possible to establish the fact that Simplicio had arrived at Forca Caruso some two days after the firing of the town hall.

"He asked me to let him sleep in my hut for the night," Carmine went on. "His teeth were chattering with fever, and so I let him come into my hut."

"He didn't tell you why it was he had taken to the mountains?"

"I asked him: 'What have you done that you're running away? Have you robbed somebody? Did you kill someone?'

He answered: 'I was making a kneading-trough for Rosa, the dye-woman. Her daughter is going to be married, and how can she marry without that trough?' I didn't bother him any more about it, because I thought he would soon be gone. He didn't get a wink of sleep, but coughed all night long."

"And it was the day after that he left?" the officials asked.

"The next day his fever was higher still; he was like a bag of straw that someone had set fire to, and I did not know what to do with the man; so I called in some of the other shepherds near here. He understood that I didn't want to get into trouble on his account. 'Let me stay here until tomorrow,' he said, 'and I'll leave in the morning.' I gave him some bread to eat, and he started to cry; he took my hand and kissed it and said, 'Man is good after all!' I talked it over with the other shepherds. 'He's certainly not a thief,' one of them said, 'he doesn't look as if he had sense enough for that.'—'And he's not a murderer, either,' said another, 'he looks like a good-hearted fellow.'—'Maybe he's murdered his wife,' somebody said. That seemed the most likely of all; so I went up to him and said: 'Tell me the truth now; did you murder your wife?' He shook his head. 'I never had a wife,' he said."

"And the day after he left?" asked the sergeant of carabineers.

"The next day," continued Carmine, "he was worse than ever; but seeing that he had promised me he would leave, he got on his feet, thanked me, said good-by, and started to walk away. He hadn't gone more than ten feet when he sank down. I stood watching him for a minute or so, waiting to see if he would get up; but he kept on coughing and wasn't able to get on his feet. I went over to him, and I saw that he was spitting blood. 'Just let me stay here alongside your hut,' he said to me; 'if I'm not inside your hut, you're not responsible, for the mountain doesn't belong to you, it belongs to everybody.' I helped him to get up and took him over into the shade beside my hut. 'Do whatever you like,' I told him; 'if you want to stay, all right; and if you want to leave, all right; the mountain belongs to everybody.' He then said to me: 'When I'm well again and back in my shop, the first thing I must do is finish that kneading-trough for Rosa, the dye-woman, because her daughter is going to be married, and she can't be married without it; but after that, I'll make you a table, or a couple of chairs, or a window-frame, or a chest, or anything you need.' With this understanding I kept on giving him a little bread every day, and every evening I would give him a glass of milk. But one day I happened to think of something; and I said to him, 'Supposing you don't get well?' He knew what I meant and thought it over for a minute. 'Haven't you a little something here that I could do? Not having any wife, I know how to cook, for one thing.' After that, I gave him some old clothes to mend; and when I saw that he did it very well, I told the other shepherds about it, and they began sending in their old clothes, and would pay him with bread or milk. All this time he had a high fever; but this didn't keep him from working, and he was in good spirits, you might say. Once in a while he would call me over, take my hand, and say, 'You know, man could be good!' It was at times like this that I tried to get the truth out of him. 'You don't need to be afraid to tell me,' I would say; 'did you kill your wife?' But he would shake his head."

"Well, then," the sergeant of carabineers interrupted him, "as I understand it, you are testifying that, from St. Augustine's Day on, this man never left the neighborhood of your hut?"

Carmine Massaro dropped to the ground, kissed the earth, then rose again.

"Not once!" he said.

"And how do you explain, then," the officer went on, "the fact that he was seen after that at Luco, at Trassacco, at Venere, and at Celano, and that yesterday, they were expecting him in his own village?"

"This man," the shepherd maintained, "never once left here after St. Augustine's Day."

"Why didn't you notify the authorities at once?" he was

asked. "Didn't you realize the risk you were running by affording shelter to a dangerous anarchist?"

"I didn't shelter anybody," was Carmine's answer. "All the time he was here, he stayed right where you see him now, outside my hut like that. He's on a rock of the mountain, and the mountain belongs to everybody, carpenters as well as anybody else."

The other shepherds there present bore out Carmine Massaro's testimony. But for all of that, Carmine was placed under arrest and had to go to Pescina with the officers. Four carabineers were left on the spot, rifles on their shoulders, stationed about Simplicio's corpse. They seemed to be saying: "If you try to get away, we'll shoot!"

But Simplicio had made his get-away.

Vladimir Voinovich

Vladimir Voinovich (1932–   ) was born in Dushanbe, Tadzhik, Soviet Union. This novelist and satirist was expelled from the Soviet Union in 1980. Among his novels are The Fur Hat *and* Moscow 2042. *This story mocks Stalin ("Comrade Koba") and his coterie.*

A CIRCLE
OF FRIENDS

(A Not Particularly Reliable Tale
concerning a Certain Historic Get-together)

The building stands behind the high red-brick wall known to the entire world. There are many windows in that building, but one was distinguished from all the others because it was lit twenty-four hours a day. Those who gathered in the evening on the broad square in front of the red-brick wall would crane their necks, strain their eyes to the point of tears, and say excitedly to one another: "Look, over there, the window's lit. He's not sleeping. He's working. He's thinking about us."

If someone came from the provinces to this city or had to stop over while in transit, he'd be informed that it was obligatory to visit that famous square and look and see whether that window was lit. Upon returning home, the fortunate provincial would deliver authoritative reports, both at closed meetings and at those open to the public, that yes, the window was lit, and judging by all appearances, he truly never slept and was continually thinking about them.

Naturally, even back then, there were certain people who abused the trust of their collectives. Instead of going to look at that window, they'd race around to all the stores, wherever there was anything for sale. But, upon their return, they, too, would report that the window was lit, and just try and tell them otherwise.

The window, of course, was lit. But the person who was said never to sleep was never at that window. A dummy made of gutta-percha, built by the finest craftsmen, stood in for him. That dummy had been so skillfully constructed that unless you actually touched it there was nothing to indicate that it wasn't alive. The dummy duplicated all the basic features of the original. Its hand held a curved pipe of English manufacture, which had a special mechanism that puffed out tobacco smoke at pre-determined intervals. As far as the original himself was concerned, he only smoked his pipe when there were people around, and his moustache was of the paste-on variety. He lived in another room, in which there were not only no windows but not even any doors. That room could only be reached through a crawl-hole in his safe, which had doors both in the front and in the rear and which stood in the room that was officially his.

He loved this secret room where he could be himself and not smoke a pipe or wear that moustache; where he could live simply and modestly, in keeping with the room's furnishings —an iron bed, a striped mattress stuffed with straw, a wash-basin containing warm water, and an old gramophone, together with a collection of records which he personally had marked—good, average, remarkable, trash.

There in that room he spent the finest hours of his life in peace and quiet; there, hidden from everyone, he would sometimes sleep with the old cleaning woman who crawled in every morning through the safe with her bucket and broom. He would call her over to him, she would set her broom in the corner in business-like fashion, give herself to him, and then return to her cleaning. In all the years, he had not exchanged a single word with her and was not even absolutely certain whether it was the same old woman or a different one every time.

One time a strange incident occurred. The old woman began rolling her eyes and moving her lips soundlessly.

"What's the matter with you?"

"I was just thinking," the old woman said with a serene smile. "My niece is coming to visit, my brother's daughter. I've got to fix some eats for her, but all I've got is three roubles. So it's either spend two roubles on millet and one on butter, or two on butter and one on millet."

This peasant sagacity touched him deeply. He wrote a note to the storehouse ordering that the old woman be issued as much millet and butter as she needed. The old woman, no fool, did not take the note to the storehouse but to the Museum of the Revolution, where she sold it for enough money to buy herself a little house near Moscow and a cow; she quit her job, and rumor has it that to this day she's still bringing in milk to sell at Tishinsky market.

Recalling this incident, he would often tell his comrades that genuine dialectical thinking had to be learned directly from the people.

One day, having parted with the cleaning woman and finding himself alone, he wound up the gramophone and began thinking great thoughts to the music. It recalled for him the far-off days of his childhood in a small town in the Caucasus: his mother, a simple woman with a wrinkled, sorrowful face; his father, a stubborn man who, through daily toil, had achieved considerable success in the art of shoemaking.

"Soso, you'll never make a real shoemaker. You're too crafty, you try to save on nails," his father would say, hitting him over the head with the last.

All this did not pass without its effect, and now, in later life, he suffered from fierce and frequent headaches. If only he could resurrect his father and ask him how was it possible to beat a child over the head with a last. How much, how passionately he wanted to resurrect his father and ask him . . .

But at that moment something else had him excited. Ominous rumors had reached his ears: Dolph, with whom he had recently become fast friends, was planning to betray their friendship and march across the border. He considered himself the most treacherous man in the world and could not bring himself to believe that there existed someone even more treacherous than he. When the others urged him to prepare to defend himself against Dolph, he treated their words as provocation and did nothing, so as not to offend Dolph with their groundless suspicions. The most suspicious man in the world was as gullible as a child in his relations with Dolph.

The closer the shortest night of the year drew, the more his soul was filled with foreboding. It would be frightening to spend that night alone.

On the eve of the shortest night of the year, he put on his faded, semi-military suit, pasted on his moustache, lit up his pipe, and became the person known to all, Comrade Koba. But before going out among people he turned to the large mirror which hung on the wall across from his bed. Pipe in hand, he ambled past the mirror a few times, gazing at his reflection out of the corner of his eye. He found his reflection satisfactory; it returned some of the grandeur the original possessed, if you didn't examine it too closely. (And who would ever allow himself the luxury of examining Comrade Koba that closely?) He grinned, nodded to his reflection, and then crawled into his office by the usual route, through his safe. He sat down at his desk and struck a pose which indicated that he'd been working days on end without a moment's rest. Without changing his position, he pressed the button on his bell. His private secretary Pokhlebyshev entered.

"Listen, my good man," said Comrade Koba to him. "Why are you always walking around with an armful of papers like some kind of bureaucrat? My word. Better you get the boys together, they can come by after work, a person has to relax somehow, get away from it all, talk, have some fun in the company of close friends."

Pokhlebyshev left and returned a short while later.

"They're all here and waiting for you, Comrade Koba."

"Very good. Let them wait a little."

For in the meantime Koba had found himself a most interesting diversion—cutting the pictures of various industrial leaders from the latest issue of *Ogonyok* and pasting the men's heads on the women's bodies and vice versa. It made for the most curious combinations, though it did use up quite a bit of his precious time.

Finally he appeared in the room where they were waiting for him. There was three rows of bottles on the table: Moskovskaya vodka, and Borzhomi, and Tsinandali dry wine. There were appetizers galore. To avoid confusion, the boys had seated themselves in alphabetical order: Leonty Aria, Nikola Borshchev, Efim Vershilov, Lazar Kazanovich, Zhorzh Merenkov, Opanas Mirzoyan, and Mocheslav Molokov. They all rose from their chairs when Koba appeared, and greeted his entrance with stormy applause and cries: "Long live Comrade Koba!" "Glory to Comrade Koba!" "Hurrah for Comrade Koba!"

Comrade Koba ran his eyes down the boys' faces noting with no little surprise the empty chair between Vershilov and Kazanovich.

"And where is our trusty Comrade Zhbanov tonight?" he asked.

Pokhlebyshev stepped out from behind Koba and reported: "Comrade Zhbanov requested permission to be late. His wife is in the hospital dying and she wanted him there in her final moments."

Comrade Koba frowned. A faint shadow flashed across his face.

"Interesting situation we have here," he said, making no attempt to conceal his bitter irony. "We're all here waiting, and as you see, some woman's whim means more to him than being with his friends. It's all right, though. We'll wait a little longer."

Shaking his head in distress, Koba left the room and returned to his office. There wasn't much he could do there. He'd already cut out all the pictures from *Ogonyok;* only the crossword puzzle was left. He pushed it over to Pokhlebyshev.

"You read them off to me, I'll try and figure them out. What's 1 across?"

"The first illegal newspaper in Georgia," read Pokhlebyshev, and shouted out the answer to himself: *"Brdzola! Brdzola!"*

"What are you giving me the answer for?" said Koba angrily. "I could have guessed it myself if I'd had time to think. All right, what's 1 down?"

"The largest prehistoric animal," read Pokhlebyshev.

"That's too easy," said Comrade Koba. "The largest animal was the elephant. Why aren't you writing 'elephant'?"

"Doesn't fit, Comrade Koba," said the secretary timidly.

"Doesn't fit? Of course, prehistoric. So write—'mammoth.' "

Pokhlebyshev bent over the crossword puzzle with his pencil, tapping the squares with the point, and then raised desperate eyes to Koba.

"Doesn't fit either?" asked Koba, amazed. "What's going on here? Was there really some animal bigger than a mammoth? Give it here." Sucking on his pipe, he examined the puzzle, counting the squares and thinking out loud: "Twelve letters. First letter—B. Could it be 'badger'? No. 'Beaver,' 'bulldog,' but they're all pretty small animals if I'm not mistaken. Why don't we call up one of our eminent biologists? Why should we rack our brains when they can give us a scientific answer if there was an animal beginning with B bigger than a mammoth. And if there wasn't, I don't envy the author of that crossword puzzle."

* * *

The telephone rang shrilly in the apartment of Academician Pleshivenko. A hoarse, imperious voice demanded that Pleshivenko come immediately to the phone. His sleepy wife answered angrily that Comrade Pleshivenko could not come to the phone, he was ill and sleeping.

"Wake him up!" An abrupt order was her reply.

"How dare you!" she said indignantly. "Do you know who you're speaking to?"

"I know," the voice answered impatiently. "Wake him up!"

"This is outrageous! I'll lodge a complaint! I'll phone the police!"

"Wake him up!" the voice insisted.

But by that time the academician was already awake.

"Trosha," said his wife, running to him, "Trosha, here, you take it."

Trosha took the phone irritably.

"Comrade Pleshivenko? Comrade Koba will speak personally with you in one moment."

"Comrade Koba?" Pleshivenko leaped out of bed as if lifted by the wind. Barefoot and naked except for his underpants, he stood on the cold floor, his wife beside him, immobile, her expression a mixture of joy and terror.

"Comrade Pleshivenko," a familiar voice with a Georgian accent boomed through the receiver. "Forgive me for calling so late . . ."

"Don't mention it, Comrade Koba," sputtered Pleshivenko. "It's my pleasure . . . mine and my wife's . . ."

"Comrade Pleshivenko," interrupted Koba, "to get right to the point, I'm calling on business. Certain of our comrades here have come up with a rather odd and unusual idea—with the aim of increasing the production of meat and milk, what if we were to somehow reintroduce to our fauna the largest prehistoric animal, what the hell is the name of it again, it's a twelve-letter word, I remember, beginning with B."

"Brontosaurus?" asked Pleshivenko uncertainly after a moment's thought.

Koba made quick use of his fingers: "B, r, o, n . . ." He covered the phone with the palm of his hand and, winking slyly, whispered to Pokhlebyshev: "Fill in 'brontosaurus.' " And then he said loudly into the phone: "Yes, exactly right, brontosaurus. And what's your reaction to this idea?"

"Comrade Koba," said Pleshivenko, all composure lost, "it's a very bold and original idea . . . That is, I mean to say it's simply an idea of . . ."

"Genius!" said the academician's wife with a little punch in his side as she awoke from her stupor. She did not know exactly what they were talking about, but she did know that the word "genius" was never out of place in such situations.

"Simply an idea of genius!" said the academician decisively, squinting off into space.

"For me it's only a working hypothesis," said Comrade Koba modestly. "We sit around, we work, we think."

"But it's a hypothesis of genius," objected the academician boldly. "It's a magnificent plan for the transformation of the animal world. If only you would permit our institute to get to work on elaborating some of the individual aspects of the problem . . ."

"I think some more hard thinking is still required. Once again I apologize for calling so late."

Pleshivenko stood for a long time with the receiver pressed to his ear and, listening intently to the distant, rapid, whistling sounds, whispered reverently but loud enough to be heard: "A genius! A genius! How fortunate I am to have the chance to live in the same era with him!"

The academician was not sure that anyone had heard him but still hoped that his words had not gone amiss.

Everything was in order when Comrade Koba returned. Anton Zhbanov had been found and installed in his usual seat. Leonty Aria had filled their tall glasses with vodka, Comrade Koba proposed the first toast.

"Dear friends," he said, "I invited you here to celebrate, among friends, the shortest night of the year, which is now beginning and which shall be followed by the longest day of the year . . ."

"Hurrah!" cried Vershilov.

"Not so fast," said Comrade Koba, knitting his brows. "You're always jumping the gun. I want to propose a toast— that all our nights be short, and that all our days be long . . ."

"Hurrah!" said Vershilov.

"You son of a bitch!" Enraged, Comrade Koba spat in his face.

Vershilov wiped the spit off with his sleeve and grinned.

"I also want to propose a toast to our wisest statesman, the staunchest revolutionary, the most brilliant . . ." began Koba.

Vershilov was about to shout "Hurrah!" just to be on the safe side, realizing that butter never spoils the porridge, but this time Comrade Koba managed to spit directly into Vershilov's open mouth.

". . . to a man great in both theory and practice, to Comrade . . ." Koba prolonged his significant pause, which he then terminated sharply: "Molokov."

The room fell silent. Merenkov and Mirzoyan exchanged glances. Borshchev unbuttoned the collar of his Ukrainian shirt. Aria clapped, then grabbed at his back pocket, which some angular object was bulging out of shape.

Two silent figures appeared in the doorway and froze.

Turning pale, Molokov set his glass aside and rose to his feet, holding on to the back of his chair so as not to fall.

"Comrade Koba," Molokov said in tongue-tied reproach, "what's this about? You're hurting my feelings without any reason to. You know I'm unworthy of all that praise, that nothing of the sort ever enters my mind. All my modest achievements are only a reflection of your great ideas. I am, if I may so express myself, merely a rank-and-file advocate of Kobaism, the greatest doctrine of our age. At your command, I am ready to give my all for you, even my life. It is you who are the staunchest revolutionary, you who are the greatest practitioner and theoretician . . ."

"A genius!" proclaimed Aria, raising his glass with his left hand since his right hand was still on his pocket.

"A marvelous architect!" acclaimed Merenkov.

"Best friend of the Armenian people!" interjected Mirzoyan.

"And the Ukrainian!" added Borshchev.

"Antosha, why aren't you saying anything?" Koba turned to Zhbanov, who had a sorrowful look about him.

"What is there left for me to say, Comrade Koba?" objected Zhbanov. "The comrades have done a first-rate job of illuminating your comprehensive role in history and contemporary life. Perhaps we say too little about it, perhaps we shy away from high-flown talk, but it's the truth all the same, that's the way it all really is. Everyday life furnishes us with dozens of striking examples which demonstrate how Kobaism is constantly penetrating deeper and deeper into the consciousness of the masses and truly becoming a guiding star for all mankind. But, Comrade Koba, here, in the free and open company of friends, I would like to point out yet another enormous talent you possess which your innate modesty prevents you from ever mentioning. It is your literary talent I have in mind. Yes, comrades," he said, elevating his tone and now addressing the entire company, "not long ago I had occasion to read once again Comrade Koba's early poetry, which he wrote under the pen name of Sosello. And in all candor I must say that this poetry, like precious pearls, could adorn the treasure house of any nation's literature, of all world literature, and if Pushkin were alive today . . ."

At that point Zhbanov burst into tears.

"Hurrah!" said Vershilov, but quietly this time and without retaliation from Koba.

The tension left the room. Leonty clapped his hands and the two silent figures by the door vanished into the air. Comrade Koba wiped away the tear running down his cheek. Perhaps he did not enjoy such things being said to him, but he enjoyed it even less when they were not.

"Thank you, dear friends," he said, though his tears interfered with his speaking. "Thank you for putting so high a value on the modest services I have rendered for the people. I personally think my doctrine, which you have so aptly named Kobaism, is truly good, not because it's mine, but because it's a progressive doctrine. And you, my dear friends, have put no little effort into making it that progressive. So, without any false modesty, let's drink to Kobaism."

"To Kobaism! To Kobaism!" They all joined in.

They drank down their vodka, knocked their glasses against the table, then drank again. After the fourth glass, Comrade Koba decided he needed a little entertainment and requested Borshchev to dance the *gopak*.

"You're Ukrainian, you'll do fine," he said encouragingly.

Borshchev hopped from his chair into a squat, Zhbanov accompanied him on the piano, and the rest of them clapped their hands in time to the music.

At that moment a messenger appeared without making a sound and handed Zhbanov a telegram informing him that his wife had just died in the hospital.

"Don't bother me," said Zhbanov. "Can't you see I'm busy."

The messenger withdrew. Then Comrade Koba personally strode over to Zhbanov. He stroked his trusty comrade's head with his rough and manly hand.

"You're a true Bolshevik, Antosha," said Koba with feeling.

Zhbanov raised his eyes, full of tears and devotion, to his teacher.

"Keep playing, keep playing," said Comrade Koba. "You could have made a name for yourself as a musician, but you chose to devote all your strength and talent to our party, our people."

Koba walked back to the table and sat down across from

Molokov, Mirzoyan, and Merenkov, who were involved in a discussion.

"And what are we talking about here?" asked Comrade Koba.

"We were just saying," Molokov, who was sitting in the middle, answered readily, "that the agreement with Dolph, concluded on your initiative, of course, was both wise and timely."

Koba glowered. Because of the reports that had recently come to his attention, there was nothing he wanted to hear about less than that blasted agreement.

"I'm curious," he said, staring at Molokov, "I'm curious to know why you wear glasses, Mocha?"

Another whiff of danger. Zhbanov began playing more softly. Borshchev, still squatting and dancing, looked from Molokov to Koba. Just to be on the safe side, Merenkov and Mirzoyan moved away, each to one end of the table, Molokov, pale as a ghost, rose on legs out of his control and, not knowing what to say, looked in silence at Comrade Koba.

"So, you cannot tell me why you wear glasses?"

Molokov remained silent.

"But I know already. I'm well aware why you wear glasses. But I won't tell you. I want you to use your head and then tell me the real reason you wear glasses."

Shaking a threatening finger at Molokov, Koba suddenly let his head drop into a plate full of green peas and immediately fell asleep.

"I've got to stretch my legs a bit," said Mirzoyan cheerfully and slipped away from the table with an independent air. Then Merenkov, too, slipped away. Taking advantage of the absence of authority, Vershilov and Kazanovich found a corner and started playing cards. Borshchev, who had not received permission to rest, continued dancing to Zhbanov's accompaniment, but he, too, had already begun to slacken off —he was no longer squatting fully, just bending his knees a little.

Aria was sitting by himself, playing mumblety-peg with his knife.

Suddenly this peaceful picture was shattered. Vershilov's hand shot out and slapped Kazanovich resoundingly across the face. This was more than Kazanovich could bear, and screeching, he dug his fingernails into Vershilov's face. They rolled on the floor.

Awakened by the commotion. Comrade Koba raised his head. Catching sight of this, Borshchev sank back into a deep squat with renewed vigor, Zhbanov began playing at a livelier tempo, and Merenkov and Mirzoyan began clapping their hands in time to the music.

"Enough." Koba waved angrily at Borshchev. "Take a break."

Borshchev staggered to the table and polished off a glass of Borzhomi. Vershilov and Kazanovich continued rolling on the floor, which was strewn with their cards. Kazanovich succeeded in grabbing hold of his opponent's right ear; Vershilov kept on trying to knee Kazanovich below the belt. Koba summoned Aria over.

"Listen, Leonty, what kind of people are these, anyway? Leaders or gladiators?"

Aria brushed off his knee and stood up in front of Koba, holding his curved Caucasian dagger, with which, a moment before, he'd been playing mumbletypeg.

"Shall I pry them apart?" he asked darkly, testing the blade with his thumbnail.

"Please. Except do me one favor and put that dagger away. God forbid something terrible might happen."

Leonty slipped the dagger into his belt, walked over to the combatants, and gave them each individually a good kick. They both hopped to their feet and made quite an unsavory sight as they presented themselves to Comrade Koba. Vershilov was smearing blood across his face, Kazanovich gently feeling the dark bruise swelling under his left eye.

"So, so," said Koba, shaking his head. "Our people have

entrusted their fate to men like you. What game were you playing?"

Embarrassed, the two enemies looked at their feet.

"Come on, I'm asking you a question."

Kazanovich glowered up sullenly at Koba.

"Blackjack, Comrade Koba."

"Blackjack?"

"Nothing to it, Comrade Koba, just a little game."

"I don't understand," said Comrade Koba, spreading out his hands. "What do we have here? Bosses? Leaders? Or just a bunch of crooks. What was the fight about?"

"That kike was cheating," answered Vershilov.

"What kind of word is that, 'kike'?" asked Koba angrily.

"I'm sorry, the Jew," Vershilov corrected himself.

"You're a stupid person." Koba sighed. "An anti-Semite. How many times have I told you to get rid of those great-power ways of yours. I'm giving you one week to study all my works on the question of nationalities, you understand me?"

"I do."

"All right, go. And you, Kazanovich, you didn't behave right either. You Jews do nothing but furnish anti-Semitism with ammunition by your appearance and provocative behavior. I'm getting tired of struggling with anti-Semitism; at some point I'll get fed up."

Koba was about to develop this thought further when Pokhlebyshev appeared. "Comrade Koba, we've just received a dispatch. Dolph's troops have moved right up to the border."

These words made Comrade Koba uneasy. "Come over here," he said to his secretary. "Bend close to me."

Koba took his pipe from the table and began knocking out the ashes on Pokhlebyshev's balding head.

"Dolph's my friend," he said as if hammering his words into his secretary's head. "It's our custom in the Caucasus to stand up for our friends with everything we've got. We can forgive someone insulting our sister or our brother, we can forgive someone insulting our father or our mother, but we cannot forgive someone insulting a friend. To insult my friend is to insult me."

He threw his pipe to the floor and raised Pokhlebyshev's head, using the one-finger-under-the-chin method. Fat tears were running down Pokhlebyshev's face.

"Oh, you're crying!" said Comrade Koba in surprise. "Tell me why you're crying."

"I'm crying because you spoke so touchingly about friendship," said Pokhlebyshev, sobbing and tugging at his nose.

Comrade Koba softened. "So, all right then," he said with a little more warmth in his voice, "I know you're a good man at heart, you're just severe on the outside. Go rest up a bit and tell the doctor to put some iodine on your head, God forbid you should get an infection."

Comrade Koba then reassembled all the boys at the table and proposed a toast to friendship.

"Comrade Koba," asked Molokov, "may I drink with you, too?"

Comrade Koba did not answer, letting the question slip in one ear and out the other. Molokov continued to hold his glass of vodka, and, unable to make up his mind one way or the other, stayed just as he was.

Next, Comrade Koba expressed a desire to play a little music. He walked over to the piano and, playing with one finger, sang the following well-known ditty:

> I was up on the hill,
> I gave Egor all I had,
> Now don't you think I was bad,
> It was just my rolling tobacco . . .

Everyone broke into amiable laughter and applauded. In a short speech Comrade Zhbanov remarked on the high artistic merits of the piece. Vershilov took out a pad of paper and a stubby indelible-ink pen from his pocket and requested permission to take down the words of the ditty on the spot.

"I'll copy them down, too," said Borshchev. "I'll sing it to Zinka tomorrow. She'll get a laugh out of it."

"Sure, let her have a laugh," said Koba, returning to his place at the table. He laid his head on his arms and again fell immediately asleep.

The earliest dawn of that summer began, the night growing gradually lighter like ink being diluted with water. Everything stood out with increasing clarity against the background of the brightening sky, the golden cupolas sharpened in relief.

No little vodka had been drunk that night, and now the group was beginning to fade. Comrade Koba was sleeping at the table. Aria, his hand still on his back pocket, had reclined on the sofa and dozed off. Mirzoyan was snoring noisily under the table, using Merenkov's cheek for a pillow. Still not daring to budge, his face like stone, Molokov was sitting in front of Comrade Koba. Kazanovich and Vershilov had made their peace and were playing cards again. Zhbanov was standing in the corner, his forehead against the cold wall, trying to vomit. Only Borshchev was still wandering quietly about the room with a look of great concentration on his face, as if he had lost something and was trying to find it. He had apparently sobered up and now a hangover was torturing his brain, which was filled with vague and gloomy thoughts. Crinkling his face in sympathy, Borshchev stood near Zhbanov and recommended the old folk remedy—two fingers down the throat. Zhbanov mooed something resembling words and shook his head. Borshchev then walked over to the card players. He started following their game out of simple curiosity, but Vershilov soon drove him away. Borshchev looked over at Leonty and, convinced that he was sleeping, sat down by Molokov, keeping, however, a certain distance. He sighed loudly in an attempt to attract Molokov's attention. Without turning his head, Molokov looked out of the corner of his eye at Borshchev, who winked back and said in a whisper: "You should take off your glasses for the time being. Comrade Koba's been a little nervous lately, you shouldn't get him riled up. Later on he'll forget all about it and you can put them back on."

Borshchev grabbed a cucumber from the table, took a bite of it, and spat it right back out. Bitter! He gave Koba a sidelong look and then sighed once again. "Of course it's tough working with him. He's not a regular person, he's a genius. But what am I doing here? I used to work in the mines, drilling coal. Not what you might call the cleanest work, but it was a living. Now look at me, I've ended up as one of the leaders, they carry portraits of me when the people parade through the streets. But what kind of leader can I be when all I've got is a third-grade education and Advanced Party School? The rest of you are all prominent people. Theoreticians. I've heard that you know twelve languages. Now take me, for example; I consider myself a Ukrainian, I lived in the Ukraine, but I couldn't speak their language if you put a gun to my head. It's a funny language they've got. We say 'staircase' and they say 'stairladder.' " Borshchev burst out laughing as if the strangeness of Ukrainian had just struck him for the first time.

Even Molokov smiled. The rumors about his knowledge of foreign languages were greatly exaggerated. The fact of the matter was that at one point, to increase the authority of the ruling body, Comrade Koba had endowed them with merits that none of them had previously even suspected themselves of possessing. Thus, Merenkov became a major philosopher and the theoretician of Kobaism; Mirzoyan became a man of business; Kazanovich a technician; Aria a psychologist; Vershilov an outstanding general; Zhbanov a specialist in all the arts; Borshchev a Ukrainian; and he, Molokov, who knew a few foreign words and expressions, a linguist.

Naturally, Molokov said nothing of this to Borshchev, remarking only that his life was no bowl of cherries either.

"There's something I don't get," sighed Borshchev. "Where's your conscience if you can pick on someone because of his glasses. He asked you why you wear glasses. Maybe you just like to. If he talked about me like that," said

Borshchev, growing heated, "I'd spit right in his face and not be shy about it either."

At that moment Comrade Koba stirred in his sleep. Borshchev froze in horror, but his fears were groundless; Koba remained asleep. "What a fool I am," thought Borshchev with a sigh of relief. "Like they say, the tongue's loose, it's got no bones in it. But with a tongue like mine, oi, what trouble you could get in!" He decided not to talk any more with his colleague who was out of favor, but he couldn't restrain himself and once again he bent close to Molokov's ear.

"Listen, Mocheslav," he whispered, "what about asking him to let us go? Look, if he's a genius, let him decide everything himself. What the hell does he need us for?"

"All right," said Molokov, "but what would we live on?"

"We'll go to the mines. I'll teach you how to mine coal, it's simple. First you dig down into the bed, then you pull out the coal from the top. The money's not like the money we're making here, but the work's less risky. Of course you might get buried in a cave-in but that's a one-time thing; here you die from terror every single day."

Borshchev shuddered, then straightened up, having heard someone breathing behind him. It was Aria. Rubbing his ear with the handle of his dagger, Aria cast a curious glance from Borshchev to Molokov. "What could you be talking about that has you so absorbed, I wonder," he said, imitating Koba's intonation.

Did he hear or not? flashed through both minds.

He heard, decided Molokov, and immediately found the surest way out of the predicament.

"Comrade Borshchev here," he said with a touch of sarcasm, "was just suggesting that he and I abandon our political activities and join the inner emigration."

But you couldn't put anything over on Borshchev either. "You fool!" he said, rising and smoothing his chest. "I only wanted to feel you out and see what makes you tick. Doesn't matter anyway, nobody's going to believe you. Everybody knows I don't wear glasses. My eyes are clear when I look into Comrade Koba's eyes and into the distance shining with our beautiful future."

"Here's the future for you," mimicked Molokov. "First learn Russian properly, and then . . ."

He never finished his sentence. Fortunately for both of them, Pokhlebyshev came flying into the room, his head swathed in bandages.

"Comrade Koba! Comrade Koba!" he shouted as he entered the room, for which he immediately received a box on the ear from Leonty.

"Can't you see that Comrade Koba's busy with his predawn sleep?" said Leonty. "What's happened now?"

Shaking with extraordinary excitement, Pokhlebyshev kept repeating one word: Dolph. It required tremendous effort to squeeze out of him the fact that Dolph's troops had poured across the border.

An urgent, special, and extraordinary meeting then took place, chaired by Leonty Aria. Comrade Koba, still sleeping in his chair, was elected honorary chairman. The group began deliberations on which course to take. Vershilov said that it was imperative to announce a general mobilization. Kazanovich proposed that all bridges and train stations should be blown up at once. Mirzoyan, taking the floor to reply, noted that although their meeting was both timely and businesslike, they should not lose sight of the presence and at the same time the absence of Comrade Koba.

"We can of course make one decision or another," he said, "but after all it's no secret that none of us has any guarantees against making some serious mistakes."

"But we'll be acting as a collective," said Kazanovich.

"A collective, Comrade Kazanovich, consists of individuals, as everyone knows. If a single individual can commit a single error, several individuals can commit several errors. Only one man can reach an infallibly wise and correct decision. And that one man is Comrade Koba. He, however, unfortunately, at the moment is busy with his pre-dawn sleep."

"Why do you say 'unfortunately'?" interrupted Leonty Aria. "I'm obliged to correct Comrade Mirzoyan here. It is truly fortunate that at a time so difficult for us all Comrade Koba is busy with his pre-dawn sleep, building up his strength for the wise decisions he will soon be making."

Merenkov requested a point of order and said: "I totally and completely support Comrade Aria for rebuffing Comrade Mirzoyan for his ill-considered words. It would appear that Comrade Mirzoyan had no criminal intentions and his statement should be considered a simple slip of the tongue, though of course at times it is quite difficult to draw a sufficiently clear boundary between a simple slip of the tongue and a premeditated offense. At the same time I think it would be advisable to acknowledge that Comrade Mirzoyan is correct in thinking that only Comrade Koba can make a correct, wise, and principled decision concerning Dolph's treacherous invasion. However, in this connection, yet another question arises, one that requires immediate resolution, one which I now propose be discussed, namely, shall we wake Comrade Koba or wait until he wakes up himself?"

The comrades' opinion was divided on the subject. Some thought he should be awakened; others proposed waiting, since Comrade Koba himself knew best when he needed to sleep and when he should wake up.

In spite of having just learned of his wife's death and in spite of being ill from alcohol poisoning, Comrade Zhbanov took an active part in the debate and said that, before deciding the question of whether or not to wake Koba, it was necessary to decide a question which preceded that one, a subquestion so to speak, concerning the seriousness of Dolph's intentions and whether this might simply be a provocation designed to interrupt Comrade Koba's sleep. But to decide whether this was a serious invasion or a mere provocation was again something that could only be determined by Comrade Koba personally.

Finally two issues were put to vote:
1. To wake Comrade Koba.

2. Not to wake Comrade Koba.

The results of the voting on both propositions were as follows: For—no one. Against—no one. Abstaining—no one.

It was noted in the minutes of the meeting that both questions had been decided unanimously and that certain of Comrade Mirzoyan's ill-considered statements had been pointed out to him. After the minutes had been drawn up, Comrade Molokov unexpectedly asked for the floor to make some supplementary remarks. He realized that now his only salvation lay in taking an active role. Molokov said that in view of the developing situation he intended to wake up Comrade Koba at once and take full responsibility for the consequences of his act.

That said, he walked decisively over to Comrade Koba and began shaking his shoulder. "Comrade Koba, wake up!"

Comrade Koba shook his head without yet waking up. His legs twitched.

"Comrade Koba, it's war!" In desperation Molokov shouted right in his ear, this time shaking him so hard that Koba woke up.

"War?" repeated Koba, looking at his comrades' faces with uncomprehending eyes. He poured a bottle of vodka over his head and halted his gaze at Molokov. "War with who?"

"With Dolph," said Molokov, who had nothing left to lose.

"So, it's war?" Comrade Koba was gradually coming around. "And when was it declared?"

"That's just it, Comrade Koba, that's the treachery of it all, war hasn't been declared."

"Hasn't been declared?" said Koba in surprise, filling his pipe with the tobacco from a pack of Kazbek cigarettes. "Interesting. And how do you know it's war if war hasn't been declared?"

"We received a dispatch," said Molokov desperately.

"But if war hasn't been declared, it means there's no war. For that reason we Kobaists do not accept or acknowledge it, for to accept something which doesn't exist is to slip into the swamp of idealism. Isn't that so, comrades?"

Everyone was staggered. A thought of such brilliance could never have entered any of their minds. Only a genius could have resolved such a complex problem with such ease.

"Hurrah!" cried Vershilov boldly.

"Hurrah!" seconded all the remaining comrades.

"And now I want to sleep," Comrade Koba announced decisively. "Who'll give me a hand?"

Molokov and Kazanovich took their teacher under the arm. Vershilov, too, rushed forward but wasn't quick enough.

"You shout louder than anybody else," Koba remarked disapprovingly, "but when it comes to action, you're not quick enough. Next time be a little faster on your feet. And you, Mocha," said Koba, giving Molokov a little slap on the cheek, "you're a true staunch warrior and Kobaist and I'll tell you straight off why you wear glasses. You wear glasses because you don't have such good eyesight. And every person who doesn't have good eyesight should wear glasses so he can see clearly what's in front of him. All right, let's get going!"

He dismissed his two helpers at the door to his office and locked himself in. He listened for a while until he was sure that Kazanovich and Molokov had walked away, and only then did he crawl into his room, taking the usual route through the safe. Upon arrival, he threw his pipe in the corner, then ripped off his moustache and flung it to the corner as well. He was perfectly sober. He had realized what was happening. He had not been sleeping when Pokhlebyshev reported Dolph's attack and he had not been sleeping during the meeting of his comrades. He had been playing the role of a drunken man asleep and he had played it very well because, of all the talents ascribed to him, he did possess one—he was an actor.

Now, with no spectators, there was no reason to play a part. Comrade Koba sat down on his bed, pulled off his boots, unbuttoned his pants, and sank into thought. Somehow things weren't turning out right. He had never trusted anybody except this once and look what had happened. How could he have any faith in people after this? Still, he had to find some way out. In this country, he thought to himself, it's you alone who does the thinking for everyone and nobody is going to do any thinking for you. What to do? Address an appeal to the people? And say what? Forgive me, my dear people, it seems I've just about fuc . . . Oh, he had almost said a dirty word. Request military assistance from the Americans? Or political asylum for himself? Then what? Settle somewhere in Florida and write his memoirs: *My Life as a Tyrant*. Or maybe go into hiding in Georgia and live there disguised as a simple shoemaker?

"Soso," his father used to tell him, "you'll never make a real cobbler."

Comrade Koba lifted his eyes and noticed a pitiable, moustacheless old man on the opposite wall. Mechanically rubbing his scrawny knees, the old man was sitting on an iron bed, his pants at his ankles. Comrade Koba smiled bitterly.

"So there it is," he said to the old man. "Now you see. You thought you were the most cunning, the craftiest. You wouldn't listen to anyone's advice or warning. You ripped out every tongue that tried to tell you the truth. And the one man in the world you trusted turned out to be more cunning and crafty than you. Who's going to help you now? Who's going to support you now? The people? They hate you. Your so-called comrades? Comrades, that's a laugh. A bunch of court flatterers and flunkies. They'd be the first to sell you out as soon as they got the chance. In the old days, at least jesters and saints were allowed to tell the truth. But who'll tell the truth now? You demanded lies; now you can choke on them. Everybody lies now—your newspapers, your public speakers, your spies, your informers. But there still is one man with the courage to tell you the truth to your face. And he's sitting right in front of you now. He sees right through you like you were his own self. Look at yourself, you who considered yourself a superman. What kind of superman are you, anyway? You're small, pockmarked, you've got aches and pains everywhere. Your head aches, your liver aches, your intestines do a lousy job of digesting what you gobble down, the meat you steal from your hungry people. Why then, if you're such a superman, are your teeth and hair falling out? Superparasite, why did you kill so many people? Mensheviks, Bolsheviks, priests, peasants, intellectuals, children, mothers . . . Why did you ruin agriculture and decapitate the army? For the sake of a brighter future? No, for your own personal power. You like it when everyone fears you like the plague. But you, the creator of an empire of fear, aren't you the most frightened person in it? What is there you don't fear? A shot from behind, poison in your wine, a bomb under your bed. You're afraid of your own comrades, guards, cooks, barbers, your own shadow and reflection. Driven by your own fear, you ferret out enemies of the people and counter-Kobaists everywhere. There's no need to. Just look at yourself—you are the number-one enemy of the people, the number-one counter-Kobaist."

While Koba was speaking, the old man's face glowered and grew increasingly malicious. It was obvious that, as usual, the truth was not to his liking. He fended off the reproaches hurled at him by flailing his arms, grimacing, and crinkling up his face. As he spoke his final words, Koba's hand began moving of its own toward the pillow. He noticed the old man doing the same thing. He had to beat him to it. Koba darted and grabbed the pistol from under the pillow. At that same instant an identical pistol flashed in the old man's hand. But Koba had already pulled the trigger.

Gunfire in an enclosed area always produces a great deal of noise. One shot followed by another and the old man's pockmarked face cracked into a web of crooked lines. The room smelled of hot gun oil. Koba's eardrums vibrated; the old man's nasty face burst apart, flew into falling pieces, creating the illusion of a living man writhing in the throes of death.

Suddenly everything was silent. The pistol was empty, Koba looked up—now there was no one there.

"That's it," said Koba sadly, and with significance, though to exactly whom was unclear. "I have saved the people from the hangman." And with those words he tossed away the pistol, which was of no further use to him.

It later appeared that no one had heard the shots. This should cause no surprise—the walls of Koba's room were so thick that even sounds of a much greater magnitude would not have escaped them.

The old woman who came the next morning to clean the room saw the slivers of glass strewn everywhere. She found the master lying on his back in bed. His left leg was on the bed, his right leg, with his pants caught around the ankle, was on the floor. His right hand hung lifelessly, almost touching the floor. At first deciding that Comrade Koba had shot himself, the old woman was about to sound the alarm, but then, convinced that the body on the bed had suffered no harm, she decided against it, not wishing to be called in as a witness. She put his arm and leg up on the bed, finished pulling off his pants, and covered Comrade Koba with a camel's hair blanket, carefully tucking it in around him. That done, she set about cleaning up the glass, hoping that Comrade Koba would certainly sleep off his drunkenness by the next day. But he did not wake up the next day, or the day after; reliable sources indicate he spent the next ten days in a lethargic sleep. They say that it was sometime during those ten days that the old woman retired and brought the note concerning the millet to the Museum of the Revolution. I, however, do not believe that. I believe the note's value would have fallen somewhat during those ten days, then risen back in value afterward. Clearly, the old woman was clever enough to bring that note to the best possible place to sell and therefore would also have waited for the best possible price. Besides, there now exist many contradictory opinions concerning the old woman. Supporters of the pro-Kobaist line in our historical scholarship, while not denying the existence of the old woman, doubt that she actually removed Comrade Koba's pants, which they consider unremovable. These scholars point out that just as Comrade Koba was born in a generalissimo's uniform, he lived his life in it as well, without ever having once removed it. The adherents of the anti-Kobaist line, on the other hand, maintain that Comrade Koba was born naked but that his body was covered with thick fur. From a distance his contemporaries mistook this fur for a common soldier's overcoat or a generalissimo's uniform. Not adhering myself to either of these versions, I admit finding each of them interesting in their own way.

(1967)

P.S. *This story is solely the product of the author's fantasy. Any resemblance of any of the characters to actual people is purely coincidental.*

George Orwell

George Orwell *(1903–1950) was born Eric Arthur Blair in Bengal. He was one of the finest English essayists of the century and his novels* Animal Farm *and* 1984 *are classics. "Shooting an Elephant" recounts his experiences as a member of the British imperial police in Burma.*

SHOOTING AN ELEPHANT

In Moulmein, in Lower Burma, I was hated by large numbers of people—the only time in my life that I have been important enough for this to happen to me. I was sub-divisional police officer of the town, and in an aimless, petty kind of way anti-European feeling was very bitter. No one had the guts to raise a riot, but if a European woman went through the bazaars alone somebody would probably spit betel juice over her dress. As a police officer I was an obvious target and was baited whenever it seemed safe to do so. When a nimble Burman tripped me up on the football field and the referee (another Burman) looked the other way, the crowd yelled with hideous laughter. This happened more than once. In the end the sneering yellow faces of young men that met me everywhere, the insults hooted after me when I was at a safe distance, got badly on my nerves. The young Buddhist priests were the worst of all. There were several thousands of them in the town and none of them seemed to have anything to do except stand on street corners and jeer at Europeans.

All this was perplexing and upsetting. For at that time I had already made up my mind that imperialism was an evil thing and the sooner I chucked up my job and got out of it the better. Theoretically—and secretly, of course—I was all for the Burmese and all against their oppressors, the British. As for the job I was doing, I hated it more bitterly than I can perhaps make clear. In a job like that you see the dirty work of Empire at close quarters. The wretched prisoners huddling in the stinking cages of the lock-ups, the grey, cowed faces of the long-term convicts, the scarred buttocks of the men who had been flogged with bamboos—all these oppressed me with an intolerable sense of guilt. But I could get nothing into perspective. I was young and ill-educated and I had had to think out my problems in the utter silence that is imposed on every Englishman in the East. I did not even know that the British Empire is dying, still less did I know that it is a great deal better than the younger empires that are going to supplant it. All I knew was that I was stuck between my hatred of the empire I served and my rage against the evil-spirited little beasts who tried to make my job impossible. With one part of my mind I thought of the British Raj as an unbreakable tyranny, as something clamped down, *in saecula saeculorum*, upon the will of prostrate peoples; with another part I thought that the greatest joy in the world would be to drive a bayonet into a Buddhist priest's guts. Feelings like these are the normal by-products of imperialism; ask any Anglo-Indian official, if you can catch him off duty.

One day something happened which in a roundabout way was enlightening. It was a tiny incident in itself, but it gave me a better glimpse than I had had before of the real nature of imperialism—the real motives for which despotic governments act. Early one morning the sub-inspector at a police station the other end of the town rang me up on the phone and said that an elephant was ravaging the bazaar. Would I please come and do something about it? I did not know what I could do, but I wanted to see what was happening and I got on to a pony and started out. I took my rifle, an old .44 Winchester and much too small to kill an elephant, but I thought the noise might be useful *in terrorem*. Various Burmans stopped me on the way and told me about the elephant's doings. It was not, of course, a wild elephant, but a tame one which had gone "must". It had been chained up as tame elephants always are when their attack of "must" is due, but on the previous night it had broken its chain and escaped. Its mahout, the only person who could manage it when it was in that state, had set out in pursuit, but he had taken the wrong direction and was now twelve hours' journey away, and in the morning the elephant had suddenly reappeared in the town. The Burmese population had no weapons and were quite helpless against it. It had already destroyed somebody's bamboo hut, killed a cow and raided some fruit-stalls and devoured the stock; also it had met the municipal rubbish van, and, when the driver jumped out and took to his heels, had turned the van over and inflicted violence upon it.

The Burmese sub-inspector and some Indian constables were waiting for me in the quarter where the elephant had been seen. It was a very poor quarter, a labyrinth of squalid bamboo huts, thatched with palm-leaf, winding all over a steep hillside. I remember that it was a cloudy stuffy morning at the beginning of the rains. We began questioning the people as to where the elephant had gone, and, as usual, failed to get any definite information. That is invariably the case in the East; a story always sounds clear enough at a distance, but the nearer you get to the scene of events the vaguer it becomes. Some of the people said that the elephant had gone in one direction, some said that he had gone in another, some professed not even to have heard of any elephant. I had almost made up my mind that the whole story was a pack of lies, when we heard yells a little distance away. There was a loud, scandalised cry of "Go away, child! Go away this instant!" and an old woman with a switch in her hand came round the corner of a hut, violently shooing away a crowd of naked children. Some more women followed, clicking their tongues and exclaiming; evidently there was something there that the children ought not to have seen. I rounded the hut and saw a man's dead body sprawling in the mud. He was an Indian, a black Dravidian coolie, almost naked, and he could not have been dead many minutes. The people said that the elephant had come suddenly upon him round the corner of the hut, caught him with its trunk, put its foot on his back and ground him into the earth. This was the rainy season and the ground was soft, and his face had scored a trench a foot deep and a couple of yards long. He was lying on his belly with arms crucified and head sharply twisted to one side. His face was coated with mud, the eyes wide open, the teeth bared and grinning with an expression of unendurable agony. (Never tell me, by the way, that the dead look peaceful. Most of the corpses I have seen looked devilish.) The friction of the great beast's foot had stripped the skin from his back as neatly as one skins a rabbit. As soon as I saw the dead man I sent an orderly to a friend's house nearby to borrow an elephant rifle. I had already sent back the pony, not wanting it to go mad with fright and throw me if it smelled the elephant.

The orderly came back in a few minutes with a rifle and five cartridges, and meanwhile some Burmans had arrived and told us that the elephant was in the paddy fields below, only a few hundred yards away. As I started forward practically the whole population of the quarter flocked out of their houses and followed me. They had seen the rifle and were all shouting excitedly that I was going to shoot the elephant. They had not shown much interest in the elephant when he was merely ravaging their homes, but it was different now that he was going to be shot. It was a bit of fun to them, as it would be to an English crowd; besides, they wanted the meat. It made me vaguely uneasy. I had no intention of shooting the elephant—I had merely sent for the rifle to defend myself if necessary—and it is always unnerving to have a crowd following you. I marched down the hill, looking and feeling a fool, with the rifle over my shoulder and an evergrowing army of people jostling at my heels. At the bottom, when you got away from the huts, there was a metalled road and beyond that a miry waste of paddy fields a thousand yards across, not yet ploughed but soggy from the first rains and dotted with coarse grass. The elephant was standing eighty yards from the road, his left side towards us. He took not the slightest notice of the crowd's approach. He was tearing up bunches of grass, beating them against his knees to clean them and stuffing them into his mouth.

I had halted on the road. As soon as I saw the elephant I knew with perfect certainty that I ought not to shoot him. It is a serious matter to shoot a working elephant—it is comparable to destroying a huge and costly piece of machinery—and obviously one ought not to do it if it can possibly be avoided. And at that distance, peacefully eating, the elephant looked no more dangerous than a cow. I thought then and I think now that his attack of "must" was already passing off; in which case he would merely wander harmlessly about until the mahout came back and caught him. Moreover, I did not in the least want to shoot him. I decided that I would watch him for a little while to make sure that he did not turn savage again, and then go home.

But at that moment I glanced round at the crowd that had followed me. It was an immense crowd, two thousand at the least and growing every minute. It blocked the road for a long distance on either side. I looked at the sea of yellow faces above the garish clothes—faces all happy and excited over this bit of fun, all certain that the elephant was going to be shot. They were watching me as they would watch a conjuror about to perform a trick. They did not like me, but with the magical rifle in my hands I was momentarily worth watching. And suddenly I realised that I should have to shoot the elephant after all. The people expected it of me and I had got to do it; I could feel their two thousand wills pressing me forward, irresistibly. And it was at this moment, as I stood there with the rifle in my hands, that I first grasped the hollowness, the futility of the white man's dominion in the East. Here was I, the white man with his gun, standing in front of the unarmed native crowd—seemingly the leading actor of the piece; but in reality I was only an absurd puppet pushed to and fro by the will of those yellow faces behind. I perceived in this moment that when the white man turns tyrant it is his own freedom that he destroys. He becomes a sort of hollow, posing dummy, the conventionalised figure of a sahib. For it is the condition of his rule that he shall spend his life in trying to impress the "natives" and so in every crisis he has got to do what the "natives" expect of him. He wears a mask, and his face grows to fit it. I had got to shoot the elephant. I had committed myself to doing it when I sent for the rifle. A sahib has got to act like a sahib; he has got to appear resolute, to know his own mind and do definite things. To come all that way, rifle in hand, with two thousand people marching at my heels, and then to trail feebly away, having done nothing—no, that was impossible. The crowd would laugh at me. And my whole life, every white man's life in the East, was one long struggle not to be laughed at.

But I did not want to shoot the elephant. I watched him beating his bunch of grass against his knees, with that preoccupied grandmotherly air that elephants have. It seemed to me that it would be murder to shoot him. At that age I was not squeamish about killing animals, but I had never shot an elephant and never wanted to. (Somehow it always seems worse to kill a *large* animal.) Besides, there was the beast's owner to be considered. Alive, the elephant was worth at least a hundred pounds; dead he would only be worth the value of his tusks—five pounds, possibly. But I had got to act quickly. I turned to some experienced-looking Burmans who had been there when we arrived, and asked them how the elephant had been behaving. they all said the same thing: he took no notice of you if you left him alone, but he might charge if you went too close to him.

It was perfectly clear to me what I ought to do. I ought to walk up to within, say, twenty-five yards of the elephant and test his behaviour. If he charged I could shoot, if he took no notice of me it would be safe to leave him until the mahout came back. But also I knew that I was going to do no such thing. I was a poor shot with a rifle and the ground was soft

mud into which one would sink at every step. If the elephant
charged and I missed him, I should have about as much
chance as a toad under a steam roller. But even then I was
not thinking particularly of my own skin, only the watchful
yellow faces behind. For at that moment, with the crowd
watching me, I was not afraid in the ordinary sense, as I
would have been if I had been alone. A white man mustn't be
frightened in front of "natives"; and so, in general, he isn't
frightened. The sole thought in my mind was that if anything
went wrong those two thousand Burmans would see me pursued, caught, trampled on and reduced to a grinning corpse
like that Indian up the hill. And if that happened it was quite
probably that some of them would laugh. That would never
do. There was only one alternative. I shoved the cartridges
into the magazine and lay down on the road to get a better
aim.

The crowd grew very still, and a deep, low, happy sigh, as of
people who see the theatre curtain go up at lasts, breathed
from innumerable throats. They were going to have their bit
of fun after all. The rifle was a beautiful German thing with
cross-hair sights. I did not then know that in shooting an
elephant one should shoot to cut an imaginary bar running
from ear-hole to ear-hole. I ought therefore, as the elephant
was sideways on, to have aimed straight at his ear-hole; actually I aimed several inches in front of this, thinking the brain
would be further forward.

When I pulled the trigger I did not hear the bang or feel
the kick—one never does when a shot goes home—but I
heard the develish roar of glee that went up from the crowd.
In that instant, in too short a time, one would have thought,
even for the bullet to get there, a mysterious, terrible change
had come over the elephant. He neither stirred, nor fell, but
every line of his body altered. He looked suddenly stricken,
shrunken, immensely old, as though the frightful impact of
the bullet had paralysed him without knocking him down. At
last, after what seemed a long time—it might have been five
seconds, I dare say—he sagged flabbily to his knees. His

mouth slobbered. An enormous senility seemed to have settled upon him. One could have imagined him thousands of years old. I fired again into the same spot. At the second shot he did not collapse but climbed with desperate slowness to his feet and stood weakly upright, with legs sagging and head drooping. I fired a third time. That was the shot that did for him. You could see the agony of it jolt his whole body and knock the last remnant of strength from his legs. But in falling he seemed for a moment to rise, for as his hind legs collapsed beneath him he seemed to tower upwards like a huge rock toppling, his trunk reaching skyward like a tree. He trumpeted, for the first and only time. And then down he came, his belly towards me, with a crash that seemed to shake the ground even wher I lay.

I got up. The Burmans were already racing past me across the mud. It was obvious that the elephant would never rise again, but he was not dead. He was breathing very rhythmically with long rattling gasps, his great mound of a side painfully rising and falling. His mouth was wide open—I could see far down into caverns of pale pink throat. I waited a long time for him to die, but his breathing did not weaken. Finally I fired my two remaining shots into the spot where I thought his heart must be. The thick blood welled out of him like red velvet, but still he did not die. His body did not even jerk when the shots hit him, the tortured breathing continued without a pause. He was dying, very slowly and in great agony, but in some world remote from me where not even a bullet could damage him further. I felt that I had got to put an end to that dreadful noise. It seemed dreadful to see the great beast lying there, powerless to move and yet powerless to die, and not even to be able to finish him. I sent back for my small rifle and poured shot after shot into his heart and down his throat. They seemed to make no impression. The tortured gasps continued as steadily as the ticking of a clock.

In the end I could not stand it any longer and went away. I heard later that it took him half an hour to die. Burmans were arriving with dahs and baskets even before I left, and I was told they had stripped his body almost to the bones by the afternoon.

Afterwards, of course, there were endless discussions about the shooting of the elephant. The owner was furious, but he was only an Indian and could do nothing. Besides, legally I had done the right thing, for a mad elephant has to be killed, like a mad dog, if its owner fails to control it. Among the Europeans opinion was divided. The older men said I was right, the younger men said it was a damn shame to shoot an elephant for killing a coolie, because an elephant was worth more than any damn Coringhee coolie. And afterwards I was very glad that the coolie had been killed; it put me legally in the right and it gave me a sufficient pretext for shooting the elephant. I often wondered whether any of the others grasped that I had done it solely to avoid looking a fool.

John Berryman

John Berryman *(1914–1972) was born in McAlester, Oklahoma. "The Imaginary Jew" received the Kenyon-Doubleday Award as the best short story of 1945. Berryman is best known as a poet, and won both the Pulitzer prize and National Book Award for his verse. He committed suicide in Minneapolis.*

THE IMAGINARY JEW

THE second summer of the European war I spent in New York. I lived in a room just below street level on Lexington above Thirty-fourth, wrote a good deal, tried not to think about Europe, and listened to music on a small gramophone, the only thing of my own, except books, in the room. Haydn's London Symphony, his last, I heard probably fifty times in two months. One night when excited I dropped the pickup, creating a series of knocks at the beginning of the last movement where the oboe joins the strings which still, when I hear them, bring up for me my low, dark, long, damp room and I feel the dew of heat and smell the rented upholstery. I was trying, as one says, to come back a little, uncertain and low after an exhausting year. Why I decided to do this in New York—the enemy in summer equally of soul and body, as I had known for years—I can't remember; perhaps I didn't, but we held on merely from week to week by the motive which presently appeared in the form of a young woman met the Christmas before and now the occupation of every evening not passed in solitary and restless gloom. My friends were away; I saw few other people. Now and then I went to the zoo in lower Central Park and watched with interest the extraordinary behavior of a female badger. For a certain time she quickly paced the round of her cage. Then she would approach the side wall from an angle in a determined, hardly perceptible, unhurried trot; suddenly, when an inch away, point her nose up it, follow her nose up over her back, turning a deft and easy somersault, from which she emerged on her feet moving swiftly and unconcernedly away, as if the action had been no affair of hers, indeed she had scarcely been present. There was another badger in the cage who never did this, and nothing else about her was remarkable; but this competent disinterested somersault she enacted once every five or ten minutes as long as I watched her—quitting the wall, by the way, always at an angle in fixed relation to the angle at which she arrived at it. It is no longer possible to experience the pleasure I knew each time she lifted her nose and I understood again that she would not fail me, or feel the mystery of her absolute disclaimer—she has been taken away or died.

The story I have to tell is no further a part of that special summer than a nightmare takes its character, for memory, from the phase of the moon one noticed on going to bed. It could have happened in another year and in another place. No doubt it did, has done, will do. Still, so weak is the talent of the mind for pure relation—immaculate apprehension of *p* alone—that everything helps us, as when we come to an unknown city: architecture, history, trade practices, folklore. Even more anxious our approach to a city—like my small story—which we have known and forgotten. Yet how little we can learn! Some of the history is the lonely summer. Part of the folklore, I suppose, is which I now unwillingly rehearse, the character which experience has given to my sense of the Jewish people.

Born in a part of the South where no Jews had come, or none had stayed, and educated thereafter in states where they are numerous, I somehow arrived at a metropolitan university without any clear idea of what in modern life a Jew was—without even a clear consciousness of having seen one. I am unable now to explain this simplicity or blindness. I had not escaped, of course, a sense that humans somewhat different from ourselves, called "Jews," existed as in the middle distance and were best kept there, but this sense was of the vaguest. From what it was derived I do not know; I do not recall feeling the least curiosity about it, or about Jews; I had, simply, from the atmosphere of an advanced heterogeneous democratic society, ingathered a gently negative attitude toward Jews. This I took with me, untested, to college, where it received neither confirmation nor stimulus for two months. I rowed and danced and cut classes and was political; by mid-November I knew most of the five hundred men in my year. Then the man who rowed Number Three, in the eight of which I was bow, took me aside in the shower one afternoon and warned me not to be so chatty with Rosenblum.

I wondered why not. Rosenblum was stroke, a large handsome amiable fellow, for whose ability in the shell I felt great respect and no doubt envy. Because the fellows in the house wouldn't like it, my friend said. "What have they against him?" "It's only because he's Jewish," explained my friend, a second-generation Middle European.

I hooted at him, making the current noises of disbelief, and went back under the shower. It did not occur to me that he could be right. But next day when I was talking with Herz, the coxswain, whom I knew very well, I remembered the libel with some annoyance, and told Herz about it as a curiosity. Herz looked at me oddly, lowering his head, and said after a pause, "Why Al *is* Jewish, didn't you know that?" I was amazed. I said it was absurd, he couldn't be! "Why not?" said Herz, who must have been as astonished as I was. "Don't you know I'm Jewish?"

I did not know, of course, and ignorance has seldom cost me such humiliation. Herz did not guy me; he went off. But greater than my shame at not knowing something known, apparently, without effort to everyone else, were my emotions for what I then quickly discovered. Asking careful questions during the next week, I learned that about a third of the men I spent time with in college were Jewish; that they knew it, and the others knew it; that some of the others disliked them for it, and they knew this also; that certain houses existed *only* for Jews, who were excluded from the rest; and that what in short I took to be an idiotic state was deeply established, familiar, and acceptable to everyone. This discovery was the beginning of my instruction in social life proper—construing social life as that from which political life issues like a somatic dream.

My attitude toward my friends did not alter on this revelation. I merely discarded the notion that Jews were a proper object for any special attitude; my old sense vanished. This was in 1933. Later, as word of the German persecution filtered into this country, some sentimentality undoubtedly corrupted my attitude. I denied the presence of obvious defects in particular Jews, feeling that to admit them would be to side with the sadists and murderers. Accident allotting me close friends who were Jewish, their disadvantages enraged me. Gradually, and against my sense of impartial justice, I became the anomaly which only a partial society can produce, and for which it has no name known to the lexicons. In one area, not exclusively, "nigger-lover" is flung in a proximate way; but for a special sympathy and liking for Jews—which became my fate, so that I trembled when I heard one abused in talk—we have no term. In this condition I still was during the summer of which I speak. One further circumstance may be mentioned, as a product, I believe, of this curious training. I am spectacularly unable to identify Jews as Jews—by name, cast of feature, accent, or environment—and this has been true, not only of course before the college incident, but during my whole life since. Even names to anyone else patently Hebraic rarely suggest to me anything. And when once I learn that So-and-so is Jewish, I am likely to forget it. Now Jewishness—the religion or the race—may be a fact as striking and informative as someone's past heroism or his Christianity or his understanding of the subtlest human relations, and I feel sure that something operates to prevent my utilizing the plain signs by which such characters—in a Jewish man or woman—may be identified, and prevent my retaining the identification once it is made.

So to the city my summer and a night in August. I used to stop on Fourteenth Street for iced coffee, walking from the Village home (or to my room rather) after leaving my friend, and one night when I came out I wandered across to the island of trees and grass and concrete walks raised in the center of Union Square. Here men—a few women, old—sit in the evenings of summer, looking at papers or staring off or talking, and knots of them stay on, arguing, very late; these the unemployed or unemployable, the sleepless, the malcontent. There are no formal orators, as at Columbus Circle in the nineteen-thirties and at Hyde Park Corner. Each group is dominated by several articulate and strong-lunged persons who battle each other with prejudices and desires, swaying with intensity, and take on from time to time the interrupters: a forum at the bottom of the pot—Jefferson's fear, Whitman's hope, the dream of the younger Lenin. It was now about one o'clock, almost hot, and many men were still out. I stared for a little at the equestrian statue, obscure in the night on top of its pedestal, thinking that misty Rider would sweep away again all these men at his feet, whenever he liked—what symbol for power yet in a mechanical age rivals the mounted man?—and moved to the nearest group; or I plunged to it.

The dictator to the group was old, with dark cracked skin, fixed eyes in an excited face, leaning forward madly on his bench toward the half-dozen men in semicircle before him. "It's bread! It's bread!" he was saying. "It's bittersweet. All the bitter and all the sweetness. Of an overture. What else do you want? When you ask for steak and potatoes, do you want pastry with it? It's bread! It's bread! Help yourself! Help yourself!"

The listeners stood expressionless, except one who was smiling with contempt and interrupted now.

"Never a happy minute, never a happy minute!" the old man cried. "It's good to be dead! Some men should kill themselves."

"Don't you want to live?" said the smiling man.

"Of course I want to live. Everyone wants to live! If death comes suddenly, it's better. It's better!"

With pain I turned away. The next group were talking diffusely and angrily about the mayor, and I passed to a third, where a frantic olive-skinned young man with a fringe of silky beard was exclaiming:

"No restaurant in New York had the Last Supper! No. When people sit down to eat they should think of that!"

"Listen," said a white-shirted student on the rail, glancing around for approbation, "listen, if I open a restaurant and put *The Last Supper* up over the door, how much money do you think I'd lose? Ten thousand dollars?"

The fourth cluster was larger and appeared more coherent. A savage argument was in progress between a man of fifty with an oily red face, hatted, very determined in manner, and a muscular fellow half his age with heavy eyebrows, coatless, plainly Irish. Fifteen or twenty men were packed around them, and others on a bench near the rail against which the Irishman was lounging were attending also. I listened for a few minutes. The question was whether the President was trying to get us into the war—or, rather, whether this was legitimate, since the Irishman claimed that Roosevelt was a goddamned warmonger whom all the real people in the country hated, and the older man claimed that we should have gone into the f—ing war when France fell a year before, as everybody in the country knew except a few immigrant rats. Redface talked ten times as much as the Irishman, but he was not able to establish any advantage that I could see. He ranted, and then Irish either repeated shortly and fiercely what he had said last, or shifted his ground. The audience were silent—favoring whom I don't know, but evidently much interested. One or two men pushed out of the group, others arrived behind me, and I was eddied forward toward the disputants. The young Irishman broke suddenly into a tirade by the man with the hat:

"You're full of s—. Roosevelt even tried to get us in with the communists in the Spanish war. If he could have done it we'd have been burning churches down like the rest of the Reds."

"No, that's not right," I heard my own voice, and pushed forward, feeling blood in my face, beginning to tremble. "No, Roosevelt, as a matter of fact, helped Franco by non-intervention, at the same time that Italian and German planes were fighting against the Government and arms couldn't get in from France."

"What's that? What are you, a Jew?" He turned to me contemptuously, and was back at the older man before I could speak. "The only reason we weren't over there four years ago is because you can only screw us so much. Then we quit. No New Deal bastard could make us go help the goddamned communists."

"That ain't the question, it's if we want to fight *now* or *later*. Them Nazis ain't gonna sit!" shouted the red-faced man. "They got Egypt practically, and then it's India if it ain't England first. It ain't a question of the communists, the communists are on Hitler's side. I tellya we can wait and wait and chew and spit and the first thing you know they'll be in England, and then who's gonna help us when they start after us? Maybe Brazil? Get wise to the world! Spain don't matter now one way or the other, they ain't gonna help and they can't hurt. It's Germany and Italy and Japan, and if it ain't too late now it's gonna be. Get wise to yourself. We shoulda gone in—"

"What with?" said the Irishman with disdain. "Pop, pop. Wooden machine guns?"

"We were as ready a year ago as we are now. Defense don't mean nothing, you gotta have to fight!"

"No, we're much better off now," I said, "than we were a

year ago. When England went in, to keep its word to Poland, what good was it to Poland? The German Army—"

"Shut up, you Jew," said the Irishman.

"I'm not a Jew," I said to him. "What makes—"

"Listen, Pop," he said to the man in the hat, "it's O.K. to shoot your mouth off, but what the hell have you got to do with it? You aren't gonna do any fighting."

"Listen," I said.

"You sit on your big ass and talk about who's gonna fight who. Nobody's gonna fight anybody. If we feel hot, we ought to clean up some of the sons of bitches here before we go sticking our nuts anywhere to help England. We ought to clean up the sons of bitches in Wall Street and Washington before we take any ocean trips. You want to know something? You know why Germany's winning everything in this war? Because there ain't no Jews back home. There ain't no more Jews, first shouting war like this one here"—nodding at me—"and then skinning off to the synagogue with the profits. Wake up, Pop! You must have been around in the last war, you ought to know better."

I was too nervous to be angry or resentful. But I began to have a sense of oppression in breathing. I took the Irishman by the arm.

"Listen, told you I'm not a Jew."

"I don't give a damn what you are." He turned his half-dark eyes to me, wrenching his arm loose. "You talk like a Jew."

"What does that mean?" Some part of me wanted to laugh. "How does a Jew talk?"

"They talk like you, buddy."

"That's a fine argument! But if I'm not a Jew, my talk only——"

"You probably are a Jew. You look like a Jew."

"I *look* like a Jew? Listen"—I swung around eagerly to a man standing next to me—"do I look like a Jew? It doesn't matter whether I do or not—a Jew is as good as anybody and better than this son of a bitch." I was not exactly excited, I was trying to adapt my language as my need for the crowd, and sudden respect for its judgment possessed me. "But in fact I'm not Jewish and I don't look Jewish. Do I?"

The man looked at me quickly and said, half to me and half to the Irishman, "Hell, I don't know. Sure he does."

A wave of disappointment and outrage swept me almost to tears. I felt like a man betrayed by his brother. The lamps seemed brighter and vaguer, the night large. Glancing 'round, I saw sitting on a bench near me a tall, heavy, serious-looking man of thirty, well dressed, whom I had noticed earlier, and appealed to him, "Tell me, do I look Jewish?"

But he only stared up and waved his head vaguely. I saw with horror that something was wrong with him.

"You look like a Jew. You talk like a Jew. You *are* a Jew," I heard the Irishman say.

I heard murmuring among the men, but I could see nothing very clearly. It seemed very hot. I faced the Irishman again helplessly, holding my voice from rising.

"I'm *not* a Jew," I told him. "I might be, but I'm not. You have no bloody reason to think so, and you can't make me a Jew by simply repeating like an idiot that I am."

"Don't deny it, son," said the red-faced man, "stand up to him."

"God damn it"—suddenly I was furious, whirling like a fool (was I afraid of the Irishman? had he conquered me?) on the red-faced man—"I'm *not* denying it! Or rather I am, but only because I'm not a Jew! I despise renegades, I hate Jews who turn on their people, if I were a Jew I would say so, I would be proud to be. What is the vicious opinion of a man like this to me if I were a Jew? But I'm not. Why the hell should I admit I am if I'm not?"

"Jesus, the Jew is excited," said the Irishman.

"I have a right to be excited, you son of a bitch. Suppose I call you a Jew. Yes, you're a Jew. Does that mean anything?"

"Not a damn thing." He spat over the rail past a man's head.

"Prove that you're not. I say you are."

"Now listen, you Jew. I'm a Catholic."

"So am I, or I was born one, I'm not one now. I was born a Catholic." I was a little calmer but goaded, obsessed with the need to straighten this out. I felt that everything for everyone there depended on my proving him wrong. If *once* this evil for which we have not even a name could be exposed to the rest of the men as empty—if I could *prove* I was not a Jew—it would fall to the ground, neither would anyone else be a Jew to be accused. Then it could be trampled on. Fascist America was at stake. I listened, intensely anxious for our fate.

"Yeah?" said the Irishman. "Say the Apostles' Creed."

Memory went swirling back. I could hear the little bell die as I hushed it and set it on the felt. Father Boniface looked at me tall from the top of the steps and smiled, greeting me in the darkness before dawn as I came to serve, the men pressed around me under the lamps, and I could remember nothing but *visibilium omnium, et invisibilium.*

"I don't remember it."

The Irishman laughed with his certainty.

The papers in my pocket; I thought them over hurriedly. In my wallet. What would they prove? Details of ritual, Church history: anyone could learn them. My piece of Irish blood. Shame, shame: shame for my ruthless people. I will not be his blood. I wish I were a Jew, I would change my blood, to be able to say *Yes* and defy him.

"I'm not a Jew." I felt a fool. "You only say so. You haven't any evidence in the world."

He leaned forward from the rail, close to me. "Are you cut?"

Shock, fear ran through me before I could make any meaning out of his words. Then they ran faster, and I felt confused.

From that point nothing is clear for me. I stayed a long time—it seemed impossible to leave, showing him victor to them—thinking of possible allies and new plans of proof, but without hope. I was tired to the marrow. The arguments rushed on, and I spoke often now but seldom was heeded except by an old fat woman, very short and dirty, who listened intently to everyone. Heavier and heavier appeared to me to press upon us in the fading night our general guilt.

In the days following, as my resentment died, I saw that I had not been a victim altogether unjustly. My persecutors were right: I was a Jew. The imaginary Jew I was was as real as the imaginary Jew hunted down, on other nights and days, in a real Jew. Every murderer strikes the mirror, the lash of the torturer falls on the mirror and cuts the real image, and the real and the imaginary blood flow down together.

Jorge Luis Borges

Jorge Luis Borges (1899–1986) was born in Buenos Aires, Argentina. He is perhaps the most acclaimed figure in Latin American literature in this century. Among his works are A Universal History of Infamy, Ficciones, *and* Labyrinths.

THEME OF THE
TRAITOR AND THE HERO

> *So the Platonic year*
> *Whirls out new right and wrong,*
> *Whirls in the old istead;*
> *All men are dancers and their tread*
> *Goes to the barbarous clangour of a gong.*
>
> W. B. YEATS: *The Tower*

Under the notable influence of Chesterton (contriver and embellisher of elegant mysteries) and the palace counsellor Leibniz (inventor of the pre-established harmony), in my idle afternoons I have imagined this story plot which I shall perhaps write some day and which already justifies me somehow. Details, rectifications, adjustments are lacking; there are zones of the story not yet revealed to me; today, 3 January 1944, I seem to see it as follows:

The action takes place in an oppressed and tenacious country: Poland, Ireland, the Venetian Republic, some South

American or Balkan state. . . . Or rather it has taken place, since, though the narrator is contemporary, his story occurred towards the middle or the beginning of the nineteenth century. Let us say (for narrative convenience) Ireland; let us say in 1824. The narrator's name is Ryan; he is the great-grandson of the young, the heroic, the beautiful, the assassinated Fergus Kilpatrick, whose grave was mysteriously violated, whose name illustrated the verses of Browning and Hugo, whose statue presides over a grey hill amid red marshes.

Kilpatrick was a conspirator, a secret and glorious captain of conspirators; like Moses, who from the land of Moab glimpsed but could not reach the promised land, Kilpatrick perished on the eve of the victorious revolt which he had premeditated and dreamt of. The first centenary of his death draws near; the circumstances of the crime are enigmatic; Ryan, engaged in writing a biography of the hero, discovers that the enigma exceeds the confines of a simple police investigation. Kilpatrick was murdered in a theatre; the British police never found the killer; the historians maintain that this scarcely soils their good reputation, since it was probably the police themselves who had him killed. Other facets of the enigma disturb Ryan. They are of a cyclic nature: they seem to repeat or combine events of remote regions, of remote ages. For example, no one is unaware that the officers who examined the hero's body found a sealed letter in which he was warned of the risk of attending the theatre that evening; likewise Julius Caesar, on his way to the place where his friends' daggers awaited him, received a note he never read, in which the treachery was declared along with the traitors' names. Caesar's wife, Calpurnia, saw in a dream the destruction of a tower decreed him by the Senate; false and anonymous rumours on the eve of Kilpatrick's death publicized throughout the country that the circular tower of Kilgarvan had burned, which could be taken as a presage, for he had been born in Kilgarvan. These parallelisms (and others) between the story of Caesar and the story of an Irish conspirator lead Ryan to suppose the existence of a secret form of time, a pattern of repeated lines. He thinks of the decimal history conceived by Condorcet, of the morphologies proposed by Hegel, Spengler and Vico, of Hesiod's men, who degenerate from gold to iron. He thinks of the transmigration of souls, a doctrine that lends horror to Celtic literature and that Caesar himself attributed to the British druids; he thinks that, before having been Fergus Kilpatrick, Fergus Kilpatrick was Julius Caesar. He is rescued from these circular labyrinths by a curious finding, a finding which then sinks him into other, more inextricable and heterogeneous labyrinths: certain words uttered by a beggar who spoke with Fergus Kilpatrick the day of his death were prefigured by Shakespeare in the tragedy *Macbeth*. That history should have copied history was already sufficiently astonishing; that history should copy literature was inconceivable. . . . Ryan finds that, in 1814, James Alexander Nolan, the oldest of the hero's companions, had translated the principal dramas of Shakespeare into Gaelic; among these was *Julius Caesar*. He also discovers in the archives the manuscript of an article by Nolan on the Swiss *Festspiele:* vast and errant theatrical representations which require thousands of actors and repeat historical episodes in the very cities and mountains where they took place. Another unpublished document reveals to him that, a few days before the end, Kilpatrick, presiding over the last meeting, had signed the order for the execution of a traitor whose name has been deleted from the records. This order does not accord with Kilpatrick's merciful nature. Ryan investigates the matter (this investigation is one of the gaps in my plot) and manages to decipher the enigma.

Kilpatrick was killed in a theatre, but the entire city was a theatre as well, and the actors were legion, and the drama crowned by his death extended over many days and many nights. This is what happened:

On 2 August 1824, the conspirators gathered. The country was ripe for revolt; something, however, always failed: there was a traitor in the group. Fergus Kilpatrick had charged James Nolan with the responsibility of discovering the traitor.

Nolan carried out his assignment: he announced in the very midst of the meeting that the traitor was Kilpatrick himself. He demonstrated the truth of his accusation with irrefutable proof; the conspirators condemned their president to die. He signed his own sentence, but begged that his punishment not harm his country.

It was then that Nolan conceived his strange scheme. Ireland idolized Kilpatrick; the most tenuous suspicion of his infamy would have jeopardized the revolt; Nolan proposed a plan which made of the traitor's execution an instrument for the country's emancipation. He suggested that the condemned man die at the hands of an unknown assassin in deliberately dramatic circumstances which would remain engraved in the imagination of the people and would hasten the revolt. Kilpatrick swore he would take part in the scheme, which gave him the occasion to redeem himself and for which his death would provide the final flourish.

Nolan, urged on by time, was not able to invent all the circumstances of the multiple execution; he had to plagiarize another dramatist, the English enemy William Shakespeare. He repeated scenes from *Macbeth*, from *Julius Caesar*. The public and secret enactment comprised various days. The condemned man entered Dublin, discussed, acted, prayed, reproved, uttered words of pathos, and each of these gestures, to be reflected in his glory, had been pre-established by Nolan. Hundreds of actors collaborated with the protagonist; the role of some was complex; that of others momentary. The things they did and said endure in the history books, in the impassioned memory of Ireland. Kilpatrick, swept along by this minutely detailed destiny which both redeemed and destroyed him, more than once enriched the text of his judge with improvised acts and words. Thus the populous drama unfolded in time, until 6 August 1824, in a theatre box with funereal curtains prefiguring Lincoln's, a long-desired bullet entered the breast of the traitor and hero, who, amid two effusions of sudden blood, was scarcely able to articulate a few foreseen words.

In Nolan's work, the passages imitated from Shakespeare are the *least* dramatic; Ryan suspects that the author interpolated them so that in the future someone might hit upon the truth. He understands that he too forms part of Nolan's plot. . . . After a series of tenacious hesitations, he resolves to keep his discovery silent. He publishes a book dedicated to the hero's glory; this too, perhaps, was foreseen.

Translated by J.E.I.

Sadat Hasan Manto

Sadat Hasan Manto (1912–1955) was born in Sambrala in the Punjab and died in Lahore, Pakistan. He was a leading short story writer and essayist in the Urdu language. This story is a commentary on the ethnic violence and population transfers that accompanied the birth of India and Pakistan in 1947.

TOBA TEK SINGH

A couple of years after the Partition of the country, it occurred to the respective governments of India and Pakistan that inmates of lunatic asylums, like prisoners, should also be exchanged. Muslim lunatics in India should be transferred to Pakistan and Hindu and Sikh lunatics in Pakistani asylums should be sent to India.

Whether this was a reasonable or an unreasonable idea is difficult to say. One thing, however, is clear. It took many conferences of important officials from the two sides to come to this decision. Final details, like the date of actual exchange, were carefully worked out. Muslim lunatics whose families were still residing in India were to be left undisturbed, the rest moved to the border for the exchange. The situation in Pakistan was slightly different, since almost the entire population of Hindus and Sikhs had already migrated to India. The question of keeping non-Muslim lunatics in Pakistan did not, therefore, arise.

While it is not known what the reaction in India was, when

the news reached the Lahore lunatic asylum, it immediately became the subject of heated discussion. One Muslim lunatic, a regular reader of the fire-eating daily newspaper *Zamindar*, when asked what Pakistan was, replied after deep reflection: "The name of a place in India where cut-throat razors are manufactured."

This profound observation was received with visible satisfaction.

A Sikh lunatic asked another Sikh: "Sardarji, why are we being sent to India? We don't even know the language they speak in that country."

The man smiled: "I know the language of the *Hindostoras*. These devils always strut about as if they were the lords of the earth."

One day a Muslim lunatic, while taking his bath, raised the slogan *"Pakistan Zindabad"* with such enthusiasm that he lost his footing and was later found lying on the floor unconscious.

Not all inmates were mad. Some were perfectly normal, except that they were murderers. To spare them the hangman's noose, their families had managed to get them committed after bribing officials down the line. They probably had a vague idea why India was being divided and what Pakistan was, but, as for the present situation, they were equally clueless.

Newspapers were no help either, and the asylum guards were ignorant, if not illiterate. Nor was there anything to be learnt by eavesdropping on their conversations. Some said there was this man by the name Mohamed Ali Jinnah, or the Quaid-e-Azam, who had set up a separate country for Muslims, called Pakistan.

As to where Pakistan was located, the inmates knew nothing. That was why both the mad and the partially mad were unable to decide whether they were now in India or in Pakistan. If they were in India, where on earth was Pakistan? And if they were in Pakistan, then how come that until only the other day it was India?

One inmate had got so badly caught up in this India—Pakistan—Pakistan—India rigmarole that one day, while sweeping the floor, he dropped everything, climbed the nearest tree and installed himself on a branch, from which vantage point he spoke for two hours on the delicate problem of India and Pakistan. The guards asked him to get down; instead he went a branch higher, and when threatened with punishment, declared: "I wish to live neither in India nor in Pakistan. I wish to live in this tree."

When he was finally persuaded to come down, he began embracing his Sikh and Hindu friends, tears running down his cheeks, fully convinced that they were about to leave him and go to India.

A Muslim radio engineer, who had an M.Sc. degree, and never mixed with anyone, given as he was to taking long walks by himself all day, was so affected by the current debate that one day he took all his clothes off, gave the bundle to one of the attendants and ran into the garden stark naked.

A Muslim lunatic from Chaniot, who used to be one of the most devoted workers of the All India Muslim League, and obsessed with bathing himself fifteen or sixteen times a day, had suddenly stopped doing that and announced—his name was Mohamed Ali—that he was Quaid-e-Azam Mohamed Ali Jinnah. This had led a Sikh inmate to declare himself Master Tara Singh, the leader of the Sikhs. Apprehending serious communal trouble, the authorities declared them dangerous, and shut them up in separate cells.

There was a young Hindu lawyer from Lahore who had gone off his head after an unhappy love affair. When told that Amritsar was to become a part of India, he went into a depression because his beloved lived in Amritsar, something he had not forgotten even in his madness. That day he abused every major and minor Hindu and Muslim leader who had cut India into two, turning his beloved into an Indian and him into a Pakistani.

When news of the exchange reached the asylum, his friends offered him congratulations, because he was now to be sent to India, the country of his beloved. However, he declared that he had no intention of leaving Lahore, because his practice would not flourish in Amritsar.

There were two Anglo-Indian lunatics in the European ward. When told that the British had decided to go home after granting independence to India, they went into a state of deep shock and were seen conferring with each other in whispers the entire afternoon. They were worried about their changed status after independence. Would there be a European ward or would it be abolished? Would breakfast continue to be served or would they have to subsist on bloody Indian chapati?

There was another inmate, a Sikh, who had been confined for the last fifteen years. Whenever he spoke, it was the same mysterious gibberish: *"Uper the gur gur the annexe the bay dhayana the mung the dal of the laltain."* Guards said he had not slept a wink in fifteen years. Occasionally, he could be observed leaning against a wall, but the rest of the time, he was always to be found standing. Because of this, his legs were permanently swollen, something that did not appear to bother him. Recently, he had started to listen carefully to discussions about the forthcoming exchange of Indian and Pakistani lunatics. When asked his opinion, he observed solemnly: *"Uper the gur gur the annexe the bay dhayana the mung the dal of the Government of Pakistan."*

Of late, however, the Government of Pakistan had been replaced by the Government of Toba Tek Singh, a small town in the Punjab which was his home. He had also begun enquiring where Toba Tek Singh was to go. However, nobody was quite sure whether it was in India or Pakistan.

Those who had tried to solve this mystery had become utterly confused when told that Sialkot, which used to be in India, was now in Pakistan. It was anybody's guess what was going to happen to Lahore, which was currently in Pakistan, but could slide into India any moment. It was also possible that the entire subcontinent of India might become Pakistan.

And who could say if both India and Pakistan might not entirely vanish from the map of the world one day?

The old man's hair was almost gone and what little was left had become a part of the beard, giving him a strange, even frightening, appearance. However, he was a harmless fellow and had never been known to get into fights. Older attendants at the asylum said that he was a fairly prosperous landlord from Toba Tek Singh, who had quite suddenly gone mad. His family had brought him in, bound and fettered. That was fifteen years ago.

Once a month, he used to have visitors, but since the start of communal troubles in the Punjab, they had stopped coming. His real name was Bishan Singh, but everybody called him Toba Tek Singh. He lived in a kind of limbo, having no idea what day of the week it was, or month, or how many years had passed since his confinement. However, he had developed a sixth sense about the day of the visit, when he used to bathe himself, soap his body, oil and comb his hair and put on clean clothes. He never said a word during these meetings, except occasional outbursts of *"Uper the gur gur the annexe the bay dhayana the mung the dal of the laltain."*

When he was first confined, he had left an infant daughter behind, now a pretty young girl of fifteen. She would come occasionally, and sit in front of him with tears rolling down her cheeks. In the strange world that he inhabited, hers was just another face.

Since the start of this India—Pakistan caboodle, he had got into the habit of asking fellow inmates where exactly Toba Tek Singh was, without receiving a satisfactory answer, because nobody knew. The visits had also suddenly stopped. He was increasingly restless, but, more than that, curious. The sixth sense, which used to alert him to the day of the visit, had also atrophied.

He missed his family, the gifts they used to bring and the concern with which they used to speak to him. He was sure they would have told him whether Toba Tek Singh was in

India or Pakistan. He also had a feeling that they came from Toba Tek Singh, where he used to have his home.

One of the inmates had declared himself God. Bishan Singh asked him one day if Toba Tek Singh was in India or Pakistan. The man chuckled: "Neither in India nor in Pakistan, because, so far, we have issued no orders in this respect."

Bishan Singh begged "God" to issue the necessary orders, so that his problem could be solved, but he was disappointed, as "God" appeared to be preoccupied with more pressing matters. Finally, he told him angrily: *"Uper the gur gur the annexe the mung the dal of Guruji da Khalsa and Guruji ki fateh . . . jo boley so nihal sat sri akal."*

What he wanted to say was: "You don't answer my prayers because you are a Muslim God. Had you been a Sikh God, you would have been more of a sport."

A few days before the exchange was to take place, one of Bishan Singh's Muslim friends from Toba Tek Singh came to see him—the first time in fifteen years. Bishan Singh looked at him once and turned away, until a guard said to him: "This is your old friend Fazal Din. He has come all the way to meet you."

Bishan Singh looked at Fazal Din and began to mumble something. Fazal Din placed his hand on his friend's shoulder and said: "I have been meaning to come for some time to bring you news. All your family is well and has gone to India safely. I did what I could to help. Your daughter Roop Kaur . . ."—he hesitated—"she is safe too . . . in India."

Bishan Singh kept quiet. Fazal Din continued: "Your family wanted me to make sure you were well. Soon you will be moving to India. What can I say, except that you should remember me to bhai Balbir Singh, bhai Vadhawa Singh and bahain Amrit Kaur. Tell bhai Bibir Singh that Fazal Din is well by the grace of God. The two brown buffaloes he left behind are well too. Both of them gave birth to calves, but, unfortunately, one of them died after six days. Say I think of them often and to write to me if there is anything I can do."

Then he added: "Here, I brought you some rice crispies from home."

Bishan Singh took the gift and handed it to one of the guards. "Where is Toba Tek Singh?" he asked.

"Where? Why, it is where it has always been."

"In India or in Pakistan?"

"In India . . . no, in Pakistan."

Without saying another word, Bishan Singh walked away, murmuring: *"Uper the gur gur the annexe the be dhyana the mung the dal of the Pakistan and Hindustan dur fittey moun."*

Meanwhile, exchange arrangements were rapidly getting finalized. Lists of lunatics from the two sides had been exchanged between the governments, and the date of transfer fixed.

On a cold winter evening, buses full of Hindu and Sikh lunatics, accompanied by armed police and officials, began moving out of the Lahore asylum towards Wagha, the dividing line between India and Pakistan. Senior officials from the two sides in charge of exchange arrangements met, signed documents and the transfer got under way.

It was quite a job getting the men out of the buses and handing them over to officials. Some just refused to leave. Those who were persuaded to do so began to run pell-mell in every direction. Some were stark naked. All efforts to get them to cover themselves had failed because they couldn't be kept from tearing off their garments. Some were shouting abuse or singing. Others were weeping bitterly. Many fights broke out.

In short, complete confusion prevailed. Female lunatics were also being exchanged and they were even noisier. It was bitterly cold.

Most of the inmates appeared to be dead set against the entire operation. They simply could not understand why they were being forcibly removed, thrown into buses and driven to this strange place. There were slogans of *"Pakistan Zindabad"* and *"Pakistan Murdabad,"* followed by fights.

When Bishan Singh was brought out and asked to give his

name so that it could be recorded in a register, he asked the official behind the desk: "Where is Toba Tek Singh? In India or Pakistan?"

"Pakistan," he answered with a vulgar laugh.

Bishan Singh tried to run, but was overpowered by the Pakistani guards who tried to push him across the dividing line towards India. However, he wouldn't move. "This is Toba Tek Singh," he announced. *"Uper the gur gur the annexe the be dhyana mung the dal of Toba Tek Singh and Pakistan."*

Many efforts were made to explain to him that Toba Tek Singh had already been moved to India, or would be moved immediately, but it had no effect on Bishan Singh. The guards even tried force, but soon gave up.

There he stood in no man's land on his swollen legs like a colossus.

Since he was a harmless old man, no further attempt was made to push him into India. He was allowed to stand where he wanted, while the exchange continued. The night wore on.

Just before sunrise, Bishan Singh, the man who had stood on his legs for fifteen years, screamed and as officials from the two sides rushed towards him, he collapsed to the ground.

There, behind barbed wire, on one side, lay India and behind more barbed wire, on the other side, lay Pakistan. In between, on a bit of earth which had no name, lay Toba Tek Singh.

Jomo Kenyatta

Jomo Kenyatta (1891–1978) was born in Ngenda, then British East Africa. He was a leading figure in the struggle for the independence of his country and became Kenya's first president in 1963. This parable, from Facing Mt. Kenya *(1938), is concerned with the African encounter with Western imperialism.*

THE GENTLEMEN
OF THE JUNGLE

Once upon a time an elephant made a friendship with a man. One day a heavy thunderstorm broke out, the elephant went to his friend, who had a little hut at the edge of the forest, and said to him: "My dear good man, will you please let me put my trunk inside your hut to keep it out of this torrential rain?" The man, seeing what situation his friend was in, replied: "My dear good elephant, my hut is very small, but there is room for your trunk and myself. Please put your trunk in gently." The elephant thanked his friend, saying: "You have done me a good deed and one day I shall return your kindness." But what followed? As soon as the elephant put his trunk inside the hut, slowly he pushed his head inside, and finally flung the man out in the rain, and then lay down comfortably inside his friend's hut, saying: "My dear good friend, your skin is harder than mine, and as there is not enough room for both of us, you can afford to remain in the rain while I am protecting my delicate skin from the hail-storm."

The man, seeing what his friend had done to him, started to grumble; the animals in the nearby forest heard the noise and came to see what was the matter. All stood around listening to the heated argument between the man and his friend the elephant. In this turmoil the lion came along roaring, and said in a loud voice: "Don't you all know that I am the King of the Jungle! How dare any one disturb the peace of my kingdom?" On hearing this the elephant, who was one of the high ministers in the jungle kingdom, replied in a soothing voice, and said: "My lord, there is no disturbance of the peace in your kingdom. I have only been having a little discussion with my friend here as to the possession of this little hut which your lordship sees me occupying." The lion, who wanted to have "peace and tranquillity" in his kingdom, replied in a noble voice, saying: "I command my ministers to appoint a Commission of Enquiry to go thoroughly into this matter and report accordingly." He then turned to the man and said: "You have done well by establishing friendship with my people, especially with the elephant, who is one of my honourable ministers of state. Do not grumble any more, your hut is not lost to you. Wait until the sitting of my Imperial Commission, and there you will be given plenty of opportunity to state your case. I am sure that you will be pleased with the findings of the Commission." The man was very pleased by these sweet words from the King of the Jungle, and innocently waited for his opportunity, in the belief that naturally the hut would be returned to him.

The elephant, obeying the command of his master, got busy with other ministers to appoint the Commission of Enquiry. The following elders of the jungle were appointed to sit in the Commission: (1) Mr. Rhinoceros; (2) Mr. Buffalo; (3) Mr. Alligator; (4) The Rt Hon. Mr. Fox to act as chairman; and (5) Mr. Leopard to act as Secretary to the Commission. On seeing the personnel, the man protested and asked if it was not necessary to include in this Commission a member from his side. But he was told that it was impossible, since no one from his side was well enough educated to understand the intricacy of jungle law. Further, that there was nothing to fear, for the members of the Commission were all men of repute for their impartiality in justice, and as they were gentlemen chosen by God to look after the interests of races less adequately endowed with teeth and claws, he might rest assured that they would investigate the matter with the greatest care and report impartially.

The Commission sat to take the evidence. The Rt. Hon. Mr. Elephant was first called. He came along with a superior air, brushing his tusks with a sapling which Mrs. Elephant had provided, and in an authoritative voice said: "Gentlemen of the Jungle, there is no need for me to waste your valuable time in relating a story which I am sure you all know. I have always regarded it as my duty to protect the interests of my friends, and this appears to have caused the misunderstanding between myself and my friend here. He invited me to save his hut from being blown away by a hurricane. As the hurricane had gained access owing to the unoccupied space in the hut, I considered it necessary, in my friend's own interests, to turn the undeveloped space to a more economic use by sitting in it myself; a duty which any of you would undoubtedly have performed with equal readiness in similar circumstances."

After hearing the Rt. Hon. Mr. Elephant's conclusive evidence, the Commission called Mr. Hyena and other elders of the jungle, who all supported what Mr. Elephant had said. They then called the man, who began to give his own account of the dispute. But the Commission cut him short, saying: "My good man, please confine yourself to relevant issues. We have already heard the circumstances from various unbiased sources; all we wish you to tell us is whether the undeveloped space in your hut was occupied by any one else before Mr. Elephant assumed his position?" The man began to say: "No, but—" But at this point the Commission declared that they had heard sufficient evidence from both sides and retired to consider their decision. After enjoying a delicious meal at the expense of the Rt. Hon. Mr. Elephant, they reached their verdict, called the man, and declared as follows: "In our opinion this dispute has arisen through a regrettable misunderstanding due to the backwardness of your ideas. We consider that Mr. Elephant has fulfilled his sacred duty of protecting your interests. As it is clearly for your good that the space should be put to its most economic use, and as you yourself have not reached the stage of expansion which would enable you to fill it, we consider it necessary to arrange a compromise to suit both parties. Mr. Elephant shall continue his occupation of your hut, but we give you permission to look for a site where you can build another hut more suited to your needs, and we will see that you are well protected."

The man, having no alternative, and fearing that his refusal might expose him to the teeth and claws of members of the Commission, did as they suggested. But no sooner had he built another hut than Mr. Rhinoceros charged in with his horn lowered and ordered the man to quit. A Royal Commission was again appointed to look into the matter, and the same finding was given. This procedure was repeated until Mr. Buffalo, Mr. Leopard, Mr. Hyena and the rest were all accommodated with new huts. Then the man decided that he must adopt an effective method of protection, since Commissions of Enquiry did not seem to be of any use to him. He sat down and said, *"Ng'enda thi ndagaga motegi,"* which literally means "there is nothing that treads on the earth that cannot be trapped," or in other words, you can fool people for a time, but not for ever.

Early one morning, when the huts already occupied by the jungle lords were all beginning to decay and fall to pieces, he went out and built a bigger and better hut a little distance away. No sooner had Mr. Rhinoceros seen it than he came rushing in, only to find that Mr. Elephant was already inside, sound asleep. Mr. Leopard next came to the window, Mr. Lion, Mr. Fox and Mr. Buffalo entered the doors, while Mr. Hyena howled for a place in the shade and Mr. Alligator basked on the roof. Presently they all began disputing about their rights of penetration, and from disputing they came to fighting, and while they were all embroiled together the man set the hut on fire and burnt it to the ground, jungle lords and all. Then he went home, saying: "Peace is costly, but it's worth the expense," and lived happily ever after.

Ngugi wa Thiong'o

Ngugi wa Thiong'o (1938–   ) was born in Limuru, Kenya. His most renowned novel is Weep Not Child. *In 1977 he was imprisoned for a period after the performance of his play* I Will Marry When I Want.

THE MARTYR

When Mr. and Mrs. Garstone were murdered in their home by unknown gangsters, there was a lot of talk about it. It was all on the front pages of the daily papers and figured importantly in the Radio Newsreel. Perhaps this was so because they were the first European settlers to be killed in the increased wave of violence that had spread all over the country. The violence was said to have political motives. And wherever you went, in the marketplaces, in the Indian bazaars, in a remote African duka, you were bound to hear something about the murder. There were a variety of accounts and interpretations.

Nowhere was the matter more thoroughly discussed than in a remote, lonely house built on a hill, which belonged, quite appropriately, to Mrs. Hill. Her husband, an old veteran settler of the pioneering period, had died the previous year after an attack of malaria while on a visit to Uganda. Her only son and daughter were now getting their education at "Home"— home being another name for England. Being one of the earliest settlers and owning a lot of land with big tea plantations sprawling right across the country, she was much respected by the others if not liked by all.

For some did not like what they considered her too "liberal" attitude to the "natives." When Mrs. Smiles and Mrs. Hardy came into her house two days later to discuss the murder, they wore a look of sad triumph—sad because Europeans (not just Mr. and Mrs. Garstone) had been killed, and of triumph, because the essential depravity and ingratitude of the natives had been demonstrated beyond all doubt. No longer could Mrs. Hill maintain that natives could be civilized if only they were handled in the right manner.

Mrs. Smiles was a lean, middle-aged woman whose tough, determined nose and tight lips reminded one so vividly of a missionary. In a sense she was. Convinced that she and her kind formed an oasis of civilization in a wild country of savage people, she considered it almost her calling to keep on reminding the natives and anyone else of the fact, by her gait, talk and general bearing.

Mrs. Hardy was of Boer descent and had early migrated into the country from South Africa. Having no opinions of her own about anything, she mostly found herself agreeing with any views that most approximated those of her husband and her race. For instance, on this day she found herself in agreement with whatever Mrs. Smiles said. Mrs. Hill stuck to her guns and maintained, as indeed she had always done, that the natives were obedient at heart and *all* you needed was to treat them kindly.

"That's all they need. *Treat them kindly.* They will take kindly to you. Look at my 'boys.' They all love me. They would do anything I ask them to!" That was her philosophy and it was shared by quite a number of the liberal, progressive type. Mrs. Hill had done some liberal things for her "boys." Not only had she built some brick quarters *(brick,* mind you) but had also put up a school for the children. It did not matter if the school had not enough teachers or if the children learnt only half a day and worked in the plantations for the other half; it was more than most other settlers had the courage to do!

"It is horrible. Oh, a horrible act," declared Mrs. Smiles rather vehemently. Mrs. Hardy agreed. Mrs. Hill remained neutral.

"How could they do it? We've brought 'em civilization. We've stopped slavery and tribal wars. Were they not all leading savage miserable lives?" Mrs. Smiles spoke with all her powers of oratory. Then she concluded with a sad shake of the head: "But I've always said they'll never be civilized, simply can't take it."

"We should show tolerance," suggested Mrs. Hill. Her tone spoke more of the missionary than Mrs. Smiles's looks.

"Tolerant! Tolerant! How long shall we continue being tolerant? Who could have been more tolerant than the Garstones? Who more kind? And to think of all the squatters they maintained!

"Well, it isn't the squatters who . . ."

"Who did? Who did?"

"They should all be hanged!" suggested Mrs. Hardy. There was conviction in her voice.

"And to think they were actually called from bed by their houseboy!"

"Indeed?"

"Yes. It was their houseboy who knocked at their door and urgently asked them to open. Said some people were after him—"

"Perhaps there—"

"No! It was all planned. All a trick. As soon as the door was opened, the gang rushed in. It's all in the paper."

Mrs. Hill looked away rather guiltily. She had not read her paper.

It was time for tea. She excused herself and went near the door and called out in a kind, shrill voice.

"Njoroge! Njoroge!"

Njoroge was her "houseboy." He was a tall, broad-shouldered man nearing middle age. He had been in the Hills' service for more than ten years. He wore green trousers, with a red clothband round the waist and a red fez on his head. He now appeared at the door and raised his eyebrows in inquiry —an action which with him accompanied the words, "Yes, Memsahib?" or "Ndio, Bwana."

"Leta Chai."

"Ndio, Memsahib!" and he vanished back after casting a quick glance round all the Memsahibs there assembled. The conversation which had been interrupted by Njoroge's appearance was now resumed.

"They look so innocent," said Mrs. Hardy.

"Yes. Quite the innocent flower but the serpent under it." Mrs. Smiles was acquainted with Shakespeare.

"Been with me for ten years or so. Very faithful. Likes me very much." Mrs. Hill was defending her "boy."

"All the same I don't like him. I don't like his face."

"The same with me."

Tea was brought. They drank, still chatting about the death, the government's policy, and the political demagogues who were undesirable elements in this otherwise beautiful country. But Mrs. Hill, maintained that these semi-illiterate demagogues who went to Britain and thought they had education did not know the true aspirations of their people. You could still win your "boys" by being kind to them.

Nevertheless, when Mrs. Smiles and Mrs. Hardy had gone, she brooded over that murder and the conversation. She felt uneasy and for the first time noticed that she lived a bit too far from any help in case of an attack. The knowledge that she had a pistol was a comfort.

Supper was over. That ended Njoroge's day. He stepped out of the light into the countless shadows and then vanished into the darkness. He was following the footpath from Mrs. Hill's house to the workers' quarters down the hill. He tried to whistle to dispel the silence and loneliness that hung around him. He could not. Instead he heard a bird cry, sharp, shrill. Strange thing for a bird to cry at night.

He stopped, stood stock-still. Below, he could perceive

nothing. But behind him the immense silhouette of Memsahib's house—large, imposing—could be seen. He looked back intently, angrily. In his anger, he suddenly thought he was growing old.

"You. You. I've lived with you so long. And you've reduced me to this!" Njoroge wanted to shout to the house all this and many other things that had long accumulated in his heart. The house would not respond. He felt foolish and moved on.

Again the bird cried. Twice!

"A warning to her," Njoroge thought. And again his whole soul rose in anger—anger against those with a white skin, those foreign elements that had displaced the true sons of the land from their God-given place. Had God not promised Gekoyo all this land, he and his children, forever and ever? Now the land had been taken away.

He remembered his father, as he always did when these moments of anger and bitterness possessed him. He had died in the struggle—the struggle to rebuild the destroyed shrines. That was at the famous 1923 Nairobi Massacre when police fired on a people peacefully demonstrating for their rights. His father was among the people who died. Since then Njoroge had had to struggle for a living—seeking employment here and there on European farms. He had met many types—some harsh, some kind, but all dominating, giving him just what salary they thought fit for him. Then he had come to be employed by the Hills. It was a strange coincidence that he had come here. A big portion of the land now occupied by Mrs. Hill was the land his father had shown him as belonging to the family. They had found the land occupied when his father and some of the others had temporarily retired to Muranga owing to famine. They had come back and *Ng'o!* the land was gone.

"Do you see that fig tree? Remember that land is yours. Be patient. Watch these Europeans. They will go and then you can claim the land."

He was small then. After his father's death, Njoroge had forgotten this injunction. But when he coincidentally came here and saw the tree, he remembered. He knew it all—all by heart. He knew where every boundary went through.

Njoroge had never liked Mrs. Hill. He had always resented her complacency in thinking she had done so much for the workers. He had worked with cruel types like Mrs. Smiles and Mrs. Hardy. But he always knew where he stood with such. But Mrs. Hill! Her liberalism was almost smothering. Njoroge hated settlers. He hated above all what he thought was their hypocrisy and complacency. He knew that Mrs. Hill was no exception. She was like all the others, only she loved paternalism. It convinced her she was better than the others. But she was worse. You did not know exactly where you stood with her.

All of a sudden, Njoroge shouted, "I hate them! I hate them!" Then a grim satisfaction came over him. Tonight, anyway, Mrs. Hill would die—pay for her own smug liberalism, her paternalism and pay for all the sins of her settler race. It would be one settler less.

He came to his own room. There was no smoke coming from all the other rooms belonging to the other workers. The lights had even gone out in many of them. Perhaps, some were already asleep or gone to the Native Reserve to drink beer. He lit the lantern and sat on the bed. It was a very small room. Sitting on the bed one could almost touch all the corners of the room if one stretched one's arms wide. Yet it was here, *here*, that he with two wives and a number of children had to live, had in fact lived for more than five years. So crammed! Yet Mrs. Hill thought that she had done enough by just having the houses built with brick.

"Mzuri, sana, eh?" (very good, eh?) she was very fond of asking. And whenever she had visitors she brought them to the edge of the hill and pointed at the houses.

Again Njoroge smiled grimly to think how Mrs. Hill would pay for all this self-congratulatory piety. He also knew that he had an axe to grind. He had to avenge the death of his father and strike a blow for the occupied family land. It was foresight on his part to have taken his wives and children back to the Reserve. They might else have been in the way and in any case he did not want to bring trouble to them should he be forced to run away after the act.

The other Ihii (Freedom Boys) would come at any time now. He would lead them to the house. Treacherous—yes! But how necessary.

The cry of the night bird, this time louder than ever, reached his ears. That was a bad omen. It always portended death—death for Mrs. Hill. He thought of her. He remembered her. He had lived with Memsahib and Bwana for more than ten years. He knew that she had loved her husband. Of that he was sure. She almost died of grief when she had learnt of his death. In that moment her settlerism had been shorn off. In that naked moment, Njoroge had been able to pity her. Then the children! He had known them. He had seen them grow up like any other children. Almost like his own. They loved their parents, and Mrs. Hill had always been so tender with them, so loving. He thought of them in England, wherever that was, fatherless and motherless.

And then he realized, too suddenly, that he could not do it. He could not tell how, but Mrs. Hill had suddenly crystallized into a woman, a wife, somebody like Njeri or Wambui, and above all, a mother. He could not kill a woman. He could not kill a mother. He hated himself for this change. He felt agitated. He tried hard to put himself in the other condition, his former self and see her as just a settler. As a settler, it was easy. For Njoroge hated settlers and all Europeans. If only he could see her like this (as one among many white men or settlers) then he could do it. Without scruples. But he could not bring back the other self. Not now, anyway. He had never thought of her in these terms. Until today. And yet he knew she was the same, and would be the same tomorrow—a patronizing, complacent woman. It was then he knew that he was a divided man and perhaps would ever remain like that. For now it even seemed an impossible thing to snap just like that ten years of relationship, though to him they had been years of pain and shame. He prayed and wished there had never been injustices. Then there would never have been this rift—the rift between white and black. Then he would never have been put in this painful situation.

What was he to do now? Would he betray the "Boys?" He sat there, irresolute, unable to decide on a course of action. If only he had not thought of her in human terms! That he hated settlers was quite clear in his mind. But to kill a mother of two seemed too painful a task for him to do in a free frame of mind.

He went out.

Darkness still covered him and he could see nothing clearly. The stars above seemed to be anxiously awaiting Njoroge's decision. Then, as if their cold stare was compelling him, he began to walk, walk back to Mrs. Hill's house. He had decided to save her. Then probably he would go to the forest. There, he would forever fight with a freer conscience. That seemed excellent. It would also serve as a propitiation for his betrayal of the other "Boys."

There was no time to lose. It was already late and the "Boys" might come any time. So he ran with one purpose—to save the woman. At the road he heard footsteps. He stepped into the bush and lay still. He was certain that those were the "Boys." He waited breathlessly for the footsteps to die. Again he hated himself for this betrayal. But how could he fail to hearken to this other voice? He ran on when the footsteps had died. It was necessary to run, for if the "Boys" discovered his betrayal he would surely meet death. But then he did not mind this. He only wanted to finish this other task first.

At last, sweating and panting, he reached Mrs. Hill's house and knocked at the door, crying, "Memsahib! Memsahib!"

Mrs. Hill had not yet gone to bed. She had sat up, a multitude of thoughts crossing her mind. Ever since that afternoon's conversation with the other women, she had felt more and more uneasy. When Njoroge went and she was left alone she had gone to her safe and taken out her pistol, with which she was now toying. It was better to be prepared. It was unfortunate that her husband had died. He might have kept her company.

She sighed over and over again as she remembered her pioneering days. She and her husband and others had tamed the wilderness of this country and had developed a whole mass of unoccupied land. People like Njoroge now lived contented without a single worry about tribal wars. They had a lot to thank the Europeans for.

Yes she did not like those politicians who came to corrupt the otherwise obedient and hard-working men, especially when treated kindly. She did not like this murder of the Garstones. No! She did not like it. And when she remembered the fact that she was really alone, she thought it might be better for her to move down to Nairobi or Kinangop and stay with friends a while. But what would she do with her boys? Leave them there? She wondered. She thought of Njoroge. A queer boy. Had he many wives? Had he a large family? It was surprising even to her to find that she had lived with him so long, yet had never thought of these things. This reflection shocked her a little. It was the first time she had ever thought of him as a man with a family. She had always seen him as a servant. Even now it seemed ridiculous to think of her houseboy as a father with a family. She sighed. This was an omission, something to be righted in future.

And then she heard a knock on the front door and a voice calling out "Memsahib! Memsahib!"

It was Njoroge's voice. Her houseboy. Sweat broke out on her face. She could not even hear what the boy was saying for the circumstances of the Garstones' death came to her. This was her end. The end of the road. So Njoroge had led them here! She trembled and felt weak.

But suddenly, strength came back to her. She knew she was alone. She knew they would break in. No! She would die bravely. Holding her pistol more firmly in her hand, she opened the door and quickly fired. Then a nausea came over her. She had killed a man for the first time. She felt weak and fell down crying, "Come and kill me!" She did not know that she had in fact killed her saviour.

On the following day, it was all in the papers. That a single woman could fight a gang fifty strong was bravery unknown. And to think she had killed one too!

Mrs. Smiles and Mrs. Hardy were especially profuse in their congratulations.

"We told you they're all bad."

"They are all bad," agreed Mrs. Hardy. Mrs. Hill kept quiet. The circumstances of Njoroge's death worried her. The more she thought about it, the more of a puzzle it was to her. She gazed still into space. Then she let out a slow enigmatic sigh.

"I don't know," she said.

"Don't know?" Mrs. Hardy asked.

"Yes. That's it. Inscrutable." Mrs. Smiles was triumphant. "All of them should be whipped."

"All of them should be whipped," agreed Mrs. Hardy.

Chinua Achebe

Chinua Achebe (1930–   ) was born in Ogidi, east Nigeria. He is one of Africa's outstanding intellectuals and the author of many works of fiction and essays. His Things Fall Apart *is one of the most celebrated contemporary African novels. "Vengeful Creditor," written in 1971, comes from* Girls at War and other Stories.

VENGEFUL CREDITOR

"Madame, this way," sang the alert, high-wigged salesgirl minding one of a row of cash machines in the supermarket. Mrs. Emenike veered her full-stacked trolley ever so lightly to the girl.

"Madame, you were coming to me," complained the cheated girl at the next machine.

"Ah, sorry my dear. Next time."

"Good afternoon, Madame," sang the sweet-voiced girl already unloading Madame's purchases on to her counter.

"Cash or account, Madame?"

"Cash."

She punched the prices as fast as lightning and announced the verdict. Nine pounds fifteen and six. Mrs. Emenike opened her handbag, brought out from it a wallet, unzipped it and held out two clean and crisp five-pound notes. The girl punched again and the machine released a tray of cash. She put Madame's money away and gave her change and a foot-long receipt. Mrs. Emenike glanced at the bottom of the long

---

strip of paper where the polite machine had registered her total spending with the words THANK YOU COME AGAIN, and nodded.

It was at this point that the first hitch occurred. There seemed to be nobody around to load Madame's purchases into a carton and take them to her car outside.

"Where are these boys?" said the girl almost in distress. "Sorry, Madame. Many of our carriers have gone away because of this free primary . . . John!" she called out, as she caught sight of one of the remaining few, "Come and pack Madame's things!"

John was a limping forty-year-old boy sweating profusely even in the air-conditioned comfort of the supermarket. As he put the things into an empty carton he grumbled aloud.

"I don talk say make una tell Manager make e go fin' more people for dis monkey work."

"You never hear say everybody don go to free primary?" asked the wigged girl, jovially.

"All right-o. But I no go kill myself for sake of free primary."

Out in the car-park he stowed the carton away in the boot of Mrs. Emenike's grey Mercedes and then straightened up to wait while she opened her handbag and then her wallet and stirred a lot of coins there with one finger until she found a threepenny piece, pulled it out between two fingers and dropped it into the carrier's palm. He hesitated for a while and then limped away without saying a word.

Mrs. Emenike never cared for these old men running little boys' errands. No matter what you gave them they never seemed satisfied. Look at this grumbling cripple. How much did he expect to be given for carrying a tiny carton a few yards? That was what free primary education had brought. It had brought even worse to the homes, Mrs. Emenike had lost three servants including her baby-nurse since the beginning of the school year. The baby-nurse problem was of course the worst. What was a working woman with a seven-month-old baby supposed to do?

However the problem did not last. After only a term of free education the government withdrew the scheme for fear of going bankrupt. It would seem that on the advice of its experts the Education Ministry had planned initially for eight hundred thousand children. In the event one million and a half turned up on the first day of school. Where did all the rest come from? Had the experts misled the government? The chief statistician, interviewed on the radio, said it was nonsense to talk about a miscalculation. The trouble was simply that children from neighbouring states had been brought in in thousands and registered dishonestly by unscrupulous people, a clear case of sabotage.

Whatever the reason the government cancelled the scheme. The *New Age* wrote an editorial praising the Prime Minister for his statesmanship and courage but pointing out that the whole dismal affair could have been avoided if the government had listened in the first place to the warning of many knowledgeable and responsible citizens. Which was true enough, for these citizens had written on the pages of the *New Age* to express their doubt and reservation about free education. The newspaper, on throwing open its pages to a thorough airing of views on the matter, had pointed out that it did so in the national cause and, mounting an old hobby-horse, challenged those of its critics who could see no merit whatever in a newspaper owned by foreign capital to come forward and demonstrate an equal or a higher order of national commitment and patriotism, a challenge that none of those critics took up. The offer of space by the *New Age* was taken up eagerly and in the course of ten days at the rate of two or even three articles a day a large number of responsible citizens—lawyers, doctors, merchants, engineers, salesmen, insurance brokers, university lecturers, etc.—had written in criticism of the scheme. No one was against education for the kids, they said, but free education was premature. Someone said that not even the United States of America in all its wealth and power had introduced it yet, how much less . . .

Mr. Emenike read the various contributions with boyish

excitement. "I wish civil servants were free to write to the papers," he told his wife at least on three occasions during those ten days.

"This is not bad, but he should have mentioned that this country has made tremendous strides in education since independence because parents know the value of education and will make any sacrifice to find school fees for their children. We are not a nation of Oliver Twists."

His wife was not really interested in all the argument at that stage, because somehow it all seemed to hang in the air. She had some vague, personal doubts about free education, that was all.

"Have you looked at the paper? Mike has written on this thing," said her husband on another occasion.

"Who is Mike?"

"Mike Ogudu."

"Oh, what does he say?"

"I haven't read it yet . . . Oh yes, you can trust Mike to call a spade a spade. See how he begins: 'Free primary education is tantamount to naked Communism?' That's not quite true but that's Mike all over. He thinks someone might come up to nationalize his shipping line. He is so scared of Communism."

"But who wants Communism here?"

"Nobody. That's what I told him the other evening at the Club. But he is so scared. You know one thing? Too much money is bad-o."

The discussion in the Emenike family remained at this intellectual level until one day their "Small Boy," a very bright lad of twelve helping out the cook and understudying the steward, announced he must go home to see his sick father.

"How did you know your Father was sick?" asked Madame.

"My brodder come tell me."

"When did your brother come?"

"Yesterday for evening-time."

"Why didn't you bring him to see me?"

"I no no say Madame go wan see am."

"Why you no talk since yesterday?" asked Mr. Emenike looking up from his newspaper.

"At first I tink say I no go go home. But today one mind tell me say make you go see-am-o; perhaps e de sick too much. So derefore . . ."

"All right. You can go but make sure you are back by to-morrow afternoon otherwise . . ."

"I must return back by morning-time sef."

He didn't come back. Mrs. Emenike was particularly angry because of the lies. She didn't like being outwitted by servants. Look at that little rat imagining himself clever. She should have suspected something from the way he had been carrying on of late. Now he had gone with a full month's pay which he should lose in lieu of notice. It went to show that kindness to these people did not pay in the least.

A week later the gardener gave notice. He didn't try to hide anything. His elder brother had sent him a message to return to their village and register for free education. Mr. Emenike tried to laugh him out of this ridiculous piece of village ignorance.

"Free primary education is for children. Nobody is going to admit an old man like you. How old are you?"

"I am fifteen years of old, sir."

"You are three," sneered Mrs. Emenike. "Come and suck breast."

"You are not fifteen," said Mr. Emenike. "You are at least twenty and no headmaster will admit you into a primary school. If you want to go and try, by all means do. But don't come back here when you've gone and failed."

"I no go fail, *oga*," said the gardener. "One man for our village wey old pass my fader sef done register everyting finish. He just go for Magistrate Court and pay dem five shilling and dey swear-am for Court juju wey no de kill porson; e no fit kill rat sef."

"Well it's entirely up to you. Your work here has been good but . . ."

"Mark, what is all that long talk for? He wants to go, let him go."

"Madame, no be say I wan go like dat. But my senior brodder . . ."

"We have heard. You can go now."

"But I no de go today. I wan give one week notice. And I fit find anoder gardener for Madame."

"Don't worry about notice or gardener. Just go away."

"I fit get my pay now or I go come back for afternoon-time?"

"What pay?"

"Madame, for dis ten days I don work for dis mont."

"Don't annoy me any further. Just go away."

But real annoyance was yet to come for Mrs. Emenike. Abigail, the baby-nurse, came up to her two mornings later as she was getting ready for work and dumped the baby in her lap and took off. Abigail of all people! After all she had done for her. Abigail who came to her full of craw-craw, who used rags for sanitary towels, who was so ignorant she gave the baby a full bowl of water to stop it crying and dropped some through its nose. Now Abigail was a lady; she could sew and bake, wear a bra and clean pants, put on powder and perfumes and stretch her hair; and she was ready to go.

From that day Mrs. Emenike hated the words "free primary" which had suddenly become part of everyday language, especially in the villages where they called it "free primadu." She was particularly angry when people made jokes about it and had a strong urge to hit them on the head for a lack of feeling and good taste. And she hated the Americans and the embassies (but particularly the Americans) who threw their money around and enticed the few remaining servants away from Africans. This began when she learnt later that her gardener had not gone to school at all but to a Ford Foundation man who had offered him seven pounds, and bought him a bicycle and a Singer sewing-machine for his wife.

"Why do they do it?" she asked. She didn't really want or need an answer but her husband gave one all the same.

"Because," said he, "back home in America they couldn't possibly afford a servant. So when they come out here and find them so cheap they go crazy. That's why."

Three months later free primary ended and school fees were brought back. The government was persuaded by then that its "piece of hare-brained socialism" as the *New Age* called it was unworkable in African conditions. This was a jibe at the Minister of Education who was notorious for his leftist sympathies and was perpetually at war with the formidable Minister of Finance.

"We cannot go through with this scheme unless we are prepared to impose new taxes," said the Finance Minister at a Cabinet meeting.

"Well then, let's impose the taxes," said the Minister of Education, which provoked derisive laughter from all his colleagues and even from Permanent Secretaries like Mr. Emenike who were in attendance and who in strict protocol should not participate in debate or laughter.

"We can't," said the Finance Minister indulgently with laughter still in his mouth. "I know my right honourable friend here doesn't worry whether or not this government lasts its full term, but some of us others do. At least I want to be here long enough to retire my election debts . . ."

This was greeted with hilarious laughter and cries of "Hear! Hear!" In debating skill Education was no match for Finance. In fact Finance had no equal in the entire Cabinet, the Prime Minister included.

"Let us make no mistake about it," he continued with a face and tone now serious, "if anyone is so foolish as to impose new taxes now on our long-suffering masses . . ."

"I thought we didn't have masses in Africa," interrupted the Minister of Education starting a meagre laughter that was taken up in good sport by one or two others.

"I am sorry to trespass in my right honourable friend's territory; communist slogans are so infectious. But as I was saying we should not talk lightly about new taxes unless we are prepared to bring the Army out to quell tax riots. One simple fact of life which we have come to learn rather painfully and reluctantly—and I'm not so sure even now that we have all learnt it—is that people do riot against taxes but not against school fees. The reason is simple. Everybody, even a motor-park tout, knows what school fees are for. He can see his child going to school in the morning and coming back in the afternoon. But you go and tell him about general taxation and he immediately thinks that government is stealing his money from him. One other point, if a man doesn't want to pay school fees he doesn't have to, after all this is a democratic society. The worst that can happen is that his child stays at home which he probably doesn't mind at all. But taxes are different; everybody must pay whether they want to or not. The difference is pretty sharp. That's why mobs riot." A few people said "Hear! Hear!" Others just let out exhalations of relief or agreement. Mr. Emenike who had an unrestrainable admiration for the Finance Minister and had been nodding like a lizard through his speech shouted his "Hear! Hear!" too loud and got a scorching look from the Prime Minister.

A few desultory speeches followed and the government took its decision not to abolish free primary education but to suspend it until all the relevant factors had been thoroughly examined.

One little girl of ten, named Veronica, was brokenhearted. She had come to love school as an escape from the drabness and arduous demands of home. Her mother, a near-destitute widow who spent all hours of the day in the farm and, on market days, in the market left Vero to carry the burden of caring for the younger children. Actually only the youngest, aged one, needed much looking after. The other two, aged seven and four, being old enough to fend for themselves, picking palm-kernels and catching grasshoppers to eat, were no problem at all to Vero. But Mary was different. She cried a lot even after she had been fed her midmorning foo-foo and soup saved for her (with a little addition of water to the soup) from breakfast which was itself a diluted left-over from last night's supper. Mary could not manage palm-kernels on her own account yet so Vero half-chewed them first before passing them on to her. But even after the food and the kernels and grasshoppers and the bowls of water Mary was rarely satisfied, even though her belly would be big and tight like a drum and shine like a mirror.

Their widowed mother, Martha, was a hard-luck woman. She had had an auspicious beginning long, long ago as a pioneer pupil at St. Monica's, then newly founded by white women-missionaries to train the future wives of native evangelists. Most of her schoolmates of those days had married young teachers and were now wives of pastors and one or two even of bishops. But Martha, encouraged by her teacher, Miss Robinson, had married a young carpenter trained by white artisan-missionaries at the Onitsha Industrial Mission, a trade school founded in the fervent belief that if the black man was to be redeemed he needed to learn the Bible alongside manual skills. (Miss Robinson was very keen on the Industrial Mission whose Principal she herself later married.) But in spite of the bright hopes of those early evangelical days carpentry never developed very much in the way teaching and clerical jobs were to develop. So when Martha's husband died (or as those missionary artisans who taught him long ago might have put it—when he was called to higher service in the heavenly mansions by Him who was Himself once a Carpenter on earth) he left her in complete ruins. It had been a bad-luck marriage from the start. To begin with she had had to wait twenty whole years after their marriage for her first child to be born, so that now she was virtually an old woman with little children to care for and little strength left for her task. Not that she was bitter about that. She was simply too overjoyed that God in His mercy had lifted her curse of barrenness to feel a need to grumble. What she nearly did grumble about was the disease that struck her husband and paralysed his right arm for five years before his death. It was a trial too heavy and unfair.

Soon after Vero withdrew from school Mr. Mark Emenike, the big government man of their village who lived in the capital, called on Martha. His Mercedes 220S pulled up on the side of the main road and he walked the 500 yards or so of a narrow unmotorable path to the widow's hut. Martha was perplexed at the visit of such a great man and as she bustled about for colanut she kept wondering. Soon the great man himself in the hurried style of modern people cleared up the mystery.

"We have been looking for a girl to take care of our new baby and today someone told me to inquire about your girl . . ."

At first Martha was reluctant, but when the great man offered her £5 for the girl's services in the first year—plus feeding and clothing and other things—she began to soften.

"Of course it is not money I am concerned about," she said, "but whether my daughter will be well cared for."

"You don't have to worry about that, Ma. She will be treated just like one of our own children. My wife is a Social Welfare Officer and she knows what it means to care for children. Your daughter will be happy in our home, I can tell you that. All she will be required to do is carry the little baby and give it its milk while my wife is away at the office and the older children at school."

"Vero and her sister Joy were also at school last term," said Martha without knowing why she said it.

"Yes, I know. That thing the government did is bad, very bad. But my belief is that a child who will be somebody will be somebody whether he goes to school or not. It is all written here, in the palm of the hand."

Martha gazed steadily at the floor and then spoke without raising her eyes. "When I married I said to myself: My daughters will do better than I did. I read Standard Three in those days and I said they will all go to College. Now they will not have even the little I had thirty years ago. When I think of it my heart wants to burst."

"Ma, don't let it trouble you too much. As I said before,

what any one of us is going to be is all written here, no matter what the difficulties."

"Yes. I pray God that what is written for these children will be better than what He wrote for me and my husband."

"Amen! . . . And as for this girl if she is obedient and good in my house what stops my wife and me sending her to school when the baby is big enough to go about on his own? Nothing. And she is still a small girl. How old is she?"

"She is ten."

"You see? She is only a baby. There is plenty of time for her to go to school."

He knew that the part about sending her to school was only a manner of speaking. And Martha knew too. But Vero who had been listening to everything from a dark corner of the adjoining room did not. She actually worked out in her mind the time it would take the baby to go about on his own and it came out quite short. So she went happily to live in the capital in a great man's family and looked after a baby who would soon be big enough to go about on his own and then she would have a chance to go to school.

Vero was a good girl and very sharp. Mr. Emenike and his wife were very pleased with her. She had the sense of a girl twice her age and was amazingly quick to learn.

Mrs. Emenike, who had almost turned sour over her recent difficulty in getting good servants, was now her old self again. She could now laugh about the fiasco of free primadu. She told her friends that now she could go anywhere and stay as long as she liked without worrying about her little man. She was so happy with Vero's work and manners that she affectionately nicknamed her "Little Madame." The nightmare of the months following Abigail's departure was mercifully at an end. She had sought high and low then for another baby-nurse and just couldn't find one. One rather over-ripe young lady had presented herself and asked for seven pounds a month. But it wasn't just the money. It was her general air—a kind of labour-exchange attitude which knew all the rights in the labour code, including presumably the right to have abortions in your servants' quarters and even have a go at your husband. Not that Mark was that way but the girl just wasn't right. After her no other person had turned up until now.

Every morning as the older Emenike children—three girls and a boy—were leaving for school in their father's Mercedes or their mother's little noisy Fiat, Vero would bring the baby out to the steps to say bye-bye. She liked their fine dresses and shoes—she'd never worn any shoes in her life—but what she envied them most was simply the going away every morning, going away from home, from familiar things and tasks. In the first months this envy was very, very mild. It lay beneath the joy of the big going away from the village, from her mother's drab hut, from eating palm-kernels that twisted the intestines at midday, from bitter-leaf soup without fish. That going away was something enormous. But as the months passed the hunger grew for these other little daily departures in fine dresses and shoes and sandwiches and biscuits wrapped in beautiful paper-napkins in dainty little school bags. One morning, as the Fiat took the children away and little Goddy began to cry on Vero's back, a song sprang into her mind to quieten him:

> Little noisy motor-car
> If you're going to the school
> Please carry me
> Pee—pee—pee!—poh—poh—poh!

All morning she sang her little song and was pleased with it. When Mr. Emenike dropped the other children home at one o'clock and took off again Vero taught them her new song. They all liked it and for days it supplanted "Baa Baa Black Sheep" and "Simple Simon" and the other songs they brought home from school.

"The girl is a genius," said Mr. Emenike when the new song finally got to him. His wife who heard it first had nearly died from laughter. She had called Vero and said to her, "So you make fun of my car, naughty girl." Vero was happy because she saw not anger but laughter in the woman's eyes.

"She is a genius," said her husband. "And she hasn't been to school."

"And besides she knows you ought to buy me a new car."

"Never mind, dear. Another year and you can have that sports car."

"Na so."

"So you don't believe me? Just you wait and see."

More weeks and months passed by and little Goddy was beginning to say a few words but still no one spoke about Vero's going to school. She decided it was Goddy's fault, that he wasn't growing fast enough. And he was becoming rather too fond of riding on her back even though he could walk perfectly well. In fact his favourite words were "Cayi me." Vero made a song about that too and it showed her mounting impatience:

> *Carry you! Carry you!*
> *Every time I carry you!*
> *If you no wan grow again*
> *I must leave you and go school*
> *Because Vero e don tire!*
> *Tire, tire e don tire!*

She sang it all morning until the other children returned from school and then she stopped. She only sang this one when she was alone with Goddy.

One afternoon Mrs. Emenike returned from work and noticed a redness on Vero's lips.

"Come here," she said, thinking of her expensive lipstick. "What is that?"

It turned out, however, not to be lipstick at all, only her husband's red ink. She couldn't help a smile then.

"And look at her finger-nails! And toes too! So, Little Madame, that's what you do when we go out and leave you at home to mind the baby? You dump him somewhere and begin to paint yourself. Don't ever let me catch you with that kind of nonsense again; do you hear?" It occurred to her to strengthen her warning somehow if only to neutralize the smile she had smiled at the beginning.

"Do you know that red ink is poisonous? You want to kill yourself? Well, little lady, you have to wait till you leave my house and return to your mother."

That did it, she thought in glowing self-satisfaction. She could see that Vero was suitably frightened. Throughout the rest of that afternoon she walked about like a shadow.

When Mr. Emenike came home she told him the story as he ate a late lunch. And she called Vero for him to see.

"Show him your finger-nails," she said. "And your toes, Little Madame!"

"I see," he said waving Vero away. "She is learning fast. Do you know the proverb which says that when mother cow chews giant grass her little calves watch her mouth?"

"Who is a cow? You rhinoceros!"

"It is only a proverb, my dear."

A week or so later Mrs. Emenike just home from work noticed that the dress she had put on the baby in the morning had been changed into something much too warm.

"What happened to the dress I put on him?"

"He fell down and soiled it. So I changed him," said Vero. But there was something very strange in her manner. Mrs. Emenike's first thought was that the child must have had a bad fall.

"Where did he fall?" she asked in alarm. "Where did he hit on the ground? Bring him to me! What is all this? Blood? No? What is it? My God has killed me! Go and bring me the dress. At once!"

"I washed it," said Vero beginning to cry, a thing she had never done before. Mrs. Emenike rushed out to the line and brought down the blue dress and the white vest both heavily stained red!

She seized Vero and beat her in a mad frenzy with both hands. Then she got a whip and broke it all on her until her face and arms ran with blood. Only then did Vero admit making the child drink a bottle of red ink. Mrs. Emenike collapsed into a chair and began to cry.

Mr. Emenike did not wait to have lunch. They bundled Vero into the Mercedes and drove her the forty miles to her mother in the village. He had wanted to go alone but his wife insisted on coming, and taking the baby too. He stopped on the main road as usual. But he didn't go in with the girl. He just opened the door of the car, pulled her out and his wife threw her little bundle of clothes after her. And they drove away again.

Martha returned from the farm tired and grimy. Her children rushed out to meet her and to tell her that Vero was back and was crying in their bedroom. She practically dropped her basket and went to see; but she couldn't make any sense of her story.

"You gave the baby red ink? Why? So that you can go to school? How? Come on. Let's go to their place. Perhaps they will stay in the village overnight. Or else they will have told somebody there what happened. I don't understand your story. Perhaps you stole something. Not so?"

"Please, Mama, don't take me back there. They will kill me."

"Come on, since you won't tell me what you did."

She seized her wrist and dragged her outside. Then in the open she saw all the congealed blood on whipmarks all over her head, face, neck and arms. She swallowed hard.

"Who did this?"

"My Madame."

"And what did you say you did? You must tell me."

"I gave the baby red ink."

"All right, then let's go."

Vero began to wail louder. Martha seized her by the wrist again and they set off. She neither changed her work clothes nor even washed her face and hands. Every woman—and sometimes the men too—they passed on the way screamed on seeing Vero's whipmarks and wanted to know who did it. Martha's reply to all was "I don't know yet. I am going to find out."

She was lucky. Mr. Emenike's big car was there, so they had not returned to the capital. She knocked at their front door and walked in. Mrs. Emenike was sitting there in the parlour giving bottled food to the baby but she ignored the visitors completely neither saying a word to them nor even looking in their direction. It was her husband who descended the stairs a little later who told the story. As soon as the meaning dawned on Martha—that the red ink was given to the baby *to drink* and that the motive was to encompass its death—she screamed, with two fingers plugging her ears, that she wanted to hear no more. At the same time she rushed outside, tore a twig off a flowering shrub and by clamping her thumb and forefinger at one end and running them firmly along its full length stripped it of its leaves in one quick movement. Armed with the whip she rushed back to the house crying "I have heard an abomination!" Vero was now screaming and running around the room.

"Don't touch her here in my house," said Mrs. Emenike, cold and stern as an oracle, noticing her visitors for the first time. "Take her away from here at once. You want to show me your shock. Well I don't want to see. Go and show your anger in your own house. Your daughter did not learn murder here in my house."

This stung Martha deep in her spirit and froze her in mid-stride. She stood rooted to the spot, her whiphand lifeless by her side. "My Daughter," she said finally addressing the younger woman, "as you see me here I am poor and wretched but I am not a murderer. If my daughter Vero is to become a murderer God knows she cannot say she learnt from me."

"Perhaps it's from me she learnt," said Mrs. Emenike

showing her faultless teeth in a terrible false smile, "or maybe she snatched it from the air. That's right, she snatched it from the air. Look, woman, take your daughter and leave my house."

"Vero, let's go; come, let's go!"

"Yes, please go!"

Mr. Emenike who had been trying vainly to find an opening for the clearly needed male intervention now spoke.

"It is the work of the devil," he said. "I have always known that the craze for education in this country will one day ruin all of us. Now even children will commit murder in order to go to school."

This clumsy effort to mollify all sides at once stung Martha even more. As she jerked Vero homewards by the hand she clutched her unused whip in her other hand. At first she rained abuses on the girl, calling her an evil child that entered her mother's womb by the back of the house.

"Oh God, what have I done?" Her tears began to flow now. "If I had had a child with other women of my age, that girl that calls me murderer might have been no older than my daughter. And now she spits in my face. That's what you brought me to," she said to the crown of Vero's head, and jerked her along more violently.

"I will kill you today. Let's get home first."

Then a strange revolt, vague, undirected began to well up at first slowly inside her. "And that thing that calls himself a man talks to me about the craze for education. All his children go to school, even the one that is only two years; but that is no craze. Rich people have no craze. It is only when the children of poor widows like me want to go with the rest that it becomes a craze. What is this life? To God, what is it? And now my child thinks she must kill the baby she is hired to tend before she can get a chance. Who put such an abomination into her belly? God, you know I did not."

She threw away the whip and with her freed hand wiped her tears.

Nadine Gordimer

Nadine Gordimer (1923–   ) was born in Springs, South Africa. The daughter of Jewish immigrants, she is not only one of South Africa's most renowned literary figures but has long been a fervent opponent of apartheid and white supremacy. Among her novels are Burger's Daughter *and* July's People. *In 1991 she won the Nobel prize for literature.*

AT THE RENDEZVOUS
OF VICTORY

A young black boy used to brave the dogs in white men's suburbs to deliver telegrams; Sinclair "General Giant" Zwedu has those bite scars on his legs to this day.

So goes the opening paragraph of a "profile" copyrighted by a British Sunday paper, reprinted by reciprocal agreement with papers in New York and Washington, syndicated as far as Australia and translated in both *Le Monde* and *Neue Züricher Zeitung*.

But like everything else he was to read about himself, it was not quite like that. No. Ever since he was a kid he loved dogs, and those dogs who chased the bicycle—he just used to whistle in his way at them, and they would stand there wagging their long tails and feeling silly. The scars on his legs were from wounds received when the white commando almost captured him, blew up one of his hideouts in the bush. But he understood why the journalist had decided to paint the wounds over as dog-bites—it made a kind of novel opening to the story, and it showed at once that the journalist wasn't on the side of the whites. It was true that he who became Sinclair "General Giant" Zwedu was born in the blacks' compound on a white man's sugar farm in the hottest and most backward part of the country, and that, after only a few years at a school where children drew their sums in the dust, he was the post office messenger in the farmers' town. It was in that two-street town, with the whites' Central Hotel, Main Road Garage, Buyrite Stores, Snooker Club and railhead, that he first heard the voice of the brother who was to become Prime Minister and President, a voice from a big trumpet on the top of a shabby van. It summoned him (there were others, but they didn't become anybody) to a meeting in the Catholic Mission Hall in Goodwill Township—which was what the white farmers called the black shanty town outside their own. And it was here, in Goodwill Township, that the young post office messenger took away the local Boy Scout troop organized by but segregated from the white Boy Scout troop in the farmers' town, and transformed the scouts into the Youth Group of the National Independence Party. Yes—he told them—you will be prepared. The Party will teach you how to make a fire the government can't put out.

It was he who, when the leaders of the Party were detained for the first time, was imprisoned with the future Prime Minister and became one of his chief lieutenants. He, in fact, who in jail made up defiance songs that soon were being sung at mass meetings, who imitated the warders, made pregnant one of the women prisoners who polished the cell floors (though no one believed her when she proudly displayed the child as his, he would have known *that* was true), and finally, when he was sent to another prison in order to remove his invigorating influence from fellow political detainees, overpowered three warders and escaped across the border.

It was this exploit that earned him the title "General Giant" as prophets, saints, rogues and heroes receive theirs:

named by the anonymous talk of ordinary people. He did not come back until he had wintered in the unimaginable cold of countries that offer refuge and military training, gone to rich desert cities to ask for money from the descendants of people who had sold Africans as slaves, and to the island where sugar-cane workers, as his mother and father had been, were now powerful enough to supply arms. He was with the first band of men who had left home with empty hands, on bare feet, and came back with AKM assault rifles, heat-guided missiles and limpet mines.

The future Prime Minister was imprisoned again and again and finally fled the country and established the Party's leadership in exile. When Sinclair "General Giant" met him in London or Algiers, the future Prime Minister wore a dark suit whose close weave was midnight blue in the light. He himself wore a bush outfit that originally had been put together by men who lived less like men than prides of lion, tick-ridden, thirsty, waiting in thickets of thorn. As these men increased in numbers and boldness, and he rose in command of them, the outfit elaborated into a combat uniform befitting his style, title and achievement. At the beginning of the war, he had led a ragged hit-and-run group; after four years and the deaths of many, which emphasized his giant indestructibility, his men controlled a third of the country and he was the man the white army wanted most to capture.

Before the future Prime Minister talked to the Organization of African Unity or United Nations he had now to send for and consult with his commander-in-chief of the liberation army, Sinclair "General Giant" Zwedu. General Giant came from the bush in his Czech jeep, in a series of tiny planes from secret airstrips, and at last would board a scheduled jet liner among oil and mineral men who thought they were sitting beside just another dolled-up black official from some unheard-of state whose possibilities they might have to look into sometime. When the consultation in the foreign capital was over, General Giant did not fidget long in the putter of official cocktail parties, but would disappear to find for himself whatever that particular capital could offer to meet his high capacities—for leading men to fight without fear, exciting people to caper, shout with pleasure, drink and argue, for touching women. After a night in a bar and a bed with girls (he never had to pay professionals, always found well-off, respectable women, black or white, whose need for delights simply matched his own) he would take a plane back to Africa. He never wanted to linger. He never envied his brother, the future Prime Minister, his flat in London and the invitations to country houses to discuss the future of the country. He went back imperatively as birds migrate to Africa to mate and assure the survival of their kind, journeying thousands of miles, just as he flew and drove deeper and deeper into where he belonged until he reached again his headquarters—that the white commandos often claimed to have destroyed but could not be destroyed because his headquarters were the bush itself.

The war would not have been won without General Giant. At the Peace Conference he took no part in the deliberations but was there at his brother's, the future Prime Minister's side: a deterrent weapon, a threat to the defeated white government of what would happen if peace were not made. Now and then he cleared his throat of a constriction of boredom; the white delegates were alarmed as if he had roared.

Constitutional talks went on for many weeks; there was a cease-fire, of course. He wanted to go back—to his headquarters—home—but one of the conditions of the cease-fire had been that he should be withdrawn "from the field" as the official term, coined in wars fought over poppy-meadows, phrased it. He wandered about London. He went to nightclubs and was invited to join parties of arabs who, he found, had no idea where the country he had fought for, and won for his people, was; this time he really did roar—with laughter. He walked through Soho but couldn't understand why anyone would like to watch couples making the movements of love-making on the cinema screen instead of doing it themselves. He came upon the Natural History Museum in South

Kensington and was entranced by the life that existed anterior to his own unthinking familiarity with ancient nature hiding the squat limpet mines, the iron clutches of offensive and defensive hand-grenades, the angular AKMs, metal blue with heat. He sent postcards of mammoths and gasteropods to his children, who were still where they had been with his wife all through the war—in the black location of the capital of his home country. Since she was his wife, she had been under police surveillance, and detained several times, but had survived by saying she and her husband were separated. Which was true, in a way; a man leading a guerrilla war has no family, he must forget about meals cooked for him by a woman, nights in a bed with two places hollowed by their bodies, and the snuffle of a baby close by. He made love to a black singer from Jamaica, not young, whose style was a red-head wig rather than fashionable rigid pigtails. She composed a song about his bravery in the war in a country she imagined but had never seen, and sang it at a victory rally where all the brothers in exile as well as the white sympathizers with their cause, applauded her. In her flat she had a case of special Scotch whisky, twelve years old, sent by an admirer. She said —sang to him—Let's not let it get any older. As she worked only at night, they spent whole days indoors making love when the weather was bad—the big man, General Giant, was like a poor stray cat, in the cold rain: he would walk on the balls of shoe-soles, shaking each foot as he lifted it out of the wet.

He was waiting for the okay, as he said to his brother, the future Prime Minister, to go back to their country and take up his position as commander-in-chief of the new state's Defence Force. His title would become an official rank, the highest, like that of army chiefs in Britain and the United States— General Zwedu.

His brother turned solemn, dark in his mind; couldn't be followed there. He said the future of the army was a tremendous problem at present under discussion. The two armies, black and white, who had fought each other, would have to be made one. What the discussions were also about remained in the dark: the defeated white government, the European powers by whom the new black state was promised loans for reconstruction, had insisted that Sinclair "General Giant" Zwedu be relieved of all military authority. His personality was too strong and too strongly associated with the triumph of the freedom fighter army for him to be anything but a divisive reminder of the past, in the new, regular army. Let him stand for parliament in the first peace-time election, his legend would guarantee that he win the seat. Then the Prime Minister could find him some safe portfolio.

What portfolio? What? This was in the future Prime Minister's mind when General Giant couldn't follow him. "What he knows how to do is defend our country, that he fought for," the future Prime Minister said to the trusted advisers, British lawyers and African experts from American universities. And while he was saying it, the others knew he did not want, could not have his brother Sinclair "General Giant" Zwedu, that master of the wilderness, breaking the confinement of peace-time barracks.

He left him in Europe on some hastily-invented mission until the independence celebrations. Then he brought him home to the old colonial capital that was now theirs, and at the airport wept with triumph and anguish in his arms, while school-children sang. He gave him a portfolio—Sport and Recreation; harmless.

General Giant looked at his big hands as if the appointment were an actual object, held there. What was he supposed to do with it? The great lungs that pumped his organ-voice failed; he spoke flatly, kindly, almost pityingly to his brother, the Prime Minister.

Now they both wore dark blue suits. At first, he appeared prominently at the Prime Minister's side as a tacit recompense, to show the people that he was still acknowledged by the Prime Minister as a co-founder of the nation, and its popular hero. He had played football on a patch of bare earth between wattlebranch goal posts on the sugar farm, as a child, and as a youth on a stretch of waste ground near the Catholic Mission Hall; as a man he had been at war, without time for games. In the first few months he rather enjoyed attending important matches in his official capacity, watching from a special box and later seeing himself sitting there, on a TV newsreel. It was a Sunday, a holiday amusement; the holiday went on too long. There was not much obligation to make speeches, in his cabinet post, but because his was a name known over the world, his place reserved in the mountain stronghold Valhalla of guerrilla wars, journalists went to him for statements on all kinds of issues. Besides, he was splendid copy, talkative, honest, indiscreet and emotional. Again and again, he embarrassed his government by giving an outrageous opinion, that contradicted government policy, on problems that were none of his business. The Party caucus reprimanded him again and again. He responded by seldom turning up at caucus meetings. The caucus members said that Zwedu (it was time his "title" was dropped) thought too much of himself and had taken offence. Again, he knew that what was assumed was not quite true. He was bored with the caucus. He wanted to yawn all the time, he said, like a hippopotamus with its huge jaws open in the sun, half-asleep, in the thick brown water of the river near his last headquarters. The Prime Minister laughed at this, and they drank together with arms round one another—as they did in the old days in the Youth Group. The Prime Minister told him—"But seriously, sport and recreation are very important in building up our nation. For the next budget, I'll see that there's a bigger grant to your department, you'll be able to plan. You know how to inspire young men . . . I'm told a local team has adapted one of the freedom songs you made up, they sang it on TV."

The Minister of Sport and Recreation sent his deputy to officiate at sports meetings these days and he didn't hear his war song become a football fans' chant. The Jamaican singer had arrived on an engagement at the Hilton that had just opened conference rooms, bars, a casino and nightclub on a site above the town where the old colonial prison used to be (the new prison was on the site of the former Peace Corps camp). He was there in the nightclub every night, drinking the brand of Scotch she had had in her London flat, tilting his head while she sang. The hotel staff pointed him out to overseas visitors—Sinclair "General Giant" Zwedu, the General Giap, the Che Guevara of a terrible war there'd been in this country. The tourists had spent the day, taken by private plane, viewing game in what the travel brochure described as the country's magnificent game park but—the famous freedom fighter could have told them—wasn't quite that; was in fact his territory, his headquarters. Sometimes he danced with one of the women, their white teeth contrasting with shiny sunburned skin almost as if they had been black. Once there was some sort of a row; he danced too many times with a woman who appeared to be enjoying this intimately, and her husband objected. The "convivial Minister" had laughed, taken the man by the scruff of his white linen jacket and dropped him back in his chair, a local journalist reported, but the government-owned local press did not print his story or picture. An overseas journalist interviewed "General Giant" on the pretext of the incident, and got from him (the Minister was indeed convivial, entertaining the journalist to excellent whisky in the house he had rented for the Jamaican singer) some opinions on matters far removed from nightclub scandal.

When questions were asked in parliament about an article in an American weekly on the country's international alliances, "General Giant" stood up and, again, gave expression to convictions the local press could not print. He said that the defence of the country might have been put in the hands of neo-colonialists who had been the country's enemies during the war—and he was powerless to do anything about that. But he would take the law into his own hands to protect the National Independence Party's principles of a people's democracy (he used the old name, on this occasion, although it had been shortened to National Party). Hadn't he fought, hadn't the brothers spilled their blood to get rid of the old laws and the old bosses, that made them *nothing?* Hadn't they fought for new laws under which they would be men? He would shed blood rather than see the Party betrayed in the name of so-called rational alliances and national unity.

International advisers to the government thought the speech, if inflammatory, so confused it might best be ignored. Members of the cabinet and Members of Parliament wanted the Prime Minister to get rid of him. General Giant Zwedu? How? Where to? Extreme anger was always expressed by the Prime Minister in the form of extreme sorrow. He was angry with both his cabinet members and his comrade, without whom they would never have been sitting in the House of Assembly. He sent for Zwedu. (He must accept that name now; he simply refused to accommodate himself to anything, he illogically wouldn't even drop the "Sinclair" though *that* was the name of the white sugar farmer his parents had worked for, and nobody kept those slave names anymore.)

Zwedu: so at ease and handsome in his cabinet minister's suit (it was not the old blue, but a pin-stripe flannel the Jamaican singer had ordered at his request, and brought from London), one could not believe wild and dangerous words could come out of his mouth. He looked good enough for a diplomatic post somewhere . . . Unthinkable. The Prime Minister, full of sorrow and silences, told him he must stop drinking. He must stop giving interviews. There was no mention of the Ministry; the Prime Minister did not tell his brother he would not give in to pressure to take that away from him, the cabinet post he had never wanted but that was all there was to offer. He would not take it away—at least not until this could be done decently under cover of a cabinet reshuffle. The Prime Minister had to say to his brother, you mustn't let me down. What he wanted to say was: What have I done to you?

There was a crop failure and trouble with the unions on the coal mines; by the time the cabinet reshuffle came the press hardly noticed that a Minister of Sport and Recreation had been replaced. Mr. Sinclair Zwedu was not given an alternative portfolio, but he was referred to as a former Minister when his name was added to the boards of multinational industrial firms instructed by their principals to Africanize. He could be counted upon not to appear at those meetings, either. His director's fees paid for cases of whisky, but sometimes went to his wife, to whom he had never returned, and the teen-age children with whom he would suddenly appear in the best stores of the town, buying whatever they silently pointed at. His old friends blamed the Jamaican woman, not the Prime Minister, for his disappearance from public life. She went back to England—her reasons were sexual and honest, she realized she was too old for him—but his way of life did not recover; could not recover the war, the third of the country's territory that had been his domain when the white government had lost control to him, and the black government did not yet exist.

The country is open to political and trade missions from both East and West, now, instead of these being confined to allies of the old white government. The airport has been extended. The new departure lounge is a sculpture gallery with reclining figures among potted plants, wearily waiting for connections to places whose directions criss-cross the colonial North-South compass of communication. A former Chief-of-Staff of the white army, who, since the black government came to power, has been retained as chief military adviser to the Defence Ministry, recently spent some hours in the lounge waiting for a plane that was to take him on a government mission to Europe. He was joined by a journalist booked on the same flight home to London, after a rather disappointing return visit to the country. Well, he remarked to the military man as they drank vodka-and-tonic together, who wants to read about rice-growing schemes instead of seek-and-destroy raids? This was a graceful reference to the ex-Chief-of-Staff's successes with that strategy at the beginning of the war, a reference safe in the cosy no-man's-land of a departure lounge, out of earshot of the new black security officials alert to any hint of encouragement of an old-guard white coup.

A musical gong preceded announcements of the new estimated departure time of the delayed British Airways plane. A swami found sweets somewhere in his saffron robes and went among the travellers handing out comfits with a message of peace and love. Businessmen used the opportunity to write reports on briefcases opened on their knees. Black children were spores attached to maternal skirts. White children ran back and forth to the bar counter, buying potato crisps and peanuts. The journalist insisted on another round of drinks.

Every now and then the departure of some other flight was called and the display of groups and single figures would change; some would leave, while a fresh surge would be let in through the emigration barriers and settle in a new composition. Those who were still waiting for delayed planes became part of the permanent collection, so to speak; they included a Canadian evangelical party who read their gospels with the absorption other people gave to paperback thrillers, a very old black woman dry as the fish in her woven carrier, and a prosperous black couple, elegantly dressed. The ex-Chief-of-Staff and his companion were sitting not far behind these two, who flirted and caressed, like whites—it was quite unusual to see those people behaving that way in public. Both the white men noticed this although they were able to observe only the back of the man's head and the profile of the girl, pretty, painted, shameless as she licked his tiny black ear and lazily tickled, with long fingers on the stilts of purple nails, the roll of his neck.

The ex-Chief-of-Staff made no remark, was not interested —what did one *not* see, in the country, now that they had taken over. The journalist was the man who had written a profile, just after the war: *a young black boy used to brave the dogs in white men's suburbs* . . . Suddenly he leant forward, staring at the back of the black man's head. "That's General Giant! I know those ears!" He got up and went over to the bar, turning casually at the counter to examine the couple from the front. He bought two more vodka-and-tonics, swiftly was back to his companion, the ice chuntering in the glasses. "It's him. I thought so. I used to know him well. Him, all right. Fat! Wearing suède shoes. And the tart . . . where'd he find her!"

The ex-Chief-of-Staff's uniform, his thick wad of campaign ribbons over the chest and cap thrust down to his fine eyebrows, seemed to defend him against the heat rather than make him suffer, but the journalist felt confused and stifled as the vodka came out distilled once again in sweat and he did not know whether he should or should not simply walk up to "General Giant" (no secretaries or security men to get past, now) and ask for an interview. Would anyone want to read it? Could he sell it anywhere? A distraction that made it difficult for him to make up his mind was the public address system nagging that the two passengers holding up flight something-or-other were requested to board the aircraft immediately. No one stirred. "General Giant" (no mistaking him) simply signalled, a big hand snapping in the air, when he wanted fresh drinks for himself and his girl, and the barman hopped to it, although the bar was self-service. Before the journalist could come to a decision an air hostess ran in with the swish of stockings chafing thigh past thigh and stopped angrily, looking down at the black couple. The journalist could not hear what was said, but she stood firm while the couple took their time getting up, the girl letting her arm slide languidly off the man; laughing, arranging their hand luggage on each other's shoulders.

Where was he *taking* her?

The girl put one high-heeled sandal down in front of the other, as a model negotiates a catwalk. Sinclair "General Giant" Zwedu followed her backside the way a man follows a paid woman, with no thought of her in his closed, shiny face, and the ex-Chief-of-Staff and the journalist did not know whether he recognized them, even saw them, as he passed without haste, letting the plane wait for him.

B. Traven

B. Traven (?–1969) is one of the most mysterious figures of modern fiction, for he refused to reveal his identity. It is widely believed that he was the anarchist Ret Marut (although this may also be an alias), who participated in the Bavarian revolution of 1919. He moved to Mexico City where he wrote The Jungle Books, *a series of novels about the Mexican revolution and the oppression of Mexican peasants, and* The Treasure of the Sierra Madre, *on which the famous film is based, among other works. He apparently wrote in both English and German.*

THE DIPLOMAT*

During the rule of the dictator Porfirio Diaz, Mexico had neither bandits nor rebels nor train robbers. Porfirio Diaz had rid the country of bandits in a very simple and effective dictatorial way. He had forbidden all newspapers to print a word about bandit attacks, unless the report was sent to them by the government itself.

Occasionally Porfirio Diaz was interested that reports should appear about bandit attacks and train robberies. He wanted, on those occasions, to provide booty for some general whom he needed for particular political purposes connected with keeping himself in power. He would then send such a general and his troops into the bandit-troubled region.

* Translated from the German by Mina C. & H. Arthur Klein

This provided such a favored general with a small additional income of several times ten thousand dollars.

When the general had finished his business and had the money in his pocket—collected from all the business people of the region, who had to pay for the anti-bandit action at the rates billed to them by the general—then all over the world appeared news reports that the great statesman Porfirio Diaz once again with iron hand had cleansed the land of bandits. Thus foreign capital was as safe in Mexico as if it lay in the vaults of the Bank of England.

Several dozen bandits had been shot—among them many who weren't bandits at all, but only agricultural laborers who had begun to rise to throw off the cruel yoke of the big land-owners, the possessors of the great *latifundia*. About fifty names of other bandits who had been executed were published in the newspapers to facilitate the general's collection of the bills he had rendered. These names seemed authentic. They suffered only from the drawback that they lacked live bearers, for the general's secretary had either copied them from old tombstones, or simply thought them up.

At that time, more than today, paymasters, managers, and engineers of big American companies in Mexico were kidnapped and carried off into the mountains, with threats that they'd be chopped into bits if their ransom wasn't delivered on the spot within six days. It was Porfirio Diaz who paid the ransom to the bandits, so that American newspapers would not learn about the kidnappings and thus frighten off foreign capital. The ransomed man, once set free, was given a small sum in cash as compensation for his pains and as hush money.

But Porfirio Diaz did not dig down into his own pocket for these ransom and hush-money payments. If he had done that, he'd not have been able to gain the reputation of administering the national treasury with exceptional economy. Consequently he collected sums equal to the expended ransom and hush money from the same American companies for whose benefit—or rather for the benefit of their kidnapped employees—he had laid it out. To these companies he sold, for large amounts of good money, special concessions and communal land that he took from the Indians.

In this way he gained two new friends who were interested in the perpetuation of his dictatorship. One new friend was the favored American company; the other new friend was the Mexican large landowner, who, because the communal land had been taken from the Indians, gained a new troop of slaves whom he worked for three centavos a day, de sol a sol —from sunrise to sunset.

What newspapers do not report, simply does not exist. Especially not for foreign countries. Thus a nation always retains its good name. All dictators operate according to the same recipe. Today, as then, all the newspapers of Mexico, without exception, are in the hands of conservatives, in the hands of members of that class which praises the dictatorship of Porfirio Diaz as "Mexico's golden age." And because in Mexico this class is beginning to totter before the onslaught of the Indian and half-Indian proletariat, so today the newspapers of this class are filled with stories about bandits, rebels, and attacks on railway trains. They glorify every shabby assassin and every dishonorable general, if he happens to be a person who makes trouble for the present government.

Today in Mexico—according to the statements of those newspapers—complete freedom of the press is constantly endangered. Under the dictatorship of Porfirio Diaz, on the other hand, in spite of the rigid bans against reports about bandits, there was no talk about threats to the freedom of the press. For in those days there existed the only true and genuine freedom of the press—that glorified freedom of the press which operates in the interests of the capitalist class and permits the press to be free only to serve that interest.

In spite of the fact that Porfirio Diaz had completely exterminated all bandits in his simple and effective fashion, things nevertheless took place from time to time which had extremely painful consequences and which threatened to cause the collapse of his beautiful gold-plated construction—a construction lovelier and more skillful than a Prince Potemkin ever managed to create.

A new trade treaty was about to be negotiated between Mexico and the United States. With regard to all such treaties, Porfirio Diaz believed that he was the sly fox and consummate statesman; but when they were concluded and one looked more closely at a treaty and all its consequences, it was always found that Mexico had been tricked and robbed.

The United States government sent to Mexico one of its best commercial diplomats, for in the commercial relationships of the United States, Mexico is always regarded as one of the most important countries. For all time—in the future far more than in the past—Mexico will remain the most important country for the United States. More important than all of Europe.

Porfirio Diaz wanted to do a good lather job on this diplomat from the United States in order—as he thought—to give him a closer shave later on. And at the same time, Diaz wanted to display for that diplomat the wealth of Mexico and of its population—or of its upper classes, constituting less than one half of one percent of its population—and to demonstrate also how cultivated and civilized they were. Therefore, Diaz arranged a luxurious banquet in honor of the commercial diplomat from the United States.

Probably few men understood so well as Diaz how to mount such affairs. The later celebration which he staged in 1910 for all the world—the so-called Centenario celebration, the centenary of the independence of Mexico from Spain—unquestionably belongs among the greatest public celebrations which until then had been staged on the American continent, if not on the entire earth. Everything so abounded in and gleamed with gold that the visitors from other countries were dazzled.

The millions of dollars which that celebration cost the people of Mexico have never been counted. The visitors saw only the rich gold façades. In exceptionally clever ways, precautions were taken so that no foreign visitor to the Centenary had an opportunity to see what really lay behind the golden façades. Behind those façades ninety-five percent of the Mexican people lived in rags and tatters; ninety-five percent of the people had no shoes or boots; ninety-five percent lived only on tortillas, frijoles, chili, pulque, and tea made from the leaves of trees; more than eighty-five percent could not read; and more than eighty-five percent could not even write their own names.

Where in all the world, civilized or uncivilized, has ever such an event been celebrated! And what a tiny, obscure village fiddler Prince Potemkin was, compared with this great blower of fanfares, Porfirio Diaz, who on the occasion of that centenary celebration of Mexican independence had his chest so loaded with medals and decorations from all the kinds and kaisers that sixty fully loaded railway freight cars would not suffice to transport those orders and symbols of honor. Such is the picture of a golden age.

You have to admit that Porfirio Diaz understood how to hold festivals, and the event which he gave a few years earlier for that diplomat from the United States was an appropriate preliminary celebration to the glorious façade-illumination of the centenary festival.

The affair in honor of the diplomat was held in the Chapultepec Palace of Mexico City. Since the Revolution that palace has been rather neglected. Celebrations are now rarely held there, because the Mexican people today have more important things to do than to celebrate glittering affairs of this kind. For the most part, the Palace of Chapultepec is only a museum for foreign tourists who want to view the bed of the Empress Carlota, wife of Maximilian, and want to feel it to find out whether Carlota's sleeping accommodations were sufficiently soft.

Here also was the summer residence of the Aztec emperor, whose bath is still to be seen and is well preserved. Although Chapultepec Palace is the official residence of the President of the Republic of Mexico, the revolutionary presidents seldom live there. President Calles, for example, never lived in that palace, but occupied a modest house nearby.

Under Porfirio Diaz, however, things went on merrily and splendidly in Chapultepec Palace. Diaz was obliged to keep the small but very fat aristocracy of his country cozy and contented, in order to maintain his rule, just as other dictators have to warm up to the Pope when the capitalists, as a result of business going ever more badly, begin to realize that dictatorship too has its disadvantages.

To the affair given in honor of the diplomat from the United States of America, only the cream of the top society of Mexico was invited, in order to intensify the diplomat's impression of how elegant, civilized, cultivated, and wealthy the Mexicans were. Glittering generals' uniforms abounded. And Porfirio Diaz himself, bedecked with gold braid and gold lace, looked like a circus ape playing the principal role in a burlesque operetta, set in some fabulous and fictitious Balkan principality.

The ladies were loaded with jewels like the main display case in the show window of a jeweler in one of the most elegant streets of Paris between two and six of an afternoon. All in all, those present were the most select society that Porfirio Diaz possibly could assemble.

It was not the first time in the life of the United States diplomat that he had been assigned to negotiate and complete trade treaties with other countries. Only a short time before he had successfully completed a trade treaty between his own nation and England. In this treaty, without the diplomat or the American government understanding quite how, England had captured the juiciest morsels, which England always succeeds in getting in all such, or similar, instances.

And in order to reward the United States diplomat for his good work and to honor him and hypnotize him until the trade treaty was signed and ratified by the legislative bodies of both countries, he was received in a private audience by the King of England. Since the King could not elevate him to a knighthood—a good republican American doesn't stand for that sort of thing—the King bestowed on him a gold pocket watch richly set with diamonds and provided with a resounding and distinguished dedication and with the engraved signature of Edward VII, King of England and Emperor of India.

The diplomat was naturally very proud of this watch, just as every good North American republican is proud when a European king or grand duke has showed him some attention. For after all, such news is carried on the front pages of all American newspapers.

It was quite natural that at the Chapultepec affair in his honor, the diplomat showed this watch to Don Porfirio Diaz. Don Porfirio was flattered that the United States government considered him important enough to send to Mexico a diplomat of such distinction as to have been signally honored by the King of England, in order to negotiate and complete a new commercial treaty with him. Thereby Porfirio Diaz felt himself highly honored, since he was being regarded as of equal importance with the King of England.

Such equal status with kings and emperors made Porfirio Diaz tractable—a fact which was well known to the governments of all foreign countries and to their diplomats, and which fact was ruthlessly exploited by all governments and diplomats to the great detriment of the people of Mexico. Because Porfirio Diaz, like the majority of all dictators, was a parvenu upstart who had no well-founded right to be included among the aristocracy of Mexico—neither by virtue of his origin, nor his family, nor his education and training, nor his wealth, nor his talents. The characteristic which he did have in greatest abundance, however, was vanity.

As Diaz looked at the diplomat's watch, he was already reflecting how he, Diaz, could surpass this gift from the King of England, and in what form so that all nations on earth could hear of it and spread the word.

All the assembled Mexican generals naturally examined the watch and admired it appropriately.

After the preliminary ceremonies of greeting and presentation were over, the company withdrew to the great banquet where many fine speeches were made about the admirable relations between Mexico and the United States and between Mexico and all the other nations. Every participating diplomat, in his formal address, praised the golden age of Mexico, and above all the man who was solely responsible for the golden age—and that, of course, was none other than Don Porfirio himself.

When this was over, all prepared for the great ball which was danced in a style modeled after receptions for ambassadors in Paris. For Don Porfirio despised everything Mexican or Indian, and was an admirer of all that had a French aroma or which resembled court life in Vienna. This admiration at times reached total idiocy. Proof: The opera house of Mexico City.

During a pause in the great ball, the United States diplomat suddenly noticed that his valuable presentation watch was not where it originally had been. In spite of long agitated searching, he found it in none of the other pockets of his dress suit. And when he looked more closely later on, he found that the watch had been very expertly severed from the gold chain to which it had been secured—and indeed, as detectives later established, with the help of a manicure scissors.

The United States diplomat had sufficient tact to know that you didn't mention such a thing if it concerns only a run-of-the-mill gold watch that is lost during so lofty a diplomatic social event. You give a little wink, perhaps, to tip off the master of ceremonies. If the watch is recovered, all well and good; if it is not found, then the loss is made good by the U.S. State Department. Such incidents occur more often than the average citizen, who has never been a guest at a diplomatic ball, would believe, for diplomats too—more than one would think—are frequently in financial difficulties, which can be taken care of only in ways that do not conform completely to the proprieties expected at ambassadors' balls.

This watch, however, could not be replaced. That a diplomat treasures so little the personal gift of the King of England as to lose it, is almost an insult to the King of England. It could result in the loss of his diplomatic good name and diplomatic position. Now, from a United States diplomat one cannot expect the tact of a French, English, or Russian diplomat. The French diplomat would find a witty excuse to explain how and in what way the watch was mislaid, an excuse so fine and elegant that it would be more likely to help than to hinder him in his diplomatic career.

But in this area we from the United States are still peasants and schoolboys, and consequently make a fuss about it.

With the blunt toughness in matters of tact that is characteristic of the people of his country, the United States diplomat turned at once to Don Porfirio, and, with the help of his Spanish-speaking secretary, asked him for a brief conference.

"Pardon me, Don Porfirio," the diplomat said. "I am truly sorry that I must bother you, but I have just been robbed, here in this room, of my watch that was presented to me by the King of England."

Porfirio Diaz did not move a muscle. He refrained from saying "That's impossible!" or "Isn't there some mistake?" He knew his people and no one was more aware than he that only in the newspaper reports had bandits been eliminated, but not, however, in the land of Mexico. For if he had wanted to exterminate all the bandits, he would have had to begin by shooting all his own generals and governors and mayors and tax administrators and secretaries of state. The ruling class robbed because of insatiable greed; and the non-ruling class robbed of bitter hunger.

Hence Porfirio Diaz said in answer to the diplomat only, "Don't worry, your Excellency. This is clearly just a little joke. I give you my word of honor that within forty-eight hours you shall have the watch in your possession once again."

The word of honor of the President! Porfirio Diaz could confidently give his word of honor. Whoever is master of all bandits and thieves, whoever knows all bandits and thieves and their tricks and dodges as well as did Porfirio Diaz—himself a master-thief in all matters not directly involving common pickpocketry—would surely be able to find the watch.

Finally, and with the politest possible manner, Porfirio Diaz said farewell to the diplomat from North America, without having mentioned, even by a tiny word, the little misfortune.

However, afterwards, though only his most intimate aides were aware of it, Don Porfirio began to rage, as only he could rage. It was the raging of a dictator whose frauds are on the verge of being exposed.

"The Old Boy is blowing his top again," the frightened servants whispered to each other, and they trembled in fear at what would happen when the ball was over. The dictator's outbursts of rage were dreaded more than earthquakes, since he became as vicious as an angry old wildcat.

What he knew from the start, and with complete certainty, was this: a Mexican had the watch; only a Mexican could have it. And, to be sure, he knew how to handle Mexican thieves.

If the watch had been taken by a member of the staff of servants in his palace, then it was already too late to order the many detectives not to allow any of the servants to leave the palace. If the watch actually had been stolen by a servant, the detectives were no longer of any use, for, in the meantime, the watch already would have been smuggled out of the palace. Admittedly, it was also possible that one of the detectives had the watch. It was by no means certain that detectives would not steal what they could get hold of easily. Porfirio Diaz, after all, had placed plenty of thieves, pickpockets, burglars, and highwaymen in the ranks of the police, because thieves often make better thief-catchers than do respectable people.

It was hardly likely that the diamonds would be pried out of the watch or that its case would be broken up so that the watch could be sold more easily and safely piece by piece. The value of the watch would be diminished too much. It was more likely that the engraved inscription would be eradicated before the watch reappeared and was offered for sale. Stripped of its engraved inscription, however, the watch would naturally be worthless to the diplomat.

Don Porfirio could have immediately got hold of another gold watch, studded with any required number of diamonds, if only that would have served the diplomat's needs. But as things were, it was necessary to recover this particular watch, and no other.

Porfirio Diaz gave way to rage not because he feared he might perhaps be unable to recover the watch. Getting it back he regarded as a problem that he could solve. No, what caused him to boil with rage was something else. The theft of the watch at such a time and place stripped off the gilt veneer from one of his gleaming façades. It exposed nakedly the ordinary and unmistakable cheap plaster beneath.

The whole world had been overawed by the legend that Porfirio Diaz, the great Mexican statesman, with iron hand and broom of steel had completely and permanently purged the country of bandits and thieves with such success as had never been attained by any other person in any other country.

According to the news reports that Porfirio Diaz had spread throughout the world, at that time in Mexico one could travel on a horse with a sack full of gold pieces on the right side and another on the left side, from one end of the Republic to the other, and when one arrived one would have additional sacks of gold pieces on the right side as well as on the left—one sack more on each side than one had on the day of one's departure.

In a certain sense this was true. A capitalist from the United States, who crossed from El Paso, Texas, into Mexico with fifty thousand dollars in checks, could leave Mexico via Nogales six weeks later with one hundred thousand dollars in checks—the surplus having been squeezed out of Mexico and its people in that short time with the help of Porfirio Diaz.

But strictly and literally speaking, under Porfirio Diaz it was unsafe to travel through Mexico with money or other valuables, without a military escort. Often enough, the military escort when still under way would begin to reflect that it was wiser to protect itself with the money than to protect the money. Then a report would appear—if the matter could not be taken care of privately by the Diaz government to the satisfaction of all concerned—that the stagecoach had bogged down in a swamp or been buried by a landslide.

However, the whole lovely web of lies in which the dictatorship had enveloped itself, was threatening to come apart, since at a diplomatic social event within Chapultepec Palace itself, a gold watch had been stolen from the pocket of so important a diplomat from the United States of America— for this meant that the property of an honored foreign diplomat was not safe even at a diplomatic party in Mexico.

If bandits were so close to the throne of the dictator himself, what must things be like elsewhere in the land of Mexico? If this incident should be reported in the American newspapers, then the whole world would learn that the iron hand of Porfirio Diaz was really only made of cardboard, and that the big foreign capitalists would be wiser to be cautious with investments, so far as Mexico was concerned.

The diplomat from the United States had the dictator's word of honor and his statement that this amounted only to a little joke. Therefore the diplomat said not a word about it to reporters because he felt that it was his duty to wait to find whether, and in what manner, Porfirio Diaz would make good his word of honor. Porfirio Diaz knew that, according to the custom in diplomatic circles, the American was bound to leak nothing to the Mexican press, as long as the matter was covered by the dictator's word of honor.

That same night, Porfirio Diaz summoned the police chief to discuss with him how the watch could be recovered without advertising in the newspapers.

The next morning began the plowing up of the Mexican land in the search for the American diplomat's stolen watch.

The police chief appeared in Belén. Belén is the largest

prison in Mexico City where all male and female criminals are held until sentenced.

The police chief had all prisoners assembled, and he addressed them as follows:

"Yesterday evening a gold watch was stolen. The watch is inlaid with diamonds. On the inside of the cover a dedication is engraved in English. This dedication includes the signature of King Edward VII.

"It is now seven o'clock in the morning. If, by seven o'clock this evening the watch is turned over to the warden of this prison, then you'll all be released tonight—and none of you will be prosecuted for the crime for which you now find yourself in Belén.

"The one who returns the watch won't be asked for his name. He'll be allowed to leave as freely as he came. He won't be asked how he got hold of the watch, and he won't be either prosecuted or imprisoned because of the watch nor for anything else he may have committed before seven o'clock this morning. Besides, he'll receive from the warden a reward of two hundred pesos in gold.

"You will now all receive writing paper and an envelope and pencils. You may write in these letters anything you want. The letters will not be read or censored. And nobody on the prison staff will be allowed to read even the address on the envelope. In an hour, the letter carriers will be here, and you personally will turn over to them the letters you have written. The letters will be handled as official state secrets and delivered as addressed.

"Here I have a certificate, signed by Don Porfirio, by me, and by the warden of this prison. This certificate has the force of law until seven-thirty this evening."

The speech by the chief of police and the certificate, which contained it all word for word, proved how intimately Don Porfirio knew his thieves and bandits. If the watch really were in the hands of common pickpockets and fences for stolen goods, then it would be delivered by seven that evening, or even earlier.

In Mexico, as in other countries, all thieves and fences are quite well acquainted with one another. If one alone does not know all the others, still he knows at least about twenty others, knows their hideouts, their hangouts, their taverns, and where they live—knows where those twenty can be found, knows their sweethearts, and knows what each one of them has to answer for. Each of these twenty, in turn, knows a number of others with whom the first one is not acquainted.

For these reasons—and here neither Don Porfirio nor the police chief was mistaken—it was certain the contents of that speech became known within only a few hours to all thieves in Mexico City as well as to all fences for stolen goods.

The letters written by the prisoners to their accomplices on the outside—and delivered without censorship or inspection—contained everything that the prisoners had long wanted to tell their accomplices living in freedom outside.

To the great distress of the prisoners, and probably to the even greater distress of Porfirio Diaz, the watch was not delivered by the stipulated time. In this instance, failure resulted from the methods that Porfirio Diaz previously had used with success in cases that seemed hopeless.

The story was later told in Mexico that the watch really was recovered in this way with the help of the prisoners, and that all the prisoners were freed as they had been promised. But this is not correct. This rumor was only spread in order to hide the truth.

When by seven o'clock that evening the stolen watch had not been returned, Porfirio Diaz knew for certain that the watch had not been stolen by common thieves and also that it was not in the hands of the fences. He concluded, and quite rightly, that the watch was in the hands of someone who needed money, but did not need it so urgently that he had to hurry to sell the watch. It was someone who knew enough to correctly assess the value of the watch, and who awaited the time when he could sell it as advantageously as possible for a second-hand timepiece.

With the common or small-time thieves now ruled out, Porfirio Diaz knew the next level of thieves who had to be considered. These were not the last resorts, but rather that group who approach most closely to the common thieves and highwaymen, in terms of morality and incessant need for money, as well as with regard to impudence in stealing whenever an opportunity presented itself.

Accordingly, Don Porfirio now summoned to an evening audience all the generals who had been present at the diplomatic party to enliven it with their gold-laden uniforms. He had a list of those generals who had been in the Palace and he saw to it that all of them attended this audience.

But as matters turned out, one was missing—a Divisional general, or Divisionario. This Divisionario sent his regrets. Don Porfirio accepted those regrets because they arose from pressing duties that could not be postponed.

To the assembled generals Don Porfirio spoke: "Caballeros, probably all of you saw here in the palace the watch that the American diplomat showed me. This watch was lost track of in the palace. I assume that one of the soldiers on guard duty or one of your orderlies found the watch. That watch must be in my hands tomorrow morning by ten o'clock. If it is in my hands by that indicated time, then, caballeros, each of you will receive a special bonus of one thousand dollars for your efforts. Also I will seek to show my appreciation to you in other ways.

"Naturally, you will take care of this matter as unobtrusively as lies within your powers; for I do not want even the tiniest stain to fall upon our glorious army. With the offenders, you will proceed according to your own judgment. I thank you, caballeros!"

Everyone who knows Mexico knows that some Mexican soldiers of the lower ranks may have every possible vice and depravity; that—especially in matters connected with their love-life—they will unhesitatingly murder a rival. Mexican soldiers steal. That is true. But they steal only that which—and not more than—their generals and other superior officers leave over for them to steal.

In their ethics, in their bravery, in their honor, in their love of their homeland, in their loyalty, they stand far higher than their generals. They are used by the false and dishonorable generals to attack and to murder their own brothers, fathers, sons, mothers, comrades in other regiments. They never know whether in fact they are on the side of rebelling generals or on the side of troops that have remained loyal. They fight, because they remain loyal to their general, because they bear within themselves a fidelity their generals do not have.

Their generals initiate a military revolt under the slogan of freeing the tormented country from tyrants and from the "Bolshies"; whereas in actual practice they perpetrate revolts only in order to plunder the banks and the prosperous business people, and they have conveyed the stolen property safely to the United States, before the troops that have remained loyal to the government can pursue and catch up with them within the remote districts of the large land of Mexico. Under generals of this sort, the Mexican soldier—who can be regarded as the bravest, most loyal, and least demanding soldier of all armies on earth—is forced to serve and to obey.

Porfirio Diaz knew well, as the assembled generals also knew, that the slandered common soldiers might have all manner of vices and depravities, but one thing they certainly were not—pickpockets.

And consequently Porfirio Diaz knew quite well that when he beat the sack, he meant the donkey. In other words, when he implicated the rank-and-file soldiers he meant the generals.

In every lost war, the rank-and-file soldiers are always blamed for the defeat. It is always the rank-and-file soldiers, the proletarians, who would not stand their ground, whose morale was shattered, who lent a willing ear to defeatist misleaders and apostles of peace, who had no love for the fatherland. Never is the blame laid on the incompetent generals, never on the politicians with hardened arteries, never on the weakspined and demoralized diplomats, never on the greedy profiteers. Always the fault is that of the soldier, the proletarian. And if the war is won, then that is wholly and solely thanks to the competent generals, the wise statesmen, and clever diplomats. The generals, statemen, and diplomats get all the honors recorded in world history and school textbooks. The ordinary soldier gets as reward a parade, which the half-starved, lousy, and crippled munitions workers are allowed to witness like obedient sheep, behind a heavily barricaded line of police who swing their clubs in order that the generals are supplied with enough "Hurrah!" shouters and wavers of red, white, and blue star-spangled flags.

The generals here knew right well that Porfirio Diaz did not for an instant mean seriously that one of the soldiers on guard or one of the generals' orderlies could have stolen the watch. Admittedly, all the generals knew what Porfirio Diaz really thought of them, just as Porfirio Diaz most certainly knew what all his generals thought of him. Master and accomplices both bore down heavily with feet, fists, and claws on the unfortunate rich land of Mexico.

By ten o'clock next morning the watch had not been returned.

For an instant—but only for an instant—Porfirio Diaz became confused, because it seemed that he had miscalculated.

Then, however, he recalled the Divisional general who had sent his regrets at being unable to be on hand the evening before, because he had to be out of the capital, in Tlalpam, on an important matter connected with the military service.

Now Porfirio Diaz speedily ordered this general to appear.

When the general stood before him, Porfirio Diaz looked at him for a while, then said, short and hard, "Divisionario, give me the watch that belongs to the American diplomat."

Without a change of expression, without in any way becoming embarrassed, the general reached under the jacket of his uniform, poked around in a pocket there, and brought out the watch.

He stepped two paces closer to the dictator and handed him the watch with the words, "A sus apreciables órdenes, Señor Presidente, at your highly valued service."

Porfirio Diaz took the watch and laid it on the table in front of him.

He felt called upon to say something. And so he said: "Divisionario, I don't understand—eh—why?"

The Divisionario thereupon answered soberly, "I was afraid Señor Presidente, that someone else would take the watch, and so I thought to myself, it may be better if I take it.

To this answer Porfirio Diaz remained silent. In so doing, he proved again most admirably that he was smarter than many of those who condemn him wish to admit. Also it is difficult to assume that Porfirio Diaz would have been involved in a matter of common pocket-picking. And certainly not in the final five years of his rule, when he had already become a little shaky.

But one thing must be said.

Porfirio Diaz had to keep the diplomat in a friendly mood and in a favorable frame of mind if the incident was not to become known. Porfirio Diaz was more concerned about the good name of his court than many a European potentate. Therefore, in order to appease the diplomat and put him in a good humor, Porfirio was obliged, when it came to the completion of the commercial treaty, to make concessions for which, it is true, the people of Mexico had to pay, but which brought to that diplomat the honor of being called one of the most skillful diplomats of the United States of America.

Carmen Naranjo

Carmen Naranjo *(1931–   ) was born in Cartago, Costa Rica. She is today one of Costa Rica's leading novelists and short story writers.*

AND WE SOLD
THE RAIN

"This is a royal fuck-up," was all the treasury minister could say a few days ago as he got out of the jeep after seventy kilometers of jouncing over dusty rutted roads and muddy trails. His advisor agreed: there wasn't a cent in the treasury, the line for foreign exchange wound four times around the capital, and the IMF was stubbornly insisting that the country could expect no more loans until the interest had been paid up, public spending curtailed, salaries frozen, domestic production increased, imports reduced, and social programs cut.

The poor were complaining, "We can't even buy beans—they've got us living on radish tops, bananas and garbage; they raise our water bills but don't give us any water even though it rains every day, and on top of that they add on a charge for excess consumption for last year, even though there wasn't any water in the pipes then either."

"Doesn't anyone in this whole goddamned country have an idea that could get us out of this?" asked the president of the republic, who shortly before the elections, surrounded by a toothily smiling, impeccably tailored meritocracy, had

444

boasted that by virtue of his university-trained mind (Ph.D. in developmental economics) he was the best candidate. Someone proposed to him that he pray to La Negrita; he did and nothing happened. Somebody else suggested that he reinstate the Virgin of Ujarrás. But after so many years of neglect, the pretty little virgin had gone deaf and ignored the pleas for help, even though the entire cabinet implored her, at the top of their lungs, to light the way to a better future and a happier tomorrow.

The hunger and poverty could no longer be concealed: the homeless, pockets empty, were squatting in the Parque Central, the Parque Nacional, and the Plaza de la Cultura. They were camping along Central and Second Avenues and in a shantytown springing up on the plains outside the city. Gangs were threatening to invade the national theater, the Banco Central, and all nationalized banking headquarters. The Public Welfare Agency was rationing rice and beans as if they were medicine. In the marketplace, robberies increased to one per second, and homes were burgled at the rate of one per half hour. Business and government were sinking in sleaze; drug lords operated uncontrolled, and gambling was institutionalized in order to launder dollars and attract tourists. Strangely enough, the prices of a few items went down: whiskey, caviar and other such articles of conspicuous consumption.

The sea of poverty that was engulfing cities and villages contrasted with the growing number of Mercedes Benzes, BMWs and a whole alphabet of trade names of gleaming new cars.

The minister announced to the press that the country was on the verge of bankruptcy. The airlines were no longer issuing tickets because so much money was owed them, and travel became impossible; even official junkets were eliminated. There was untold suffering of civil servants suddenly unable to travel even once a month to the great cities of the world! A special budget might be the solution, but tax revenues were nowhere to be found, unless a compliant public were to go along with the president's brilliant idea of levying a tax on air—a minimal tax, to be sure, but, after all, the air was a part of the government's patrimony. Ten *colones* per breath would be a small price to pay.

July arrived, and one afternoon a minister without portfolio and without umbrella, noticing that it had started to rain, stood watching people run for cover. "Yes," he thought, "here it rains like it rains in Comala, like it rains in Macondo. It rains day and night, rain after rain, like a theater with the same movie, sheets of water. Poor people without umbrellas, without a change of clothes, they get drenched, people living in leaky houses, without a change of shoes for when they're shipwrecked. And here, all my poor colleagues with colds, all the poor deputies with laryngitis, the president with that worrisome cough, all this on top of the catastrophe itself. No TV station is broadcasting; all of them are flooded, along with the newspaper plants and the radio stations. A people without news is a lost people, because they don't know that everywhere else, or almost everywhere else, things are even worse. If we could only export the rain," thought the minister.

Meanwhile, the people, depressed by the heavy rains, the dampness, the lack of news, the cold, and their hunger and despair without their sitcoms and soap operas, began to rain inside and to increase the baby population—that is, to try to increase the odds that one of their progeny might survive. A mass of hungry, naked babies began to cry in concert every time it rained.

When one of the radio transmitters was finally repaired, the president was able to broadcast a message: He had inherited a country so deeply in debt that it could no longer obtain credit and could no longer afford to pay either the interest or the amortization on loans. He had to dismiss civil servants, suspend public works, cut off services, close offices, and spread his legs somewhat to transnationals. Now even these lean cows were dying; the fat ones were on the way, encouraged by the International Monetary Fund, the AID and the IDB, not to mention the EEC. The great danger was that the fat cows had to cross over the neighboring country on their way, and it was possible that they would be eaten up—even though they came by air, at nine thousand feet above the ground, in a first class stable in a pressurized, air-conditioned cabin. Those neighbors were simply not to be trusted.

The fact was that the government had faded in the people's memory. By now no one remembered the names of the president or his ministers; people remembered them as "the one with glasses who thinks he's Tarzan's mother," or "the one who looks like the baby hog someone gave me when times were good, maybe a little uglier."

The solution came from the most unexpected source. The country had organized the Third World contest to choose "Miss Underdeveloped," to be elected, naturally, from the multitudes of skinny, dusky, round-shouldered, short-legged, half-bald girls with cavity-pocked smiles, girls suffering from parasites and God knows what else. The prosperous Emirate of the Emirs sent its designée, who in sheer amazement at how it rained and rained, widened her enormous eyes—fabulous eyes of harem and Koran delights—and was unanimously elected reigning Queen of Underdevelopment. Lacking neither eyeteeth nor molars, she was indeed the fairest of the fair. She returned in a rush to the Emirate of the Emirs, for she had acquired, with unusual speed, a number of fungal colonies that were taking over the territory under her toenails and fingernails, behind her ears, and on her left cheek.

"Oh, Father Sultan, my lord, lord of the moons and of the suns, if your Arabian highness could see how it rains and rains in that country, you would not believe it. It rains day and night. Everything is green, even the people; they are green people, innocent and trusting, who probably have never even thought about selling their most important resource, the rain. The poor fools think about coffee, rice, sugar, vegetables, and lumber, and they hold Ali Baba's treasure in their hands without even knowing it. What we would give to have such abundance!"

Sultan Abun dal Tol let her speak and made her repeat the

part about the rain from dawn to dusk, dusk to dawn, for months on end. He wanted to hear over and over about that greenness that was forever turning greener. He loved to think of it raining and raining, of singing in the rain, of showers bringing forth flowers . . .

A long distance phone call was made to the office of the export minister from the Emirate of the Emirs, but the minister wasn't in. The trade minister grew radiant when Sultan Abun dal Tol, warming to his subject, instructed him to buy up rain and construct an aqueduct between their countries to fertilize the desert. Another call. Hello, am I speaking with the country of rain, not the rain of marijuana or cocaine, not that of laundered dollars, but the rain that falls naturally from the sky and makes the sandy desert green? Yes, yes, you are speaking with the export minister, and we are willing to sell you our rain. Of course, its production costs us nothing; it is a resource as natural to us as your petroleum. We will make you a fair and just agreement.

The news filled five columns during the dry season, when obstacles like floods and dampness could be overcome. The president himself made the announcement: We will sell rain at ten dollars per cc. The price will be reviewed every ten years. Sales will be unlimited. With the earnings we will regain our independence and our self-respect.

The people smiled. A little less rain would be agreeable to everyone, and the best part was not having to deal with the six fat cows, who were more than a little oppressive. The IMF, the World Bank, the AID, the Embassy, the International Development Bank and perhaps the EEC would stop pushing the cows on them, given the danger that they might be stolen in the neighboring country, air-conditioned cabin, first class stable and all. Moreover, one couldn't count on those cows really being fat, since accepting them meant increasing all kinds of taxes, especially those on consumer goods, lifting import restrictions, spreading one's legs completely open to the transnationals, paying the interest, which was now a little higher, and amortizing the debt that was increasing at a rate only comparable to the spread of an epidemic. And as if this were not enough, it would be necessary to structure the cabinet a certain way, as some ministers were viewed by some legislators as potentially dangerous, as extremists.

The president added with demented glee, his face garlanded in sappy smiles, that French technicians, those guardians of European meritocracy, would build the rain funnels and the aqueduct, a guarantee of honesty, efficiency and effective transfer of technology.

By then we had already sold, to our great disadvantage, the tuna, the dolphins, and the thermal dome, along with the forests and all Indian artifacts. Also our talent, dignity, sovereignty, and the right to traffic in anything and everything illicit.

The first funnel was located on the Atlantic coast, which in a few months looked worse than the dry Pacific. The first payment from the emir arrived—in dollars!—and the country celebrated with a week's vacation. A little more effort was needed. Another funnel was added in the north and one more in the south. Both zones immediately dried up like raisins. The checks did not arrive. What happened? The IMF garnisheed them for interest payments. Another effort: a funnel was installed in the center of the country; where formerly it had rained and rained. It now stopped raining forever, which paralyzed brains, altered behavior, changed the climate, defoliated the corn, destroyed the coffee, poisoned aromas, devastated canefields, dessicated palm trees, ruined orchards, razed truck gardens, and narrowed faces, making people look and act like rats, ants, and cockroaches, the only animals left alive in large numbers.

To remember what we once had been, people circulated photographs of an enormous oasis with great plantations, parks, and animal sanctuaries full of butterflies and flocks of birds, at the bottom of which was printed, "Come and visit us. The Emirate of Emirs is a paradise."

The first one to attempt it was a good swimmer who took the precaution of carrying food and medicine. Then a whole family left, then whole villages, large and small. The population dropped considerably. One fine day there was nobody left, with the exception of the president and his cabinet. Everyone else, even the deputies, followed the rest by opening the cover of the aqueduct and floating all the way to the cover at the other end, doorway to the Emirate of the Emirs.

In that country we were second-class citizens, something we were already accustomed to. We lived in a ghetto. We got work because we knew about coffee, sugar cane, cotton, fruit trees, and truck gardens. In a short time we were happy and felt as if these things too were ours, or at the very least, that the rain still belonged to us.

A few years passed; the price of oil began to plunge and plunge. The emir asked for a loan, then another, then many; eventually he had to beg and beg for money to service the loans. The story sounds all too familiar. Now the IMF has taken possession of the aqueducts. They have cut off the water because of a default in payments and because the sultan had the bright idea of receiving as a guest of honor a representative of that country that is a neighbor of ours.

Translated by Jo Anne Engelbert

Gabriel García Márquez

Gabriel García Márques (1928–) was born in Aracataca, Colombia. One of the foremost writers in the Spanish language, he is the author of One Hundred Years of Solitude, No One Writes to the Colonel *and* Autumn of the Patriarch, *and numerous other works.*

ONE OF THESE DAYS

Monday dawned warm and rainless. Aurelio Escovar, a dentist without a degree, and a very early riser, opened his office at six. He took some false teeth, still mounted in their plaster mold, out of the glass case and put on the table a fistful of instruments which he arranged in size order, as if they were on display. He wore a collarless striped shirt, closed at the neck with a golden stud, and pants held up by suspenders. He was erect and skinny, with a look that rarely corresponded to the situation, the way deaf people have of looking.

When he had things arranged on the table, he pulled the drill toward the dental chair and sat down to polish the false teeth. He seemed not to be thinking about what he was doing, but worked steadily, pumping the drill with his feet, even when he didn't need it.

After eight he stopped for a while to look at the sky through the window, and he saw two pensive buzzards who were drying themselves in the sun on the ridgepole of the house next door. He went on working with the idea that before lunch it would rain again. The shrill voice of his eleven-year-old son interrupted his concentration.

"Papá."

"What?"

"The Mayor wants to know if you'll pull his tooth."

"Tell him I'm not here."

He was polishing a gold tooth. He held it at arm's length, and examined it with his eyes half closed. His son shouted again from the little waiting room.

"He says you are, too, because he can hear you."

The dentist kept examining the tooth. Only when he had put it on the table with the finished work did he say:

"So much the better."

He operated the drill again. He took several pieces of a bridge out of a cardboard box where he kept the things he still had to do and began to polish the gold.

"Papá."

"What?"

He still hadn't changed his expression.

"He says if you don't take out his tooth, he'll shoot you."

Without hurrying, with an extremely tranquil movement, he stopped pedaling the drill, pushed it away from the chair, and pulled the lower drawer of the table all the way out. There was a revolver. "O.K.," he said. "Tell him to come and shoot me."

He rolled the chair over opposite the door, his hand resting on the edge of the drawer. The Mayor appeared at the door. He had shaved the left side of his face, but the other side, swollen and in pain, had a five-day-old beard. The dentist saw many nights of desperation in his dull eyes. He closed the drawer with his fingertips and said softly:

"Sit down."

"Good morning," said the Mayor.

"Morning," said the dentist.

While the instruments were boiling, the Mayor leaned his skull on the headrest of the chair and felt better. His breath was icy. It was a poor office: an old wooden chair, the pedal drill, a glass case with ceramic bottles. Opposite the chair was a window with a shoulder-high cloth curtain. When he felt the dentist approach, the Mayor braced his heels and opened his mouth.

Aurelio Escovar turned his head toward the light. After inspecting the infected tooth, he closed the Mayor's jaw with a cautious pressure of his fingers.

"It has to be without anesthesia," he said.

"Why?"

"Because you have an abscess."

The Mayor looked him in the eye. "All right," he said, and tried to smile. The dentist did not return the smile. He brought the basin of sterilized instruments to the worktable and took them out of the water with a pair of cold tweezers, still without hurrying. Then he pushed the spittoon with the tip of his shoe, and went to wash his hands in the washbasin. He did all this without looking at the Mayor. But the Mayor didn't take his eyes off him.

It was a lower wisdom tooth. The dentist spread his feet and grasped the tooth with the hot forceps. The Mayor seized the arms of the chair, braced his feet with all his strength, and felt an icy void in his kidneys, but didn't make a sound. The dentist moved only his wrist. Without rancor, rather with a bitter tenderness, he said:

"Now you'll pay for our twenty dead men."

The Mayor felt the crunch of bones in his jaw, and his eyes filled with tears. But he didn't breathe until he felt the tooth come out. Then he saw it through his tears. It seemed so foreign to his pain that he failed to understand his torture of the five previous nights.

Bent over the spittoon, sweating, panting, he unbuttoned his tunic and reached for the handkerchief in his pants pocket. The dentist gave him a clean cloth.

"Dry your tears," he said.

The Mayor did. He was trembling. While the dentist washed his hands, he saw the crumbling ceiling and a dusty spider web with spider's eggs and dead insects. The dentist returned, drying his hands. "Go to bed," he said, "and gargle with salt water." The Mayor stood up, said goodbye with a casual military salute, and walked toward the door, stretching his legs, without buttoning up his tunic.

"Send the bill," he said.

"To you or the town?"

The Mayor didn't look at him. He closed the door and said through the screen:

"It's the same damn thing."

Luisa Valenzuela

Luisa Valenzuela *(1938–   ) was born in Buenos Aires, Argentina. A novelist and short story writer, her collection of stories,* Open Door, *has been translated into English.*

THE CENSORS

Poor Juan! One day they caught him with his guard down before he could even realize that what he had taken as a stroke of luck was really one of fate's dirty tricks. These things happen the minute you're careless, as one often is. Juancito let happiness—a feeling you can't trust—get the better of him when he received from a confidential source Mariana's new address in Paris and knew that she hadn't forgotten him. Without thinking twice, he sat down at his table and wrote her a letter. *The* letter that now keeps his mind off his job during the day and won't let him sleep at night (what had he scrawled, what had he put on that sheet of paper he sent to Mariana?).

Juan knows there won't be a problem with the letter's contents, that it's irreproachable, harmless. But what about the rest? He knows that they examine, sniff, feel, and read between the lines of each and every letter, and check its tiniest comma and most accidental stain. He knows that all letters pass from hand to hand and go through all sorts of tests in the huge censorship offices and that, in the end, very few continue on their way. Usually it takes months, even years, if there aren't any snags; all this time the freedom, maybe even the life, of both sender and receiver is in jeopardy. And that's why Juan's so troubled: thinking that something might happen to Mariana because of his letters. Of all people, Mariana, who must finally feel safe there where she always dreamt she'd live. But he knows that the *Censor's Secret Command* operates all over the world and cashes in on the discount in air fares; there's nothing to stop them from going as far as that hidden Paris neighborhood, kidnapping Mariana, and returning to their cozy homes, certain of having fulfilled their noble mission.

Well, you've got to beat them to the punch, do what everyone tries to do: sabotage the machinery, throw sand in its gears, get to the bottom of the problem so as to stop it.

This was Juan's sound plan when he, like many others, applied for a censor's job—not because he had a calling or needed a job: no, he applied simply to intercept his own letter, a consoling albeit unoriginal idea. He was hired immediately, for each day more and more censors are needed and no one would bother to check on his references.

Ulterior motives couldn't be overlooked by the *Censorship Division*, but they needn't be too strict with those who applied. They knew how hard it would be for the poor guys to find the letter they wanted and even if they did, what's a letter or two when the new censor would snap up so many others? That's how Juan managed to join the *Post Office's Censorship Division*, with a certain goal in mind.

The building had a festive air on the outside that contrasted with its inner staidness. Little by little, Juan was absorbed by his job, and he felt at peace since he was doing everything he could to get his letter for Mariana. He didn't even worry when, in his first month, he was sent to *Section K* where envelopes are very carefully screened for explosives.

It's true that on the third day, a fellow worker had his right hand blown off by a letter, but the division chief claimed it was sheer negligence on the victim's part. Juan and the other employees were allowed to go back to their work, though feeling less secure. After work, one of them tried to organize a strike to demand higher wages for unhealthy work, but Juan didn't join in; after thinking it over, he reported the man to his superiors and thus got promoted.

You don't form a habit by doing something once, he told himself as he left his boss's office. And when he was transferred to *Section F,* where letters are carefully checked for poison dust, he felt he had climbed a rung in the ladder.

By working hard, he quickly reached *Section E* where the job became more interesting, for he could now read and analyze the letters' contents. Here he could even hope to get hold of his letter, which, judging by the time that had elapsed, had gone through the other sections and was probably floating around in this one.

Soon his work became so absorbing that his noble mission blurred in his mind. Day after day he crossed out whole paragraphs in red ink, pitilessly chucking many letters into the censored basket. These were horrible days when he was shocked by the subtle and conniving ways employed by people to pass on subversive messages; his instincts were so sharp that he found behind a simple "the weather's unsettled" or "prices continue to soar" the wavering hand of someone secretly scheming to overthrow the Government.

His zeal brought him swift promotion. We don't know if this made him happy. Very few letters reached him in *Section B*—only a handful passed the other hurdles—so he read them over and over again, passed them under a magnifying glass, searched for microprint with an electronic microscope, and tuned his sense of smell so that he was beat by the time he made it home. He'd barely manage to warm up his soup, eat some fruit, and fall into bed, satisfied with having done his duty. Only his darling mother worried, but she couldn't get him back on the right track. She'd say, though it wasn't always true: Lola called, she's at the bar with the girls, they miss you, they're waiting for you. Or else she'd leave a bottle of red wine on the table. But Juan wouldn't overdo it: any distraction could make him lose his edge and the perfect censor had to be alert, keen, attentive, and sharp to nab cheats. He had a truly patriotic task, both self-denying and uplifting.

His basket for censored letters became the best fed as well as the most cunning basket in the whole *Censorship Division*. He was about to congratulate himself for having finally discovered his true mission, when his letter to Mariana reached his hands. Naturally, he censored it without regret. And just as naturally, he couldn't stop them from executing him the following morning, another victim of his devotion to his work.

tr. David Unger

Nawal el-Saadawi

Nawal el-Saadawi (1923–   ) is an Egyptian feminist, born in the village of Kafr Tahla. She served as Egypt's Director of Public Health but was dismissed for her book Woman and Sex *and was detained for a period under Sadat. She is the author of numerous works including* Woman at Point Zero *and* God Dies by the Nile.

THE DEATH OF
HIS EXCELLENCY
THE EX-MINISTER

Put your hand on my head, Mother, and stroke my hair and neck and chest gently, just as you used to when I was a child, for you're the only one I have left and your face is the only one in the whole world that I see or want to see in these final moments. How I used to want you to scold me for not having visited you for five years. But you were not the only one I neglected. I neglected the whole world, including myself, my house, my wife and my friends. Golf, which was my hobby, I haven't played once during these past five years. Even my little daughter whom I loved so much, I haven't seen. My own face, Mother, I haven't seen my own face. As I used to rush out of the house, I'd take a quick look in the mirror, not to look at my face but to adjust the tie around my neck or to check that the colour of my shirt didn't clash with that of my tie. And when I did look at my face in the mirror, I still didn't see it. When I looked at the faces of people in the office or in the street through the windscreen of my car, I didn't see them. If they spoke to me, I didn't hear them, even if they spoke loudly. The loudest hooting from any car, even if it was directly behind me, I didn't hear. So often did a car catch me unawares that I stopped walking.

I was, Mother, like one who neither sees nor hears nor lives in this world. In what world was I living then? Is there any other world in which a person lives, apart from that of people, unless God has taken him? I knew, Mother, that God hadn't yet taken me, because I didn't see my obituary in the newspaper. It's not possible for a man in my position to die like that, without a large and prominent obituary in the papers and a large funeral procession in which the leading statesmen walk, the head of state in their midst and the whole world crying. The scene used to move me so much, Mother, that as I walked in such awe-inspiring funeral processions, I wished that it was I in the box. But since I don't remember ever being inside that box and since I always used to walk along behind it, it follows that I am alive.

But I didn't live in the world in which you people live. I wasn't concerned with the matters that concern you, but with more important issues. My concerns were limitless and were more than my mind and body could bear. Sometimes my body would seize up and stop moving, even though my mind would continue. At other times, it was my mind which would seize up until it stopped thinking, while my body kept on moving and coming and going. It would go to the office and attend meetings and head conferences and receive official guests at the airport and attend receptions and travel abroad on official missions. When I saw my body, Mother, moving like this of its own accord, without my mind, I was amazed and even scared, especially if I was in an important meeting which demanded my concentration and attention. And the only really important meeting was one in which I was a subordinate. . . .

From the time I became a government employee, I hated being subordinate. I got used to repressing my feelings of hatred before my superiors and would give vent to them only in my office with my subordinates, or at home with my wife, just like I saw Father do with you, Mother. I was unable to express my hatred before my superior, even if he was an ordinary employee, like a head of department or a managing director. And what if my superior were not simply an employee, any employee of state, but the head of the whole state? What's that you say, Mother? Yes, my dear. I used to sit in my chair before him, my mind and body tense, senses alert and wide awake, fearful that he'd suddenly ask me a question to which I wouldn't know the answer, that if I knew the answer it wouldn't be the right one and that if it were the right one it wouldn't be the required one.

What's that you say, my dear? Yes, Mother. That's the ABC of politics which we learn in the first lesson. The right answer isn't always the required answer, but the required answer is always the right one. Men like us must always be alert, in mind and body, to distinguish the right truth from the wrong truth—and that's a tough job, Mother, tougher than any other in life. I had to sit in meetings, alert in both mind and body. I'd sit in my chair, my left hand lying in my lap, my right hand holding a pen poised above a sheet of paper, ready and prepared to pick up a gesture, any gesture, be it a nod of the head, a movement of hand or finger or a bottom lip tightening ever so slightly or a small contraction of a muscle around the mouth or nose or eye. I had to distinguish the movement of the right eye from that of the left. If I saw a movement the moment it happened, or even before it happened, I had to interpret it quickly in my mind. My mind had to be even quicker than me and interpret it before I did. My eyes had to be quicker than my mind and had to see a movement even before it took place. My ears had to be fast and hear a sound even before it was made.

What's that you say, Mother? Yes, my dear. During these important meetings I relied on my five senses. My mind and body were transformed, as I sat in my chair, into a mass of hypersensitive nerves, as if naked radar wires wrapped around each other were making my head and arms and chest and stomach work. I was so sensitive, Mother, that I would feel my stomach tremble as if it contained an electrical circuit, especially when I stood next to or near him. I'd feel the fingers of my right hand tremble, even though I'd clasp them with my left hand, with both the right and left pressed against my chest or stomach. My legs would also be pressed together, whether I was sitting or standing. That's how I was, Mother, when I was with him. My body was unable to adopt any other position. When the light fell on my face and the lens was focused on my body to photograph me for the people, I tried to release my right hand from the left and lift it off my chest or stomach, but I couldn't. I'd find them heavy, as though paralysed. What's that you say, Mother? Yes, my dear. That was the picture I saw of myself in the newspapers and I was ashamed. I tried to hide the paper from my family, especially from my young daughter who, with her little fingers, pointed to my face amongst the others in the paper and said to her mother, "Isn't that Father, Mama?" And she, with the pride of wives of great men, replied, "Yes, that's your father, my darling. Look how great he is, standing there with the president of state!"

My wife's voice rang in my ears and I realized it wasn't her real voice, that beneath the voice there was another that she had been hiding since time began and would continue to hide for all eternity, from the time we married until our death, hiding her real self and my real self in a deep and remote recess inside her. I sometimes felt it beneath my hand, like a chronic and hardened swelling which would not dissolve.

What's that you say, Mother? No, my dear. I was ashamed only in front of my little daughter, for even though her eyes are those of a child, perhaps for that very reason, they can always see through me and expose my real self which no one on this earth, not even I myself, can uncover. Do you remember, Mother, you always used to tell me that the veil was transparent for a child? I didn't believe you at the time, but I've realized since that sometimes, when my little daughter looked me in the face with those wide and steady eyes of hers, I felt frightened. At times I thought that this strong and steady look was not that of a child, especially not of a girl, or more exactly, a natural girl. The look of a natural girl, or even of a natural boy, ought to be less penetrating, less steady, less impudent, especially when directed at a larger and older person in authority. And what if this person is the father, master of the family and its provider, who works and who spends and whose right it is to be respected and obeyed by all the members of his family, big or small, especially the young ones . . . ?

What's that you say, Mother? Yes. That's exactly what you used to tell me when I was a child. It has always stayed in my mind, to the extent that I used to tell it to my wife and repeat it to my daughter, and I'd even say it to those employees under my leadership or authority. I felt pleased with myself saying it, like a child pleasing its mother. I even felt admiration for myself, to the point of vanity, when I saw the admiration in the eyes of the employees around me, and I grew more confident that what I was saying was absolute truth for all eternity and that whoever said anything different was mistaken or blasphemous.

What's that, Mother? Yes, my dear. All my life, from the time I was a junior employee until I became minister, I could not befriend any employee who contradicted me. And that's why, Mother, I couldn't stand that woman, why I couldn't bear to remain sitting in my chair, keeping my normal composure, as dignified as any other minister in the presence of his employees. I could only bear it, Mother, by jumping to my feet and shouting with anger unusual for me, losing my dignity and my nerve, saying nothing meaningful, unlike what I was used to saying. I don't know, Mother, why I couldn't bear it nor how I deviated from my usual calm and dignity. I wasn't angry with her for expressing an opinion different from mine, or because she was a junior employee whose view differed from that of a minister, or because she was a woman holding her own opinion before a man, or because she called me "Sir" whereas all the other employees addressed me as "Your Excellency the Minister." But I was angry, Mother, because when she talked to me she raised her eyes to mine in a way I'd never seen before. Such a gaze, such a strong and steady look, is daring in itself, even impudent, when it comes from a man. So what if it comes from an employee, from a woman? I wasn't angry *because* she did it, but because I didn't know *how* she did it, how she dared do it.

What's that? Yes, Mother. I wanted to understand how that woman did it. The desire to know took hold of me to the point of anger, anger with myself for not knowing and because I wasn't capable of knowing. Anger overcame me to the point that, the following day, I issued her with an order to come to my office. I left her standing before me whilst I sat and made her feel that she didn't exist. And I kept her standing whilst I sat talking on the telephone, laughing with the person who was speaking to me. The strange thing was she remained standing. She just didn't hear my voice nor did she look at me, but gazed at a picture hanging on the wall. I thought she'd look at me when I'd finished on the phone, but she kept staring at that picture on the wall as though I didn't exist. I tried to study her features before she moved and saw me, but she turned her head and her strong, steady eyes fixed themselves on mine. I jumped, as though all my clothes had dropped off me, all of a sudden. I felt ashamed; it reminded me in a flash of my little daughter's eyes. In one moment, the shame turned to anger and in another fleeting moment, the anger turned into the desire to shame her as she had shamed me. I found myself shouting in her face, in an unusually loud voice, "How dare you? Who do you think you are? Don't you know that whoever you are, you're nothing but a junior employee and I am a minister and that no matter how far up the ladder you go, in the end you're a woman whose place is in bed underneath a man?"

What's that you say, Mother? Yes. Any woman hearing

such words from any man would have died of shame, or would at least have fainted, especially if the man saying such things were not just any man but her superior in the government, who is not merely a manager or head of department, but a minister in person. And she didn't hear those words being said in an empty or closed room, but in my office, full of men, all of them senior employees. Yes, Mother, any woman in her place would surely have died of shame. I wanted to kill her by any means, even by shame. But the strange thing was, Mother, that nothing could kill this woman. She wasn't overcome by shame, didn't even lower her eyes, didn't blink an eyelid. Perhaps, Mother, you can imagine how much anger any man in my place, in my position, of my status and manliness and pride in my own eyes and in those of the employees in my ministry, would feel? And also because, Mother, I had never in all my life seen an employee raise his eyes to those of his superior, certainly never a woman raise hers to those of a man, not to her brother or father or superior, not even to her son. And what if that man were more important than her father or superior or any other man in his own and other people's opinion and in his self-respect and in people's respect for him?

Each time I remembered, Mother, how much respect I had for my masculinity and the respect people had for my position, my anger grew more intense. How could this woman do what she did? My anger, Mother, may have cooled a bit if I'd seen her blink, just once, or if her eyelids had trembled for just one second. But, Mother, she stood before me, her eyes raised to mine, as though I were not her boss and she not my subordinate, as though I were not a minister and she not a junior employee, as though I were not a man and she not a woman, as though I were not myself and she not herself. My anger grew each time I felt that I wasn't myself, that she wasn't herself. I asked myself who she was to make me feel that I was not myself. Or perhaps it was that I got more angry each time I remembered that I was indeed myself, with all the status, authority, masculinity and self-respect that is mine. I was absolutely sure, Mother, that I was myself, with all that meant. But, Mother, and this is what drove me crazy, at the same time I felt equally sure that I was not myself, that I would never be the same again. Maybe, Mother, you can appreciate my situation and can forgive me for hating this woman so much that the following day my temperature rose to 40°c and I had to stay at home, with my head burning under an ice-pack. And, Mother, my temperature did not go down until after I'd issued all the ministerial decisions in my power to break that woman and utterly destroy her.

What's that? No, not at all, Mother. I wasn't able to destroy her. She remained in existence, that woman. I happened to overhear some people say that she still existed. I didn't exactly overhear it, for I used to snoop around for information about her, fearful that someone would notice me, hoping to hear bad news or that she'd been destroyed in an accident. But no, Mother, that woman remained in existence. Not only did she remain as alive as any other woman but, Mother, I happened to see her once and she hadn't changed in the slightest. Her eyes were still raised and her eyelids did not tremble, even though, Mother, for all that, she was a woman like any other. I wasn't angry because she was a woman and I had never seen a woman do what she did. I wasn't angry because she was an employee and I had never seen an employee do what she did. No, what angered me and made me crazy was that I was incapable of destroying her by any decision or any authority and that she remained in existence. Her existence drove me mad, made me lose my dignity, my mind. I wanted to retrieve myself and my composure. But, Mother, she remained in existence and her existence began to threaten my own.

What's that? Yes, Mother. I don't know how I got into such a state. How could a junior employee, in the fifth or sixth grade, threaten the existence of any great man such as myself in a ministerial position. But I was really angry, more angry than I'd ever been in my life. I wasn't angry because I couldn't destroy her, with all the power at my disposal, nor because she did something no one else had done. No, what really angered me, Mother, was that she had done something I myself had never done. I have never, in all my life, been able to raise my eyes to those of any one of my superiors, even if he were a junior employee with only slight power over me. My anger grew, Mother, each time I tried to understand why I was incapable of doing that while she could, even though I'm a man and she's a woman, just like any other woman!

What's that? Yes, Mother. She was like any other woman. Like you, Mother, yes, like you. But I've never seen you, Mother, raise your eyes to anyone the way that woman did to me. Maybe if I'd seen you do it just once, I'd have been able to stand that employee. If you'd raised your eyes once to Father's, maybe I too would have been able to raise my eyes to his. Maybe I'd have been able to raise my eyes to those of any man in a position of authority. But, Mother, I've never seen you do it. If you'd done it only once, it may have been possible for me to do it too, because I did everything like you. Because, Mother, you were my sole example when I was a child and I used to imitate you, to imitate your every movement. I learned how to speak by moving my lips as you moved yours. I learned to walk by moving my legs as you moved your legs. I learned everything from you, Mother. So why didn't you raise your eyes to Father's so that I could have learned how to do it? Maybe if you'd done it just once, I'd have been able, as a child, to overcome my fear of him just once. And maybe, as an employee, I'd have been able to overcome my fear of any person in a position of authority.

What's that, Mother? No, my dear. I'm not blaming you. All I ask is that you stroke my head and neck and chest with your tender hand as you used to when I was a child, for you're the only one to whom I can open my heart, and to whom I can reveal my real tragedy. And the real tragedy is not that I lost my position as minister, but *how* I lost it. Perhaps the tragedy would have been somewhat lessened if I'd lost it for a serious or important or even plausible reason. The tragedy, Mother, is that the reason was not plausible and nobody can understand or believe it. Perhaps I did not know, Mother, that the reason was implausible until the day I opened the morning paper and did not find my name included amongst those of the new ministry. I suddenly felt absolutely sunk, as if my very name had fallen from my body. Every day, as I searched the papers for my name and did not find it, my feeling that I'd become a nameless body was confirmed. The telephone, Mother, which used to ring each day and at each moment, calling my name, fell silent, deaf, inarticulate, as if it too were bringing me down, bringing down my name. Such a bitter feeling of downfall, Mother, I've never experienced in all my life.

What's that, Mother? Yes, my dear, I didn't know the taste of that which I'd lost until that moment. And I fear, Mother, that that's the way of all life. We don't know the taste until after we've lost it. That in itself, Mother, is a catastrophe, because time passes and the opportunity may be lost for ever. That was how it was as I sat by the silent telephone, waiting, scared that one of my family would notice me sitting and waiting. Then I'd act as if I wasn't waiting, even though I was. If only the phone had rung, just once, in any way, made any sound, man or woman, relative or stranger, big or small, human or animal, any voice, even the braying of a donkey. If only the phone had rung, just one time, and called my name.

What's that, Mother? No, my dear. The catastrophe was not that the telephone did not ring, nor that I wanted it to ring. The tragedy, Mother, was that I discovered that the ringing of the telephone, which I'd always said I hated, I didn't hate at all, but loved. The sound of the bell used to send a quiver of delight through my body which, had I only known it at the time, no power on earth could have taken from me. That delight, Mother, was greater than the delight of sex and the delight of love and the delight of food and of everything in the world. It was an unearthly, inhuman delight, unknown to human instincts, an instinct without feeling and non-instinctual, an instinct which annihilated feeling, annihilated instincts. It alone remained strong, gigantic, tremendous, capable of annihilating anything in the world, wiping out tiredness, the pressure of work, wiping out dignity, insults, making my body capable of movement and activity even as I slept, making my mind work even in my dreams, making me stand on my feet in the airport under the rays of the sun after non-stop effort, features relaxed to welcome some official guest, making me sit with back and neck tensed up at some meeting or some reception, making me ready, at any moment of the day or night, to adopt the official position of legs pressed together and hands clasped over the chest or stomach. Yes, Mother. This gigantic delight was capable of wiping out any tiredness or effort, was even capable of wiping itself out, and myself with it, if it so desired.

What's that, Mother? Yes, my dear. I lost all this delight for the sake of some insignificant thing. And what is not insignificant compared to such delight? But, to tell the truth, Mother, that thing was not insignificant. It was not something simple, ordinary. No, it was not simple and not ordinary. It was the most serious thing that ever happened to me, the most serious thing I could ever face. Like death, Mother. Sometimes I used to believe I could face even death itself. But at the time I did not know what was happening to me. I sat in my chair as usual, alert in mind and body, my nerves and senses awake. My mind and body had turned into that nervous radar mass, naked and sensitive to any gesture or movement. I sat in my chair as normal, certain that I was normal, whilst with equal certainty, I knew that I was not normal and that, despite the fact that I was extremely alert, I was incapable of being alert and that, for the first time in my life, I was incapable of focusing my mind or of controlling it. My mind had begun to think by itself without me and was preoccupied with something with which I did not want to be preoccupied. That in itself would be a catastrophe if it happened to any employee in a meeting. So what about me, a minister, in this only meeting of importance, in which I was turned into a subordinate? The catastrophe, Mother, was not that my mind was out of my control, for had it been so in order to think of something important, like the annual report which I was to present or the new budget for which I was to ask, then maybe I'd have felt a little relaxed and comforted. But the catastrophe was that my mind did not think of anything important, but of something insignificant, the most insignificant thing that the mind of a man in a position such as mine, and particularly at such a meeting, could be occupied with.

What's that you say, Mother? No, my dear. I wasn't thinking about anyone. I was thinking about myself. I wanted to work out how to sit in my chair as normal, despite the fact that I wasn't normal. I wanted to work out whether it was me sitting in my chair or some other person and which of them was me. The problem, Mother, was not that I couldn't work it out, but rather that I knew that the reason for this catastrophe was none other than that junior employee. I curse the day I set eyes on her, for since then my mind has not stopped thinking about her. Perhaps I'd have found a little peace or comfort if what engrossed me was that she was a woman or a female. After all, I am a man and any man, no matter what his position, can still sometimes be engrossed in a woman. But the tragedy, Mother, was that at the time she didn't preoccupy me as a woman or a female because, in my view, she wasn't female at all. She was perhaps the only woman I've ever met in my life whom I did not feel for a second was a female. But what occupied and dominated my mind to the extent of stripping me of my willpower was that, although she was a female and although she was a junior employee, the most junior official who could enter a minister's office, she had managed to do something out of the ordinary, breaking every convention with which we are brought up from the time we're born, all the values we have known since the time we found ourselves alive and became human. The tragedy, Mother, was not that she did that and not that she did what no one else had done or what I myself had not done, but that from the time she'd done it, I was no longer myself. Whoever it was ~~sitting~~ in my chair was not me, but another person whom I hardly knew. I didn't even know which of the two was me. That, Mother, was the precise question which dominated my mind and body and all my senses at that meeting.

I tried so hard, Mother, to fight it. I mustered all my strength to resist it, to drive it from my mind, so that my left hand moved of its own accord as though to drive it out of my head. My right hand was, as usual, holding a pen over a piece of paper, poised and ready for any sign or sound. My left hand should have remained lying in my lap as normal, but it did not lie there. Whoever saw it move the way it did must have thought I was brushing away an obstinate fly from my face, but since the meeting hall was clean and completely free of flies, the cleanest hall in the whole country and the last hall on earth that a fly could enter, the movement of my left hand must have appeared abnormal. And since it was abnormal, it began to attract attention. I used to hate, Mother, to draw attention to myself at such important meetings, and always preferred to remain sitting in my chair completely unobtrusive or unnoticed until the meeting was over and I had not had to face any questions.

What's that, Mother? No, my dear. I wasn't frightened of questions and I wasn't afraid of not knowing the right answer, since the right answer was common knowledge and easy, easier than any other answer, easier than any maths problem I had to solve as a pupil, as easy as the simplest step in a multiplication table, two times two equals four. The difficulty, Mother, was that I wasn't scared of *not* giving the right answer but of *giving* the right answer.

What's that, my dear? Yes, Mother. That was the real catastrophe that happened that day. I don't know how it happened and I don't know if it was me who said it or the other person occupying my chair. I was still sitting in my chair, like I told you, and it seems that the repeated movement of my left hand had attracted attention because suddenly, he turned his eyes towards me, reminding me in a flash of my father's

eyes when I was a child. As his eyes turned towards me, I
tried to shrink back slightly or to move forward, just as I used
to do as a pupil sitting in class, and hoped that his eyes would
fall on the one sitting in front of me or behind me, and not on
me. But that day I didn't move in my chair. Maybe I didn't
notice the movement of his eyes at the right time, before they
turned in my direction. Or perhaps I wasn't in full possession
of my faculties at that moment. Or perhaps I was sick with
fever and my temperature had risen. Or perhaps there was
some other reason. The important thing, Mother, was that I
didn't move in my chair and the full weight of his eyes fell on
me, like the fall of death. When he asked me the question, my
mouth opened of its own accord, involuntarily, as if it were
the mouth of another person, an unthinking person quick to
answer without much thought or great effort. And since it
was an answer without much thought or great effort, it was
the easy answer, the easiest and simplest of answers. It was,
Mother, the obvious answer.

What's that, my dear? No, Mother. The obvious answer
was not the right answer. The right answer is not the required
answer. That, Mother, is the ABC of politics, as I told you at
the start. It's the first lesson we learn in politics. How did I
come to forget it, Mother? I don't know. But I did forget it at
that moment. How it grieved me, Mother, to forget it. And
my grief was so very, very strong that all feelings of grief
disappeared, so much so that my feelings of relief were almost akin to joy. I felt, Mother, that a heavy burden had been
lying on my chest and stomach, heavier than my two
paralysed hands clasped over my chest and stomach, heavier
even than my body sitting paralysed in my chair, heavier even
than the chair and the earth beneath it, as if the earth itself
were weighing on me.

What's that, Mother? Yes, my dear. I relaxed and what
relaxation! How I feel this relaxation in these final moments
as I leave the world and everything in it. But the catastrophe,
Mother, is that despite this relaxation and although I'm leaving this world, I still put the telephone beside my head and

I'm still waiting for it to ring, just once. To hear the bell, just once. To hear a voice, any voice, say in my ear: "Your Excellency, the Minister," How I'd love to hear it, Mother, one time, only one time before I die.

Mike Thelwell

Mike Thelwell *(1938–) was born in Jamaica, the West Indies. He was a leading activist in the American civil rights movement in the 1960s and now teaches in the Afro-American Studies Department at the University of Massachusetts at Amherst.*

DIRECT ACTION

We were all sitting around the front room the night it started. The front room of the pad was pretty kooky. See, five guys lived there. It was a reconstructed basement and the landlord didn't care what we did, just so he got his rent.

Well, the five guys who lived there were pretty weird, at least so it was rumored about the campus. We didn't care too much. Lee was on a sign kick, and if he thought of anything that appeared profound or cool—and the words were synonymous with him—wham! we had another sign. See, he'd write a sign and put it up. Not only that; he was klepto about signs. He just couldn't resist lifting them, so the pad always looked like the basement of the Police Traffic Department, with all the DANGER NO STANDING signs he had in the john, and over his bed he had a sign that read WE RESERVE THE RIGHT TO DENY SERVICE TO ANYONE. Man, he'd bring in those silly freshman girls who'd think the whole place was "so-o-o bohemian," and that sign would really crack them up.

Anyway, I was telling you about the front room. Lee had put up an immense sign he'd written: IF YOU DON'T DIG KIKES,

DAGOS, NIGGERS, HENRY MILLER, AND J. C., YOU AIN'T WELCOME! Across from that he had another of his prize acquisitions; something in flaming red letters issued a solemn WARNING TO SHOPLIFTERS. You've probably seen them in department stores.

Then there was the kid in art school, Lisa, who was the house artist and mascot. Man, that kid was mixed up. She was variously in love with everyone in the pad. First she was going with Dick—that's my brother. Then she found that he was a "father surrogate"; then it was Lee, but it seems he had been "only an intellectual status symbol." Later it was Doug "the innocent." After Doug it was Art—that's our other roomie— but he had only been an expression of her "urge to self-destruction." So now that left only me. The chick was starting to project that soulful look, but hell, man, there was only one symbol left and I wasn't too eager to be "symbolized." They should ban all psychology books, at least for freshman girls.

Anyway, I was telling you about the room. When Lisa was "in love" with Dick she was in her surrealist period. She used to bring these huge, blatantly Freudian canvases, which she hung on the walls until the room looked, as Doug said, like "the pigmented expression of a demented psyche." Then Lisa started to down Dick because of his lack of "critical sensitivity and creativity." She kept this up, and soon we were all bugging Dick. He didn't say too much, but one day when he was alone in the pad, he got some tins of black, green, yellow, and red house paint, stripped the room, and started making like Jackson Pollock. The walls, the windows, and dig this, even the damn floor was nothing but one whole mess of different-colored paint. Man, we couldn't go in the front room for four days; when it dried, Dick brought home an instructor from art school to "appraise some original works."

I was sorry for the instructor. He was a short, paunchy little guy with a bald patch, and misty eyes behind some of the thickest lenses you ever saw. At first he thought Dick was joking, and he just stood there fidgeting and blinking his watery little eyes. He gave a weak giggle and muttered something that sounded like, "Great . . . uh . . . sense of humor. Hee."

But Dick was giving him this hurt-creative-spirit come-on real big. His face was all pained, and he really looked stricken and intense.

"But, sir, surely you can see some promise, some little merit?"

"Well, uh, one must consider, uh, the limitations of your medium, uh . . . hee."

"Limitations of medium, yes, but surely there must be *some* merit?"

"Well, you must realize—"

"Yes, but not even *some* spark of promise, some faint, tiny spark of promise?" Dick was really looking distraught now. The art teacher was visibly unhappy and looked at me appealingly, but I gave him a don't-destroy-this-poor-sensitive-spirit look. He mopped his face and tried again.

"Abstractionism is a very advanced genre—"

"Yes, yes, advanced," Dick said, cutting him off impatiently, "but not even the faintest glimmer of merit?" He was really emoting now, and then he started sobbing hysterically and split the scene. I gave the poor instructor a cold how-could-you-be-so-cruel look, and he began to stutter. "I had n-no idea, n-no idea. Oh, dear, so strange . . . Do you suppose he is all right? How d-do you explain . . . Oh, dear."

"Sir," I said, "I neither suppose nor explain. All I know is that my brother is very high-strung and you have probably induced a severe trauma. If you have nothing further to say, would you . . . ?" and I opened the door suggestively. He looked at the messed-up walls in bewilderment and shook his head. He took off his misty glasses, wiped them, looked at the wall, bleated something about "all insane," and scurried out. He probably heard us laughing.

Man, these white liberals are really tolerant. If Dick and I were white, the cat probably would have known right off that we were kidding. But apparently he was so anxious not to hurt our feelings that he gave a serious response to any old crap we said. Man, these people either kill you with intolerance or they turn around and overdo the tolerance bit. However, as Max Shulman says, "I digress."

The cats in our pad were kind of integrated, but we never thought of it that way. We really dug each other, so we hung around together. As Lee would say, "We related to each other in a meaningful way." (That's another thing about Lee. He was always "establishing relationships." Man, if he made a broad or even asked her the time, it was always, "Oh, I established a relationship today.") Like, if you were a cat who was hung up on this race bit, you could get awfully queered up around the pad. The place was about as mixed up as Brooklyn. The only difference, as far as I could see, was that we could all swear in different languages. Lee's folks had come from Milan, Dick and I were Negro, and Art, with his flaming red head and green Viking eyes, was Jewish.

The only cat who had adjustment problems was Doug. He was from sturdy Anglo-Saxon Protestant stock; his folks still had the *Mayflower* ticket stub and a lot of bread. When he was a freshman in the dorm, some of the cats put him down because he was shy and you could see that he was well off. And those s.o.b.'s would have been so helpful if the cat had been "culturally deprived" and needed handouts. Man, people are such bastards. It's kind of a gas, you know. Doug probably could have traced his family back to Thor, and yet he had thin, almost Semitic features, dark brown hair, and deep eyes with a dark rabbinical sadness to them.

Anyway, we guys used to really swing in the pad; seems like we spent most of the time laughing. But don't get the idea that we were just kick-crazy or something out of Kerouac, beat-type stuff. All of us were doing okay in school—grades and that jazz. Take Art, for instance: most people thought that because he had a beard and was always playing the guitar and singing, and ready to party, he was just a campus beatnik-in-residence. They didn't know that he was an instructor and was working on his doctorate in anthropology. ~~Actua~~lly, we were really more organized than we looked.

Anyway, this thing I'm telling you about happened the summer when this sit-in bit broke out all over. Since Pearl Springs was a Midwestern college town, there was no segregation of any kind around—at least, I didn't see any. But everyone was going out to picket Woolworth's every weekend. At first we went, but since there was this crowd out each week, and nobody was crossing the line anyway, we kind of lost interest. (Actually, they had more people than they needed.)

So we were all sitting around and jiving each other, when I mentioned that a guy we called "The Crusader" had said he was coming over later.

"Oh, no," Dick groaned; "that cat bugs me. Every time he sees me in the cafeteria or the union he makes a point of coming over to talk, and he never has anything to say. Hell, every time I talk to the guy I feel as if he really isn't seeing me, just a cause—a minority group."

"Yeah, I know," Art added. "Once at a party I was telling some broad that I was Jewish and he heard. You know, he just had to steer me into a corner to tell me how sympathetic he was to the 'Jewish cause' and 'Jewish problems.' The guy isn't vicious, only misguided."

Then Lee said, "So the guy is misguided, but, hell, he's going to come in here preaching all this brotherly love and Universal Brotherhood. And who wants to be a brother to bums like you?"

That started it.

Dick was reading the paper, but he looked up. "Hey, those Israelis in Tel Aviv are really getting progressive."

"Yeah, them Israelis don't mess around. What they do now?" Art asked. He was a real gung-ho Zionist, and had even spent a summer in a kibbutz in Israel.

"Oh," said Dick, "they just opened a big hydroelectric plant."

Art waded in deeper. "So what?"

"Nothing, only they ain't got no water, so they call it The Adolf Eichmann Memorial Project."

Everybody cracked up. Art said something about "niggers and flies."

"Niggers and kikes," I chimed in. "I don't like them, either, but they got rights . . . in their place."

"Rights! They got too many rights already. After all, this is a free country, and soon a real American like me won't even have breathing room," cracked Lee.

"Hey, Mike," someone shouted, "you always saying some of your best friends are dagos, but would you like your sister to marry one?"

"Hell no, she better marryink der gute Chewish boy," I replied.

"And for niggers, I should of lynched you all when I had the chance . . ." Art was saying when The Crusader entered. This was the cat who organized the pickets—or at least he used to like to think he did. A real sincere crusading-type white cat. He looked with distaste at Lee's sign about kikes and niggers.

"Well, fellas, all ready for the picket on Saturday?"

"Somebody tell him," said Lee.

"Well, you see," I ventured, "we ain't going."

"Ain't going!" The Crusader howled. "But why? Don't you think—"

"Of course not. We are all dedicated practitioners of nonthink. Besides, all our Negrahs are happy. Ain't yuh happy, Mike?" Art drawled.

"Yeah, but I don' like all these immigran's, kikes, dagos, an' such. Like, I thinks—"

"And Ah purely hates niggers: they stink so," Lee announced.

The Crusader didn't get the message. "Look, guys, I know you're joking, but . . . I know you guys are awful close—hell, you room together—but you persist in using all these derogatory racial epithets. I should think that you of all people . . . I really don't think it's funny."

"Man," said Dick, "is this cat for real?"

I knew just what he meant: I can't stomach these crusading liberal types, either, who just have to prove their democracy.

"Okay, can it, guys. I think we ought to explain to this gentleman what we mean," Art said. "Look, I don't think I have to prove anything to anyone in this room. We're all in favor of the demonstrations. In fact, nearly half the community is, so we don't think we need to parade our views. Besides, you have enough people as it is. So we're supporting the students in the South, but why not go across the state line into Missouri and really do something? That's where direct action is needed."

"Oho, the same old excuse for doing nothing," The Crusader sneered.

I could see that Lee over in his corner was getting mad. Suddenly he said, "So you accuse us of doing nothing? Well, we'll show you what we mean by direct action. We mean action calculated to pressure people, to disrupt economic and social functions and patterns, to pressure them into doing something to improve racial relations."

"Very fine, Comrade Revolutionary, and just what do you propose to do, besides staying home and lecturing active people like me?" The Crusader's tone dripped sarcasm.

Lee completely lost control. "What do we propose to do?" he shouted. "We'll go across the state line and in two weeks we'll integrate some institution! That'll show you what direct action means."

"Okay, okay, just make sure you do it," said The Crusader as he left.

Man, next day it was all over campus that we had promised to integrate everything from the State of Georgia to the White House main bedroom—you know how rumors are. We were in a fix. Every time Lee blew his top we were always in a jam. Now we had to put up or shut up.

The pressure was mounting after about a week. We were all sitting around one day when Doug proclaimed to Lee, "We shall disrupt their social functions, we shall disrupt their human functions—You utter nut, what the hell are you going to do?"

Lee was real quiet, like he hadn't heard; then he jumped up. "Human functions! Doug—genius. I love you!" Then he split the scene, real excited-like.

About an hour later Lee came back still excited, and mysterious. "Look," he said, "we're cool. I have it all worked out. You know that big department store in Deershead? Well, they have segregated sanitary facilities."

Dick interrupted, "So? This is a Christian country. You expect men and women to use the same facilities?"

"Oh, shut up, you know what I mean. Anyway, we're going to integrate them. All you guys have to do is get ten girls and five other guys and I'll do the rest."

"Oh, isn't our genius smart," I snarled. "If you think that, hot as it is, I'm going to picket among those hillbillies, you're out of your cotton-chopping little mind."

"Who's going to picket?" Lee said. "Credit me with more finesse than that. I said direct action, didn't I? Well, that's what I meant. All you guys have to do is sit in the white johns and use all the seats. I'll do the rest."

"And the girls?" I asked.

"They do the same over in the women's rest rooms. Oh, is this plan a riot!" The cat cracked up and wouldn't say any more. Nobody liked it much. Lee was so damn wild at times. See, he was a real slick cat. I mean, if he had ten months with a headshrinker he'd probably end up President. But, man, most of the jams we got into were because the cat *hadn't* seen a headshrinker. Anyway, we didn't have any alternative, so we went along.

The morning we were ready to leave, Lee disappeared. Just when everyone was getting real mad, he showed, dragging two guys with him. One was The Crusader and the other cat turned out to be a photographer from the school paper. So we drove to Deershead, a hick town over in Missouri. All the way, Lee was real confident. He kept gloating to The Crusader that he was going to show him how to operate.

When we arrived at the "target," as Lee called it, he told everyone to go in and proceed with stage one. All this means is that we went and sat in the white johns. The girls did the same. Lee disappeared again. We all sat and waited. Soon he showed up grinning all over and said:

"Very good. Now I shall join you and wait for our little scheme to develop." He told The Crusader and the photographer to wait in the store for our plan to take effect. Man, we sat in that place for about an hour. It was real hot, even in there. The guys started to get restless and finally threatened to leave if Lee didn't clue us in on the plan—if he had one.

Just as he decided to tell us, two guys came into the john real quick. We heard one of them say, "Goddamn, the place is full." They waited around for a while, and more guys kept coming in. All of a sudden the place was filled with guys. They seemed real impatient, and one of them said, "Can't you fellas hurry up? There's quite a line out here."

"Wonder why everyone has such urgent business?" drawled Lee. "Must be an epidemic."

"Must be something we ate," the guy said. His voice sounded strange and tense. "Hurry up, fellas, will you?"

I peeped through the crack in the door and saw the guys outside all sweating and red in the face. One cat was doubled up, holding his middle and grimacing. I heard Lee say in a tone of real concern, "I tell you what, men, looks like we'll be here for some time. Why don't you just go down to the other rest room?"

"What!" someone shouted. "You mean the nigger john?"

Then Lee said ever so sweetly, "Oh, well . . . there's always the floor." And he started laughing softly.

The guys got real mad. Someone tried my door, but it was locked. I heard one guy mutter, "The hell with this," and he split. For a minute there was silence; then we heard something like everyone rushing for the door.

Lee said, "C'mon, let's follow them." So we all slipped out.

Man, that joint was in an uproar. There was a crowd of whites milling around the door of both colored johns. The Crusader was standing around looking bewildered. Lee went over to the photographer and told him to get some pictures. After that, we got the girls and split the scene.

In the car coming back, Lee was crowing all over the place about what a genius he was. "See," he said, "I got the idea from Doug when he was saying all that bit about 'human functions.' That was the key: all I had to do then was figure out some way to create a crisis. So what do I do? Merely find a good strong colorless laxative and introduce it into the drinking water at the white coolers—a cinch with the old-fashioned open coolers they got here. Dig? That's what I was doing while you guys were sitting in."

Just then The Crusader bleeped, "Hey—would you stop at the next service station?"

The guy did look kinda pale at that. I thought, "And this cat always peddling his brotherhood and dragging his white man's burden behind him all the time." Oh, well, I guess I might have used the cooler, too.

Well, there was quite a furor over the whole deal. The school newspaper ran the shots and a long funny story, and the local press picked it up. Deershead was the laughingstock of the whole state. The management of the store was threatening to sue Lee and all that jazz, but it was too late to prove any "willful mischief or malice aforethought," or whatever it is they usually prove in these matters. The Negro kids in Deershead got hep and started a regular picket of the store. Man, I hear some of those signs were riots: LET US SIT DOWN TOGETHER, and stuff like that. The store held out a couple of months, but finally they took down the signs over the johns. Guess they wanted to forget.

That's the true story as it happened. You'll hear all kinds of garbled versions up on campus, but that's the true story of the "sitting" as it happened. Oh, yeah, one other thing: the Deershead branch of the N.A.A.C.P. wanted to erect a little statue of either me or Dick sitting on the john, the first Negro to be so integrated in Deershead. You know how they dig this first Negro bit. We had to decline. Always were shy and retiring.

Ward Just

Ward Just *(1935–   ) was born in Michigan City, Indiana. He worked as a journalist for* The Washington Post *and* Newsweek *and is the author of many works of political fiction, including* Jack Gance *and* The American Ambassador.

THE CONGRESSMAN WHO
LOVED FLAUBERT

The deputation was there: twelve men in his outer office and he would have to see them. His own fault, if "fault" was the word. They'd called every day for a week, trying to arrange an appointment. Finally his assistant, Annette, put it to him: Please see them. Do it for me. Wein is an old friend, she'd said. It meant a lot to Wein to get his group before a congressman whose name was known, whose words had weight. LaRuth stood and stretched; his long arms reached for the ceiling. He was his statuesque best that day: dark suit, dark tie, white shirt, black beard neatly trimmed. No jewelry of any kind. He rang his secretary and told her to show them in, to give them thirty minutes, and then ring again; the committee meeting was at eleven.

"What do they look like?"

"Scientists," she said. "They look just as you'd expect scientists to look. They're all thin. And none of them are smoking." LaRuth laughed. "They're pretty intense, Lou."

"Well, let's get on with it."

He met them at the door, as they shyly filed in. Wein and his committee were scientists against imperialism. They were physicists, biologists, linguists, and philosophers. They introduced themselves, and LaRuth wondered again what it was that a philosopher did in these times. It had to be a grim year for philosophy. The introductions done, LaRuth leaned back, a long leg hooked over the arm of his chair, and told them to go ahead.

They had prepared a congressional resolution, a sense-of-the-Congress resolution, which they wanted LaRuth to introduce. It was a message denouncing imperialism, and as LaRuth read it he was impressed by its eloquence. They had assembled hard facts: so many tons of bombs dropped in Indochina, so many "facilities" built in Africa, so many American soldiers based in Europe, so many billions in corporate investment in Latin America. It was an excellent statement, not windy as so many of them are. He finished reading it and turned to Wein.

"Congressman, we believe this is a matter of simple morality. Decency, if you will. There are parallels elsewhere, the most compelling being the extermination of American Indians. Try not to look on the war and the bombing from the perspective of a Westerner looking East but of an Easterner facing West." LaRuth nodded. He recognized that it was the war that truly interested them. "The only place the analogy breaks down is that the Communists in Asia appear to be a good deal more resourceful and resilient than the Indians in America. Perhaps that is because there are so many more of them." Wein paused to smile. "But it is genocide either way. It is a stain on the American Congress not to raise a specific voice of protest, not only in Asia but in the other places where American policy is doing violence . . ."

LaRuth wondered if they knew the mechanics of moving a congressional resolution. They probably did; there was no need for a civics lecture. Wein was looking at him, waiting for a response. An intervention. "It's a very fine statement," LaRuth said.

"Everybody says that. And then they tell us to get the signatures and come back. We think this ought to be undertaken from the inside. In that way, when and if the resolution is passed, it will have more force. We think that a member of Congress should get out front on it."

An admirable toughness there, LaRuth thought. If he were Wein, that would be just about the way he'd put it.

"We've all the people you'd expect us to have." Very rapidly, Wein ticked off two dozen names, the regular antiwar contingent on the Democratic left. "What we need to move with this is not the traditional dove, but a more moderate man. A moderate man with a conscience." Wein smiled.

"Yes," LaRuth said.

"Someone like you."

LaRuth was silent a moment, then spoke rapidly. "My position is this. I'm not a member of the Foreign Affairs Committee or the Appropriations Committee or Armed Services or any of the others where . . . war legislation or defense matters are considered. I'm not involved in foreign relations, I'm in education. It's the Education and Labor Committee. No particular reason why those two subjects should be linked, but they are." LaRuth smiled. "That's Congress for you."

"It seems to us, Congressman, that the war—the leading edge of imperialism and violence—is tied to everything. Education is a mess because of the war. So is labor. And so forth. It's all part of the war. Avoid the war and you avoid all the other problems. The damn thing is like the Spanish Inquisition, if you lived in Torquemada's time, fifteenth-century Spain. If you did try to avoid it you were either a coward or a fool. That is meant respectfully."

"Well, it is nicely put. Respectfully."

"But you won't do it."

La Ruth shook his head. "You get more names, and I'll think about cosponsoring. But I won't front for it. I'm trying to pass an education bill right now. I can't get out front on the war, too. Important as it is. Eloquent as you are. There are other men in this House who can do the job better than I can."

"We're disappointed," Wein said.

"I could make you a long, impressive speech." His eyes took in the others, sitting in chilly silence. "I could list all the reasons. But you know what they are, and it wouldn't do either of us any good. I wish you success."

"Spare us any more successes," Wein said. "Everyone wishes us success, but no one helps. We're like the troops in the trenches. The Administration tells them to go out and win the war. You five hundred thousand American boys, you teach the dirty Commies a lesson. Storm the hill, the Administration says. But the Administration is far away from the shooting. We're right behind you, they say. Safe in Washington."

"I don't deny it," LaRuth said mildly.

"I think there are special places in hell reserved for those who see the truth but will not act." LaRuth stiffened, but stayed silent. "These people are worse than the ones who love the war. You are more dangerous than the generals in the Pentagon, who at least are doing what they believe in. It is because of people like you that we are where we are."

Never justify, never explain, LaRuth thought; it was pointless anyway. They were pleased to think of him as a war criminal. A picture of a lurching tumbrel in Pennsylvania Avenue flashed through his mind and was gone, an oddly comical image. LaRuth touched his beard and sat upright. "I'm sorry you feel that way. It isn't true, you know." One more number like that one, he thought suddenly, and he'd throw the lot of them out of his office.

But Wein would not let go. "We're beyond subtle distinctions, Mr. LaRuth. That is one of the delightful perceptions that the war has brought us. We can mumble all day. You can tell me about your responsibilities and your effectiveness, and how you don't want to damage it. You can talk politics and I can talk morals. But I took moral philosophy in college. An interesting academic exercise." LaRuth nodded; Wein was no fool. "Is it true you wrote your Ph.D. thesis on Flaubert?"

"I wrote it at the Sorbonne," LaRuth replied. "But that was almost twenty years ago. Before politics." LaRuth wanted to give them something to hang on to. They would appreciate the irony, and then they could see him as a fallen angel, a victim of the process; it was more interesting than seeing him as a war criminal.

"Well, it figures."

LaRuth was surprised. He turned to Wein. "How does it figure?"

"Flaubert was just as pessimistic and cynical as you are."

LaRuth had thirty minutes to review his presentation to the committee. This was the most important vote in his twelve years in Congress, a measure which, if they could steer it through the House, would release a billion dollars over three years' time to elementary schools throughout the country. The measure was based on a hellishly complicated formula which several legal experts regarded as unconstitutional; but one expert is always opposed by another when a billion dollars is involved. LaRuth had to nurse along the chairman, a volatile personality, a natural skeptic. Today he had to put his presentation in exquisite balance, giving here, taking there, assuring the committee that the Constitution would be observed, and that all regions would share equally.

It was not something that could be understood in a university, but LaRuth's twelve years in the House of Representatives would be justified if he could pass this bill. Twelve years, through three Presidents. He'd avoided philosophy and concentrated on detail, his own time in a third-rate grade school in a southern mill town never far from his mind: that was the reference point. Not often that a man was privileged to witness the methodical destruction of children before the age of thirteen, before they had encountered genuinely soulless and terrible events: the war, for one. His bill would begin the process of revivifying education. It was one billion dollars' worth of life, and he'd see to it that some of the money leaked down to his own school. LaRuth was lucky, an escapee on scholarships, first to Tulane and then to Paris, his world widened beyond measure; Flaubert gave him a taste for politics. *Madame Bovary* and *A Sentimental Education* were political novels, or so he'd argued at the Sorbonne; politics was nothing more or less than an understanding of ambition, and the moral and social conditions that produced it in its various forms. The House of Representatives: *un stade des arrivistes.* And now the press talked him up as a southern liberal, and the northern Democrats came to him for help. Sometimes he gave it, sometimes he didn't. They could not understand the refusals—Lou, you won with sixty-five percent of the vote the last time out. What do you want, a coronation? They were critical that he would not get out front on the war and would not vote against bills vital to southern interests. (Whatever they were, now that the entire region was dominated by industrial combines whose headquarters were in New York or Chicago—and how's that for imperialism, Herr Wein?) They didn't, or couldn't, grasp the paper-thin depth of his support. The Birchers and the segs were everywhere, and each time he voted with the liberals in the House he'd hear from a few of them. *You are being watched.* He preferred a low silhouette. All those big liberals didn't understand that a man with enough money could still buy an election in his district; he told them that LaRuth compromised was better than no LaRuth at all. That line had worked well the first four or five years he'd been in Washington; it worked no longer. In these times, caution and realism were the refuge of a scoundrel.

The war, so remote in its details, poisoned everything. He read about it every day, and through a friend on the Foreign Affairs Committee saw some classified material. But he could not truly engage himself in it, because he hadn't seen it firsthand. He did not know it intimately. It was clear enough that it was a bad war, everyone knew that; but knowing it and feeling it were two different things. The year before, he'd worked to promote a junket, a special subcommittee to investigate foreign aid expenditures for education. There was plenty of scandalous rumor to justify the investigation. He tried to promote it in order to get a look at the place first-hand, on the ground. He wanted to look at the faces and the villages, to see the countryside which had been destroyed by the war, to observe the actual manner in which the war was being fought. But the chairman refused, he wanted no part of it; scandal or no scandal, it was not part of the committee's business. So the trip never happened. What the congressman knew about the war he read in newspapers and magazines and saw on television. But that did not help. LaRuth had done time as an infantryman in Korea and knew what killing was about; the box did not make it as horrible as it was. The box romanticized it, cleansed it of pain; one more false detail. Even the blood deceived, coming up pink and pretty on the television set. One night he spent half of Cronkite fiddling with the color knob to get a perfect red, to insist the blood look like *blood*.

More: Early in his congressional career, LaRuth took pains to explain his positions. He wanted his constituents to know what he was doing and why, and two newsletters went out before the leader of his state's delegation took him aside one day in the hall. Huge arms around his shoulders, a whispered conference. Christ, you are going to get killed, the man said. *Don't do that.* Don't get yourself down on paper on every raggedy-ass bill that comes before Congress. It makes you a few friends, who don't remember, and a lot of enemies, who do. Particularly in your district: you are way ahead of those people in a lot of areas, but don't advertise it. You've a fine future here; don't ruin it before you've begun. LaRuth thought the advice was captious and irresponsible and disregarded it. And very nearly lost reelection, after some indiscretions to a newspaperman. *That* son of a bitch, who violated every rule of confidence held sacred in the House of Representatives.

His telephone rang. The secretary said it was Annette. "How did it go?" Her voice was low, cautious.

"Like a dream," he said. "And thanks lots. I'm up there with the generals as a war criminal. They think I make lamp-shades in my spare time."

Coolly: "I take it you refused to help them."

"You take it right."

"They're very good people. Bill Wein is one of the most distinguished botanists in the country."

"Yes, he speaks very well. A sincere, intelligent, dedicated provocateur. Got off some very nice lines, at least one refer-ence to Dante. A special place in hell is reserved for people like me, who are worse than army generals."

"Well, that's one point of view."

"You know, I'm tired of arguing about the war. If Wein is so goddamned concerned about the war and the corruption of the American system, then why doesn't he give up the fat government contracts at that think tank he works for—"

"That's unfair, Lou!"

"Why do they think that anyone who deals in the real world is an automatic sellout? Creep. A resolution like that one, *even if passed,* would have no effect. Zero effect. It would not be binding, the thing's too vague. They'd sit up there and everyone would have a good gooey warm feeling, *and nothing would happen.* It's meaningless, except of course for the virtue. Virtue everywhere. Virtue triumphant. So I am supposed to put my neck on the line for something that's meaningless—" LaRuth realized he was near shouting, so he lowered his voice. "Meaningless," he said.

"You're so hostile," she said angrily. "Filled with hate. Contempt. Why do you hate everybody? You should've done what Wein wanted you to do."

He counted to five and was calm now, reasonable. His con-gressional baritone: "It's always helpful to have your political advice, Annette. Very helpful. I value it. Too bad you're not a politician yourself." She said nothing, he could hear her breathing. "I'll see you later," he said, and hung up.

* * *

LaRuth left his office, bound for the committee room. He'd gone off the handle and was not sorry. But sometimes he indulged in just a bit too much introspection and self-justification, endemic diseases in politicians. There were certain basic facts: his constituency supported the war, at the same time permitting him to oppose it so long as he did it quietly and in such a way that "the boys" were supported. Oppose the war, support the troops. A high-wire act—very Flaubertian, that situation; it put him in the absurd position of voting for military appropriations and speaking out against the war. Sorry, Annette; that's the way we think on Capitol Hill. It's a question of what you *vote* for. Forget the fancy words and phrases, it's a question of votes. Up, down, or "present." Vote against the appropriations and sly opponents at home would accuse him of "tying the hands" of American troops and thereby comforting the enemy. Blood on his fingers.

II

LaRuth was forty; he had been in the House since the age of twenty-eight. Some of his colleagues had been there before he was born, moving now around the halls and the committee rooms as if they were extensions of antebellum county courthouses. They smelled of tobacco and whiskey and old wool, their faces dry as parchment. LaRuth was amused to watch them on the floor; they behaved as they would at a board meeting of a family business, attentive if they felt like it, disruptive if their mood was playful. They were forgiven; it was a question of age. The House was filled with old men, and its atmosphere was one of very great age. Deference was a way of life. LaRuth recalled a friend who aspired to a position of leadership. They put him through his paces, and for some reason he did not measure up; the friend was told he'd have to wait, it was not yet time. He'd been there eighteen years and was only fifty-two. Fifty-two! Jack Kennedy was President at forty-three, and Thomas Jefferson had written the preamble when under thirty-five. But then, as one of the senior men put it, this particular fifty-two-year-old man had none of the durable qualities of Kennedy or Jefferson. That is, he did not have Kennedy's money or Jefferson's brains. Not that money counted for very much in the House of Representatives; plutocrats belonged in the other body.

It was not a place for lost causes. There were too many conflicting interests, too much confusion, too many turns to the labyrinth. Too many *people:* four hundred and thirty-five representatives and about a quarter of them quite bright. Quite bright enough and knowledgeable enough to strangle embarrassing proposals and take revenge as well. Everyone was threatened if the eccentrics got out of hand. The political coloration of the eccentric didn't matter. This was one reason why it was so difficult to build an ideological record in the House. A man with ideology was wise to leave it before reaching a position of influence, because by then he'd mastered the art of compromise, which had nothing to do with dogma or public acts of conscience. It had to do with simple effectiveness, the tact and strength with which a man dealt with legislation, inside committees, behind closed doors. That was where the work got done, and the credit passed around.

LaRuth, at forty, was on a knife's edge. Another two years and he'd be a man of influence, and therefore ineligible for any politics outside the House—or not ineligible, but shopworn, no longer new, no longer fresh. He would be ill-suited, and there were other practical considerations as well, because who wanted to be a servant for twelve or fourteen years and then surrender an opportunity to be master? Not LaRuth. So the time for temporizing was nearly past. If he was going to forsake the House and reach for the Senate (a glamorous possibility), he had to do it soon.

LaRuth's closest friend in Congress was a man about his own age from a neighboring state. They'd come to the Hill in the same year, and for a time enjoyed publicity in the national press, where they could least afford it. *Two Young Liberals from the South,* that sort of thing. Winston was then a bachelor, too, and for the first few years they shared a house in Cleveland Park. But it was awkward, there were too many women in and out of the place, and one groggy morning Winston had come upon LaRuth and a friend taking a shower together and that had torn it. They flipped for the house and LaRuth won, and Winston moved to grander quarters in Georgetown. They saw each other frequently and laughed together about the curiosities of the American political system; Winston, a gentleman farmer from the plantation South, was a ranking member of the House Foreign Affairs Committee. The friendship was complicated because they were occasional rivals: who would represent the New South? They took to kidding each other's press notices: LaRuth was the "attractive liberal," Winston the "wealthy liberal." Thus, LaRuth became Liberal Lou and Winston was Wealthy Warren. To the extent that either of them had a national reputation, they were in the same category: they voted their consciences, but were not incautious.

It was natural for Wein and his committee of scientists to go directly to Winston after leaving LaRuth. The inevitable telephone call came the next day, Winston inviting LaRuth by for a drink around six; "small problem to discuss." Since leaving Cleveland Park, Warren Winston's life had become plump and graceful. Politically secure now, he had sold his big house back home and bought a small jewel of a place on Dumbarton Avenue, three bedrooms and a patio in back, a mirrored bar, and a sauna in the basement. Winston was drinking a gin and tonic by the pool when LaRuth walked in. The place was more elegant than he'd remembered; the patio was now decorated with tiny boxbushes and a magnolia tree was in full cry.

They joked a bit, laughing over the new southern manifesto floating around the floor of the House. They were trying to find a way to spike it without seeming to spike it. Winston mentioned the "small problem" after about thirty minutes of small talk.

"Lou, do you know a guy named Wein?"

"He's a friend of Annette's."

"He was in to see you, then."

"Yeah."

"And?"

"We didn't see eye to eye."

"You're being tight-lipped, Liberal Lou."

"I told him to piss off," LaRuth said. "He called me a war criminal, and then he called me a cynic. A pessimist, a cynic, and a war criminal. All this for some cream-puff resolution that will keep them damp in Cambridge and won't change a goddamed thing."

"You think it's *that* bad."

"Worse, maybe."

"I'm not sure. Not sure at all."

"Warren, *Christ.*"

"Look, doesn't it make any sense at all to get the position of the House on record? That can't fail to have some effect downtown, and it can't fail to have an effect in the country. It probably doesn't stand a chance of being passed, but the effort will cause some commotion. The coon'll be treed. Some attention paid. It's a good thing to get on the record, and I can see some points being made."

"What points? Where?"

"The newspapers, the box. Other places. It'd show that at least some of us are not content with things as they are. That we want to change . . ."

LaRuth listened carefully. It was obvious to him that Winston was trying out a speech; like a new suit of clothes, he took it out and tried it on, asking his friend about the color, the fit, the cut of it.

". . . the idea that change can come from within the system . . ."

"Aaaaaoh," LaRuth groaned.

"No?" Innocently.

"How about, *and so, my fellow Americans, ask not what you can do for Wein, but what Wein can do for you.* That thing is loose as a hound dog's tongue. Now tell me the true gen."

"Bettger's retiring."

"You don't say." LaRuth was surprised. Bettger was the state's senior senator, a living southern legend.

"Cancer. No one knows about it. He'll announce retirement at the end of the month. It's my only chance for the next four years, maybe *ever.* There'll be half a dozen guys in the primary, but my chances are good. If I'm going to go for the Senate, it's got to be now. This thing of Wein's is a possible vehicle. I say possible. One way in. People want a national politician as a senator. It's not enough to've been a good congressman, or even a good governor. You need something more: when people see your face on the box they want to think *senatorial,* somehow. You don't agree?"

LaRuth was careful now. Winston was saying many of the things he himself had said. Of course he was right, a senator needed a national gloss. The old bulls didn't need it, but they were operating from a different tradition, pushing different buttons. But if you were a young man running statewide for the first time, you needed a different base. Out there in television land were all those followers without leaders. People were pulled by different strings now. The point was to identify which strings pulled strongest.

"I think Wein's crowd is a mistake. That resolution is a mistake. They'll kill you at home if you put your name to that thing."

"No, Lou. You do it a different way. With a little rewording, that resolution becomes a whole lot less scary; it becomes something straight out of Robert A. Taft. You e-*liminate* the fancy words and phrases. You steer *clear* of words like 'corrupt' or 'genocide' or 'violence.' You and I, Lou, we know: our people *like* violence, it's part of our way of life. So you don't talk about violence, you talk about American traditions, like 'the American tradition of independence and individuality. Noninterference!' Now you are saying a couple of *other* things, when you're saying that, Lou. You dig? That's the way you get at imperialism. You don't call it imperialism because that word's got a bad sound. A foreign sound."

LaRuth laughed. Winston had it figured out. He had to get Wein to agree to the changes, but that should present no problem. Wealthy Warren was a persuasive man.

"Point is, I've got to look to people down there like I can make a difference . . ."

"I think you've just said the magic words."

"Like it?"

"I think so. Yeah, I think I do."

"To make the difference. Winston for Senator. A double line on the billboards, like this." Winston described two lines with his finger and mulled the slogan again. *"To make the difference, Winston for Senator.* See, it doesn't matter what kind of difference. All people know is that they're fed up to the teeth. *Fed up and mad at the way things are.* And they've got to believe that if they vote for you, in some unspecified way things will get better. Now I think the line about interference can do double duty. People are tired of being hassled, in all ways. Indochina, down home." Winston was a gifted mimic, and now he adopted a toothless expression and hooked his thumbs into imaginary galluses. "Ah think Ah'll vote for that-there Winston. Prob'ly won't do any harm. Mot do some good. Mot mek a diff'rence."

"Shit, Warren."

"You give me a little help?"

"Sure."

"Sign the Wein thing?"

LaRuth thought a moment. "No," he said.

"What the hell, Lou? Why not? If it's rearranged the way I said. Look, Wein will be out of it. It'll be strictly a congressional thing."

"It doesn't mean anything."

"Means a whole lot to me."

"Well, that's different. That's political."

"If you went in too, it'd look a safer bet."

"All there'd be out of that is more gold-dust-twins copy. You don't want that."

"No, it'd be made clear that I'm managing it. I'm out front.

I make all the statements, you're back in the woodwork. Far from harm's way, Lou." Winston took his glass and refilled it with gin and tonic. He carefully cut a lime and squeezed it into the glass. Winston looked the part, no doubt about that. Athlete's build, big, with sandy hair beginning to thin; he could pass for an astronaut.

"You've got to find some new names for the statement."

"Right on, brother. Too many Jews, too many foreigners. Why are there no scientists named Robert E. Lee or Thomas Jefferson? Talmadge, Bilbo." Winston sighed and answered his own question. "The decline of the WASP. Look, Lou. The statement will be forgotten in six weeks, and that's fine with me. I just need it for a little national coverage at the beginning. Hell, it's not decisive. But it could make a difference."

"You're going to *open* the campaign with the statement?"

"You bet. Considerably revised. It'd be a help, Lou, if you'd go along. It would give them a chance to crank out some updated New South pieces. The networks would be giving that a run just as I announce for the Senate and my campaign begins. See, it's a natural. Bettger is Old South, I'm New. But we're friends and neighbors, and that's a fact. It gives them a dozen pegs to hang it on, and those bastards love *you,* with the black suits and the beard and that cracker accent. It's a natural, and it would mean a hell of a lot, a couple of minutes on national right at the beginning. I wouldn't forget it. I'd owe you a favor."

LaRuth was always startled by Winston's extensive knowledge of the press. He spoke of "pieces" and "pegs," A.M. and P.M. cycles, facts "cranked out" or "folded in," who was up and who was down at CBS, who was analyzing Congress for the editorial board of *The Washington Post.* Warren Winston was always accessible, good for a quote, day or night; and he was visible in Georgetown.

"Can you think about it by the end of the week?"

"Sure," LaRuth said.

* * *

He returned to the Hill, knowing that he thought better in his office. When there was any serious thinking to be done, he did it there, and often stayed late, after midnight. He'd mix a drink at the small bar in his office and work. Sometimes Annette stayed with him, sometimes not. When LaRuth walked into his office she was still there, catching up, she said; but she knew he'd been with Winston.

"He's going to run for the Senate," LaRuth said.

"Warren?"

"That's what he says. He's going to front for Wein as well. That statement of Wein's—Warren's going to sign it. Wants me to sign it, too."

"Why you?"

"United front. It would help him out. No doubt about that. But it's a bad statement. Something tells me not to do it."

"Are you as mad as you look?"

He glanced at her and laughed. "Does it show?"

"To me it shows."

It was true; there was no way to avoid competition in politics. Politics was a matter of measurements, luck, and ambition, and he and Warren had run as an entry for so long that it disconcerted him to think of Senator Winston; Winston up one rung on the ladder. He was irritated that Winston had made the first move and made it effortlessly. It had nothing to do with his own career, but suddenly he felt a shadow on the future. Winston had seized the day all right, and the fact of it depressed him. His friend was clever and self-assured in his movements; he took risks; he relished the public part of politics. Winston was expert at delivering memorable speeches on the floor of the House; they were evidence of passion. For Winston, there was no confusion between the private and the public; it was all one. LaRuth thought that he had broadened and deepened in twelve years in the House, a man of realism, but not really a part of the apparatus. Now Winston had stolen the march, he was a decisive step ahead.

LaRuth may have made a mistake. He liked and understood the legislative process, transactions which were only briefly political. That is, they were not public. If a man kept himself straight at home, he could do what he liked in the House. So LaRuth had become a fixture in his district, announcing election plans every two years from the front porch of his family's small farmhouse, where he was born, where his mother lived still. The house was filled with political memorabilia; the parlor walls resembled huge bulletin boards, with framed photographs, testimonials, parchments, diplomas. His mother was so proud. His life seemed to vindicate her own, his successes hers; she'd told him so. His position in the U.S. Congress was precious, and not lightly discarded. The cold age of the place had given him a distrust of anything spectacular or . . . capricious. The House: no place for lost causes.

Annette was looking at him, hands on hips, smiling sardonically. He'd taken off his coat and was now in shirtsleeves. She told him lightly that he shouldn't feel badly, that if *he* ran for the Senate he'd have to shave off his beard. Buy new clothes. Become prolix, and professionally optimistic. But, as a purchase on the future, his signature . . .

"Might. Might not," he said.

"Why not?"

"I've never done that here."

"Are you refusing to sign because you don't want to, or because you're piqued at Warren? I mean, Senator Winston."

He looked at her. "A little of both."

"Well, that's foolish. You ought to sort out your motives."

"That can come later. That's my business."

"No. Warren's going to want to know why you're not down the line with him. You're pretty good friends. He's going to want to know *why.*"

"It's taken me twelve years to build what credit I've got in this place. I'm trusted. The Speaker trusts me. The chairman trusts me."

"Little children see you on the street. Gloryosky! There goes trustworthy Lou LaRuth—"

"Attractive, liberal," he said, laughing. "Well, it's true. This resolution, if it ever gets that far, is a ball-buster. It could distract the House for a month and revive the whole issue. Because it's been quiet we've been able to get on with our work, I mean the serious business. Not to get pompous about it."

"War's pretty important," she said.

"Well, is it now? You tell me how important it is." He put his drink on the desk blotter and loomed over her. "Better yet, you tell me how this resolution will solve the problem. God forbid there should be any solutions, though. Moral commitments. Statements. Resolutions. They're the great things, aren't they? Fuck solutions." Thoroughly angry now, he turned away and filled the glasses. He put some ice and whiskey in hers and a premixed martini in his own.

"What harm would it do?"

"Divert a lot of energy. Big play to the galleries for a week or two. Until everyone got tired. The statement itself? No harm at all. Good statement, well done. No harm, unless you consider perpetuating an illusion some kind of harm."

"A lot of people live by illusions, *and what's wrong with getting this House on record?*"

"But it won't be gotten on record. That's the point. The thing will be killed. It'll just make everybody nervous and divide the place more than it's divided already."

"I'd think about it," she said.

"Yeah, I will. I'll tell you something. I'll probably end up signing the goddamned thing. It'll do Warren some good. Then I'll do what I can to see that it's buried, although God knows we won't lack for gravediggers. And then go back to my own work on the school bill."

"I think that's better." She smiled. "One call, by the way. The chairman. He wants you to call first thing in the morning."

"What did he say it's about?"

"The school bill, dear."

Oh shit, LaRuth thought.

"There's a snag," she said.

"Did he say what it was?"

"I don't think he wants to vote for it anymore."

III

Winston was after him, trying to force a commitment, but LaRuth was preoccupied with the school bill, which was becoming unstuck. It was one of the unpredictable things that happen; there was no explanation for it. But the atmosphere had subtly changed and support was evaporating. The members wavered, the chairman was suddenly morose and uncertain; he thought it might be better to delay. LaRuth convinced him that was an unwise course and set about repairing damage. This was plumbing, pure and simple; talking with members, speaking to their fears. LaRuth called it negative advocacy, but it often worked. Between conferences a few days later, LaRuth found time to see a high-school history class, students from his alma mater. They were touring Washington and wanted to talk to him about Congress. The teacher, sloe-eyed, stringy-haired, twenty-five, wanted to talk about the war; the students were indifferent. They crowded into his outer office, thirty of them; the secretaries stood aside, amused, as the teacher opened the conversation with a long preface on the role of the House, most of it inaccurate. Then she asked LaRuth about the war. What was the congressional role in the war?

"Not enough," LaRuth replied, and went on in some detail, addressing the students.

"Why not a congressional resolution demanding an end to this terrible, immoral war?" the teacher demanded. "Congressman, why can't the House of Representatives take matters into its own hands?"

"Because"—LaRuth was icy, at once angry, tired, and bored—"because a majority of the members of this House do not want to lose Asia to the Communists. Irrelevant, perhaps. You may think it is a bad argument. I think it is a bad argument. But it is the way the members feel."

503

"But why can't that be *tested?* In votes."

The students came reluctantly awake and were listening with little flickers of interest. The teacher was obviously a favorite, their mod pedagogue. LaRuth was watching a girl in the back of the room. She resembled the girls he'd known at home, short-haired, light summer dress, full-bodied; it was a body that would soon go heavy. He abruptly steered the conversation to his school bill, winding into it, giving them a stump speech, some flavor of home. He felt the students with him for a minute or two, then they drifted away. In five minutes they were somewhere else altogether. He said good-bye to them then and shook their hands on the way out. The short-haired girl lingered a minute; she was the last one to go.

"It would be good if you could do something about the war," she said.

"Well, I've explained."

"My brother was killed there."

LaRuth closed his eyes for a second and stood without speaking.

"Any gesture at all," she said.

"Gestures." He shook his head sadly. "They never do any good."

"Well," she said. "Thank you for your time." LaRuth thought her very grown-up, a well-spoken girl. She stood in the doorway, very pretty. The others had moved off down the hall; he could hear the teacher's high whine.

"How old was he?"

"Nineteen," she said. "Would've been twenty next birthday."

"Where?"

"They said it was an airplane."

"I'm so sorry."

"You wrote us a letter, don't you remember?"

"I don't know your name," LaRuth said gently.

"Ecker," she said. "My brother's name was Howard."

"I remember," he said. "It was . . . some time ago."

"Late last year," she said, looking at him.

"Yes, that would be just about it. I'm very sorry."

"So am I," she said, smiling brightly. Then she walked off to join the rest of her class. LaRuth stood in the doorway a moment, feeling the eyes of his secretary on his back. It had happened before; the South seemed to bear the brunt of the war. He'd written more than two hundred letters, to the families of poor boys, black and white. The deaths were disproportionate, poor to rich, black to white, South to North. Oh well, he thought. Oh hell. He walked back into his office and called Winston and told him he'd go along. In a limited way. For a limited period.

Later in the day, Winston called him back. He wanted LaRuth to be completely informed, and up-to-date.

"It's rolling," Winston said.

"Have you talked to Wein?"

"I've talked to Wein."

"And what did Wein say?"

"Wein agrees to the revisions."

"Complaining?"

"The contrary. Wein sees himself as the spearhead of a great national movement. He sees scientists moving into political positions, cockpits of influence. His conscience is as clear as rainwater. He is very damp."

LaRuth laughed; it was a private joke.

"Wein is damp in Cambridge, then."

"I think that is a fair statement, Uncle Lou."

"How wonderful for him."

"He was pleased that you are with us. He said he misjudged you. He offers apologies. He fears he was a speck . . . harsh."

"Bully for Wein."

"I told everyone that you would be on board. I knew that when the chips were down you would not fail. I knew that you would examine your conscience and your heart and determine where the truth lay. I knew you would not be cynical or pessimistic. I know you want to see your old friend in the Senate."

They were laughing together. Winston was in one of his dry, mordant moods. He was very salty. He rattled off a dozen names and cited the sources of each member's conscience: money and influence. "But to be fair—always be fair, Liberal Lou—there are a dozen more who are doing it because they want to do it. They think it's *right.*"

"Faute de mieux."

"I am not schooled in the French language, Louis. You are always flinging French at me."

"It means, 'in the absence of anything better.'"

Winston grinned, then shrugged. LaRuth was depressed, the shadow lengthened, became darker.

"I've set up a press conference, a half dozen of us. All moderate men. Men of science, men of government. I'll be out front, doing all the talking. OK?"

"Sure." LaRuth was thinking about his school bill.

"It's going to be jim-dandy."

"Swell. But I want to see the statement beforehand, music man."

Winston smiled broadly and spread his hands wide. Your friendly neighborhood legislator, concealing nothing; merely your average, open, honest fellow trying to do the right thing, trying to do his level best. "But of course," Winston said.

Some politicians have it; most don't. Winston has it, a fabulous sense of timing. Everything in politics is timing. For a fortnight, the resolution dominates congressional reportage. "An idea whose time has come," coinciding with a coup in Latin America and a surge of fighting in Indochina. The leadership is agitated, but forced to adopt a conciliatory line; the doves are in war paint. Winston appears regularly on the television evening news. There are hearings before the Foreign Affairs Committee, and these produce pictures and newsprint. Winston, a sober legislator, intones *feet to the fire.* There are flattering articles in the newsmagazines, and editorial support from the major newspapers, including the most influential paper in Winston's state. He and LaRuth are to appear on the cover of *Life*, but the cover is scrapped at the last minute. Amazing to LaRuth, the mail from his district runs about even. An old woman, a woman his mother has known for years, writes to tell him that he should run for President. Incredible, really: the Junior Chamber of Commerce composes a certificate of appreciation, commending his enterprise and spirit, "an example of the indestructible moral fiber of America." When the networks and the newspapers cannot find Winston, they fasten on LaRuth. He becomes something of a celebrity, and wary as a man entering darkness from daylight. He tailors his remarks in such a way as to force questions about his school bill. He finds his words have effect, although this is measurable in no definite way. His older colleagues are amused; they needle him gently about his new blue shirts.

He projects well on television, his appearance is striking; his great height, the black suits, the beard. So low-voiced, modest, diffident; no hysteria or hyperbole (an intuitive reporter would grasp that he has contempt for "the Winston Resolution," but intuition is in short supply). When an interviewer mentions his reticent manner, LaRuth smiles and says that he is not modest or diffident, he is pessimistic. But his mother is ecstatic. His secretary looks on him with new respect. Annette thinks he is one in a million.

No harm done. The resolution is redrafted into harmless form and is permitted to languish. The language incomprehensible, at the end it becomes an umbrella under which anyone could huddle. Wein is disillusioned, the media looks elsewhere for its news, and LaRuth returns to the House Education and Labor Committee. The work is backed up; the school bill has lost its momentum. One month of work lost, and now LaRuth is forced to redouble his energies. He speaks often of challenge and commitment. At length the bill is cleared from committee and forwarded to the floor of the House, where it is passed; many members vote aye as a favor, either to LaRuth or to the chairman. The chairman is quite good about it, burying his reservations, grumbling a little, but going along. The bill has been, in the climactic phrase of the newspapers, watered down. The three years are now five. The billion is reduced to five hundred million. Amendments are written, and they are mostly restrictive. But the bill is better than nothing. The President signs it in formal ceremony, LaRuth at his elbow. The thing is now law.

The congressman, contemplating all of it, is both angry and sad. He has been a legislator too long to draw obvious morals, even if they were there to be drawn. He thinks that everything in his life is meant to end in irony and contradiction. LaRuth, at forty, has no secret answers. Nor any illusions. The House of Representatives is no simple place, neither innocent nor straightforward. Appearances there are as appearances elsewhere: deceptive. One is entitled to remain fastidious as to detail, realistic in approach.

Congratulations followed. In his hour of maximum triumph, the author of a law, LaRuth resolved to stay inside the belly of the whale, to become neither distracted nor moved. Of the world outside, he was weary and finally unconvinced. He knew who he was. He'd stick with what he had and take comfort from a favorite line, a passage toward the end of *Madame Bovary*. It was a description of a minor character, and the line had stuck with him, lodged in the back of his head. Seductive and attractive, in a pessimistic way. *He grew thin, his figure became taller, his face took on a saddened look that made it nearly interesting.*

John Sayles

John Sayles *(1950–   ) was born in Schenectady, New York. He is a filmmaker and author. Among his works are the novel* Union Dues *and the films* Return of the Secaucus Seven, Brother from Another Planet, Matewan, *and* City of Hope.

AT THE
ANARCHISTS' CONVENTION

Sophie calls to ask am I going by the Anarchists' Convention this year. The year before last I'm missing because Brickman, may he rest in peace, was on the Committee and we were feuding. I think about the Soviet dissidents, but there was always something so it's hard to say. Then last year he was just cooling in the grave and it would have looked bad.

"There's Leo Gold," they would have said, "come to gloat over Brickman."

So I tell Sophie maybe, depending on my hip. Rainy days it's torture, there isn't a position it doesn't throb. Rainy days and Election Nights.

But Sophie won't hear no, she's still got the iron, Sophie. Knows I won't be caught dead on the Senior Shuttle so she arranges a cab and says, "But Leo, don't you want to see *me?*"

Been using that one for over fifty years.

Worked again.

We used to have it at the New Yorker Hotel before the Korean and his Jesus children moved in. You see them on the streets peddling flowers, big smiles, cheeks glowing like Hitler Youth. High on the Opiate of the People. Used to be the New Yorker had its dopers, its musicians, its sad sacks and marginal types. We felt at home there.

So this year the Committee books us with the chain that our religious friends from Utah own, their showpiece there on Central Park South. Which kicks off the annual difficulties.

"That's the bunch killed Joe Hill," comes the cry.

"Corporate holdings to rival the Pope," they say, and we're off to the races.

Personally, I think we should have it where we did the year the doormen were on strike, should rent the Union Hall in Brooklyn. But who listens to me?

So right off the bat there's Pinkstaff working up a petition and Weiss organizing a counter-Committee. Always with the factions and splinter groups those two, whatever drove man to split the atom is the engine that rules their lives. Not divide and conquer but divide and subdivide.

First thing in the lobby we've got Weiss passing a handout on Brigham Young and the Mountain Meadow Massacre.

"Leo Gold! I thought you were dead!"

"It's a matter of days. You never learned to spell, Weiss."

"What, spelling?"

I point to the handout. "Who's this Norman? 'Norman Hierarchy,' 'Norman Elders.' And all this capitalization, it's cheap theatrics."

Weiss has to put on his glasses. "That's not spelling," he says, "that's typing. Spelling I'm fine, but these new machines —my granddaughter bought an electric."

"It's nice she lets you use it."

"She doesn't know. I sneak when she's at school."

Next there's the placard in the lobby—WELCOME ANARCHISTS and the caricature of Bakunin, complete with sizzling bomb in hand. That Gross can still hold a pen is such a miracle we have to indulge his alleged sense of humor every year. A malicious man, Gross, like all cartoonists. Grinning, watching the hotel lackeys stew in their little brown uniforms, wondering is it a joke or not. Personally, I think it's in bad taste, the bomb-throwing bit. It's the enemy's job to ridicule, not ours. But who asks me?

They've set us loose in something called the Elizabethan Room and it's a sorry sight. A half-hundred old crackpots tiptoeing across the carpet, wondering how they got past the velvet ropes and into the exhibit. That old fascination with the enemy's lair, they fit like fresh kishke on a silk sheet. Some woman I don't know is pinning everyone with name tags. Immediately the ashtrays are full of them, pins bent by palsied fingers. Name tags at the Anarchists' Convention.

Pearl is here, and Bill Kinney in a fog and Lou Randolph and Pinkstaff and Fine, and Diamond tottering around flashing his new store-boughts at everyone. Personally, wearing dentures I would try to keep my mouth shut. But then I always did.

"Leo, we thought we'd lost you," they say.

"Not a word, it's two years."

"Thought you went just after Brickman, rest his soul."

"So you haven't quit yet, Leo."

I tell them it's a matter of hours and look for Sophie. She's by Baker, the Committee Chairman this year. Always the Committee Chairman, he's the only one with such a streak of masochism. Sophie's by Baker and there's no sign of her Mr. Gillis.

There's another one makes the hip act up. Two or three times I've seen the man since he set up housekeeping with Sophie, and every time I'm in pain. Like an allergy, only bone-deep. It's not just he's CP from the word go—we all had our fling with the Party, and they have their point of view. But Gillis is the sort that didn't hop off of Joe Stalin's bandwagon till after it nose-dived into the sewer. The deal with Berlin wasn't enough for Gillis, or the Purges, no, nor any of the other tidbits that started coming out from reliable sources.

Not till the Party announced officially that Joe was off the Sainted list did Gillis catch a whiff. And him with Sophie now.

Maybe he's a good cook.

She lights up when she sees me. That smile, after all these years, that smile and my knees are water. She hasn't gone the Mother Jones route, Sophie, no shawls and spectacles, she's nobody's granny on a candy box. She's thin, a strong thin, not like Diamond, and her eyes, they still stop your breath from across the room. Always there was such a crowd, such a crowd around Sophie. And always she made each one think *he* was at the head of the line.

"Leo, you came! I was afraid you'd be shy again." She hugs me, tells Baker I'm like a brother.

Sophie who always rallied us after a beating, who bound our wounds, who built our pride back up from shambles and never faltered a step. The iron she had! In Portland they're shaving her head, but no wig for Sophie, she wore it like a badge. And the fire! Toe-to-toe with a fat Biloxi deputy, head-to-head with a Hoboken wharf boss, starting a near-riot from her soapbox in Columbus Circle, but shaping it, turning it, stampeding all that anger and energy in the right direction.

Still the iron, still the fire, and still it's Leo you're like a brother.

Baker is smiling his little pained smile, looking for someone to apologize to, Blum is telling jokes, Vic Lewis has an aluminum walker after his stroke and old Mrs. Axelrod, who knew Emma Goldman from the Garment Workers, is dozing in her chair. Somebody must be in charge of bringing the old woman, with her mind the way it is, because she never misses. She's our museum piece, our link to the past.

Not that the rest of us qualify for the New Left.

Bud Odum is in one corner trying to work up a sing-along. Fifteen years younger than most here, a celebrity, still with the denim open at the chest and the Greek sailor cap. The voice is shot though. With Harriet Foote and old Lieber joining they sound like the look-for-the-Union-label folks on television. Determined but slightly off-key. The younger kids aren't so big on Bud anymore, and the Hootenanny Generation is grown, with other fish to fry.

Kids. The room is crawling with little Barnard girls and their tape recorders, pestering people for "oral history." A pair camp by Mrs. Axelrod, clicking on whenever she starts awake and mutters some Yiddish. Sophie, who speaks, says she's raving about the harness-eyes breaking and shackles bouncing on the floor, some shirt-factory tangle in her mind. Gems, they think they're getting, oral-history gems.

There are starting to be Rebeccas again, the little Barnard girls, and Sarahs and Esthers, after decades of Carol, Sally and Debbie. The one who tapes me is a Raisele, which was my mother's name.

"We're trying to preserve it," she says with a sweet smile for an old man.

"What, Yiddish? I don't speak."

"No," she says. "Anarchism. The memories of anarchism. Now that it's served its dialectical purpose."

"You're a determinist."

She gives me a look. They think we never opened a book. I don't tell her I've written a few, it wouldn't make an impression. If it isn't on tape or film it doesn't register. Put my name in the computer, you'll draw a blank.

"Raisele," I say. "That's a pretty name."

"I learned it from an exchange student. I used to be Jody."

Dinner is called and there's confusion, there's jostling, everyone wants near the platform. The ears aren't what they used to be. There is a seating plan, with place cards set out, but nobody looks. Place cards at the Anarchists' Convention? I manage to squeeze in next to Sophie.

First on the agenda is fruit cup, then speeches, then dinner, then more speeches. Carmen Marcovicci wants us to go get our own fruit cup. It makes her uneasy, she says, being waited on. People want, they should get up and get it themselves.

A couple minutes of mumble-grumble, then someone points out that we'd be putting the two hotel lackeys in charge of the meal out of a job. It's agreed, they'll serve. You could always reason with Carmen.

Then Harriet Foote questions the grapes in the fruit cup. The boycott is over, we tell her, grapes are fine. In fact grapes were always fine—it was the labor situation that was no good, not the *fruit*.

"Well I'm not eating *mine*," she says, blood pressure climbing toward the danger point, "it would be disloyal."

The Wrath of the People. That's what Brickman used to call it in his articles, in his harangues, in his three-hour walking diatribes. Harriet still has it, and Carmen and Weiss and Sophie and Bill Kinney on his clear days and Brickman had it to the end. It's a wonderful quality, but when you're over seventy and haven't eaten since breakfast it has its drawbacks.

Baker speaks first, apologizing for the site and the hour and the weather and the Hundred Years' War. He congratulates the long travelers—Odum from L.A., Kinney from Montana, Pappas from Chicago, Mrs. Axelrod all the way in from Yonkers. He apologizes that our next scheduled speaker, Mikey Dolan, won't be with us. He apologizes for not having time to prepare a eulogy, but it was so sudden—

More mumble-grumble, this being the first we've heard about Mikey. Sophie is crying, but she's not the sort you offer your shoulder or reach for the Kleenex. *If steel had tears,* Brickman used to say. They had their battles, Brickman and Sophie, those two years together. '37 and '38. Neither of them known as a compromiser, both with healthy throwing arms, once a month there's a knock and it's Sophie come to borrow more plates. I worked for money at the moviehouse, I always had plates.

The worst was when you wouldn't see either of them for a week. Phil Rapf was living below them then and you'd see him in Washington Square, eight o'clock in the morning. Phil who'd sleep through the Revolution itself it it came before noon.

"I can't take it," he'd say. "They're at it already. In the

morning, in the noontime, at night. At least when they're fighting the plaster doesn't fall."

Less than two years it lasted. But of all of them, before and after, it was Brickman left his mark on her. That hurts.

Bud Odum is up next, his Wisconsin accent creeping toward Oklahoma, twanging on about "good red-blooded American men and women" and I get a terrible feeling he's going to break into "The Ballad of Bob LaFollette," when war breaks out at the far end of the table. In the initial shuffle Allie Zaitz was sitting down next to Fritz Groh and it's fifteen minutes before the shock of recognition. Allie has lost all his hair from the X-ray treatments, and Fritz never had any. More than ever they're looking like twins.

"You," says Allie, "you from the Dockworkers!"

"And you from that yellow rag. They haven't put you away from civilized people?"

"They let *you* in here? You an *an*archist?"

"In the fullest definition of the word. Which you wouldn't know. What was that coloring book you wrote for?"

At the top of their voices, in the manner of old Lefties. What, old—in the manner we've always had, damn the decibels and full speed ahead. Baker would apologize but he's not near enough to the microphone, and Bud Odum is just laughing. There's still something genuine about the boy, Greek sailor cap and all.

"Who let this crank in here? We've been infiltrated!"

"Point of order! Point of order!"

What Allie is thinking with point of order I don't know, but the lady from the name tags gets them separated, gives each a Barnard girl to record their spewings about the other. Something Fritz said at a meeting, something Allie wrote about it, centuries ago. We don't forget.

Bud gets going again and it seems that last year they weren't prepared with Brickman's eulogy, so Bud will do the honors now. I feel eyes swiveling, a little muttered chorus of "Leoleoleo" goes through the room. Sophie knew, of course, and conned me into what she thought would be good for me. Once again.

First Bud goes into what a fighter Brickman was, tells how he took on Union City, New Jersey, single-handed, about the time he organized an entire truckload of scabs with one speech, turning them around right under the company's nose. He can still rouse an audience, Bud, even with the pipes gone, and soon they're popping up around the table with memories. Little Pappas, who we never thought would survive the beating he took one May Day scuffle, little one-eyed, broken-nosed Pappas stands and tells of Brickman saving the mimeograph machine when they burned our office on 27th Street. And Sam Karnes, ghost-pale, like the years in prison bleached even his blood, is standing, shaky, with the word on Brickman's last days. Tubes running out of him, fluids dripping into him, still Brickman agitates with the hospital orderlies, organizes with the cleaning staff. Then Sophie takes the floor, talking about spirit, how Brickman had it, how Brickman was it, spirit of our cause, more spirit sometimes than judgment, and again I feel the eyes, hear the Leoleoleo and there I am on my feet.

"We had our troubles," I say, "Brickman and I. But always I knew his heart was in the right place."

Applause, tears, and I sit down. It's a sentimental moment. Of course, it isn't true. If Brickman had a heart it was a well-kept secret. He was a machine, an express train flying the black flag. But it's a sentimental moment, the words come out.

Everybody is making nice then, the old friendly juices flowing, and Baker has to bring up business. A master of tact, a genius of timing. A vote—do we elect next year's Committee before dinner or after?

"Why spoil dinner?" says one camp.

"Nobody will be left awake after," says the other. "Let's get it out of the way."

They always started small, the rifts. A title, a phrase, a point of procedure. The Chicago Fire began with a spark.

It pulls the scab off, the old animosities, the bickerings, come back to the surface. One whole section of the table splits off into a violent debate over the merits of syndicalism, another forms a faction for elections *during* dinner, Weiss wrestles Baker for the microphone and Sophie shakes her head sadly.

"Why, why, why? Always they argue," she says, "always they fight."

I could answer, I devoted half of one of my studies to it, but who asks?

While the argument heats another little girl comes over with used-to-be-Jody.

"She says you're Leo Gold."

"I confess."

"The Leo Gold?"

"There's another?"

"I read *Anarchism and the Will to Love.*"

My one turkey, and she's read it. "So you're the one."

"I didn't realize you were still alive."

"It's a matter of seconds."

I'm feeling low. Veins are standing out in temples, old hearts straining, distemper epidemic. And the sound, familiar, but with a new, futile edge.

I've never been detached enough to recognize the sound so exactly before. It's a raw-throated sound, a grating, insistent sound, a sound born out of all the insults swallowed, the battles lost, out of all the smothered dreams and desires. Three thousand collective years of frustration in the room, turning inward, a *can*cer of frustration. It's the sound of parents brawling each other because they can't feed their kids, the sound of prisoners preying on each other because the guards are out of reach, the sound of a terribly deep despair. No quiet desperation for us, not while we have a voice left. Over an hour it lasts, the sniping, the shouting, the accusations and countercharges. I want to eat. I want to go home. I want to cry.

And then the hotel manager walks in.

Brown blazer, twenty-dollar haircut and a smile from here to Salt Lake City. A huddle at the platform. Baker and Mr. Manager bowing and scraping at each other, Bud Odum looking grim, Weiss turning colors. Sophie and I go up, followed by half the congregation. Nobody trusts to hear it secondhand. I can sense the sweat breaking under that blazer when he sees us coming, toothless, gnarled, suspicious by habit. Ringing around him, the Anarchists' Convention.

"A terrible mistake," he says.

"All my fault," he says.

"I'm awfully sorry," he says, "but you'll have to move."

Seems the Rotary Club, the Rotary Club from Sioux Falls, had booked this room be*fore* us. Someone misread the calendar. They're out in the lobby, eyeballing Bakunin, impatient, full of gin and boosterism.

"We have a nice room, a smaller room," coos the manager, "we can set you up there in a jiffy. Much less drafty than this room, I'm sure the older folks would feel more comfortable."

"I think it stinks," says Rosenthal, every year the Committee Treasurer. "We paid cash, the room is ours."

Rosenthal doesn't believe in checks. "The less the Wall Street Boys handle your money," he says, "the cleaner it is." Who better to be Treasurer than a man who thinks gold is filth?

"That must be it," says Sophie to the manager. "You've got your cash from us, money in the bank, you don't have to worry. The Rotary, they can cancel a check, so you're scared. And maybe there's a little extra on the side they give you, a little folding green to clear out the riffraff?"

Sophie has him blushing, but he's going to the wire anyhow. Like Frick in the Homestead Strike, shot, stomped and stabbed by Alexander Berkman, they patch him up and he finishes his day at the office. A gold star from Carnegie. Capitalism's finest hour.

"You'll have to move," says the manager, dreams of corporate glory in his eyes, the smile hanging on to his face by its fingernails, "it's the only way."

"Never," says Weiss.

"Out of the question," says Sophie.

"Fuck off," says Pappas.

Pappas saw his father lynched. Pappas did three hard ones in Leavenworth. Pappas lost an eye, a lung and his profile to a mob in Chicago. He says it with conviction.

"Pardon?" A note of warning from Mr. Manager.

"He says to fuck off," says Fritz Groh.

"You heard him," echoes Allie Zaitz.

"If you people won't cooperate," huffs the manager, condescension rolling down like a thick mist, "I'll have to call in the police."

It zings through the room like the twinge of a single nerve.

"Police! They're sending the police!" cries Pinkstaff.

"Go limp!" cries Vic Lewis, knuckles white with excitement on his walker. "Make em drag us out!"

"Mind the shuttles, mind the shuttles!" cries old Mrs. Axelrod in Yiddish, sitting straight up in her chair.

Allie Zaitz is on the phone to a newspaper friend, the Barnard girls are taping everything in sight, Sophie is organizing us into squads and only Baker holding Weiss bodily allows Mr. Manager to escape the room in one piece. We're the Anarchists' Convention!

Nobody bickers, nobody stalls or debates or splinters. We manage to turn the long table around by the door as a kind of barricade, stack the chairs together in a second line of defense and crate Mrs. Axelrod back out of harm's way. I stay close by Sophie, and once, lugging the table, she turns and gives me that smile. Like a shot of adrenaline, I feel fifty again. Sophie, Sophie, it was always so good, just to be at your side!

And when the manager returns with his two befuddled street cops to find us standing together, arms linked, the lame held up out of their wheelchairs, the deaf joining from memory as Bud Odum leads us in "We Shall Not Be Moved," my hand in Sophie's, sweaty-palmed at her touch like the old days, I look at him in his brown blazer and think *Brickman,* I think, *my God if Brickman was here we'd show this bastard the Wrath of the People!*